PRISONER OF LUST

"We all share the same fate," said the Athenian. "The Scarlet Pirate, you see, rarely kills her victims. She shrewdly uses them, first here on Phalus to keep her mates happy, and then—"

Sinbad leaned forward inquisitively. "Keep them happy, how?"

The Athenian chuckled. "You'll learn that for yourself, my friend. But the rigors of satisfying a hundred women and more can be quite taxing . . . some nearly die from the strain. . . ."

Sinbad knew now that he was trapped—just as he knew exactly what he had to do to escape. . . .

About the Author

GRAHAM DIAMOND has been inventing incredible tales and writing them down since he was ten years old. He is the author of THE THIEF OF KALIMAR (14214, $1.95). Born in London, he now lives in Queens, N.Y., with his wife and his two daughters, Rochelle and Leslie.

8999

CAPTAIN SINBAD

by

Graham Diamond

FAWCETT GOLD MEDAL • NEW YORK

CAPTAIN SINBAD

Copyright © 1980 Graham Diamond

Published by Fawcett Gold Medal Books, a unit of CBS Publications, the Consumer Publishing Division of CBS Inc.

ISBN: 0-449-14341-4

Printed in the United States of America

First Fawcett Gold Medal printing: June 1980

10 9 8 7 6 5 4 3 2 1

INTRODUCTION

Nearly two centuries before Marco Polo began his wondrous travels to Cathay, at a time of history when the new religion of Islam was sweeping the world from Persia to the peninsula of Iberia, there lived in the fabled city of Baghdad a merchant by the name of Sinbad. An adventurer, a soldier of fortune, a poet in the caliph's court, Sinbad sailed the Seven Seas in search of fame and fortune, which he quickly acquired.

The tale told in these pages is nothing like those told by the lovely Scheharazade in *The Thousand and One Nights*. It is a new and accurate account of Sinbad the man, whose true exploits have never before been recounted.

This story reveals him as he actually was— hero and daring adventurer, yes—but no less a man, and thus as fallible and vulnerable as we all are. None of these facts was ever told by Scheherazade; indeed, the beautiful princess would surely have been dismyed to hear of them. Here for the first time are the most extraordinary exploits of the world's most courageous mariner.

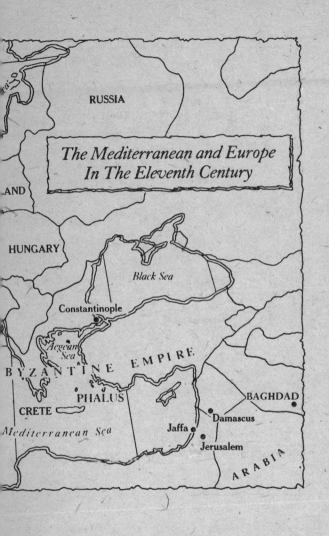

RUSSIA

The Mediterranean and Europe In The Eleventh Century

...AND

HUNGARY

Black Sea

Constantinople

Aegean Sea

BYZANTINE EMPIRE

PHALUS

BAGHDAD

CRETE

Mediterranean Sea

Jaffa

Damascus

Jerusalem

ARABIA

PART ONE:

HOW SINBAD FOUND HIMSELF SHIPWRECKED IN BARCELONA, CAUGHT BETWEEN THE WARRING MOORS OF CÓRDOBA AND THE KNIGHTS OF CHRISTENDOM.

Thunder had rolled and lightning had flashed; the tempest had struck suddenly and violently, catching the fishermen of Pansa off guard. They had rowed in a frenzy back toward home while wives and children stood waiting in fear along the chilly shore.

The storm had been especially bad for this time of year. It was told that at least three of the fishing boats had nearly capsized, their crews almost lost. But, of course, this had been recounted well after everyone had made it back safely, so the actual truth of the tale was difficult to determine with any certainty. The fishermen of Pansa, you see, are renowned for their bragging, even as far away as the walled city of Barcelona itself, some twenty kilometers to the north. Still, there was no question but that this particular storm had been the worst Pansa had encountered in some years, and that the dawn Mass had been held in the great relief of knowing that no one had been lost.

Pansa was a tiny village, its people numbering perhaps five hundred, all good and worthy Christians, living out their lives in peace with hardly a thought to the turbulent world around them. Just a few days' ride to the south stood the borders of the caliphate of Córdoba, and there it was said the Moors were preparing for war again, intent on sweeping over the county of Barcelona and then moving to take the kingdom of Navárre, thereby laying claim to almost all the Iberian peninsula in the name of their holy Prophet. Indeed, the Mother Church in distant Rome was said to fear for her flock, for should Barcelona and Navarre fall to the heathens, what army was there to stop the followers of Islam from striking throughout all of Europe? Rome itself might not be safe.

Although caught in the very center of this battle of religions and armies, the gentle folk of Pansa gave little thought to any of these matters. Little could be gained in worrying, they reasoned, for, in truth, what could be done? Pansa had no army of her own to call upon, only the bold knights of Barcelona and the village's prayers that all would finish well. Besides, there were so many other matters to contend with: the fields needed harvesting; the sheep and goats had to be tended; the fishing boats had to be kept ever seaworthy and trim. And such labors were enough by far for the quiet village to manage. Little time was left over for anything else.

So life was for Pansa during the early years of the eleventh century, a time when most of the world found itself in turmoil and chaos. Pansa's people went about their small lives happily, celebrating births and grieving deaths, basking in the warm Mediterranean sun, always looking to the bright side of things while the shadows loomed around them and waited.

Mass had been said early this morning after the storm, and the fishermen had long since rowed back out to sea. As the village prepared for a new day, María Victoria de León, seventeen years of age and marriageable, finished with her varied chores at home and began her morning stroll along the beach. She had stolen these precious moments alone as she always did, musing upon the life that would lie before her, contemplating, as young women often do, just what happiness her future might bring.

The waves were rolling softly onto the shore now, white froth foaming and splashing over the golden sand. Above, the sky was a cloudless blue, hinting at the warm spring months ahead. María Victoria de León danced at the water's edge, laughing and humming while a flock of seagulls dived down to the sea. She was a lovely girl; some would even have said stunning. She pulled the scarf from her hair and let it flow free and windblown, her face aglow at the beauty of the new day. She had her mother's eyes, it was well known, black as coals, ever flashing with vitality. Her skin was dark, stirred to deep cream by the warm Barcelona sun; she had a scattering of birthmarks across her supple breasts and over her face which always darkened noticeably whenever she blushed. Her full lips were warm and inviting, the color of deep Castilian wine, and in the brightness of morning, her tawny hair glistened with hints of scarlet and amber when sunlight touched its edges.

María Victoria de León carried herself nobly, as if she strove to rise above her station as an innkeeper's daughter. But in the village of Pansa, where there were no nobles, her father, Manuel de León, being a man of means, was himself considered as close to aristocracy as the town might have.

A seagull squawked in the sky. María Victoria looked up and watched its flight downward toward the end of the beach. She laughed as the great bird closed its wings and came to an awkward landing beside a pile of driftwood, where it pecked its beak at some undefined form. A large fish must have washed ashore, she was certain; it was a frequent occurrence. Once she had even seen the stiff carcass of a shark washed up on the sand.

María Victoria scratched her head in recollection. If memory served, the shark had come after a storm, a bad storm such as last night's. Then, with curiosity overwhelming her, she walked briskly toward the driftwood and the pecking gull.

The figure was covered with sand; she had to shade her eyes from the sun to get the briefest glimpse of it. It wasn't a fish, she realized, that was certain.

Then she put her hand to her mouth and gasped. *"Dios mío!"*

The half-buried figure was a man.

13

At first glance it seemed as though he were dead, but then she saw his arms suddenly begin to move, his fingers reaching out as if to grasp at the driftwood. Helplessly he writhed in the sand, amid the various debris of what must have once been boards of a ship.

Panting, María Victoria knelt down beside the struggling figure. She pulled her shawl from her shoulders and wiped the caked sand from his face and shirtless body. Biting her lips, she looked about in frustration while her shouts for assistance went unheeded.

The man began to moan softly in a delirium; seawater flushed from the corners of his mouth as he coughed with every breath. María Victoria made the sign of the cross and thanked Heaven that at least he was still breathing. Then, using the techniques for rescue that the fishermen had taught her, she managed to roll the stranger onto his stomach and place the palms of her hands firmly beneath his shoulder blades. With strong, deliberate movements, she pushed up, forcing the salt water from his lungs, releasing as he vomited it up, and then repeating the procedure. The man spewed up more water and fell back, breathing clearly. She turned him around carefully and placed his head upon a small rise of wet sand. With worry-filled eyes she gazed deeply into his face. A young face, windblown and handsome, yet filled with worry lines as prominent as the thin streaks of silver in his trimmed black beard.

"You're alive," she whispered, as he tried to open his eyes. "Don't be afraid. We've found you, you're safe."

The man, barely conscious, forced open bloodshot eyes, black eyes like her own, and tried to say something. Then he sighed deeply and fell asleep.

María Victoria covered his chest with her shawl and leaped to her feet. Several children had come to the beach, and she shouted to them frantically, pointing to her discovery. It was only a matter of minutes before a small crowd had gathered, made up mostly of old women and young children, all staring down in wonder at the helpless survivor of the terrible storm.

"Who do you think he might be?" asked one.

"And where could he have come from?" wondered another.

María Victoria de León looked on at the women with growing frustration. "What matter does any of that make?" she flared, biting her lips. "He needs our help. He could die if we leave him like this!"

The old women shook their heads sadly. "Such a young man, to die," one said. "Yes," agreed another. "Young—and handsome as well."

María Victoria felt tears come to her eyes. Where were the village men? Why hadn't they come to the beach? But the answer was plain—the fishermen were in their boats, already far out to sea, the shepherds and farmers already in their pastures and fields. There was no one else. No one but . . .

"Send for my father!" María Victoria demanded of a small, wide-eyed boy standing barefoot beside the sleeping stranger. "Tell him he must come here at once!"

"Sí, sí!" replied the youth, and María Victoria sighed thankfully as he ran off in the direction of her home.

Manuel de León was a stout, robust man who looked far younger than his fifty-seven years. As a youth he had served as both footman and soldier in many wars, defending his beloved Barcelona against the heathen hordes. Castilian knights had ofttimes praised him for his valor in combat, once even promising to make of him a squire and bring him into the service of Navarre. But a Moorish blade had cut short the young man's promising career, and he had been forced to return to his home, Pansa. Now he thought not of war, nor of glory or honor, or even of gold or women. Only of his small inn and the family he had raised. Three daughters he had been blessed with. Three beautiful girls, no sons to carry his name. Only dowries for his sons-in-law to be, and, God willing, that day was close at hand.

It took Manuel long minutes to hobble from the inn down to the beach, his bad leg throbbing with pain every step of the way. At sight of María Victoria, Manuel picked up in speed, giving no thought to his aches. Had the girl been hurt in some way? Molested? The boy who had come for him had spoken like an idiot, giving no details, saying only that he, Manuel, had better come to the beach at once because his youngest girl was crying. Leaving the horses of his single guest unattended in the stable, he had raced to find her. And now there she was, tearful and distraught, kneeling over the corpse of some drowned sailor washed ashore.

"But he's alive!" protested the girl as Manuel made to drag her away.

"It is true," offered one of the old women solemnly.

Manuel gazed down at the sleeping man and let go of María's hand. "You're right!" he exclaimed, reaching down and feeling the weakened pulse beat. Then he looked sternly to the old women and snapped his fingers. "Go and find Pepe—and Domingo as well!"

Respectful of Manuel de León, the crowd quickly scattered, shouting loudly for the men in the fields to come. And so it happened that the stranger was at last carried from the beach and brought to rest at the humble way station of Manuel de León.

That first night, while the stranger rested in a fretful sleep, María Victoria refused to leave his side even for a moment. She guarded him jealously, like a lover, tending his every need, mopping his brow and putting a cup of sweet wine to his lips to quench his thirst. In the small hours before dawn, when María Victoria herself fell into an uneasy sleep, her sister María Vanessa came into the room. With dampened cloth she washed the sweaty foreigner, covering every inch of his body, her eyes wide in admiration of his manly build. Then when Vanessa had finished and Victoria had almost woken, the eldest of the three, María Elisa, came in as well. She carried a bowl of hot

16

broth, and, shooing Vanessa away, she spoon-fed the stranger, carefully keeping a napkin beneath his chin to soak the spillage.

With the rooster's crow at dawn, Manuel de León woke as usual, drank a glass of wine and ate a piece of cheese, and prepared for his morning chores. But there was no sign of his daughters. With a furrowed brow, he searched their rooms, finding each one empty. He strode from the hall, crossing the garden to the small guest house and opened the stranger's door without knocking. Much to his chagrin—although not his surprise—the girls were busily doting over the sleeping man, nearly fighting among themselves to determine which might have the honor of combing his hair, who should be allowed to trim his shaggy beard, which would change the dirty linen. They were certainly giving no thought whatsoever to their duties in the house.

Fuming at the scene, Manuel de León put his fists to his hips and bellowed: "Get out of here, all of you!"

The girls looked up startled. "Yes, Papá!" they cried, and then ran one by one from the room with downcast eyes.

After they had gone, Manuel folded his arms and leaned his weight against the frame of the opened door, his gaze fixed sternly at the sleeping stranger. In the garden trees, small birds had begun to chirp, and a full sun washed the stones of the walls and patio with bright light. Mumbling quietly to himself, Manuel assessed his unexpected house guest. The man was muscular and strong, with a good firm back, a good worker if not a potential son-in-law.

"I hope you appreciate all of this," Manuel said gruffly as the stranger yawned and smiled in his sleep. Then, with a shrug, Manuel turned and shut the door, leaving the sleeping guest to his dreams.

It was nearly midafternoon by the time María Victoria had finished preparing the noon meal for the paying travelers at the inn, and she eagerly looked forward to spending a free hour with the man whose life she was positive she had saved. The morning had been hot—spitefully hot. As if the sun itself had somehow conspired to make the weather intolerable so that every hour felt as long as a day. Usually, María Victoria would go down to some secluded spot on the beach and, assured she was alone, slip out of her dress to take a refreshing swim. Today, though, it was only her stained apron that she shed; she hurried from the kitchen, where the aroma of fresh bread still filled her nostrils, ran across the garden without pausing to throw breadcrumbs into the fountain for the hungry birds, and quickly entered the small room set at the back of the stable.

It was with considerable surprise that she saw the guest sitting up in the bed, his eyes fully open, gazing peacefully from the window out at the trimmed hedges and trees along the road.

When the guest heard her enter, he turned slowly and smiled.

"Ah, you must be the girl on the beach," he said.

The girl was frozen on the threshold, amazed at his rapid recovery. In her fantasies she had pictured herself tending him for days—weeks, perhaps—until that first moment when he would open his eyes and see only her.

The man looked at her quizzically. "It *was* you, wasn't it?" he asked, with an accent that told her he came from someplace very far away.

María Victoria summoned her courage and nodded. The guest smiled fully and held out his hand for her to come closer. "I think I should thank you," he said, taking her small hand in his own.

"At first . . . at first I thought you were dead," she stammered.

The man laughed. "I thought so, too. That was some storm we had. Took us totally by surprise; there was hardly time to trim our sails, not that it did much good . . ."

María Victoria smiled at the soft singsong quality of

18

his deep voice. "Then you are a sailor?" she asked.

"Oh, yes. Almost all of my life. Born to the sea. My friends say I'm wedded to her. She waits for me always, like a wife."

María Victoria giggled and sat gently on the edge of the bed. The stranger straightened himself up a bit and inhaled deeply, feeling the tinge of salt carried on the breeze. "It's good to be alive," he told her solemnly. "How long have I been here?"

"Since yesterday morning. You were running a high fever; last night was especially bad. I stayed up with you—" She blushed girlishly and corrected: "My . . . er . . . sisters and I stayed up with you."

The stranger nodded knowingly. "It's always to be expected after you've had your lungs filled with seawater. I've seen it happen time and again. And I don't have to tell you how grateful I am for what you've done. Now maybe I should try to have a look around." He started to get off the bed but fell back feebly, his face breaking out in a sudden sweat.

"You still must rest," said the girl anxiously.

"A little more sleep, perhaps. That's all . . ."

Her eyes flashed sternly. "Papá says you're not to move for at least three days."

"Papá?" He looked at her questioningly, then smiled with dawning comprehension. "Ah, so this is your father's house. I see. Then I must be even more grateful. Not every man would trust a sailor with such a beautiful woman."

María Victoria flushed crimson. "You flatter me, señor. . . ."

The constant use of Castilian words in her expressions puzzled him somewhat. He put his hands to his temples and shut his eyes, as if trying to dispel the last of the fog from the edges of his mind. But everything was still quite dim. The last thing he could remember was being some fifty or sixty kilometers off the coast of Córdoba when the storm had hit. The rest remained a blank.

19

At length he opened his eyes again, and smiled. The girl was watching him fretfully, clearly concerned for a relapse. "What's your name?" he asked.

"María Victoria de León." She lowered her head politely, sunlight casting a shadow across her soft features. "My friends call me Victoria . . ."

His smile deepened; small dimples burrowed into his cheeks. "My ship must have been thrown way off course, Victoria. Tell me, what place is this?"

"The village of Pansa," she replied proudly, without hesitation.

The sailor nodded slowly, deep in thought. "Pansa? Hmmm. Forgive a stranger's ignorance, Victoria, but exactly where is Pansa?"

"You must indeed be from very far away, señor," she replied, seeming puzzled. "We are on the main road. All travelers pass this way, my father says."

"And what road might that be?"

"Why the road to the city, señor! The road to Barcelona!"

His smile vanished briefly, unnoticed by the perplexed girl.

"Surely you know of Barcelona?" she went on. "They say it is the greatest city in the world!"

The sailor sighed a long sigh and then grinned. "Yes, Victoria, I *have* heard of Barcelona. Many times. And indeed, they do speak of it as being beautiful."

"Then perhaps you are not quite as lost as you thought."

Her companion's eyes danced with merriment. How young and precious this girl was, so innocent, so full of life and its joys. She reminded the sailor of another; a girl quite similar in appearance to this Castilian beauty. Gazing upward, he recalled the image of that other girl—the scent of her hair, softness of her mouth, the serene touch of her fingertips. Then he awoke from his daydream and frowned. "Fate often plays strange tricks with the lives of mortal men, María Victoria," he said in a serious tone. "Never forget that."

Victoria remained completely attentive. "You sound very sad," she said. "Is something wrong?"

"Not with you, by Allah!" he said, the mirth returning to his dark features. He leaned on one elbow and studied her face intently, focusing on the pupils of her eyes as they caught the sun. "It's just that I find myself very far from where I had thought myself to be—and farther than ever from attaining my goals."

Victoria looked at him with large, hopeful eyes. "But surely you can resume your journey when you are well?"

"Yes, dear girl. I can look for my friends—if they're not all drowned." He shrugged. "Who can tell? Maybe they are already searching for *me*."

The girl squealed with excitement at the possibility of having other handsome sailors come to her home. "Perhaps they'll come to Pansa to find you!" she exclaimed.

He shrugged again. "I suppose it is possible, although I greatly doubt it."

"But why? They'll be more than welcome here. My father would be delighted to find them lodgings, I'm sure."

He smiled at her again. "Perhaps you're right. As I said, Fate enjoys her little games . . ."

Although much of his behavior seemed curious to her, María Victoria shrugged it off, thinking it surely due to his ordeal and fatigue. Still, this sailor did seem a peculiar sort, unlike anybody she had come across in all her years. And as the daughter of an innkeeper, she had met just about every type there was.

She had many more questions to ask of the stranger and was about to begin when she heard Elisa shout her name. She got up swiftly and peered from the window. Her sister was coming from the walk behind the stable, carrying a hefty load of dirty linen in a sack. Elisa was half dragging her burden behind as she searched for her younger sister.

"I had better be going," Victoria told the sailor.

"Yes," he agreed. "I wouldn't want you to get into any

trouble over me. But come back, if you like, and we can chat some more."

Her eyes brightened appreciably, and again she was a painful reminder of his love far away across two seas.

"I'll bring you your supper," she promised. Then, turning to go, she added: "That is, if my sisters don't insist on taking it to you themselves."

The sailor smiled warmly. "I'll still wait for you," he told her. "If I feel better and your father doesn't object, maybe we can sit in the garden for a while."

María Victoria nodded dramatically, even as her heart beat faster. "Until this evening," she said. Stars glittered in her eyes as she left.

"Until this evening," he repeated. Then, after she was gone, he sat back up in the bed and groaned. *Heaven's mercy!* he told himself in his moment of solitude. *I've been shipwrecked in Barcelona! What else can happen to me now?*

In the scrubby hills of the countryside near the Moorish city of Tarragona, there dwelt a bandit and thief who called himself Suliman the Noble, the Eye of the Prophet, although exactly what was noble about either him or his ragtag band of cutthroats had never been established. Nevertheless, Suliman, an illiterate, pompous, potbellied man, smelling of sheep and goats, had over the years established himself as a feared foe among the scattered Christian settlements of the county of Barcelona. Preying mostly by night, in places known to be unprotected by Barcelonan knights, Suliman made his living for the most part by abducting young women and selling them into slavery for the vast markets of North Africa.

His forays across the ill-defined boundary between the Christian and Moorish kingdoms were a topic of frequent discussion. Many a mother would shudder in fear for her daughters at the mere mention of his name. Of course, he was known by many, many names—even among his fellow

Moors, most of whom looked down upon him with contempt and disdain. Suliman the Swineherd was an often-heard favorite; Suliman the Foul, the Gutter Rat of Tarragona, and the Camel of Córdoba were other choices. In tiny Pansa they had their own local favorite, Suliman the Filthy, a fitting description for both his deeds and his habits.

During the time of this tale, it was an ill-concealed secret that the princes of Córdoba were quietly massing their forces for yet another battle in the ever continuing struggle against the kingdoms of Navarre and Barcelona. The knights of Christendom, therefore, were again forced to raise new armies of their own in response to the threat, a happenstance that would soon leave much of the countryside virtually unprotected.

It had often been claimed that Suliman was a dimwitted man; if so, he certainly was not a fool, for, while these forces gathered to meet in combat, he formulated his own plans with painstaking care. With banners aflutter, the armies of both sides would carry on the holy war in the name of religion, while he would sit back and bide his time. Then, while Barcelona lay defenseless before him, unplucked and ripe, he would lay waste to every village from the border to the walled city of Barcelona itself, plundering and raping his way to a fortune—a fortune guaranteed in gold, readily paid by the slave traders of Tangier.

And now, the moment of opportunity was nearly at hand; his dreams at night were filled with the names of villages he would destroy, and at the head of the list was Pansa.

A melody of splashing water and laughing girls could be heard from the garden. Sinbad put aside the simple fare of his supper and gazed bemusedly from the window. María Victoria, her damp dress clinging seductively to her firm breasts and thighs, pranced away from the fountain while Vanessa threatened to douse her again. The two girls paid little notice to the soft pleasures of the evening. With the sun almost set, the western sky glowed awash in scarlet as dying flames of sunburst sprayed across night-tinted clouds. A sublime breeze rustled leisurely between the branches of the tall junipers and oaks lining the road, carrying a delightful fragrance of roses upon it from Manuel de León's flower bed.

As Sinbad watched the girls enjoying the simple pleasures of an early spring night, his troubled thoughts again carried him home, back to gardens of his beloved Baghdad, and the beautiful woman he had left behind. He pictured her for the thousandth time since leaving home. The memory was as painful as ever, his mind tormented with recollections. What price would he not pay to be with her at this moment? To share with her his dreams, to be lost in the warmth of her embrace? Sinbad scowled. The past was behind. All of it. His concentration must not be divided. Not now, not while new dangers loomed everywhere.

Pushing his memories away, he got up from the bed, stretched cramped muscles, and quietly stepped into the night. Flickering candlelight danced across the spare windows of the inn, misty glimpses of silhouettes crossed his vision from inside. Supper finished, the few guests were preparing to retire. While fireflies danced and crickets sang from the grass, he saw Manuel de León blow out the parlor candle and, a long day almost done, retreat toward the stable to attend the horses.

Their game done, Vanessa and María Victoria returned to the kitchen, leaving Sinbad alone and unseen in the garden. Night was full now, a hazy moon glowing dimly above the treetops. Sinbad eyed his surroundings carefully, making a mental note of his new environs. From where he stood, the road was a few dozen meters away. Distant lights from the village glimmered on one side, and along the other stood a series of low, dark hills leading inland. He studied the landscape slowly, reflecting upon the best avenue of escape.

He could try to make his escape right now, he knew, running under the shroud of darkness for the hills and then working his way south. It might even be possible to steal a horse from the stable; he could reach the border of Córdoba by daybreak if he stayed with the road. But that would be risky; he could be seen by anyone, perhaps even stopped and questioned—and at all costs that must be avoided. Holding back the truth from girls like María Victoria and her sisters was one matter, keeping silent in the face of an inquisition quite another. He had heard tales of the interrogations of foreigners and shuddered at the thought. No one would believe him; they would laugh at his story, call him a spy, and likely as not throw him into a castle dungeon for his efforts.

No, it was more prudent to stay. At least for a day or two, until his strength fully returned. Then, with any luck, he might manage to steal one of the village's fishing boats and sail it south along the coast until he was out of danger. The sea had always been his luck; he would trust her again now.

"You should be resting."

He turned abruptly to find a woman facing him from the gate to the garden. A tall woman, with hair almost as dark as his, and eyes keener. Full-bosomed, shoulders back and her head slightly tilted to the side, she stood with her hands on her hips and an enticing smile upon her warm lips. Even though her features were covered by the soft shadows of night, Sinbad recognized her at once—María Elisa, the oldest of the three, had caught his eye a number of times today, passing so close to his opened window on so many occasions that he had been sure it was more than just coincidence.

"I found the evening too lovely to spend it locked inside the four walls of a room," he replied, looking directly at her and holding her gaze. Then he cast his look toward the glittering stars, fixing upon familiar planets the way he would when navigating. "The sky is a man's finest roof," he added thoughtfully, recalling a poem he had once written. "Don't you agree?"

Elisa grinned, displaying deep dimples. "I do," she answered, "But Papá might not. I don't think he would be very pleased to see you out of bed like this, walking around alone—"

"Ah, but I'm not alone. You're with me."

Elisa laughed gaily, tossing back her hair so that dark curls spilled majestically across her eyes. "Well, I suppose a few minutes won't do much harm . . ."

Sinbad bowed graciously; he glanced to the small stone bench at the edge of the gate. "May I sit?"

She gestured politely with her arm. "You are our guest," she told him, tightening her lace shawl around her shoulders as a sudden gust swept through the garden.

Sinbad stretched out leisurely and Elisa leaned forward over the low gate, close enough so that he could have reached out and touched her. Brazenly her eyes locked with his. There was a defiance in her air, Sinbad observed as she stood before him in the subdued moonlight. A defiance and pride very much like Victoria's, only somehow fiercer.

Her scented hair fell in lush waves over her shoulders as she moved her head; her high breasts rose and fell with her quick, deep breaths. Then, with a taunting deliberateness, she placed her slender hands behind her neck, closed her eyes, and slowly rubbed at taut muscles. After a time her long lashes lifted, and she smiled at the mariner with an unmistakable glint. At nineteen years, María Elisa was very much a woman.

"So you are a mariner," Elisa said suddenly.

Sinbad nodded. "Almost all my life. I made my first voyage when I was sixteen."

Rubbing at her shoulders, Elisa peered out in the direction of the sea. The dark water was calm, reflecting dully the mist-covered moon. The several dozen fishing boats bobbed gently against the aging wharf.

"Would that I could go to sea," said the girl in a whisper. "Sail the ocean, spend my life upon the water, see for myself the wonderous cities of the world . . ."

"You can," Sinbad told her.

"No," Elisa answered. "A woman can't do these things, but"—she looked at him sharply—"if I were a *man!* Oh, if I were a man!" And she lifted her gaze toward the stars, hands on her hips, and sighed wistfully.

"There are women who do as they please," he assured her knowingly. "In fact, once I knew a woman who captained her own ship."

Elisa glanced at him questioningly. "You're making fun of me, aren't you?"

He held up open palms and shook his head. "My word on it, Elisa! From Corsica to Alexandria, she's seen it all. And her name is known in every port."

"What about you?" she asked.

Sinbad leaned back and smiled a sad smile. There were deep shadows beneath his eyes; his face became drawn and tight and his paled lips parted slightly with his bitter mirth. "I, too, have seen it all," he acknowledged, heaving a sigh. "From the Sea of India to the Pillars of Hercules. There is little upon the face of the earth I have not greeted."

Elisa was impressed. "You've done much for one so young."

The mariner shrugged, looking away disconsolately. How many lifetimes of adventure had been crammed into his thirty-two years he could not say; only that he would gladly give it all up here and now for the peaceful life he had planned with the woman he loved.

Sensing his unhappiness, María Elisa opened the gate and slipped silently to his side. She drew close to him upon the bench and boldly took his hand into her own.

Sinbad lifted his head and gazed deeply into her eyes—
eyes that had begun to burn with tiny fires.

"You seem troubled," she said, her voice a soft shade
higher than a whisper. "Will you not share your thoughts
with me?" And slowly she ran her fingernails across his
palm and over his wrist.

Sinbad stirred; the girl was a beauty, no question of
that, and her overtures more than enticing. Still, too many
burdens lay heavily upon his brow to seek a deeper
involvement with Manuel de León's eldest daughter.

Undaunted by his aloofness, Elisa pressed in closer, so
that her breasts crushed against his arm. She ran her
fingers through the thick hair at the nape of his neck,
murmuring in his ear: "Is there nothing I can do to ease
your sadness?"

Her tongue darted briefly between her rose-tinted lips,
and with quickening breath she closed her eyes.

In a moment of passion, Sinbad leaned forward and
kissed her, delighted and surprised at the sweetness of her
mouth. Like honeyed wine it tasted, while the fragrance
of her perfume dizzily captured his imagination.

Her arms tightened around him and then suddenly
loosened. Elisa looked at him and drew away with a feline
smile. "Papá will go to bed soon," she whispered. "Wait
for me. I'll come to your room before midnight." And
before the startled sailor could reply, she was up, dress
twirling in the breeze, and hurrying through the gate back
to the house. With raised brows, Sinbad folded his arms
and grinned. Then he shook his head in wonder. Indeed,
life was filled with surprises!

The breeze turned chilly as he sat for a while on the
bench, pondering his flight from Pansa, when from very
far off the first hint of the trumpets came, so distant that at
first it sounded like little more than the twitter of tiny
birds. But seconds later it was louder and closer, shrill
blasts accompanied by the low rumble of a snare drum.

Sinbad rose to his feet quickly, his face tense again

within the shadows. Unconsciously, his right hand slid to his belt, seeking the twin-edged dagger that had been lost during the storm.

Lights were being lit everywhere. Peering down the road, Sinbad saw dozens of villagers running out of their houses, staring in surprise and joy as the silhouettes of great stallions appeared from the night. Children ran to the road amid cheers from the townsfolk, shouting and gleefully laughing while dogs barked and yapped at their heels.

The front door to the inn flew open; Manuel de León's guests and daughters filed out hurriedly and began to take part in the merrymaking. María Victoria stood away from the others, her eyes fixed on the gloomy road. Sinbad quickly came to her side. "What's going on?" he asked in perplexion.

The girl looked at him as though he were demented. "But surely you know!" she exclaimed.

Sinbad shook his head as the blare of trumpets grew louder, the clatter of hooves filled his ears.

"The war!" said the girl dramatically. "Barcelona's army is marching to fight. Look!"

Sinbad's eyes popped at the sight. Riding three abreast at a slow pace came the knights of Christendom. Stout, brave young men, sons of princes and dukes, barons, counts, all dressed in silver and purple breastplates, each adorned with plumed helmets and chain mail, crimson and velvet cloaks swirling behind. They held tall lances proudly within gloved fists; they wore long, gleaming broadswords, thick bejeweled sheaths dangling from their waists. Brass-spiked spurs glittered from their cumbersome boots, and they sat in saddles of the finest leather, holding metal shields emblazoned with the colors and insignias of their fiefdoms.

The forefront of trumpeters and drummers repeated their call. Banners flew high into the night, fluttering in strong winds sweeping down from the sea. There were priests carrying mighty crosses, each carved intricately with the body of their savior, proclaiming boldly that this war was fought in the name of God. The priests wore long black frocks with hoods pulled tightly over their heads. They somberly chanted in unison a prayer for the bold forces of Barcelona to prevail against the heathens on the battlefield.

Marching both alongside and behind the array of mounted knights came the squires and pages, themselves bedecked in the finery and splendor of their respective lords, each with head held high, proudly in service of Church and country. Behind them, under the careful eyes of lesser captains, came the footmen, a rabble of archers and weapons-bearers and messengers, all in a line stretching from one end of the village to the other. Bringing up the rear of the procession came the camp followers—young women, younger boys, beggars and ballad singers, each come to seek adventure and riches that were surely waiting once the despised Moors were beaten and expelled.

The exalted knights never wavered in stride, even as fisherwives and shepherds' daughters threw flowers and garlands. Men and boys stood with tears in their eyes, looking on with unabashed admiration. How the beat of the drums stirred their hearts, quickened their pulses, and filled them with both respect and gratitude to these noble protectors of the realm! A day such as this was never to be forgotten; children would one day tell their grandsons how they had witnessed with their own eyes the knights of Barcelona riding through Pansa, on their way to destroy the dreaded heathens of the south.

The horses strode over the dusty road and across the tiny plaza, where Father Augusto already had lined up the choir and led them in tuneful songs of praise. Chickens and pigs dodged the clattering hooves, scurrying away from the crowds and the sharp-eyed rabble eager to steal a free meal.

Sinbad, dizzied by this awesome display of pomp and

regalia, worked his way closer to the forefront, where Manuel de León and other respected members of the community had gathered to greet the noble visitors. A standard bearer smartly slapped the flanks of his mount and, riding to a point in front of the trumpeters and drummers, raised his barred banner higher. At the sight of the colors, the army halted. The standard bearer thrust the staff of his banner into the ground, where the flag slapped gently in the wind. The crowd hushed.

The front knight took off his velvet-plumed helmet and tucked it under his arm. He was young, Sinbad saw, but cold-eyed and stern, a true son of the aristocracy. The knight flexed his jaw and gazed upon the silent crowd. "God's grace to all of you," he said, flashing a grim smile to the host of well-wishers.

Two squires at his side held the reins of his nervous horse firmly, while two priests came forward, each making the sign of the cross before the peaceful gathering.

"What village is this?" inquired the knight of the grouped patrons.

"Pansa, your lordship," replied Manuel de León, bowing deeply.

The knight thought briefly and then nodded, as if finally recalling the name. Then he held out a ringed hand and permitted Manuel to kiss it, while the innkeeper fell humbly to his knees.

When the little ceremony was done and Manuel had stood, the knight held out his arms imperiously. "I am Don Carlos de Varga de Asunción," he proclaimed. And the villagers oohed and ahhed, although few had ever heard the name. "And for five days now my army has been on the march to reach Navarre."

Manuel cast down his eyes and said with humility: "Then would your lordship do me the great honor of passing the night within the walls of my humble inn?"

The knight lowered his head in a respectful gesture. "Alas, good landlord, but I cannot. Truly, there is little time for sleep when the hellish forces of our enemies gather near our borders."

The crowd gasped; no one had dared dream the Moors were so close. Many villagers clasped their hands in prayer, others wept openly.

"But be not disheartened," added the knight hastily. "Barcelona shall not stand idly by in the face of plunder. From Castile has come the word—a new leader has arisen among the believers in Christ. A man who shall carry our armies to victory upon the fields of battle. A man whose followers already number in the many thousands—"

"Who is the man?" cried Pepe the shepherd.

At this, the young knight smiled broadly, a look of satisfaction written into his boyish features. "I know not his true name," he acknowledged, "But to the people of Castile he is called *el Cid*." He leaned forward in his saddle and peered down at the questioning faces. "All of Castile is behind this man, this Cid, who has come to save us. But even one such as he is in need of an army—a brave and stout army of true men who shall not run in face of the Moors. Now, who among you will join me in my cause? Who among you will ride with me to Navarre and greet el Cid?"

For a long moment the crowd remained sullen and quiet, then: "I will come!" shouted the son of Alfonso the fisherman. "And I!" chimed newlywed Pablo the cobbler. And soon no less than thirty men, the cream of Pansa's manhood, had eagerly volunteered to walk beside the knights of Barcelona to join the holy war. Mothers and wives sobbed, even as Father Augusto tried to give them solace and comfort.

"Who else shall be with me?" called the knight, looking around for further adherents to his cause. A few boys were quick to raise their hands, but Don Carlos scowled and refused. There was little point in taking a boy under the age of ten.

"Has Pansa no more sons to offer?" questioned the

knight at Don Carlos' side. He crossed his arms over his plum-colored breastplate and gazed sternly at the elders.

Manuel opened his palms in a furtive gesture. "We are a tiny village, my lord. We cannot give what we do not have. But those whom you have so graciously permitted to walk beside you shall proudly do your honor. Had I sons of my own, I would gladly send them. But as you see . . ." He smiled wanly, shrugging his shoulders, and gestured to the three lovely girls standing together at the side of the road.

Don Carlos let his eyes linger appreciatively over their shapely forms, thinking it truly a pity he could not spend the night. Each girl would insure a most pleasant diversion, he realized, finding himself hard pressed to decide just which one he would favor, should he ever return. It was then that he caught sight of the muscular man beside the girl at the end.

Sinbad knew he had been seen. His heart was beating like a drum; he began to make rash plans for a sudden dash into the night if matters got out of hand.

"You! Yes, you! Come closer!"

At Don Carlos' beckoning, Sinbad stepped forward. The knight scrutinized him carefully, noting the well-tanned skin, the broad sweep of his shoulders, the cocky, almost arrogant way in which this peasant held himself.

"You seem a healthy specimen," he said gruffly, posing his body so that his shadow was cast over the standing figure. "Will you not heed my offer to fight?" Sinbad hesitated, and the knight smiled cruelly. "Or are you a coward?"

Manuel de León gasped; he had not nursed this sailor back to health just to have him put on a spit by Barcelona's aristrocrats.

"He is ill, my lord," stammered the innkeeper, stepping between the knight and the unhumbled mariner.

"Ill? Ill, you say?" Don Carlos raised a lofty brow. He looked to his closest companion and snickered. "What sort

33

of illness, eh? What sort of illness that a son of Pansa will not carry God's flag into glorious combat against the Moorish devils?"

Sinbad flinched. This fellow grated his nerves. Were circumstances a bit different, and he would not have to face an entire army intent on retribution, he would teach Don Carlos de Varga de Asunción a well deserved lesson or two.

María Victoria quickly stepped forward to Sinbad's side. Not to be outdone, María Elisa was right on her heels. "Forgive him, my lord!" cried Victoria with a curtsy and a smile for the incensed knight. "He is our cousin, nearly drowned in the terrible storm of this past week. Seawater has filled his lungs and left him dazed; I doubt he can even recall his own name. . . ."

"This is so," chimed Elisa, her eyes flashing at Don Carlos. "If you like, I can explain the matter to you in private."

Although her words were plain, her undertone was unmistakable, and Don Carlos stirred in his exquisitely carved saddle.

Vanessa also rushed from her place to stand beside Sinbad and her sisters. With a face as innocent as a rainbow, she pleaded with the displeased knight. "Do what you will with us, sire," she panted, "but ask not of our poor, sick cousin more than he can give."

With a dark scowl and a mistrust for the three sharp-witted women, Don Carlos pondered what he should do. Sinbad stood tense and angry, trying to subdue his growing rage. But on this occasion, he realized, silence was by far the better part of valor; Manuel de León's daughters had acted wisely and properly, although just why they would want to shield him like this was a puzzlement. Still, fortune was on his side so far, and it was better to play stupid if he must, letting these knights pass the village in peace.

At length, Don Carlos turned back to the agitated innkeeper. "You vouch for this man's infirmity?" he asked.

Manuel mopped a sweaty brow and nodded vehemently. "I do, my lord. The girls have spoken nothing but truth."

For a time Don Carlos seemed to waver; he leaned forward again, straining to look Sinbad in the eye. "So you don't even know your name, eh?" he chortled mockingly.

Amidst the darkness, María Victoria reached out and squeezed Sinbad's hand, her eyes imploring him not to say a word, lest it make matters worse. Sinbad swallowed his anger and stood mute. The knight fondled his sword, pretending to draw it from its scabbard. Then he glanced to his friends and winked, "A pity such a man must stay here among the women, wouldn't you say?"

The bold knights of Barcelona snickered among themselves. Don Carlos sighed and shook his head. "Very well," he relented. "We need not debate the matter. Time presses, Castile is waiting." He glanced down at the priests and made an imperial gesture, at which point the revered fathers gave a quick benediction. They blessed Pansa for the gift of her finest sons and extolled the armies of both Barcelona and Navarre to unite without jealousy behind el Cid, so that together they might enjoy great success against the enemy.

The people of the village stood silent and grim, remembering other leaders and other wars, each time praying that this would be the last. Finally, when the ceremony was done, Father Augusto said his own blessings for Don Carlos de Varga de Asunción and his army, and waited while mothers and fathers kissed their children good-bye. As the tearful crowd waved farewell, the young men of Pansa eagerly received weapons and took up places beside the footmen.

"Take care, good proprietor," said Don Carlos to Manuel, his eyes still on the girls. "And beware! Keep your daughters safe from those such as Suliman!"

"Suliman?" gasped Manuel, his mouth dropping. "Suliman is near?"

The knight nodded severely. "Protect yourselves, good villagers. The bandit is in the hills, waiting. You cannot be too careful."

"But will not Barcelona protect us as she has always done?" cried the anguished wife of Pablo the cobbler, whose husband stood beaming with his new shiny sword.

"Barcelona must fight upon the fields of battle," replied Don Carlos. "We have no forces to spare."

"But how are we to protect ourselves, when you have taken our sons and husbands?"

"Dear women, you are beside yourself," rebuked the knight. "Prayer is the answer. Seek your salvation in prayer."

The young woman cast down her eyes in shame and said no more. And with that, Don Carlos gave the signal; the standard bearer swept up his banner and raised it high. Trumpets blasted; the snare drums began their roll.

Don Carlos de Varga de Asunción sat straight in his saddle. He carefully placed his helmet back on and peered at the troops behind him through the slit in the shiny metal. Then he lifted his arm and lowered it abruptly. With the jab of spurs in their flanks, the fine steeds of Barcelona lurched ahead.

Dust clouds swirled everywhere. The villagers of Pansa stepped back, coughing and shielding their eyes while squires and pages cleared the way of stray pigs and chickens. The priests had resumed their chant, still making the sign of the cross as they passed, and Sinbad stood back watching while the tiny army made its way along the coastal road, slowly heading toward the walled city and other waiting forces. Soon they were gone from sight, the last roll of the drums faded into the night.

As Sinbad started to walk back to the inn, he became aware of the flurry of activity among the village elders, especially Manuel de León, who was busily trying to calm the anxious crowd.

"What's the matter?" Sinbad asked of María Vanessa, who was the closest to him at the moment.

The redheaded girl regarded him with a measure of shock. "But didn't you hear?" she protested. "Suliman the Filthy is close by!"

Sinbad scratched his head. "Suliman? I don't think I know the name . . ."

"You must indeed be from very far away, señor. He is the scourge of Córdoba. A murderer. A thief. An abductor and a slave trader."

Sinbad listened and nodded knowingly; there were such as Suliman throughout the world, touching every land with their vileness and cruelties. Brigands one and all, like vultures they hovered when there was strife, and even like those foul carrions, they swept down among the dead and helpless, plucking without conscience the fruits of honest men's toil.

Ingrained in the mariner from Baghdad was a loathing for pirates like that, and indeed he felt true anguish for the peaceful village. But he was in no position to help, he knew. With the aid of Manuel de León's charming daughters, he had barely escaped one close call; he could not afford another.

The night was alive with sound—crickets in the grass, owls hooting from the distant trees, the occasional barking of dogs, and the soft patter of restless horses in the stables. The wind whistled its way over the hills and the surf along the beach sang a soothing and familiar song.

Sinbad turned restlessly in his bed, gazing up at the moon, filling in with his mind's eye the missing stars among the constellations. The scent of roses was still in the air, and he smiled at the recollection of María Elisa's perfumed hair. What was the hour? How close to midnight was it? he wondered. And would she still keep her secret appointment in face of the evening's other events? Women had always been both his fortune and his bane, bringing life's joys in fruitful abundance, but also causing him his greatest sorrows and pain. Sinbad was no philosopher, not by any means, but he had always tried to heed the advice of Baghdad's wise men, knowing that although they spoke of theory and supposition, such wisdom could provide infinite value in an ordinary man's life when applied with thought.

When he was young, his own parents had had him well schooled in such matters. He counted among his tutors the finest historians, mathematicians, and men of science. Not to mention his early years when he dabbled in the arts. Painting and sculpture always left him bored; ah, but poetry, that was another matter entirely. In fact, if the sea had not lured him to her bosom like an errant wife, this very day he might still be at the caliph's court, a happy man, spinning his verse daily to the pleasure of all. Yet the men of philosophy had always held a special fascination for him, for they alone dealt with man and his imperfection striving to make sense out of a senseless world.

Sinbad mused upon his memories, wondering just what advice those aging sages might have for him now. It was a pleasant diversion, a way he frequently had passed lonely hours while sailing across the oceans. It took but a single rap on his door to yank him away from his thoughts.

"Come in," he said in a low voice.

The wooden door slowly opened, revealing a tall, divine silhouette against the backdrop of the garden. Sinbad smiled wolfishly. She had come after all!

The girl tiptoed inside and silently shut the door behind. Then she peered down at the sailor and grinned.

Sinbad's eyes widened. It was the wrong visitor!

"Victoria! What are you doing here?"

"Shhh," she whispered, putting a finger to her sensuous mouth. "I couldn't sleep, and I thought perhaps . . ." Her eyes kindled spryly.

"Won't your father be angry?"

María Victoria shrugged carelessly. She tilted her head so that her long hair tumbled over her uplifted breasts.

38

Then she came closer and seated herself at the corner of the bed.

Sinbad straightened up, eager to have her gone before her sister arrived, yet not wishing to make her feel unwelcome. "You should be long asleep by now," he told her in a brotherly fashion.

The girl shook her head and faced him sharply. With a degree of surprise, he realized that there were tears flowing from her black eyes. Ever the gallant gentleman, he offered her the handkerchief from the bed table and put a hand to her soft shoulder, saying: "What's wrong? Is there anything I can do?"

Victoria sniffed and forced a smile, reclining so that she rested against the propped pillows. "I'm frightened," she admitted, looking at him like a lost child.

"Of what? Suliman?"

María Victoria scoffed, waving a contemptuous hand. "Never of him—or any others like him."

"Then what?"

She reached out and placed the palm of her hand over his own. "Take me away from here," she pleaded. "I don't want to spend my life in Pansa. I want to be free, like you. I want to see the world, feel that I'm alive—oh, please, won't you take me with you? I'll do anything. *Anything!*"

"It wouldn't be possible, Victoria," he said gently, aware of her sensitivity. "You wouldn't be happy on the sea, never seeing your family or loved ones. And as for me," he sighed, "you don't even know me. Don't know anything about me."

"I know that you're a sailor. And I know that you're as daring as you are handsome . . ."

"Little enough to want to leave your home for," he pointed out.

But María Victoria remained undaunted. "I saw your face when Don Carlos made fun of you. A lesser man would have groveled at his feet. You didn't. If it wasn't for me and my sisters, you would have fought him man to man, isn't that so?"

Sinbad nodded. "You're very astute," he observed.

Victoria smiled. "That alone told me many things," she continued. "Few men would face up to so esteemed a nobleman on his own terms. But you did. Why?"

"I sought no confrontation," Sinbad stressed. "And I'm not as brave as you make me out to be."

At this her eyes rekindled with renewed flame. "I know one other thing," she said coyly. "I know that you've been purposely holding back information about yourself. You won't even tell me your name!"

Sinbad's casual manner suddenly vanished into a mood of deep concern. His hands took a firm grip on her arms and he gazed deeply into her luminous eyes. "I would gladly tell you everything there is to know about myself," he said. "I only fear that knowing about me might cause you and your sisters harm. And that is something I don't wish to see happen. You've been good to me, Victoria, and I'll never forget. But having one such as me in your house could cause great problems for your father—"

"Why, because you're not a Christian?"

His face grew impassive, and he studied the girl with a growing sense of trepidation. "How do you know that?"

María Victoria smiled like a cat. "I've suspected it from the very beginning. This morning, when I told you you were in Barcelona, I could see the shock on your face. And then again tonight, when Barcelona's army appeared so suddenly." Her smile deepened. "And earlier today I heard you swear by Allah. It was not so difficult to figure out. You're a Moor, stranded against his will in a land as alien to you as yours is to us."

Sinbad ran a dry tongue over drier lips. "Does . . . does anyone else share this discovery?"

Victoria's smile disappeared. "Elisa suspects, I'm sure. But she hasn't said anything, and neither shall I. There is no need for you to worry, your secret is safe."

Sinbad nodded gratefully, but inwardly he groaned. For all of his painstaking care, the girls had found out anyway. It wasn't that he did not trust them; quite the contrary, he did. But how long might it be before Manuel de León began to suspect? And would his reaction be quite so calm as that of his daughters? Then it was only a matter of time until others in the village started to wonder about the stranger in their midsts; it wouldn't take much for some reward-seeking villager to light out for Don Carlos' campsite and inform the already inflamed noble that a follower of Islam was hiding, and spying, in Pansa.

He shuddered at the thought. It could cost not only his own head, but those of the three sisters as well. "I must leave here at once," he stated flatly.

María Victoria shook her head. "It's foolish to run while you're still weak from your ordeal. Stay here. You'll be safe, I promise. And when the time comes, I'll help you in every way I can."

Sinbad was in a quandary. What was he to do? Events were becoming more complicated by the minute, and he cursed his ill-fortune.

Victoria wet her lips pensively, and her young heart looked with hunger to the man from the forbidden world she had been taught to mistrust and hate. Moonlight filtered through the branches of the trees, falling unevenly across her generous breasts like a sash of silver. Drawing a deep breath, she leaned over and kissed the sailor softly. "Trust me," she whispered. "Trust me. . . ."

The knock on the door startled her and she half jumped off the bed. "Quick," said Sinbad, thinking fast. He pulled the sheet off himself and quickly covered her. As the girl squirmed nervously, he got up and walked silently to the door.

"Who's there?"

"It's me," came a familiar whisper.

Sinbad put a hand to his forehead and moaned. It was Elisa.

"Let me in," she demanded.

María Victoria poked her head out from under the sheet and stared with startled eyes. "It's my sister!" she squealed. "The bitch!"

"Shhh!" Sinbad quickstepped back to the bed and pulled off the cover where Victoria lay waiting. He pointed to the open window. "Better get out before you're caught."

María Victoria fumed. "I'm not leaving," she rasped. "Tell Elisa to go away."

"Is someone inside there with you?" came the voice from behind the door. Elisa held her ground, tapping a foot nervously against the pebble-strewn path. "Are you letting me in or not?"

"Yes, yes. Just a second." Then he turned back to the girl planted firmly upon his bed. "Please, Victoria. Don't cause me problems. You promised to help me, right? If Elisa finds you here, she could get so angry that she'll tell your father everything." He gazed down at the girl pleadingly but sternly. "That wouldn't help either one of us very much, would it?"

Victoria chewed stubbornly at her lip; she was furious at this unexpected turn of events. Absolutely livid. Enraged to the point of wanting to tear out her sister's hair. But her house guest was right, she knew. If Papá were to hear about this, it would be the worst possible thing that could happen. She would most likely find herself confined to the kitchen for a month, and cause the sailor to be thrown out of the villa tied to a burro.

As Sinbad waited anxiously, she said: "All right, I'll go—*if* you give your word to help me leave Pansa also."

Without thinking, Sinbad agreed, feeling that by tomorrow he could talk her out of it. Then, with a heave of her shoulders, María Victoria got up; she threw him a hasty kiss and hurried to the window, through which she climbed into the night without making a sound. Sinbad watched for a moment as she ran along the row of hedges and finally reached the darkened house. With a long sigh of relief, he wiped the perspiration from his brow and opened the door for the waiting Elisa.

The girl came in mumbling about his delay in receiving her. Sinbad, feigning being woken from a sound sleep, half listened, his eyes widening as he realized that Victoria had left her scarf where it had fallen to the floor at the side of the bed.

Elisa glanced about the dark room, and noticed the askew sheets. "Has someone been here?" she asked.

Sinbad shook his head.

She looked at him thoughtfully, trying to decide whether to believe him or not. Then, as she basked in the slanting moonbeams, she grinned and held out her arms. Sinbad's eyes were glued to her scanty nightdress and the exposed mounds of her breasts gently rising and falling with her quick breaths. He drew her close to him in a tender embrace, carefully kicking the fallen scarf under the bed.

Elisa moaned softly as his mouth came down upon hers; she dug her fingernails into his muscles. At the feel of her supple flesh pressed so closely against him, Sinbad felt his sapped energies beginning to return.

"It seemed the night would last forever, *mi amor*," Elisa whispered in his ear. The moon rode high on the back of a passing white cloud as he arched her body forward, leading her gently to the bed. She looked at him breathlessly, passionately, her eyes smoldering with liquid fires.

Sinbad pressed his lips to the cleavage of her breasts, feeling her heartbeat quicken as he slipped the flimsy strap from her shoulders. The nightgown tumbled to the floor; she stood naked before him, a silver silhouette, perfectly carved, like a perfect living sculpture.

Elisa groaned deep in her throat, slitting her eyes as Sinbad's hands gently explored her secrets. In these moments of shared desire, time and circumstance lost all meaning. Entwined in each other's arms, they fell to the bed, bodies glistening with the heat of their need. Hips swaying rhythmically, Elisa gasped at the feel of him,

43

living in a moment of ecstasy that rose to heights of burning emotion hungrily aching to be consumed.

Like a volcano their passion exploded, and down, down they descended, still tingling with the afterglow. Then side by side they lay, unspeaking, gazing deeply into each other's faces.

Sinbad closed his eyes contentedly; Elisa purred as she snuggled her head in the crook of his arm. She had wondered what being with this nameless stranger would be like; dreamed about it since the moment she had seen him. Now those questions had been answered and she smiled with satisfaction. She had not been disappointed.

"Are you asleep, *amor?*"

Sinbad drew a deep breath of the crisp night air and shook his head. Elisa drew little circles on his chest with her finger. Then she reached out and touched his cheek. "When will you leave?" she asked.

The question caught him off guard. In these past minutes he had all but forgotten his surroundings and dangers, losing himself completely to Elisa's gentle touch. Suddenly—and regretfully—he had been snapped back to reality, to facing decisions he must not delay.

"Tomorrow, if I can," he answered.

Elisa sighed. "So soon? Must it be so? Can't you stay just a few days longer?"

"The longer I stay, the worse for all." He kissed the top of her head and mussed her hair. Elisa, eyes open wide, grinned girlishly. "And I can't . . . er . . . persuade you otherwise?"

He laughed, fondly slapping her on the buttocks. "I think not, my Barcelonian princess. Tomorrow it must be."

"Where will you go?"

"South, where I'll be safe. And then perhaps I can look for my ship. Our destination had been the Pillars of Hercules, but likely as not my crew has taken to harbor for repairs. With luck I can rejoin them before they set sail again."

"They say there is only the edge of the world beyond the Pillars of Hercules," she told him.

Sinbad laughed again and shrugged. "Who knows? A mariner will sail any sea that lies before him."

"And if there is no sea to sail, then what?"

"Then, maybe we shall go home at last."

His eyes had brightened noticeably at the mention of home, Elisa saw, and it was a wistful, if not sad, smile that came to his lips. Elisa propped herself up and, resting her chin in an open hand, she looked at him with a woman's curiosity. "I think you must miss you home very much," she said.

"More than I can tell you, Elisa. No matter how many leagues a man may travel, no matter how many years of his life he spends in other cities or climes, home is still the center of a man's universe. Without it, he is lost."

Elisa smiled, touching his face lightly with her fingertips. For all his courage and daring, he struck her as a gentle man, of far deeper emotion than appeared on the surface. Such sensitivity was unusual in a sailor, she thought, but then, everything she had so far learned about him assured her he was no ordinary mariner. But exactly what—and who—he was remained a mystery.

"Where is this home of yours?" she asked suddenly.

"Very far away, Elisa. Across the world . . ."

"Then you are not a Moor of Córdoba?"

Sinbad seemed genuinely amused. "Hardly. Their land is as far from mine as Barcelona is."

Elisa became more intrigued than ever. "Won't you speak to me of it?" she entreated. "Tell me all about this place you miss so dearly? About your life and the loved ones you left behind?"

His smile turned sour. "I left only one person behind," he admitted. "Only one. But even should I return, there would be no one waiting."

45

"Why must you speak in riddles? Has your land not a name? Have you not a name?"

Sinbad was forced to laugh; this girl was determined in having her way with him, one way or another. The more questions he answered, the more she found to ask. Still, it could do little harm, he reasoned, and he owed her far more.

"My name is Sinbad," he told her, "and I come from a city called Baghdad . . ."

"*Sinbad, Baghdad.*" Elisa repeated the names, rolling them off her tongue. "I have heard of the city," she said proudly. "They say it is ↑ beautiful city of the East."

"Perhaps the most be. tiful in the world. The rival of Damascus. The center of culture and art, of trade, of philosophy. Where there has been no war since before my father's lifetime, where the rivers flow in serenity and the lands bloom in fertility. All the nations of the world converge at Baghdad's door. Our caravans travel daily to India, to Persia, to the deserts of Arabia. Our ships are laden with cargo for Abyssinia and the Dark Continent, for Tripoli and Alexandria. Even for Tangier, Valencia . . ."

"You sound very proud of your home," she interrupted.

Sinbad nodded. "Forgive me, Elisa, if I've become carried away but once you have seen Baghdad, she is never to be forgotten. She burns like a candle forever in your soul."

"Then going home will certainly be a joyous occasion," said the girl with admiration.

But Sinbad frowned when she said that. "I think not, Elisa."

"But why? If Baghdad is all you say—"

"She is. Indeed she is! But I have reasons of my own, you see. Reasons that make my journey home perilous to myself and my friends."

This all seemed very puzzling and mysterious to this daughter of Pansa who had never traveled more than a few kilometers beyond her village. Yet there are some things

46

in the world that are universal, as much a fact in tiny Pansa as they were in mighty Baghdad. Elisa forced him to gaze at her and nodded knowingly. "It is the one you left behind," she said.

"You are very wise for one so young."

Elisa laughed. "No, not really. But I recognize the look of love in your eyes even as I recognize it in my own. Can't you tell me your tale?"

"Is it not enough to know that I was forced to flee Baghdad a virtual criminal?"

His words were meant to shock her, but Elisa remained unperturbed. "Sometimes it is good to bare one's heart," she said contemplatively. "They say it cleanses the soul . . ."

Sinbad's eyes danced and he grinned. "So you are something of a poet yourself?"

Elisa shared his brief moment of laughter. "I want to hear," she insisted. "I want to hear it all."

"All?" He glanced from the window at the moon, hazy and low, hanging above the treetops. "It's a long story," he said with a chuckle. "It could take me all night."

The girl leaned back, staring up at the needles of light fading across the shadowed ceiling. "We have all night," she replied. "Please, Sinbad! What matter to you now? Tomorrow by this time you shall be gone from Pansa, a memory in my heart and nothing more. But *tonight*,"—her face glowed with excitement—"ah, tonight we share together, the two of us, alone with only our thoughts and dreams."

Sinbad hesitated, and she took his hand, locking her dark eyes with his own. "Tell me, Sinbad," she implored. "Speak to me of this city called Baghdad, of your adventures, of all the strange and wondrous things you've seen. Tell me, Sinbad, of friends and foes, of honesty and deceit, of glories and defeats, of riches and nobles, of beggars and thieves. Tell me all this and more, entrust to me everything, and I can gaze into your life the way a Gypsy gazes into her crystal of magic. The very secrets of your being, Sinbad. I shall settle for no less."

Sinbad listened to her, enchanted by her charms and wiles. Her eagerness reminded him in some ways of himself and his own thirst to know the world's mysteries. The matters that Elisa had asked about were often painful for him, though, and never before had he shared them with anyone. Yet here he was, beside this Castilian beauty, so distant from home and about to bare his soul. He never would have thought it possible.

"All right," he said with a sigh. "I'll tell you all. Some will seem strange, I know, much even unbelievable. But I ask that you listen and trust that all spoken tonight is truth. I would have it no other way."

Elisa readily nodded, thrilled at the prospect.

Sinbad sat back comfortably, his eyes now closed, ready to start the story. But where was he to begin? Should it be in those early days when adventure was new and his exploits sung in ballads by pretty handmaidens at the caliph's court? Should he recount to Elisa each of his fabled world voyages, telling the incredible perils he surmounted to achieve fame and fortune?

These tales were all but meaningless now, he decided. His real story began only later—much later, in fact. Perhaps on the same day that he returned home from the voyage that was to be his final one. His ship had sailed from the port of Basra, up the Tigris River to Baghdad itself, beneath purple skies and a golden sun. How bright the future had seemed! How wonderful the world and life! And how invincible he had thought to himself. There was nothing not his for the asking, and his life was about to bloom.

Yes, that was the place to begin. But was it merely a year ago that all this happened, or countless lifetimes? Perhaps both, perhaps neither. Perhaps existence itself was only a dream. . . .

PART TWO:

WHY SINBAD WAS FORCED TO
FLEE HIS BELOVED BAGHDAD
AND HOW HE MET DON GIO-
VANNI, AND HOW THEY BOTH
DECIDED TO SHARE THE FU-
TURE.

A serene quiet lay over the ancient city of Baghdad that early dawn. It was summer, and the heat waves had already begun to dance from roof to roof and shimmer in the pale light of polished marble walls. Dozens of spires and minarets cast the purple shadows of morning, while the domes of mosques and public buildings were softened by the lingering haze of the night before. Few citizens had yet roused from their slumber on this holiday, and only the occasional clatter of hooves against flagstone broke the tranquil silence.

Rubbing the sleep from his eyes, Schahriar, caliph of all Baghdad, drew aside the embroidered curtains of his resplendent bedchamber and peered over the balcony wall, beyond the courtyard and park below, beyond the gardens and well-tended hedges, past the palace grounds with its fine statues and spouting fountains, and out toward the city itself. His beloved city.

Each morning, throughout all the twenty-seven years since he had taken the throne, his routine rarely varied. He enjoyed gazing upon the city when he awoke, just as he did at night, before he retired. He loved his city, and guarded her interests with jealousy, even as his soldiers alertly guarded her from harm. Justice for every man had been his guiding principle since the beginning—justice for all, not merely for those of wealth and powerful position within the court. And because of this, his people loved him dearly.

Yet Schahriar was unhappy. Nearing the twilight of his years, he now wished only two wishes: first, that his memory remain strong; second, that before he died Allah might grant him an heir. A son. For although his wives had borne him sixty-three beautiful and clever daughters, he had no male to carry on in his place. And so it was that the mighty caliph, despite his abundance, grew tense and bitter in the short time left to him.

As he gazed somberly at the sun, rising majestically over the turquoise waters of the Tigris River, he was hardly aware when the doors to his bedroom opened and a dark-faced, turbaned man came to his side. Although his dress was that of the court, his very stance readily told that he once had been a soldier. Now in his middle years, it was only the deep lines in his face that betrayed his advancing age. He held himself proudly, chin always high, wide shoulders thrown back, chest expansive, and bowed respectfully before his liege.

"Good morning, sire," he said in a husky voice.

Schahriar turned to him in greeting. "Ah, good minister, you startled me."

"Forgive me, my liege, but your thoughts must have been most intent not to have heard me knock."

The caliph put his palms to his rounded belly and smiled. "Old age does many strange things to men," he observed.

The minister frowned, seemingly offended. "You are as trim as your palace captains," he snorted. "Let no man tell you otherwise." He had served his caliph for every one of the twenty-seven years of his reign, shared with Schahriar both fortune and misfortune, fought as a brother at his side, stood by him through times of peril and luck. And now it saddened him greatly to see his liege so despondent, lost in morbid thought about his death, and his sorrow for the lack of an heir.

Still smiling, the caliph grasped him by the shoulders.

"Thank you, dear friend and lifetime companion. Of all my flock, you are without question the most faithful."

The minister shook his head firmly. "No, sire. You are wrong. All your people love you and admire you. They always have, and they always shall."

Schahriar nodded sadly and turned his gaze back to his panoramic view. By now the sun was full and blazing; he could hear the call to prayer issued by the holy men quite plainly, and sleepy-eyed citizens were already leaving their homes and taking to the busy thoroughfares. " 'Tis true they may love me now," he said. "Yet, without the heir I seek, I will soon be forgotten. Lost to the pages of history, a brief chapter in Baghdad's glorious past."

Beneath heavy black brows, the minister's gray eyes grew cold. "Never, sire! With my own hand I would strangle the man who dared utter such untruths before me. I could name for you a hundred men—nay, a thousand!—who would take their very lives gladly if you so required it!"

The weary caliph drummed his fingers against his thighs, knowing that in his heart this was so. Yet . . .

"You mean me well, Dormo. You are the best friend I have ever had. My cousin chose well in taking you for a husband . . ."

"Sire—" The minister flushed in humility, and the caliph raised an imperial hand for him to hold his tongue. "But alas," Schahriar continued, "my people have memories shorter than your own. As long as their bellies are filled and our troops protect their land and homes, they care not the name of the man who rules them."

Dormo the Greek responded angrily. "It's not so, my liege! I recall the day we fought the Assyrian barbarians; the people kissed your feet, throngs lined the streets to greet your triumphant homecoming, throwing flowers and kisses, reciting ballads, praising your name as though you were the Prophet of Islam himself!"

The caliph sighed. "Yes, minister," he murmured, recalling that day of glory. "But that was long, long ago. We were both young men then."

"And what of the years since? See for yourself, sire!" Dormo's arm gestured grandly, sweeping across the city, encompassing the mountain lands in the distance and the nearby river. "Baghdad can sleep peacefully because of your reign, my lord. Is this not true? Strike out my tongue if I lie! We have no famine, our storage houses are bulging with produce, and no man, save for the lowest of beggars, knows the meaning of hunger. And look to our ships! Even as we speak, they ply the river from the coast, laden with goods and trade, each cargo furnishing Baghdad with greater variety than even Damascus can boast." He bowed stiffly. "All this is because of you, sire. No man can claim to replace you."

Schahriar eyed him skeptically. "*No man,* loyal soldier and friend?" He glanced again at the calm waters, singling out a ship larger than the others. The ship flew golden banners from its highest mast as it cut sharply through the water toward the city. Already small crowds of people were lining the banks of the Tigris, cheering and applauding while the sleek, fast vessel sailed toward its berth.

"*There* be one man who might take my place," he said.

The caliph's First Minister also recognized the ship at once—he knew there were few men in all of Baghdad who could not. The return of this ship had become a cause of great festivity.

"Captain Sinbad," mumbled Dormo.

Schahriar nodded dourly. "Aye. Captain Sinbad."

The minister shook his head. "I still say you are wrong, sire. Sinbad is counted among your most worthy and loving subjects. Never once has he begrudged your coffers their share of his fortunes. Gladly he has given, and does give. There is no malice in his heart, I assure you. He seeks naught for himself, not even the riches he acquires.

Why, all men know that of each gold piece of profit, fully one third he gives to the poor."

"And my people adore him for it," grumbled the caliph. "Be not misled, my friend. I, too, love Sinbad. In many ways I regard him as of my own family." He shook his head ruefully. "Yet I fear his name shall one day over-shadow my own."

"Never!" flared the minister with indignation. "As much as I regard the man, I would see him exiled or dead before letting that happen."

Schahriar eyed his companion keenly. Cheers were resounding more loudly now from all quarters of the city; criers joyously ran through the streets issuing the tidings: "Sinbad is back! Captain Sinbad has returned!"

"Do you see?" said the caliph.

Dormo, who had once been a slave, freed by Schahriar thirty years before, nodded gloomily. "What is to be done?" he asked in a whisper.

The caliph stood thoughtful and silent for a time, and then he said: "I must have an heir. I must find for myself a new wife, one who can surely bear me a son while there is yet time."

Dormo sighed with relief that the request was only this. "I shall scour the kingdom for a woman to please you, sire."

Schahriar waved a hand. "That will not be necessary, minister. I have given the matter careful consideration." He leaned in closer to his friend. "And I have already chosen."

The First Minister's eyebrows rose. "My lord?"

The caliph chuckled. "I have chosen a girl, perhaps the fairest in the land. The daughter of a man dear to me, whom I know shall respect my wishes to the letter and see to it his child comes to me willingly."

A thin smile crossed the First Minister's lips. As long as he had known the caliph, Schahriar had never failed to surprise him.

"I have stood by you all my life, sire," Dormo said. "First as palace captain, then as general of your army. Now as minister and trusted vizier, keeper of your state. Let me wonder no longer; my curiosity cannot be contained. Whose daughter have you chosen to be your bride?"

The Caliph of Baghdad grinned. "Your own."

At first Dormo laughed, but the caliph's stony expression indicated that humor had definitely not been intended, and as this realization dawned, Dormo visibly paled. "You . . . you cannot be serious, sire . . ."

"Ah, but I am. Scheherazade must wed me before the week is done."

"But—but—" sputtered Dormo, "she is already betrothed! Since childhood! Surely you know that!"

The caliph looked at him callously. "That vow is voided by imperial edict. It no longer exists. Both parties shall be so informed today."

Dormo swallowed hard. He loved the caliph, he truly did. If Schahriar were to demand his head, he would chop it off himself if necessary. But to do this? To tear his beloved daughter away from the man she adored . . . It was a higher price than he could ever have imagined.

"I beg you, sire," he pleaded, falling to his knees and kissing both of the caliph's bejeweled hands. "Do not ask this of me. Do not force my child to be wrenched from the man who has sworn to wed her. The man who—"

But Schahriar was unrelenting. He had made up his mind and no power on earth could alter it. "Speak not to me of this man!" he barked in anger, veins popping from his thick throat. "This man must keep forever silent! And he must bless this wedding even as I know you shall."

"But sire!"

The caliph's face darkened with contempt. "Don't grovel like a dog, Dormo. You should be pleased. Your daughter shall bear the future caliph of all Baghdad!"

"I am pleased," he stammered, seeking words not to offend. "But I am also concerned. Sire, both my daughter and her betrothed are deeply in love. Would you rob the young of happiness?"

"For an heir, yes!" boomed the caliph, his voice thundering through the hallways of the grand palace. "You shall depart for your home at once—and tell Scheherazade of my decision."

Dormo nodded, his face broken out in a cold sweat. "And what shall I tell her betrothed?"

The caliph's eyes flickered. He would have his bride and his heir, and be rid of a thorn in his side forever. "Tell our daring Captain Sinbad whatever you will—but inform him that should he argue the point, my executioners shall gladly finish the debate for him. Now go!"

Dormo, the Greek vizier, First Minister of the caliph's court, bowed low. Then, as he hurried from the chamber to carry the shattering tidings, he realized, for perhaps the first time in his life, just how evilly fate could deal with those who greeted it with innocent smiles.

From where Scheherazade stood in the cool shadows of the roofless gallery, she could see against the evening sky the hills leading away toward the desert. She closed her eyes, aware of the tears, and drew a deep breath of fragrant air rising from the lush gardens below. She was not only weary, but sick in spirit as well. Her entire world had come crashing in on her, violently, terrifyingly. This wasn't really happening, she told herself over and over, hoping somehow to convince her broken heart that the news her father had brought this afternoon had only been an illusion. It couldn't be otherwise. It *couldn't!*

A servant quietly entered the open chamber, lighting the lamps on the pedestals, opening the curtains more fully so that sunset could be observed in all its glorious splendor. Scheherazade loved to watch the sun go down and the stars rise. As a child she had spent countless hours in this very room, gazing and musing, listening to the birds sing and observing the breathtaking beauty of the day's end. This evening, though, her thoughts were far from the glitter of stars and the shine of the moon. Rubbing nervously at her arms, biting hard on trembling lips, she bowed her head and cried softly to herself. For her, life had come to an end; the future was past and she was doomed.

Dormo entered the room without a sound and beckoned for the servant to leave. His heart ached as he looked at his daughter, feeling her pain and sympathizing with her misery. But what was there for him to do? None of this had been his own idea, in front of almighty Allah he had fallen before the caliph and begged him to change his mind. All his efforts had been futile, though; the caliph was resolute. To try and deceive Schahriar would only make matters worse, and heads would roll for it.

Dormo stepped lightly over the maroon and gold rugs scattered across the mosaic floor, his eyes glancing fretfully at the colorful frescos and tapestries that clung to the walls. Paintings and tapestries that his daughter had painstakingly designed and woven herself during the long months of Sinbad's many voyages. In the corners of the huge chamber stood tall and unusual vases of the highest quality and symmetry, Scheherazade's favorites, brought to her from the farthest-flung empires of the globe— Persia, Arabia, India, Athens—each a gift from Sinbad upon his return, each attesting to a different exotic spot to which the mariner had journeyed.

A small ivory taboret stood beside the grand marble columns; Dormo glanced at the untouched setting upon it and frowned. His servant had brought the girl the lightest of suppers—cheese, fruit, a pitcher of the finest honey-flavored juice. But the girl had not taken a thing. With a heavy sigh, Dormo picked up a crystal goblet and sipped slowly, struggling within himself to find the right words to comfort her.

Scheherazade heard as he replaced the goblet and turned toward her father abruptly. Her black hair, so long and

58

silkysmooth, was totally disheveled, her normally bright and pensive eyes now glassy and red from crying. She made to speak, but the only sound to come from her soft throat was a squeal. Her lips quivered and she put her hands to her face, weeping a new flood of tears.

Anguished Dormo reached out to touch her. "Sherry, don't," he beseeched. "It won't be so awful. You'll see. And think of it! The caliph's wife—his First Wife. And the son you bear him will make the other harem wives howl with envy." His hand took the sleeve of her costly and fashionable dress.

"Don't you touch me!" she flared, pulling away fiercely as though her father were a wild animal.

Shock and hurt mingled in his sharply etched features. "Please, Sherry. Listen to me. I did my best. Truly—"

"I hate you!" she cried, sobbing and ranting, banging her open palms against the Doric columns.

Dormo hung his head, shaking it slowly. How could this have happened? he wondered. How could such a perfect life be so suddenly spoiled at the whim of an old, jealous, spiteful man? Still, the caliph's word was law. His own duty, and Sherry's—whether they liked it or not—was to obey and keep silent.

"You are very young, child," he said. "You don't understand these matters. Listen to me, let me be the one to break the news to Sinbad. Let me—"

Dormo ducked as a crystal goblet went flying, shattering into a thousand pieces as it sailed past his head and smashed against the wall.

"Get out of here! Leave me alone, do you hear!"

Dormo held out his hands. "Sherry, you don't mean that—"

This time the bowl of fruit went flying, pears and grapes and oranges tossed and tumbling, the wooden bowl skidding and bouncing across the floor and finally coming to rest at the extreme end of the resplendent chamber.

Scheherazade balled her hands into tiny fists and glared

menacingly at her father. As distraught as she was, though, she still managed to hold herself erect and proud. Dormo could see in the defiant girl the traits of her mother, that stunning and rebellious Arabian girl he had married so long before. If only she had lived to see Sherry become a woman, to see her now . . .

Sherry picked up a large vase with both her hands and held it high above her head. "I'm not joking with you, Father," she hissed. "I'm never going to speak to you again! Now be gone before I do something we'll both regret!"

Dormo drew back hastily as the girl motioned to heave the vase. "All right, I'll go! But I'll be back," he warned, shaking his index finger at her. "And when the caliph beckons, you'll come to him sweet and blushing like a proper bride—on your knees and kissing his hand for the honor he has bestowed upon you!"

"Never!" she vowed, her eyes flashing with fiery intensity. "I'll never submit myself willingly to that bloated old goat!"

"You will, Scheherazade!"

"*I won't!* They'll have to carry me in—kicking and screaming every step of the way!"

Dormo flushed crimson with anger. He knew his daughter well enough to know that she would keep such a promise—thereby insuring a swift end to the family line. The enraged caliph would demand both their heads for such defiance; he was a man who minced no words with women, be they vizier's daughters or no.

Why has Allah both blessed and cursed me with such a headstrong child? Dormo moaned to himself. His strong-willed daughter would be the death of him yet!

"You're being very foolish about this, Sherry—"

The girl laughed bitterly, her curly black hair forming a curtain across half of her face. "Am I?" she snapped, with a glare so icy that it sent shivers down Dormo's spine. "Or is it that you're just too afraid to be a real man for once—to

60

stand up to the caliph and tell him that your daughter's hand is already promised to another."

Dormo threw up his hands in exasperation, taxed to the limit. He swung himself onto the velvet divan and gazed at Sherry, his face filled with foreboding.

Still shaking, Sherry put down the vase and knelt at the feet of her father, clasping his fingers between her soft, slim hands. "Please, Father," she begged. "Let me marry Sinbad; we can be wed immediately, the caliph will find another. He needs me not . . ."

"He needs an heir," mumbled Dormo softly, patting her unruly hair.

Sherry's eyes flashed hotly. "Am I a mare to be wed merely to bear him a son? The caliph can find someone else—he has but to snap his finger and a thousand women will gladly obey."

"But he has chosen you, my child. It's you he desires."

The girl looked at him mockingly. "You are a poor diplomat, Father. Our caliph cares not for me one whit!"

"That isn't so!" protested Dormo.

"It is so! Why, in court he barely ever gave me a second glance, so preoccupied is he with his toy soldiers and other affairs of state."

The minister glanced about the room uneasily. "Hush, child! The caliph has many spies. Let not your angry words be overheard lest they be repeated with more malice than you had intended."

Sherry sighed, shaking her head disconsolately. Even in her own home she dared not speak her mind openly! "Oh, Father," she went on, lowering her voice, "Don't you see? Schahriar forces this marriage not out of love for me, but to get even with Sinbad. He is jealous, Father. *Jealous!*"

Dormo put his head in his hands and groaned, softly weeping before his only daughter. "Dear, dear child," he muttered, "the caliph remains my closest friend. Without him I might yet be a slave here in Baghdad. And I understand him better than you give me credit for. Schahriar has been a good ruler for us; he has been a noble caliph. Alas,"—and here he sighed deeply—"his heart has hardened in his later years; he can see only what he wishes to see." Sherry squeezed her father's hand and Dormo looked at her painfully. "He has made his decision, child, one as firm and resolute as he has ever made. *You* shall be his bride."

"To force me to marry the caliph is to sign for me a warrant of death," said the girl.

"Oh, no, Sherry. You're wrong. Believe me, you're wrong. Think upon the future—and the child of your own flesh who shall one day sit upon Baghdad's throne. You will be the most important woman in our empire."

"Without Sinbad I am nothing," she lamented. A dark cloud crossed the face of the dipping sun and Sherry watched as it shadowed the gallery. It portended only grief, she was sure, darkening the sky as it did this very moment.

"Will you dry your tears, daughter, and come tomorrow with me in joy to your new husband?"

She shook her head firmly. "Father, no. I can't . . ." She cried again, like a little girl caught alone in a thunderstorm, only this time the maelstrom would last a lifetime.

As the girl buried her head against his breast and sobbed, Dormo ran his fingers through her long hair, soothing her as best he could in the same fashion he had always done when she was a child.

"It is better if I be the one to speak with Sinbad," he said after a time, when Sherry was cried out.

She peered up at him through watery, luminous eyes. "No, Father I shall tell him; I owe him at least that."

Dormo nodded reluctantly. The caliph would certainly be displeased if word of this rendezvous reached his ears, yet how could he, Dormo, deny his daughter this small wish? Sinbad would be greatly grieved, of course—he would return to his home, get drunk, and then sulk. But the pain would pass, and the captain would one day find another. It would be much the same for Sherry, and although he knew his daughter would never be able to love the caliph in the same way she did the bold mariner, he hoped that with time her heart would mellow and she would accept what destiny had chosen for her.

It was almost night outside; Dormo kissed the girl and slowly stood. Sinbad would be due at any moment, he knew. The dashing sailor never failed to visit their house upon the day of his arrival home.

He took his daughter's hands into his own and forced her to look at him. "You'll say what must be told immediately upon his arrival?"

Sherry nodded. "I promise. No time shall I waste." Then she dried her eyes with her silk handkerchief and gazed at the glittering stars. "Leave me now," she asked. "Sinbad shall be coming, and until he does, I prefer to be alone."

Captain Sinbad's arrival home had Baghdad humming with speculation. Although no one knew of Schahriar's plan to wed the mariner's betrothed, many suspected the caliph's jealousy and pondered what he might do.

The heat was intense in the late afternoon when Sinbad's ship had finally berthed and been unloaded. As the turbaned captain happily completed his arrangements to sell his cargo to the city's eager merchants, he thought not one iota of the handsome profit he would reap, but only of the waiting girl at the vizier's grand estate outside the palace walls.

Business finished at last, he returned to the city, preferring to walk among the milling throngs of his people rather than ride to Sherry's arms. Crowds of citizens jostled each other uneasily amid the bazaars and markets; Sinbad took it all in with exhilaration, thinking how good it felt to be back home at last. Needless to say, the perils of his last voyage had been many; he had barely escaped with his life on more than one occasion. This was behind him now, though, and he felt only the joy of Baghdad encompassing him.

He crossed the main thoroughfares, paying no attention to the cries of vendors hawking their wares, the acrobats and jugglers and magicians performing on virtually every corner. The memory of Sherry's scented hair held him captive, the recollection of her honeyed lips on his, her warm and tender embrace. Sinbad walked quickly through the city, waving hello to friends and a multitude of well-wishers, but never once pausing to speak. Under his arm he carried a single package, a special gift that would put to shame anything he had brought her before. It was a dazzling diadem—stolen from the caves of the Cyclops—a priceless gift unlike any other in all of Araby.

With a merry tune upon his lips and a new poem working at the corners of his mind, he came at last to the spacious home of the vizier. He plucked a rose from the garden, inhaled the sweet fragrance, and hurried up the stone steps two at a time. He gazed briefly at the moon, sighing wistfully, then knocked upon the carved bronze doors.

The servant bowed in greeting and led the way in. Sinbad bantered with the man, whom he had known for all the years since, as a young boy, he had first come here and seen Sherry. The servant, although willingly exchanging small talk, would not meet Sinbad's eyes with his own.

Peculiar, thought the mariner as he followed him along the wide, well lit corridors. But he decided that it was a matter unworthy of dwelling upon. Passing the courtyard, he greeted several other servants, all well known and trusted by him. They, too, seemed pleased to see him, yet they, too, shied from direct confrontation. At this, Sinbad's thick black brows furrowed. A nagging feeling somewhere deep in his gut cautioned him that something was amiss.

Into the spacious chamber he was swiftly taken, whereupon he was left standing alone in the shadows of the brazier. His eyes scanned the room slowly, taking in the familiar artifacts and recalling the pleasant memories that were associated with them all.

Then, as he gazed to the balcony, he saw Sherry, her

back to him, her dress gently flowing in the breeze, her face lifted to peer at the multitude of beguiling stars shining on this clear, perfect night.

His sandals pattered softly across the stone, and Sherry turned to greet him. As Sinbad came closer he saw that her eyes were bloodshot, her small mouth turned down in a frown, and her lips slightly quivering.

"Sherry! What's wrong?"

"Oh, Sinbad," she sniffed as she held out her arms and ran to him. The lovers embraced closely; Sinbad swept her off her feet and kissed her again and again.

"How I've missed you," she wept, clinging to him fiercely. "How much I've longed for this moment when we could be together—"

"Forever, Sherry. *Forever*."

She burst into sudden tears again, and Sinbad, his features darkening, held her at half arms' length. "What is it, beloved?" he asked worriedly, wondering if perhaps during his absence some grave illness had stricken her family.

She shook her head from side to side, delaying the inevitable moment. "I'm . . . I'm so frightened," she cried, her hand to her mouth. "So frightened and so ashamed . . ."

Sinbad was bewildered. "Ashamed? Sherry, what has happened? Why are you acting like this?"

"The caliph had demanded my appearance in court tomorrow—"

Sinbad laughed and held her close again. "Is *that* all? Ah, my sweet! Do you still fear the old man the way you used to when you were a child?" He put a finger to her chin and lifted her head. "There is no need for these tears, my darling. The caliph means you no ill."

Sherry's heart beat faster. "I know," she whispered. "But he does mean ill for you."

The mariner looked at her incredulously. "Don't be silly, Sherry. I know the rumors about his envy; I know he grumbles and barks, sulks and schemes. But he's really quite harmless, I assure you. Listen, tomorrow I go to court as well. Shall we not go together and announce our wedding date?"

The girl gasped and turned away. Sinbad's face contorted into a mask of puzzlement.

"We . . . we cannot be married," she whimpered, struggling not to weep again.

"*What?* What in the name of the Prophet are you talking about, girl? Not be wed? You and I? Is this a joke or a game? If so, I find little humor."

Sherry burst into sobs and crushed herself as tightly against him as she possibly could. "Would that I were jesting!" she wailed. "Would that today was but an evil dream!"

He took her by the shoulders, more roughly than he had intended, and forced her to look at him. "What's happened in my absence, Sherry? What has transpired that you say these terrible things?"

"Sinbad, Sinbad! What can I do? What can I do?" She choked on her tears. "The caliph has choosen a new bride—and *I* am to be the one!"

Sinbad gaped in astonishment. He felt as though a mighty fist had just smashed into his gut, sweeping the breath from his lungs, wreaking pain throughout his body, rendering him as helpless as a newborn infant.

"It's true, it's true!" she moaned. "Tomorrow my father presents me officially for the caliph's inspection. But this is only a formality; he has already informed my father that the wedding shall take place within a single week's time."

His head was reeling, his mind a foggy blur. Could this be so? Schahriar knew full well that he and Scheherazade were betrothed, and he had heartily approved. How could he now claim her as his own? Had the caliph gone mad? Was he out to destroy two loyal servants who had been his friends?

"I shall talk to our caliph at once," he hissed, his face stern and cold.

Sherry pulled at his sleeve and looked at him pleadingly.

"No, Sinbad! You must not! The caliph expects such a gesture from you; he shall use your anger to his own advantage—accuse you of treachery against him. You shall be banished from Baghdad—or worse!"

Sinbad was aghast. "No, Sherry. You're wrong. I know him—"

"And I know him better!" flared the girl. "I understand his wicked heart. Through me he means to get at you! Oh, Sinbad, what are we to do?" And she fell against him, her graceful body shaking with terrible spasms.

Sinbad tried to calm her anguish with soft words and kisses. "And what of your father?" he asked at length.

Sherry shook her head. "He is powerless. There is no more to be done on the matter. Our caliph will not listen to him or to any other." She sucked in air and shut her eyes. "I fear for you, Sinbad. Baghdad turns against you."

"Never! I have many friends, powerful friends. They will stand by me, you'll see. They will speak before Schahriar in my name and make him realize the folly of what he does."

She sniffed and drew away from him sharply. "Sinbad, dear lover, are you so blind? All Baghdad trembles in fear of the caliph's wrath—and with good reason. No man, no matter how much he may truly love you, shall come forward in your behalf. They dare not! Lest they face the same fate as you."

Sinbad had no words. The view of the city was magnificent from where he stood. The domes and steeples glimmered in moonlight, soft shadows danced across the countless roofs, the waters of the river reflectly brightly the torchlight of the piers. Yet Sinbad was blind to this all. With anguish tearing at him from within, he stood frozen like a statue.

"What is left for us?" he mumbled, his dark eyes staring aimlessly at the carved stones of the balcony.

"We must flee," came the brief, hushed reply.

Sinbad looked at his beloved.

Sherry glanced around nervously, making certain that no one stood hidden among the shadows.

"Tomorrow shall be too late," she continued, in a low voice. "We must act fast—that is, if you still want me . . ."

"Want you? I want you more than anything upon the world's surface; more than any treasure, more than any gift that even Allah himself might bestow. . . ."

"I love you, Sinbad. Take me away forever. What difference shall it make where we go? Our lives will never again be parted. Promise me, Sinbad, we shall leave all this behind and never return."

His mouth pressed upon hers; his hands clutched her to him until they had entwined almost as one. "Yes, Sherry," he vowed. "What good is life itself without you? Tonight we shall run—flee with a thousand soldiers after us, if necessary. And never will we come back."

For the first time Scheherazade smiled. She closed her eyes in a quick, thankful prayer, then said: "Find horses for us both. Tonight, before midnight, I shall slip from my rooms and seek you at the fountain of the Garden of Miracles. No one shall see us—I shall dress myself in the robes of a house slave, not even my brother would recognize me. Then I will wait beneath the willows for your arrival . . ."

Sinbad nodded. "Agreed. At midnight, then. Everything shall be prepared."

Sherry stood upon her toes and kissed him fleetingly. "Go, my love," she whispered. "Breathe not a word of this to anyone. Our caliph has spies everywhere."

And without another word, Sinbad passed from her arms and strode from the chamber, his mind a flurry of activity, preparing for this sudden and unexpected new adventure.

Sherry watched until he had gone. She sighed and, with a hand to her bosom, ran from the room to gather a few belongings.

Beneath the shadow of the balcony a small, wispish

fellow with a devious smile chuckled. *So they escape, do they?* he mumbled. Already he could feel the jingle of gold coins in his pocket; this time the caliph would reward him well for his little errand. Indeed, Baghdad's ruler would no doubt be willing to part with a fortune for news such as this.

The palace spy, dressed in the ragged garb of a gardener, grinned and rubbed his hands together. *The caliph shall never forgive you for this, Dormo. You shall be a broken man—and I a rich one! But never mind. I deserve it more than thee.*

Then he looked at the position of the moon and frowned. Time was passing too swiftly; he must hasten to the palace at once. There would be plenty of time for gloating tomorrow.

Scheherazade was tense and frightened that night as the hours slowly ticked away and the appointed time grew close. But, sincere in her devotion to Sinbad, she had not a single doubt in her heart as she stole from her bed and slipped silently out of the house, dressed in the rough cloth garb of a kitchen slave. She slinked under the cover of night to her father's favorite stable, where she saddled his finest stallion. Sherry was more than excited when she rode onto the quiet, tree-lined street—but how slow these minutes seemed to pass!

The hour was very late—long past eleven by the position of the moon. Soon she and Sinbad would be reunited, she was certain, and no one would ever force them apart again. By dawn they would be well away from this accursed city where separated lovers found no sympathy.

In the enlightened city of Baghdad it was not totally unusual for a woman to be out alone after dark. So she rode from her home secure in the knowledge that few citizens would take much notice, although as a precaution she pulled her veil securely over her face. She galloped the horse well away from the main thoroughfares that crisscrossed the city, keeping well out of sight of the looming stone walls of the palace and toward the oldest section of Baghdad, where few of her breeding were ever to be found.

It was here that she would soon come to the ancient place known as the Garden of Miracles, a curious and foreboding place. Once upon a time, when Baghdad flowered in its youth, these fabled gardens were numbered among the most beautiful on earth. So reknown were they that the disciples of the Prophet Mohammed himself had come there to instruct in the sacred teachings of the Koran. Princes and noblemen were frequently seen in the company of beggars as all listened to the holy word. And the Garden of Miracles blossomed as did Baghdad itself.

Yet black days soon followed.. It was said that a prince, finding his wife in the arms of another, slew the lovers as they lay in these very gardens. The soil was fouled with their blood and the dying lovers swore never to rest. Subsequent lovers who visited the garden reportedly vanished, and the laughter of ghosts was said to echo cruelly each third night. Although this had happened many years before, it was never forgotten, and now the Garden of Miracles lay fallow and wasted, unvisited save by the most hardy souls.

Sherry scoffed at such nonsense of ghosts and witchcraft, yet she knew that the folk of Baghdad were a superstitous lot, and that no one would suspect her coming here for her secret escape with Sinbad.

A strange wind had begun to blow, and there were eerie rustlings and whistlings from among the aged and bent trees as she reached the garden entrance. Her horse scuffed its hooves and whinnied when she reached down and opened the squeaky gate. Sherry dismounted; she tethered the horse outside and proceeded ahead on her own. She stepped lightly over the weedy grass searching out the row of wisping willows where her appointment would take place.

"Sinbad? Sinbad?" she called.

There was no answer and she moved deeper inside, oblivious of the fearful shadows that swept down from the trees and shrubs. Signs of decay were everywhere. Fountains set in tiny plazas crumbled; gazebos, worn and ruined, were covered by thick, slimy vines that clung like leeches; walks were cluttered with grim weeds that sprouted haphazardly throughout. A jungle in miniature spread before her, and she shuddered in trepidation.

She crossed a corroded stretch of tiled walk and climbed the hill leading to the willows. Leaves danced and swayed in a macabre ballet in front of her startled eyes. Sherry gulped, admitting to herself for the first time that perhaps the sight of the rendezvous might have been better chosen. Still, it was too late to turn back now, when midnight was so close.

She made herself as comfortable as possible beside the gnarled roots of an enormous willow, and, chewing her nails, she searched the scape below for the coming of her lover.

But where was he? Why was he so late? Had something gone wrong—had Sinbad been delayed by the caliph's soldiers? Perhaps the truth was even worse, she thought. Perhaps he had been arrested. . . . Perhaps he was dead!

The thought made her squeal with fear. Then suddenly there came a sound, which made her eyes widen and her heart fly into her throat. A hoofbeat? Or the heavy tread of boots.

Silhouettes jumped from behind. Sherry whirled and tried to run. As she made to scream, a large, calloused hand grabbed hold of her and spun her around. She kicked and fought, banged her fists against a shirtless chest, but all to no avail. Her captor grappled her down to the ground and roughly pinned her by the shoulders.

"Gag her!" he barked throatily.

Sherry squirmed as the second silhouette drew closer. Grinning in the moonlight, he withdrew a dirty rag from his robe and stuffed it inside her mouth. Then he laughed

71

malevolently. The girl stared and gasped. She recognized him at once to be a former captain of the caliph's guard, taken from that position to serve his leige as a spy among the people. A rank and foul man who had earned little respect even among his peers.

"What do we do with her?" growled the other man, the one who held her to the ground.

The spy put his hands on his hips and sighed deeply. "We keep her out of sight for now," he replied in a low voice. "Once Captain Sinbad's been caught, we can take her back to the palace. The caliph will want to decide himself what's to be done with her."

Sherry wanted to scream. Her lungs were bursting to break free, to cry out in warning. And the folly of her scheme became all too plain. These brutes—and no doubt others as well—lay in waiting to pounce upon the mariner the moment he showed. They would bind him and drag him to the palace, throwing him before the caliph as though he were a rag. "Here is your bold captain," they would snarl, "caught in the act of stealing your bride. Decide, O Schahriar, what price you would have him pay." To which the caliph would feign pity and summarily condemn Sinbad to lose his head.

Her hands were bound. Her captors had to drag her kicking and fighting all the way to a small crumbled gazebo near the top of the hillock, completely hidden from sight by weedy vines and lumbering branches. Sherry's very soul flooded with desperation—she must somehow warn Sinbad of this treachery, signal to him from afar and make him flee while there was yet time.

Along the deserted highway Sinbad rode, his horse's hooves clattering against flagstone. Behind him trailed a mule with saddlebags fully packed for the long journey ahead. The youthful mariner bore no arms, save for the fine curved dagger that he always wore strapped to his belt. He slowed down before reaching the gardens, carefully scanning the distant foliage and tree lines for sight of his betrothed. Moments later he came upon Sherry's tethered horse beside the gate and he smiled. Like himself, it seemed she enjoyed a touch of the melodramatic, choosing such a spot as this for their midnight rendezvous.

He dismounted quickly and passed through the rusted gate, paying no attention to the weird rustlings of the unpruned grasses. With any luck at all, he reasoned, by this time tomorrow they could be close to the borders of Persia. Sinbad had many friends in that nearby land, good friends whom he could count on. There he and Sherry could safely be wed. Let the caliph's soldiers try and follow! To the ends of the world they would flee, if need be. Together, bound by love and free of any king's whim. Ah, it would be wonderful. . . .

The path to the willows lay directly ahead; Sinbad crossed the muddied banks of the walk, a new poem beginning to form in his mind. Then he stopped. Before him lay a series of footprints—a man's footprints, if size were any gauge. Odd that they should be here, he mused. A brief shower had passed over Baghdad only hours before; therefore these tracks were undoubtedly fresh. But whose? What manner of man might be out in the night visiting the forbidding Garden of Miracles?

Sinbad pressed his lips together tightly and narrowed his eyes. Something was amiss; it wasn't just the track that bothered him, there was more. Something insidious.

His hand slipped to his knife and he pressed his fingers lightly against the hilt. Looking up to the crest of the hill, he called: "Sherry, are you there?"

Only the wind replied. A fleeting shadow passed between trees; Sinbad cautiously walked forward. He reached the top long moments later and studied the foliage around him. It was then that he saw the shattered gazebo, its dulled stone roof faintly reflecting moonlight. And he proceeded closer with deliberate care.

The girl sat numb in her corner, watching fearfully as

her lover made his way toward her. If only she could scream! *Run, my love, run!* she cried in her anguished thoughts. *Please, hear me and run!*

A twig snapped. Sinbad spun, his dagger already drawn. From behind a willow the spy came surging, a curved sword in his hand. "Catch him!" he bellowed to his cronies, and from everywhere they sprang, five brutish wrestlers of the caliph's service.

Sinbad's fist lashed out, catching the first off balance. The hefty wrestler took the blow squarely on the mouth and reeled backwards. A sword whistled by; Sinbad ducked and brought the dagger up in full strength. The spy groaned and fell back, his blade falling from his limp hands. Clutching the gaping wound in his belly, he doubled over.

From behind, another wrestler leaped on Sinbad's back. The mariner whirled him with a sudden jerk and sent him flying against the trunk of a tree. As the wrestler thudded to the grass, the quick-thinking mariner brought his dagger back up and fended off two more charging wrestlers.

With grins and grunts, the hirsute foe encircled Sinbad, steadily pressing in and closing off any avenue of escape. Sinbad's eyes darted into the night; he saw yet other shadows come racing from down the hill. Burly men with cloaks swirling behind and plumed helmets upon their heads. *The caliph's guard!* he realized. Perhaps a full squad of them, all having hidden and waited for his arrival.

This was no time for games. Sinbad darted forward and kicked high, in the manner of Chinese fighters. *"Ooof!"* groaned the oaf at the receiving end of Sinbad's foot. His heel had caught the man dead in the solar plexus, and now he fell to his knees gasping for air.

Sinbad swung a fast chop at the second attacker, delivering it with such speed and force that the man's collarbone snapped. He howled like an animal and fell writhing to the floor. There was an instant of respite. Sinbad raced to the gazebo and tried to free the bound Scheherazade.

"Save yourself, Sinbad," she cried as he loosened her gag.

He picked her up abruptly and cut through her bonds. "I'll not leave without you," he hissed in reply. And he roughly grabbed hold of her hand and pulled her from the gazebo.

"I want them alive!" came a cry from the racing soldiers. And the front line advanced with swords drawn menacingly.

Sinbad held the girl tightly and made a frantic dash toward the trees. The wrestlers had begun to pick themselves up and give chase. Through the maze of branches, roots, and trunks the lovers ran, panting, sweating, struggling to find a way to reach their waiting horses.

From all sides the troops began to converge. Sinbad fended off a host of blows, fighting like a cornered leopard. But the soldiers were everywhere, forming a vise around him and closing in fast.

"It's no good!" wept Sherry, her soiled dress tattered and swirling in the demonic wind.

"Then we die together!" rejoined the fabled captain.

In a flashing instant Sinbad was sent flying back by the unseen hammer chop of an advancing wrestler. He groveled on the ground, then leaped to his feet dizzily, despair etched sharply into his handsome features.

"Run, Sinbad!" shrieked the girl, and he looked on aghast while a handful of soldiers snatched her away, dragging her toward their waiting horses.

"Sherry!" he wailed in surging sorrow. He tried vainly to break his way through the host of armored flesh before him, but they held firm, parrying his thrusts easily with their curved swords. Sinbad wielded his dagger to and fro, slashing at grasping hands trying to bind him. As the swirling wind tossed dead leaves about, Sinbad knocked an advancing soldier over and swept up the fallen sword. Then he scrambled and thrust wildly, keeping the host at bay. Sinbad was reknowned throughout Baghdad for his prowess with weaponry, but none had ever dreamed he could fight with such abandon. Again and again they pressed, again

75

and again he held them off, fighting more as ten than one.

The tip of a sword grazed his cheek, another slashed through his shirt. The turbaned mariner winced at the feel of his own warm blood and quickly retreated toward the wall of bushes behind him.

"He's trapped!" shouted someone with glee and malice.

Sinbad grunted, conceding his plight. But, like the cornered rat they had made of him, he sought to free himself. Twisting, he dived over the bushes and took refuge among the thick, tall weeds.

"After him, you fools!" came an urgent cry. And while the troops frantically leaped the shrubs, Sinbad crawled on his belly along the downward slope. His catlike eyes glowed, following the dark figures as they beat swords against the bushes. He arched his body lithely and slipped beneath the gnarled roots of an especially large willow, watching searching troops run helter-skelter in their frustration to catch him.

His body began to ache from the blows he had received. He glanced down at his torn shirt with surprise at the spreading red stains. The cut was deeper than he had realized; it was a thin, wisping line running from his shoulder almost to his belly. A hairsbreadth deeper and he would probably be dead.

He stayed in position for what seemed a long time, while the soldiers continued combing the gardens. Then came the critical moment. Peering up, Sinbad saw a cloud pass before the face of the moon, shrouding the Garden of Miracles in total blackness. It was now or never—he must make it back to the gate and his waiting horse. Lingering would only give the caliph's men more time to send for reinforcments.

He slinked out from among the roots, cleaning mud off his bloody clothes. Then, sticking close to the overgrowth, he inched his way lower, dagger in hand. The soldiers still maneuvered between the willows; Sinbad reached the bottom, drew a deep breath, and mustered all his energy. Then he bolted for the gate with all his speed.

"There he is!" someone shouted.

Sinbad cursed as he stumbled, jumped the gate, and leaped for the waiting horse. A line of troopers dropped to one knee and drew bows. His stallion reared in panic at the *twang* of loosed arrows. Then it raced off into the night, Sinbad's hand slapping fiercely at its flanks.

Snub-nosed arrows whistled above the crouching rider's horse. Sinbad deftly zigged and zagged along the street, riding recklessly, his mind a blur of surging emotion. He must free Sherry! he told himself. *He must!* Yet even as he repeated this, his heart sank with the knowledge of futility. By now she had been whisked well away—perhaps already to Schahriar himself, awaiting the judgment of his wrath. *Save yourself, Sinbad!* he heard her cry in his troubled thoughts. *Save yourself!*

He must leave Baghdad now—forever, he knew. Never look back, never again return to the home of his birth. Tears flooded his eyes; he wished his heart would stop beating. *Sherry,* he wept, *how am I to live without you? Must I spend my entire life in solitude—while knowing you live in a marriage against your will?*

Suddenly more arrows were sailing, this time from in front rather than behind. Sinbad pulled in sharply at the reins and stared ahead. Directly before him stood a hastily constructed barricade, and behind it a handful of archers intent on bringing him down. They shouted frantically among themselves at the sight of him. Sinbad crouched as low as he could manage and clutched tightly at the reins. Then into the stallion's flanks he dug his boots and the horse lurched ahead. High he hurdled, over the turned wagon and crates, soldiers screaming as hooves and horseflesh slammed them about. Blades and daggers flashed, lashing the animal as he landed safely over. Sinbad urged the horse on with a slap and a whoop, and again they escaped amidst whistling arrows which fell harmlessly close by.

Or had they been harmless? As he passed from the city, thundering through the gate like a witless tiger, he noticed that the stallion's breathing grew heavy and labored. Sinbad leaned forward, ran his hand through the matted mane, looked sorrowfully at the curdling blood. Only then did he realize just how badly hurt his favorite stallion had been on this daring ride to freedom.

He slowed to a trot and steered the animal away from the caravan road, taking a shortcut to a small oasis he was familiar with. There he dismounted and examined the injury. The stallion's chest pulsed with dark blood; he saw the broken shaft of an arrow with its head firmly implanted near the animal's heart.

Sinbad tearfully stroked the trusted steed and sighed. He led it among the fig trees and to the pond, where the dying horse refused to drink. How boldly this horse had run, Sinbad thought. A lesser steed would have collapsed and died long before.

He tried to soothe the agonized horse, watching as it kicked its heels into dirt and shook its mane in terrible pain. Sinbad drew his knife. He could not let the poor creature suffer; he whispered a few gentle words of endearment into its ear and plunged the dagger deeply into its heart. The animal kicked its hind legs, jerked spasmodically, then fell with a thud at Sinbad's feet.

The despondent mariner leaned down and shut the glassy eyes forever. "Good-bye, faithful friend," he mumbled as he went through the saddlebags, taking only a water flask and a small bag of silver. "You were a better friend to me than any before; I shall never forget."

Then he stood and gazed forlornly back toward the walls of the city, now glimmering brightly under ten thousand stars.

"And farewell to you, beloved Baghdad," he sighed. "Fate, it seems, has ordained that we never see each other again. . . ." He hung his head and fought back rising sobs. "Be kind to fair Scheherazade, let her life know only joy. May Sherry be blessed with—" He could not go on. With his head against the bark of a fig tree, he wept as he had never wept before. His body was wracked with the pain of his wounds and bruises, his brow burned with fever; but nothing could compare to the anguish and hurt within his soul. He was now a man without a home, without a country, without the woman for whom he lived. In but a single day's time, he had lost everything. Only a shallow and empty life lay before him now. One devoid of any true love, devoid of any dreams on which to build. Sinbad was shattered—for what good is the poet without his dreams?

After a time he lifted himself up, straightened his shoulders, and sighed with deep resignation. Then he headed from the oasis toward the west. Toward the road to Damascus, toward the ever-hot sands of the endless Arabian desert.

All through the night Sinbad wandered across the shifting dunes in a state of bewilderment and shock. Dawn spread gaily along the eastern horizon, where the high walls of Baghdad had all but disappeared from view. That the caliph's soldiers would be in pursuit was all but a certainty, and Schahriar, although gloating over having foiled the lovers' plan, now would demand justice for the sailor who tried to steal his bride. All caravans leaving the city would be stopped; soldiers would be sent to inspect every barge and boat upon the Tigris; and palace spies would comb every inch of Baghdad in search of the wily captain. Thus Sinbad had correctly taken to the desert, knowing that only there might he slip away unseen, lost among the endless sands, doomed to a nomad's existence.

Oh, Fortune, how unfaithful thou art! Sinbad ruminated as he languished in misery. *Thou hadst charmed me with thy wiles, enticed and blessed me like no other, then like a harlot hardened thy heart and cast me adrift upon this barren sea.*

The only reply to his grief was the rising of the wind, growing like a sirocco, while Sinbad shivered with his fever beneath the blazing sun of the morning.

Half in a delirium, he crossed the dunes, aching in body and spirit as never before, wishing he were dead and forgotten to the world, his name but a memory. And so he wandered.

The sun was nearing its noon height when Sinbad came to a large flat where lay an oasis. As in a dream he stared at the fig and fruit trees and the fresh-water ponds nestled beside the grassy knolls. Sinbad gratefully washed his wounds, drank long draughts of the cool, clear water, and ate a few pieces of fruit. Then he searched for a shady place to lay down and sleep. It wasn't difficult to find.

The grasses were deep and rich beside a small lily pond, and he stretched out luxuriously, his body well shaded by the leaves of a thick, aged tree.

How tranquil this little spot was, he mused, staring expressionlessly at the deep water of the pond and watching the lily pads go floating by. Butterflies were dancing, their colorful wings catching streams of sunlight pouring down between the branches; tiny sparrows twittered carelessly from their nests in the trees. Sinbad smiled at the sight of a frog hopping along the gravelly banks.

Ah, what a peaceful place, he said to himself, relaxing and shutting his eyes. *I truly do like it here; perhaps I shall never leave. . . .*

And then he fell asleep.

It was a disturbed sleep, though, for in it he saw Sherry, her gentle features etched with grief, tears pouring from her eyes. She was clad in a wedding gown, and with her face veiled and her brooding eyes downcast, she came beside the caliph and gave him her hand. Schahriar took it greedily, a victorious glint in his eyes. And he proclaimed before Allah that the girl was his wife.

No, Sherry, no! cried Sinbad, watching from afar. But

the girl did not hear and his plea went unnoticed. Then the caliph lifted the veil and kissed her.

Sinbad jumped from his slumber, his heart thumping wildly. Seconds passed and he fell back and sighed, realizing it had only been a dream. He was still in the oasis, beside the lily pond; nothing had changed at all except that the sun had already begun to dip. Evening was upon the desert.

Sinbad sat back up, cross-legged, and put his head in his hands. "Ah, me," he mumbled sorrowfully. "What am I to do? Returning shall mean the loss of my head, but if I don't I shall never gaze into Sherry's eyes again. Not even for a fleeting moment. . . ."

And in his despair he began to create a poem, one which would forever explain to the world his shattered heart.

"It sounds as though you have a problem," said a sudden nearby voice.

Startled, Sinbad tensed, expecting to find he was not alone. Had the soldiers tracked him here? Had the caliph known of his route?

Sinbad looked around slowly, slanting his black brows and carefully examining the landscape. But all there was to see was the lily pond, the butterflies, the exotic flowers and shrubs, and, at the edge of the bank, an enormous bullfrog sitting upon his hind legs and staring at him. There was no sight of another human being.

I must still be dreaming, he told himself, forgetting about the strange voice. Then he shrugged and went back to composing his sad poem.

"Don't you want to tell me what's wrong?" came the peculiar voice again.

This time Sinbad's hand slid to his dagger. He definitely was *not* dreaming. He gazed out toward the pond and the direction of the voice. "Who . . . who said that?" he called nervously.

"I did."

The mariner's jaw hung limply; he peered long and hard at the scaly frog with bulging eyes and a tongue as long as a lizard's. It was a big frog, dark and light green in color, with numerous black spots scattered across its back and the largest webbed feet Sinbad had ever seen.

"You?" he gasped. "You spoke to me."

The frog nodded evenly.

Sinbad scratched his head in wonder. "I must be losing my mind. . . ."

The frog sighed. "No, I don't think so. It was me you heard."

Sinbad was incredulous—the world must have gone insane during his slumber! Turned topsy-turvy in a nightmare. He collected himself and narrowed his eyes at the creature. "It was *you*," he asked.

"Oh, yes. It was me all right. Take my word for it."

"But . . . but that's impossible!" he sputtered. "*Frogs* can't speak!"

"Well, dear fellow," replied the frog haughtily, "as you see, this one *can*." And then he shrugged his shoulders matter-of-factly.

Sinbad whistled and shook his head, suddenly positive that his ordeal had left him demented. Sitting here and having a conversation with a toad was just too much to accept; he had seen many, many strange and wondrous things in the world during the adventures of his voyages. Beasts of all sorts, monsters, demons, rocs, and Cyclopes— but a talking frog? Never!

But the frog seemed to pay little attention to Sinbad's quandary. With a single push of his long hind legs, he leaped from the bank and landed beside the amazed sailor.

"You must be a devil!" cried Sinbad. "An evil wizard, taken this vile guise to trick me!" He pulled his blade and wielded it menacingly. "Tell me before I slit that tongue of yours—are you an agent of the caliph?"

The frog remained cool. Shaking his head, he said:

"Nothing like that, I assure you. I'm only a common bullfrog, no different from any other."

Sinbad laughed hollowly. "Not quite so common, I'll wager," he said. "How many of your fellows converse like a man? *Hmm?*"

The frog chuckled in a curious fashion. "Well," he drawled, "I suppose you're right. I guess it would seem strange to you. But everyone here," his eyes swept the oasis in two different directions, "knows all about it. Really they do. Why, they hardly give it a second thought any more." The bullfrog sat back and stared up at Sinbad again. "But never mind me. Who are *you*, pray tell? What are you doing at my pond? And what causes you such distress?"

His fear gone, Sinbad sheathed his dagger and looked at his companion with a slightly bemused grin. "I am called Sinbad," he announced proudly. "Captain Sinbad, merchant of Baghdad, adventurer and poet, mariner and soldier of fortune."

The frog remained docile and still beside Sinbad's leg. He put a webbed foot to his head and scratched it, deep in thought. "Sinbad? Sinbad, eh?" he said. "*Hmmm.* Yes, yes; I think I've heard that name before. Why, I'm sure of it!"

Sinbad's eyes widened in disbelief. "You've actually heard of me?" he questioned.

The frog bobbed his head strongly. "I daresay the name has passed my ears now and again. After all, when you spend your whole life sitting around in a pond, you have lots of time for gossip. One hears all kinds of things, let me tell you. So is it such a surprise that the famous name of Captain Sinbad may have come this way once or twice?" The frog leaned back and blinked his eyes, which he did habitually whenever he was thinking hard.

"If memory serves," he went on after a time, "I think it was a sparrow who first mentioned you. Yes, yes. Or was it a grasshopper?"

But Sinbad remained unconvinced; this toad seemed a bit too knowledgeable for his own good. And, wary of what might happen next, he let his hand drift back toward his knife.

The bullfrog observed his nervousness and smiled in the peculiar way that only frogs do. "You needn't be afraid of me, Captain Sinbad," he said kindly. "Neither I, nor any of this oasis, mean you any harm."

Sinbad leaned forward. He put his head in his hands and sighed. "I know you don't," he told his companion. "You must excuse me. I'm not myself today—and I doubt I ever will be again." And he stared blankly out toward the brilliant sunset, unmoved and uninspired.

"What is the matter, Sinbad?" asked the frog. "What makes the most admired man in all Baghdad so saddened?"

"I am crushed," admitted the mariner. "My life is near its end, I'm sure. There is no future for me, nor can there ever be without *her* . . ."

The frog nodded knowingly; he had suspected that a female was the reason for such anguish. Somehow that was always the case, even here in the pond.

"Won't you tell me about it?" he asked.

"What good would it do? The memory is too fresh, too painful. . . ."

"Sometimes it helps to tell someone," replied the frog wisely. "It eases the pain to share it with another."

Sinbad reached over and patted his head. "You are a very clever frog—and very understanding." Then he smiled. "Why not? All right, my friend. I'll tell you my tale—all of it. And then you'll come to see why I weep as I do."

It took quite some time for Sinbad to explain the details, how he had heard of the caliph's decision, and of Sherry's plan for their escape to freedom. Sinbad left nothing unsaid; he told the frog every last point, minor and major, and when he had finished they both hung their heads.

"Love is both the joy and the bane of the world," the frog said with a sigh.

Sinbad nodded. "How true! alas. A broken heart cannot twice be endured. So now I must go far, far away. As far as I possibly can. Maybe, with time, some of the wounds shall heal—although the scars shall always remain." As Sinbad forced a smile, he tossed a few pebbles into the pond and stared at the widening ripples of water. Then he turned back to his companion. "Now you know everything there is to know," he said. "But what about your own tale? Surely it must be a strange and wondrous story. How it came about that a toad can converse."

The frog looked up indignantly. "I am *not* a toad!" he huffed.

"Forgive me. A frog, then,"

"A bullfrog!" snapped the bullfrog.

"All right, a bullfrog!" He leaned in closer, looking his companion straight in the eye. "But you still haven't answered my question."

The bullfrog grimaced and heaved a lengthy sigh. Resting back on his haunches, he croaked deeply and, as Sinbad clearly noted, very sadly.

"My fate was due to a practical joke," the frog confided at last.

"What sort of joke?"

"A poor one, surely. Once, some seasons ago, one of Baghdad's mighty wizards passed this way with a caravan. While his camels and servants rested, the fellow decided to practice his wizardry. It was my fortune to fall victim; he put a curse upon me."

"Aha!" said Sinbad, snapping his fingers. "I suspected as much! Tell me, were you indeed not once a man? But now condemned to dwell forever inside this scaley body?"

The bullfrog rolled his eyes wildly. "Heavens forbid, no!" he cried. "I was never a man—nor would I want to be. A bullfrog I was born and a bullfrog I hope to die. But this witty magician of the caliph's court thought it might be amusing to cast a spell and give to me the voice of a man."

Although the frog's plight was understandable, Sinbad could hardly refrain from a snicker.

"It's no laughing matter!" bemoaned the bullfrog. "Just take a look at me! What do you see? Do you think it's easy for me being like this? Why, my own family avoids me. Most of my friends won't even talk to me any more—and don't even ask about the problems I have during mating time!" He shuddered. "It isn't fair! I tell you, it just isn't fair!"

Sinbad listened with a sense of absolute understanding. Indeed, the poor little frog's woes were in many respects similar to his own. Both lived in misery, both had found themselves outcasts through no fault of their own.

"Do you have a name, little friend?" Sinbad asked. "Or do they just refer to you as 'Frog'?"

His companion for the first time avoided meeting the sailor's gaze. "I do have a name," he confided, "but I rarely tell it to anyone—particularly strangers. They laugh at me."

Captain Sinbad smiled warmly. "You needn't fret. You can trust me."

The frog looked up doubtfully. "You promise not to laugh?"

"I give my word."

"All right, then," he said reluctantly. "I was named . . . Giovanni. Don Giovanni."

Sinbad put his hands to his face and roared. He laughed so hard and so loud that tears were streaming from his eyes and he thought his ribs might crack.

"You promised!" wailed Don Giovanni. "You gave your *word!*"

Sinbad nodded and dried his eyes, managing to subdue his merriment to an occasional chuckle. "You are right, my friend. I beg your forgiveness. I was rude to you but I won't be any more."

The frog sniffed and sulked. He made to leave.

"Don't!" cried Sinbad, reaching out. "Don't hop away angry. I really didn't mean to make fun of you."

Don Giovanni pouted and looked at Sinbad dejectedly. "Oh, it really doesn't matter. I suppose I'm accustomed to it by now. They all used to do it, you know. They would chase me out of the pond and force me to sleep in the grass." He shut his bulging eyes and rolled them beneath heavy green lids. "What I wouldn't give to be rid of this miserable curse," he moaned. "If only I could go back to being just what nature intended for me to be."

Sinbad felt truly ashamed for his crude behavior. He fully understood how cruel one's fellow creatures can be when you are different than they are—even if your home was only a lily pond.

"And there is no way for you to have this wish granted?" he asked.

"Alas, the wizard who cast his spell has died, and his antidote is unknown."

"But surely there are other wizards," protested Sinbad. "Other potions and other spells to disperse this one. The world is vast, good frog. *Somewhere* . . ."

Slumping, Giovanni sighed. "There is said to be one cure," he confided. "But how shall I, a simple bullfrog, ever hope to find it?"

"Perhaps I can be of assistance to you," said Sinbad.

The little frog's eyes widened. "*You* would help *me*?"

Sinbad nodded. "If I can, yes."

Don Giovanni hopped onto Sinbad's shoulder and put his face close to the mariner's ear. "Have you ever heard of the flower called the Red Dahlia?"

Sinbad thought deeply for a moment, then slowly nodded. Somewhere or other in the course of his adventures he had been told of the mysterious flower which only grew upon the shores of a forbidden island. Never had he seen one with his own eyes, but it was reliably reported that the owner of such a flower might have any wish granted—

any wish at all, no matter how strange or difficult. Then the Red Dahlia would wither and die. But upon this unknown island there were said to be fields of them, thousands begging to be plucked from their roots. Why, the very thought of what a man could do with such an incredible gift boggled the mind.

Sinbad frowned. "I have sailed almost all of the world," he said, "and not once have I met a man who claims to have owned one."

Giovanni seemed disappointed. "Then you don't believe it really exists?"

The mariner folded his arms and shrugged. "Who knows? Some claim it can be found only in a man's dreams . . ."

"I have heard it can be found at World's Edge," countered the frog. "Past the Limits of Chaos, beyond the Pillars of Hercules."

"An almost impossible quest," said Sinbad.

"Even for the mighty captain," rejoined Giovanni, "whose glories and past adventures are sung upon the lips of every woman in Baghdad?"

Sinbad flushed and grinned. "Ah, you flatter me, my friend. It's true that ballad singers have for some reason taken a liking to my exploits—but don't believe everything you hear. My adventures weren't really half as dangerous or glamorous as these reciters of verse would have you believe."

Don Giovanni let his head sink dejectedly. "Then there is no hope for me at all," he lamented. "I can never have my wish granted." He glanced slyly up at Sinbad. "Nor you your own. . . ."

Sinbad scratched his chin. "What do you mean?"

"Think, Captain Sinbad—if *you* held a Red Dahlia in your hand, what would you wish for?"

"Ah, if only I had one! I would command the flower's magic to hasten Sherry to my side. We could be free, she and I, free to sail the seas and be together always. . . ."

"Yes," said the frog, "Think of it, Sinbad! Both our

desires could be answered instantly. That and more. The world would be at your command, Sinbad. Anything you wanted . . ." And he tapped a nervous webbed foot on Sinbad's shoulder.

At length the mariner spoke. "To set out upon a quest for the Red Dahlia might last a lifetime," he said. "And I must admit that I have serious doubts about the flower's existence . . ." Don Giovanni frowned, and Sinbad patted his head again. "But listen: There is always hope—even when despair is at its greatest. One must never lose belief in himself. . . ."

"You did, when you lost Scheherazade."

Sinbad laughed. "So I did, good frog! So I did! But I see now that life must continue, no matter what adversity greets us. Such is Allah's will." Then he peered at the frog and scratched his chin, his mind working out a little escapade. "I am forced to leave Baghdad in any case," he told Giovanni, "so why not come with me? There will be adventures aplenty for us both, I promise you, and who knows? Maybe someday we shall pass the Pillars of Hercules and reach the land of the Red Dahlia—or maybe find some unknown magic potion to cast off your spell. Well, frog? What do you say?"

Giovanni shuffled his feet tensely. Sinbad could see the reluctance in his eyes. "I . . . I don't know . . ."

"Is it better to stay in this pond? To bemoan your fate and do nothing to alter it?" He leaned closer. "Or do you enjoy being miserable and helpless?"

Giovanni gazed at the sailor with steadily brightening eyes. "You really mean it, Sinbad? About the adventure, about leaving this accursed pond forever? You'll take me sailing the world with you?"

"I meant every word, my friend. You'll see more than any frog has ever seen before."

A small wasp buzzed nearby and Don Giovanni watched him carefully for a moment. Then he lashed out his tongue and caught the insect in mid-flight, gulping it down with a single swallow. "All right, Sinbad!" he cried with excitement. "When can we be off? The sooner I'm away from here, the better!"

Sinbad's eyes danced merrily. "There's no better time to start than now," he said. "Come, Giovanni, sit firmly on my shoulder."

The bullfrog snobbishly flared his nostrils at the other frogs, all staring from the lily pond. "Good-bye, good-bye," he called, as Sinbad stood, collected his gear, and walked briskly from the oasis into the cool desert night.

"Where are we going?" asked Giovanni.

"To sail the sea we must first reach it," answered the mariner, peering into the endless western dunes. "Drink your fill of water while you can. We seek a caravan to Damascus. Then it's on to Tripoli or Jaffa and the Mediterranean beyond."

PART THREE:

FROM DAMASCUS TO JAFFA
UPON A JOURNEY THAT CAPTAIN
SINBAD NEVER WOULD FOR-
GET.

Damascus—mysterious city of Araby, home of countless sultans, caliphs, and kings, whose fame was merely the setting for the jeweled enchantment of its capital. Damascus, whose peoples had been conquered again and again through the ages, by King David of Israel, Alexander of Macedonia, Pompey of Rome. Damascus, melting pot of cultures and religions, the crossroads of the world to which all of Islam looked for guidance. City of secrets and enigmas, its age-less history buried deep beneath its streets, where unseen artifacts told of countless battles and the strife of war. Blessed and cursed, bled and nurtured, swollen but lean, only Damascus could conjure in men's hearts the epitome of civilization. From these dark alleys had arisen the finest minds upon the earth, from these festering slums had come wise men of science and philosophy, religion and art. Greeks and Hebrews mingled with Turks and Phoenicians, adding cosmopolitan adornment to the already richly woven tapestry of the city's life.

Men have cried at the sight of her; few who came ever wished to leave, and those who did did so reluctantly, never forgetting all they had seen. Set beside the rich plains said to be the most fertile in all of Arabia's vastness, its stone walls beckoned to all who would be free. Damascus—capital of knowledge and civilization.

A dozen caravans daily camped before her massive gates, each laden with goods and burdened with wide-eyed pilgrims come to pray at any of the more than two hundred mosques. Exhausted after long journeys begun in every known land, these new arrivals would gape in awe at the sheer majesty of the city spread before them. It was an incredible sight to behold, this metropolis of kings and beggars side by side, resplendent palaces and dingy hovels. Never before had the weary travelers seen such a thing. And so it was also for Sinbad and his tiny companion.

It had been only a few days after the mariner and the frog had left the oasis that they came across a slow caravan heading west. Sinbad, after cautioning Don Giovanni not to speak and giving a false name, offered the caravan master several pieces of silver to take them with him. Being experienced in the desert and its ways, he had no trouble in securing the passage.

The journey proved arduous and boring. Days were insufferably hot, nights frigid. There was little diversion for the mariner, save for sitting around the dung fires at night and listening to the boastful tales of the various merchants. As for Giovanni, well, the frog had even less to be joyful about. Used to spending his time beside the cool pond, he was not at all fond of the sand, which burned his webbed feet and congested his little lungs. More than once he had even considered abandoning this venture for a more tranquil life at home. Sinbad, though, constrained him, and while the sailor languished amid boring banter, the frog contented himself by burrowing beneath Sinbad's shirt during the day and blanket at night, passing the time in daydreams and slumber.

Then, almost miraculously, the caravan reached the plain, and the fabulous city lay before them. The long journey was done at last, and, thanking the caravan master and merchants, Sinbad jumped from his camel, collected his small amount of gear, and disembarked before the stolid gates. Don Giovanni was more than gleeful, longing only to be placed down beside some cool pond where he might frolic for a time. Sinbad, meanwhile, remained wistful and concerned, for, although they had safely eluded the caliph and his soldiers and crossed the border without problems, they had now come to a place where they had no friends and little money left to support themselves.

With the frog perched on his shoulder, the turbaned mariner sighed and passed through the massive black iron gates, heedless of the stares he received from the sultan's black-caped guards posted along the walls.

Immediately they were greeted with a horrendous roar of city life. Camels were snorting, dogs barked, horses whinnied and jostled through unbelievable crowds. The streets were as busy as Sinbad could imagine. Veiled dark-skinned women carrying baskets and urns under their arms hurried among the endless rows of canopied stalls, inspecting fruit and dried meats, while potbellied butchers and farmers waved frantic hands to chase away buzzing flies. Beggars, ranging in age from the smallest of children to the oldest of men, lined the walks like a solid wall, pitiful hands out as they begged all passersby for alms. Some were blind, others crippled, still others deformed. Sinbad shuddered, thinking how such misery might have befallen these poor souls, and thanking Allah that despite all, he had not yet sunk to such straits.

The air reeked with the scent of perfumes mixed with the foul odors of droppings and cheap wine spilled into the clogged gutters and sewers.

Is this the noble Damascus? he asked himself, sickened by it all, sorely disappointed at the world's most famous city.

"Come Giovanni," he said with a disdainful grimace. "Let's be off down another avenue; this one leaves me ill."

The frog nodded, equally as repulsed. This was his very first visit to a city of men, and from the looks of this one he hoped he would never have to gaze upon another.

Down a narrow byway they walked, crossing crooked streets of clustered stone houses whose windowless fronts were plain and somber. Sinbad scratched his head as he went by. If his own eyes bore witness, he decided, the repeatedly splendorous Damascus could not hold a candle to Baghdad.

It did not take long before their street opened onto a wide and spacious square. Against the backdrop of a domed mosque set at the farthest corner stood the largest and most fabulous open-air market the sailor had ever seen. Stall after stall, displayed a plethora of merchandise that left him breathless. Here was the fame of Damascus—silks and wool, and the softest linen, brought from every corner of the world to be sold at the bazaar. Marble and porcelain artifacts resting beside exquisite handcrafted gold jewelry. Rings, bracelets, pins, brooches, necklaces studded with pearls and rubies, all intricately and beautifully designed by Damascus's most renowned jewelers. And the weaponry! Sinbad gawked at the fine blades of steel, bejeweled scimitars, scabbards of silver.

Ah, the gifts I could bring home to Sherry, he thought with wonder, before remembering they were parted forever.

"A gift for a lady, perhaps?" said an eager merchant, holding out an enameled set of serpent earrings.

Sinbad smiled and shook his head, moving deftly out of the way while more obnoxious shoppers brushed past to get a better look at the offered merchandise.

The merchant frowned. "Something else, perhaps?" he asked, gesturing to the wide variety of goods available upon his counters. Then he pointed to a pair of fine leather riding boots. "Three pieces of silver, for you," he told Sinbad. "A better price cannot be found in all Damascus."

"I regret to say no again," said Sinbad, "although I agree that your price is most fair."

The merchant remained unmiffed. "Ah, wait a moment," he said snapping a finger. Then he bent down beneath his shelves and came up holding a small gold-inlaid knife, the size of a child's toy but with a blade as sharp as a razor. "A man could hide this from the sharpest eyes," the merchant assured him. "Perchance are you a traveler?"

Sinbad admitted that he was, allowing that he had come to Damascus less than an hour before.

The merchant beamed, his dark eyes gleaming. "The roads are most unsafe, my friend," he cautioned. "A man needs to be armed—and needs to bear a weapon others cannot see." He stuck the knife under Sinbad's nose and the sailor took it warily. He examined it slowly, truly admiring the fine detail of work and the sharpness of both edges. It could prove a valuable asset, he thought, wondering if he should barter.

"How much, merchant?"

The stall-keeper grinned. "A small price, good sir. Four pieces of silver."

Sinbad felt the coins in his purse. "I'll give you two."

The merchant held up his hands and rolled his eyes toward the perfect blue sky. "Allah be my judge, I make no profit," he swore. "Do you wish to insult me? Better that you steal it!"

Sinbad held back a smile; merchants were merchants, be it in Baghdad, Damascus, or any civilized city on the face of the earth. "I am hurt by your own hurt," he quickly said, playing the game with skill. "But I can do no better."

"I am a poor man. Yes, a very poor man. Ten children and three wives count on me for their bellies to be filled. Would you wish that my children cry and their mothers sit silently in grief?" And as he spoke, a black-haired young girl of about six came out from behind the curtain and stood meekly in front of her father, staring at Sinbad with the biggest and saddest eyes he had ever seen.

"Have *you* wives and children to care for?" asked the merchant, patting his daughter's hair.

Sinbad shook his head. "Allah has seen fit to bless me with neither," he replied. "All I have to care for is myself," he glanced sheepishly to the silent frog on his shoulder, "and my little—er—pet. . . ."

"Three and no less!" cried the merchant, hands on hips. "What do you say?"

Sinbad scratched his chin and mulled it over. In truth he could not afford the price, yet somehow he felt that such a knife might well come in handy during the unknown adventures ahead.

"*Help me!*" came a cry from behind.

Sinbad spun without answering the merchant. An unescorted young woman had been knocked to the ground by a brutish assailant who, having swept a small bag from her hand was trying to break through the crowds.

"Stop him!" shouted the veiled woman. "He's stolen my purse!"

Sinbad lunged forward as Don Giovanni astutely hopped off his shoulder. The mariner caught the brute by the collar of his dirty robe and swung him harshly around.

The petty thief grunted as Sinbad's fist smacked into his belly; he pushed off the sailor and dodged another blow, jamming a forearm into Sinbad's face. Sinbad staggered back momentarily, then, regaining his senses, jumped for the thief and delivered a swift Chinese chop to the brute's neck. The thief moaned; Sinbad grappled him to the ground and punched him squarely in the face. The thief sprawled unconscious, a thin trickle of blood dripping from the side of his mouth.

Seconds later a group of the sultan's soldiers, swords drawn, were on the scene to take the thief to custody. The crowd of onlookers quickly dispersed. Sinbad got up, placed the frog back on his shoulder, and dusted off his robe.

"Oh, thank you, sir," said the woman, her hands clasped together as if in prayer, her eyes batting wildly. "I would have been in great trouble had that rogue gotten away."

Sinbad drew a deep breath and wiped perspiration from his forehead. "You should be more careful, dear lady," he reprimanded. "From what I've been told, Damascus is rife with such bandits."

"I know, I know. It was most foolish of me. It won't happen again."

Sinbad scooped up the fallen purse and handed it to her. "Well, at least no harm was done . . ." He waved a finger in her face, saying: "But next time I may not be so near to help you."

The girl laughed—a full and proud laugh, filled with spirit. "Such gallantry should not go unrewarded," she said. "You deserve more than a mere thank-you for what you did."

Sinbad looked at her questioningly, noting her smile through the veil. "I would never ask payment for coming to the aid of one so lovely in distress," he replied.

Recognizing his pride, the young woman boldly took his sleeve. "No insult was intended, stranger. Believe me. It is only that you have done me a great kindness, which I would like to return if I can."

Sinbad smiled. "Forgive me. I am weary from travel and forgot my manners—"

The green-eyed girl peered carefully at the weave of his garment, recognizing the colorful design at once. "Are you a visitor of our fair city?" she asked.

Sinbad bowed graciously, and Don Giovanni politely lowered his head. The girl laughed with delight and clapped her hands. "Your pet is well trained!" she exclaimed. "Surely in your own land your are a gentleman of quality."

"Captain Sinbad at your service, madam," said the sailor happily. "Come all the way from Baghdad to admire her illustrious rival at first hand."

"Captain Sinbad!" cried the girl. "I have heard tell of you! Indeed, our meeting here is most fortunate. Tell me, Captain, have you yet found lodgings in Damascus?" She was clearly impressed by her unexpected company.

99

"No, my lady," Sinbad admitted. "I have not yet had time to seek quarters."

"Then my home shall be your own," she replied firmly. "Never let it be said that such a famous visitor was ill-treated in Damascus."

"You are very kind, madam, and I am most unworthy."

The girl tossed off his humility with a wave of her aristocratic hand. "Nonsense, Captain. We are honored to have you. Come." And she turned to leave the bazaar, offering Sinbad her arm.

The mariner hesitated. He was grateful for her offer, of course—more than grateful—still, he was concerned about burdening her household with a man who, after all, was now a fugitive from the justice of his caliph. Giovanni, though, was less doubtful; he prodded the sailor to accept by nudging at Sinbad with his head.

The waiting girl stared up at the sailor. "Well?" she asked in a half-command, "aren't you coming?" She threw back her head and stood with her tiny hands placed upon her well-rounded hips, impatiently tapping her sandaled foot.

"You're certain it will be all right?"

Her eyes sparkled with her mirth. "Oh, yes," she said. "There is plenty of room, for you and your—er—friend both."

Sinbad met her steady gaze for a long moment and then took her arm to leave.

"Wait a moment!" called the rotund merchant, who had been standing quietly and observing all the while. "What about the knife? Have we a bargain for it or not?"

Sinbad slapped a careless hand against his head. "Ah, me, I completely forgot! How much did you say?" And he turned back toward the stall with his hand upon his purse.

"Three pieces of silver," said the merchant, his pudgy hands prepared to receive payment.

"Just a minute," said the girl, stepping brazenly between the two men. She held out her own hand. "Let me see the merchandise," she demanded.

The merchant handed it over reluctantly, then grew nervous as recognition of who she was finally dawned. "Yes, yes, my lady," he stammered, placing the knife in her open palm. "A fair price is all I've asked."

Ignoring his remarks, the girl subjected the knife to a thorough inspection. Sinbad looked on with puzzlement, wondering just who his sudden benefactor might be that she so frightened the clever merchant.

"Two pieces of silver shall suffice," she said with an air of finality.

The merchant reddened. "But my lady—"

"Two is the price," she snapped, haughtily adding, "Deliver it this evening. Your money shall be waiting."

The shopkeeper gritted his teeth and nodded. "As you wish, Lady Avilia," he answered. "It shall be an honor."

Avilia smiled; she gave Sinbad her arm again, turning her back on the bowing merchant. "It's getting late," she said.

Sinbad grinned. "Lead and I shall follow," he said. "I've never been one to keep a woman waiting."

Sinbad stood on the terrace of his spacious rooms, in the magnificent house to which Lady Avilia had brought him. It was a huge stone structure in a neighborhood of incredible wealth, and Sinbad marveled that such opulence could exist side by side with the terrible squalor he had seen earlier.

Here, within sight of the sultan's palace glimmering in the early evening light, lay lands as beautiful as he had ever seen. Rolling hills of green were capped with tall fruit trees and tended hedges. Little gardens resplendent with blooming flowers dotted both sides of the walk. A winding bridle path led to large stables stocked with the best stallions of Arabia. Corinthian columns stood stoically beside the bronze entrance doors, servants constantly scurrying in and out of the house to do their mistress's bidding.

The shallow water of the garden pond reflected the ebbing sun as Sinbad smiled at the sight of Don Giovanni, frolicking away along the banks beneath the shade of a tall oak. It was a peaceful pastoral setting, the likes of which Sinbad had yearned for. Yet he found himself feeling restless, not at all sure that coming here was the proper thing to do. Still, he had accepted the invitation and now he was Lady Avilia's guest. He only hoped to learn something more about her later.

Since being brought to this fashionable home some hours earlier, he had not seen his hostess at all. A cheerful Cypriot slave had taken him to his rooms, whereupon he had bathed luxuriously in a marble bath, then napped upon a handsome feathered bed, browsing afterwards at leisure through the multitude of books in the adjacent library. It was quite an impressive collection, Sinbad soon discovered, with volumes not only in Arabic but many in classical Greek and in Hebrew as well, rare books covering a wealth of knowledge and philosophy. Thoroughly fascinated, he thumbed among the well-worn pages of both the familiar and unfamiliar, contentedly passing the time until he was to be called for supper—a grand supper in his honor, the servant had said.

As the last minutes of daylight ticked away, Sinbad paced back and forth across his balcony, his body refreshed and his mind alive with ideas. It was while musing upon a new poem that he suddenly stood still and forgot his verse.

At the end of his balcony, where a broad stone staircase with carved balustrades led down to the garden, he caught a fleeting glimpse of a figure dashing between the lengthening shadows. Although the light was poor, he had little difficulty in discerning that the figure belonged to a woman—a youthful woman hastily making her stealthy way across the estate grounds.

Growing curious, Sinbad slipped behind a pillar and peered down. The girl proved to be younger than Avilia but certainly no less lacking in beauty. She leaned against the trunk of an oak, her face half cast in shadow, panting and catching her breath. She wore a softly brocaded yellow dress, Persian in design, and a golden Egyptian shell necklace that hung below her breasts. Unbound cocoa-colored hair cascaded over slim shoulders and down her back. With slightly slanted eyes that made Sinbad wonder if perhaps she had a touch of Far Eastern blood, she glanced across the gardens before preparing to run back inside the house.

Sinbad moved from the pillar and continued to watch, admiring her profile and wondering who she might be. He would have thought little of this episode of uncertain intrigue had he not suddenly noticed the tears welling within her hazel eyes. As she turned to leave, she cast her gaze momentarily toward the balcony. For just an instant their eyes met, hers wet and wide, his as dark and brooding as always. She squealed slightly, startled at his presence, and then ran off. Sinbad stepped fully into the open to call her back, but turned at the sound of his name.

The servant stood meekly inside the room, indicating the hour had come to dine. Sinbad shrugged, then smiled, putting the incident out of his mind. But as he was led down the grand steps into the dining hall a nagging thought played around the corners of his mind. He wondered what peculiar doings might be taking place within Lady Avilia's household.

The dining hall itself was somewhat smaller than Sinbad might have anticipated, though by no means lacking in finery. Tapestries from places as diverse as Cathay and Algiers hung from the yellow-painted walls, and great intricately designed braziers bathed the room in soft, delightful light. As in Dormo's home, there were delicately painted figurines and statues placed randomly about, each in itself a fine and unusual piece of art.

Except for two, each of the seven seats at the long oak table had been taken. Several servants moved gracefully among the guests, spreading rare delicacies, filling wine glasses and anticipating every want.

At sight of the mariner, Lady Avilia burst into a laugh of joy. "Ah, Captain," she cried gleefully, standing and holding out her hand. Sinbad kissed it, looking deeply into her eyes, waiting politely for her to regain her place before he sat.

"Here, do sit beside me," she said, gesturing to the comfortable leather-cushioned chair at her right. And then in quick succession she introduced the others. A mixed lot, Sinbad observed, all close friends of Avilia. Present were the renowned ambassador from Tripoli with his wife, he a celebrated and eloquent spokesman for his land, she a vital and vibrant woman whose looks must have hidden her true age by at least a decade. Also on hand was a youth called Dionatus, a poet at the sultan's court and an engaging wit. Sinbad took a liking to him right away. Of the last guest, though, he reserved his judgment. The fellow was about his own age, dark-complexioned and masculine. He looked at Sinbad with mistrustful, if not envious eyes, and greeted the mariner coldly. It did not take long for Sinbad to realize that this fellow, Argulo he was called, was Lady Avilia's lover.

Avilia pretended not to notice the hostility, and, raising her glass, toasted both her house guest and Baghdad, to which all but Argulo eagerly drank. Sinbad put his goblet to his lips and downed the sweet brew, thinking his hostess was lovely indeed and that Argulo was a fortunate man.

The banter was moderate and cheerful as the various courses of duck and meat were served, with Sinbad cheerfully answering a hundred questions of Baghdad and his own famous voyages, tales of which had evidently reached the sultan's court. The mariner spoke truthfully on all matters under discussion, although carefully avoiding any mention of his recent downfall.

"You are a lucky man, Captain Sinbad," said the poet Dionatus with a sigh. "I do envy you."

Sinbad laughed, avoiding Argulo's icy stare. "I think perhaps I envy you more," he replied. "I too love poetry, and would be more than content to give up the bridge of a ship for pen and paper to recount my thoughts."

Dionatus flushed with the compliment. Argulo growled, saying: "A man's duty is to protect his home, his king, not to waste his life in dreams."

Avilia shot him an angered glance. "What I think Lord Argulo means," she broke in, "is that art can only be a secondary concern while a nation seeks to build its strength."

"But my lady," protested the poet, "man needs beauty as surely as he needs the ability to laugh at himself. A warlike people is an unhappy people."

"Hear, hear," agreed the ambassador.

"Bah," grumbled Argulo. He looked sharply at Sinbad. "I would have thought a man of your stature had little time for such foolish diversion."

Sinbad was not sure if he was being purposely goaded. In any case, while under Avilia's roof he was not about to get himself into a brawl. "A pen is no less foolish than a sword," he replied to the dour man opposite. "One is an instrument of man's anger, the other of his soul."

Argulo laughed contemptuously. "And when the war comes,"—he leaned across the table—"shall you fight it with a pen or a weapon?"

Sinbad held his temper.

"Then you fear this war?" interjected the ambassador.

Avilia's lover's face darkened and he nodded grimly. "These madmen of the south seek nothing else. From Acre to Jerusalem—"

"Of what war are we speaking?" asked Sinbad with interest.

"Ah, forgive us," said the ambassador. "We forget that you are from so far away; our petty strife is of little concern to Baghdad. But you see," he explained, "Damascus finds herself faced with tribes of fanatics from across the Jordan river, intent on destroying the will of Allah."

"Hebrews?"

The ambassador shook his head. "Karmathians. Heathens, worse than the Christians, worse than the Turks. Their tactics are not very pleasant; they attack mostly at night, preying upon innocent victims, butchering them like goats."

The ambassador's wife shivered. She glanced at Avilia. "Must Diona leave for Jerusalem under these conditions?" she asked.

Lady Avilia nodded. "The marriage cannot be postponed."

"Where *is* Diona?" the ambassador said suddenly, looking to the single empty chair. "Your cousin will not be present at our table?"

At this, Avilia smiled apologetically and sighed. "My cousin is not feeling very well, she tells me. She's spent the entire day inside her room and asked your forgiveness for tonight."

"A pity," commented the young poet, looking to Sinbad. "Diona's company is something to be cherished." He smiled and turned to his hostess. "Should perchance this offer of marriage not work out to your satisfaction, I know another interested party more than eager to ask for her hand."

Except for Sinbad, everyone laughed.

Avilia reached out and placed her hand on top of the poet's. "Poor dreamy-eyed Dionatus," she cooed, "in love with my cousin since childhood. But alas, the bargain is all but sealed. Diona leaves for Jerusalem in three days' time; Sheik Kahlil is not the sort of man to be kept waiting."

"Especially when his dowry is most handsome," added Argulo with a measure of scorn which was not lost on Sinbad.

Lady Avilia looked at him sharply, briefly reddening. "We don't want to bore our special guest with matters as trivial as these," she rebuked. "Particularly when life affords us so many other diversions." She snapped her fingers, calling for more wine to be brought. "A very special brew," she told Sinbad while the servants began to pour. "A secret concoction of Alexandria."

Sinbad gleamed. "Ah, dear lady! I know it well—and I promise not to be disappointed."

From the very first goblet of the potent and heady stuff, the atmosphere at the table became more relaxed. Chatter increased, laughter abounding at the ambassador's clever jokes. Even stolid Argulo let down his guard and enjoyed the company. And soon it was well into evening, the moon obscured by thick clouds rolling in from the west, the air growing stagnant and clammy.

At length Avilia stood up and bade them all to follow. She led them from the stuffy chamber to an adjoining one where thick ostrich-feathered cushions lay scattered across the floor and a large water pipe in the center provided the only furniture. A soothing cool breeze blew through opened windows, and one by one the guests took places in the dimly lighted room.

"Come, Captain," whispered Avilia, beckoning to Sinbad as she stretched out seductively over three cushions. "Come and sit beside me."

Sinbad took her hand and sat, the others forming a semicircle around him. Several servants slipped inside the room, one bringing more Egyptian wine, the other filling the water pipe and lighting it. Avilia was the first to smoke. She drew in deeply, filling her lungs and then blowing a cloud of blue-tinted smoke toward the ceiling. Then she passed the pipe around. Sinbad had never been a partaker of hashish, knowing its prolonged effects clouded the mind. But in the company of these noble Damascans it would be too impolite to refuse. He took several lungfuls of the weed and then declined more, preferring instead to nurture his huge goblet of the Alexandrian wine.

The effects of the drug were not long in coming upon them. Flushed, the supple-bosomed wife of the ambassador began to unfasten the clasps of her garment until both

107

cleavage and nipples were well exposed. Avilia's feline smile to Sinbad assured the sailor that the long night's enjoyments had yet to begin.

Argulo leaned back with closed eyes, the pipe to his lips. His own contented smile told of most pleasant and fanciful dreams dancing within his mind. As for the ambassador, he nestled his cherubic face against his wife's breasts, his forefinger drawing invisible images into the haze-filled room.

Avilia closed her eyes and leaned back dreamily, purring and sinking deeper into the cushions as she pulled Sinbad closer to her. Sinbad stirred as her long fingers began a slow catwalk down his neck and over his throat, a most subtle touch of gentle caresses filled with promise. The mariner glanced to see what effect this affection might have upon Argulo, and was relieved to find that the jealous lover was now fast asleep with his dreams.

The room was swimming in a delightful mist, the single flame of the candle swaying in the breeze, shadows cascading colorfully over the walls and ceiling. Avilia clapped her hands once, and a young girl deftly slipped into the room, a small flute to her lips. The melodious tune hung in the air as the girl expertly raised and lowered the pitch. All the candles had now been blown out by the attending servants, and only dim starlight tempered the darkness. Avilia ran her fingertips over Sinbad's lips and, cradling his head into her bosom, kissed his brow.

Unsteadily, Dionatus lifted himself and stood erect before Avilia. "I . . . I have composed a new poem in honor of this night," he announced haltingly, gazing at the still couple through red, bloodshot eyes.

Lady Avilia grinned. "A poem of love, Dionatus?" she asked.

The youthful poet smiled shyly.

His hostess laughed grandly. "Then begin!" she replied with a sweeping gesture.

Dionatus folded his arms and cast his gaze toward the night.

Tis the promise of heros unscarred,
To drink of nature's golden privilege, so oft
Wasted upon the young . . .

Avilia listened attentively, smiling as the poet began to slur in his verse and sway tipsily from the combination of Alexandrian wine and the water pipe. Suddenly Dionatus chuckled to himself, then, closing his eyes and sighing, dropped to the floor, verse unfinished.

The ambassador rose up on one elbow. "The dancers, my lady?" he mumbled.

Avilia snapped her fingers and a black-haired Bedouin girl came inside. Scantily clad in long veils of scarlet and amber, she moved enticingly among the drowsy guests, swinging her hips in slow, rhythmic fashion. Her jeweled navel quivered.

"Do you like her?" Avilia asked the watchful sailor beside her.

"A very lovely girl, my lady. An asset to any household."

Avilia smiled coyly. "Take her if you like. She is yours as a gift."

Sinbad returned her smile and shook his head. "Thank you for the offer, but as I must soon leave Damascus it would be better if I declined."

The dancer shook her shoulders before the mariner, swinging a veil above her head, brushing her breasts fleetingly against him, teasing him with outstretched arms. Sinbad, his eyes glued to her shapely form, gulped.

"Are you certain you won't change your mind?" said Avilia.

The sailor from Baghad sighed. "I have sworn off women, my lady," he admitted. "A broken heart has caused me to take a vow of celibacy."

Avilia raised her brows. "Chastity is a dubious virtue," she remarked. "It bodes no man or woman well."

"Alas, that may be true. But true love cannot be denied. I shall remain constant to my Sherry for as long as I live."

With a decidedly feline smile Avilia began to run her hand gently along the inside of Sinbad's thigh, briefly brushing her palm against his crotch. "Your heart is of one mind, your body another," she wryly observed. And she poured his goblet to the brim with the exotic sweet wine of Egypt. "Share this with me," she whispered, sipping and putting the cup to his lips. Sinbad drank a long draught, feeling the brew l rn through his veins.

"You must forget this jilting lover," said Avilia, stroking his chest with her fingernails.

"Forget her? Never."

"Then you must let me help. . . ."

Avilia unfastened the thin strap of her dress and let it slide over her body. Glistening, supple breasts, firm and youthful with round, darkened nipples, pressed lightly against him.

"Come with me to my private rooms, Sinbad," she entreated, her hand again upon his manhood.

"I don't think I should," he answered feebly.

"Then you would deny a woman all she offers?" She nibbled at his neck, her tongue darting between moist, wine-flavored lips. "Can you not be chaste anew tomorrow, and spend this summer's night with me?"

Sinbad looked over his shoulder to the dreaming Argulo. "What about him?" he asked. "I fear your lover would be most displeased with you."

Avilia frowned. "Argulo is a fool. I only keep him around because he holds powerful sway at the sultan's court. Such men are—er—useful. But in truth he means nothing to me. Nothing. A woman can find greater pleasure with a palace eunuch."

She half closed her green eyes and gazed longingly at

Sinbad. With mortal man's weakness, Sinbad took her in his strong arms and kissed her passionately, desire overwhelming the reluctance of his heart.

"Come, my darling," she whispered. And while the dancer continued to cavort among the guests, Avilia coaxed Sinbad up and led him by the hand from the chamber and to her lavish private quarters.

There, flesh hungrily seeking the touch of flesh, Sinbad swam within her delights, his rapture rising like a floodtide, lost within the feel of her hips and womanhood, which encompassed his entire body and mind until her secrets unfolded their pleasure and gratification.

Bodies glowing in perspiration, they lay silently side by side, gazing deeply into each other's eyes, panting for breath in the afterglow of contentment.

Avilia purred anew, laying her head across his breast, letting her unbound hair spill over the side of the feathered bed. All now was total silence, as outside the first hints of dawn had begun to crack the black horizon of the starry sky.

"Stay with me, Sinbad," she asked as the sailor sat up against the pillows and stroked her hair. "Stay here in Damascas. You'll find the sultan most amiable. Certainly you would be an asset to his court."

Sinbad sucked in a breath of cool air from between clenched teeth. "Your offer is most kind," he replied, kissing the top of her head. "But as I've said before, I have other matters to tend."

Avilia scoffed. "What can be so important?"

"To reach the sea," he replied. "I have an ocean to cross and a flower to find . . ."

Lady Avilia glanced up with puzzlement; Sinbad laughed, not bothering to explain about Don Giovanni and their search for the elusive Red Dahlia.

"When do you leave?" she asked.

He shrugged. "In a few days' time."

"And have you a ship waiting in port?"

111

Sinbad sighed glumly. He had neither ship nor crew, all his wealth having been left behind—and most likely confiscated—in Baghdad.

"I have very little waiting," he admitted. "My hopes are to earn the money I need for my own vessel."

Avilia nodded. She wet her lips with her tongue and slitted her eyes. "Perhaps I can be of help," she said.

"You? How so?"

"A business transaction between us. . . ."

Sinbad leaned forward, brows furrowed with interest. "What sort of transaction do you have in mind?"

Avilia smiled her cat's smile. She locked her eyes with Sinbad's, and the sailor saw a shrewd mind behind them.

"I will pay you to go to Jerusalem for me," she said flatly.

"Jerusalem? What for?"

She sat up straight, brushing back her hair with her hand, easily making the transition from lovemaking to business.

"I will not lie to you, Sinbad," she said. "As you heard before, my young cousin, Diona, is set to wed Sheik Kahlil. There is little time for Diona to be transported safely to her husband, and I want to insure that she reaches him safely and soundly"—her voice grew colder now—"as intact as the day she leaves."

"Are you asking me to take her?" asked Sinbad.

Avilia nodded firmly. "There are few in Damascus I can trust. And, as you know, the roads are unsafe because of the Karmathian bandits." She leaned in closer and started to whisper. "Diona is a valuable prize, Sinbad. These hillmen would give much to capture her and hold her for ransom. You see, by marriage she is also related to the sultan himself, who entrusted her into my care. Should anything happen to Diona . . . She indicated her fate by crossing a finger over her throat.

"So you would entrust the girl to me?"

Avilia threw back her head and laughed. "To the famous

112

Sinbad? Why not? Of course I would! Why, one man like you is worth fifty of Argulo's ilk. I'll give you all the escorts you need. Well-trained and armed palace guards. . ."

Sinbad, mulling over the matter, shook his head. "Too many troops would only attract attention. It would make these Karmathians most curious. Best for the girl to be escorted by only a single companion and arouse no suspicions."

Avilia smiled at the mariner's cunning. "You're right, of course," she said. "Then you'll do it? You'll bring Diona to the sheik?"

Sinbad held up his hands. "Hold on. I didn't say that. My plans were to reach Tripoli—"

"I'll pay you well," reminded Avilia. "Almost any price you ask. Diona's safe delivery to Jerusalem is far too important to me to leave it to chance. But think, Sinbad! This little errand for me will pay more than enough to secure your ship—you would be a fool to refuse."

Sinbad sighed and leaned back, deep in contemplation of Avilia's offer. This certainly seemed more than a fair bargain, a single week's journey out of his way and a generous payment in return. Yet he had to wonder about Lady Avilia's own motive in the matter. Could it have something to do with the dowry Sheik Kahlil had promised, as Argulo had hinted earlier?

The clever girl lost no time in realizing her companion's reluctance. "I haven't been completely honest with you," she admitted, avoiding his eyes.

"I suspected as much," replied Sinbad. "Before I even consider this offer of yours, I want to know everything. The full truth, otherwise the bargain is off. Now, what is it about Diona that makes you so afraid she'll never reach her destination safely?"

"My cousin has no intention of reaching Jerusalem," Avilia responded simply.

Sinbad winced. "What do you mean?"

Avilia laughed a curt, cold laugh. "Ah, men! Are they all so blind? Is it so hard to understand? My young, pure cousin claims the shiek is 'too old' for her. Imagine! But it's only a child's romanticisms, Sinbad, I assure you. Diona dreams of . . . well, of a prince. You know what I mean, don't you, *hmmmm?*" She cuddled closer and flashed her luminous eyes.

"So I'm to be your insurance marker against her trying to run away, is that it?"

"Yes, you could put it that way. Is it so wrong? So wrong to stop her from being so rash? Diona is hardly a woman of the world, Sinbad. She doesn't understand these things; she hasn't yet seen or experienced life, never known its cruelties." Her eyes were damp. "Sheik Kahlil is a fine and generous man, and he'll make her a *perfect* husband! He's not so old—not *so* old. Most women think he's—er—quite handsome and dashing for his age—and everything a girl like Diona could ask. Please, Sinbad. You know I only want what's best for the child. Please help me to do the right thing. . . ."

"A woman's heart is hers alone to give," he observed wisely. "Maybe this sheik really would be better off with another bride, a more willing bride."

Avilia shook her head vehemently. "Sheik Kahlil is a most astute and beneficient man, and he knows how to forgive the foolishness of youth. While visiting here in Damascus, his eyes chanced upon the fair Diona, and immediately he fell in love with her. Why, his very breath is for her, Sinbad. Gladly does he overlook whimsies and flutters of a child's untrained heart. He asks only that she be brought to him pure—and that, dear Sinbad, is one promise I fully intend to keep. No living man shall ever touch Diona, save for him, her husband-to-be." She took Sinbad's hand in her own, held it tightly. "Will you consider helping me, or"—and here she looked away with a distasteful frown—"or must I leave the job to someone

114

like Argulo? A man without finesse, without your character and understanding."

Sinbad drummed his fingers, deciding. Avilia had made a powerful case, he knew. A most convincing case. And the simple fact was that if he didn't do the job, someone else would, and he would have thrown away his chance of quickly acquiring a ship.

"All right, my lady," he said at length, hoping he would not regret the deal. "I'll take Diona to her husband—but it has to be done my way. Quietly, alone, with no fanfare or caravans."

"As you will, Captain. I place the child in your competent hands. But remember to be careful. This leader of the rabble is a cunning devil. If Ben Abdul finds out the indentity of your charge . . ."

"Leave it to me," rejoined Sinbad. "I'll have Diona in her husband's house within a week."

Avilia squealed with delight. "Thank you, Sinbad," she cried. "Now I can sleep in peace, knowing all is well cared-for."

Sinbad grinned as she smothered him with kisses, pushing him back down upon the bed. Moments later her artistic hands had easily prepared him again and they shared another round of each other's bountiful pleasures. Avilia moaned softly at his touch, clinging wildly, calling out with her passion as the sailor felt his strength return.

The sun had long risen by the time their lovemaking had ended, and, while tiny birds sang pretty songs in the trees, both Sinbad and Avilia fell asleep in each other's arms.

Eighteen-year-old Diona, the pretty and mysterious young woman Sinbad had seen that evening in the garden, stood pouting with folded arms in the morning shadows of the portico, watching with disdain as three cud-chewing camels were watered, packed, and prepared for the journey.

Cajoled into a kneeling position, the double-humped

animals remained still while busy servants tied the various trunks upon the baggage camel's back with braided twine.

Diona smiled thinly as she watched Sinbad move from beast to beast, examining teeth, forcing open droopy eyelids, running his hands along the thick muscle of their legs and thin cloven feet. At times he grimaced, at others he smiled. Then he stood, and called to the nearby skinner that they had passed his inspection. All camels were deemed desertworthy.

So, thought Diona with a glare nothing short of contempt, *you are the famous Captain Sinbad, eh? Come as my cousin's lackey to force me to Jerusalem. Was it Avilia's lips that enticed you? Or the lure of her gold? Perhaps both? Enjoy it while you can, good sailor. The desert is a strange and cruel sea.*

The sound of sandals upon the portico caused Diona to turn abruptly. Dressed in a flimsy robe that brazenly hinted at the golden, supple flesh beneath, came Lady Avilia, eager to see the departure.

Diona regarded her silently, with a baleful eye.

"Good morning, dear cousin," said Avilia with a light laugh, one that left little doubt of her sense of victory. "I trust that you slept well last night and are prepared for your travel?"

Gloat while you can, slut! thought Diona. "Yes, my lady," she said with a slight but polite curtsy. "As much as I am loath to depart this happy home, I am even more pleased to be upon my way."

Avilia met her eyes evenly and smiled. "Grieve not, young cousin. Yor husband will quickly make you forget all you leave behind." Her soft voice was filled with sarcasm and venom, not unlost upon the seething girl.

Diona clasped her hands as if in prayer and bowed her head. "I hope my husband shall not be disappointed . . ."

Avilia laughed grandly, pouring her gaze up and down Diona's well-developed body. "The sheik admires things of beauty; his hands fondle with the greatest care."

Diona sneered. "You should know, sweet cousin."

Avilia flushed. She drew back a hand to strike the bold girl, then thought better of it and smiled complacently. "I shall warn your escort to take extra-special care," she whispered in a husky voice. "We must see that the blushing virgin remains intact—"

Tears came to Diona's eyes and Avilia chortled. She turned her back upon the girl with a brisk move that sent her robe twirling behind and moved quickly toward the small gathering.

Besides Sinbad and the various attendants, Argulo stood aloof at the side of the path. He and Avilia exchanged brief secret glances before she went on to greet Sinbad.

"Almost ready I see, Captain," she said, batting her eyes.

Sinbad, hands on hips, nodded, his tanned features in stark contrast to to his sand-colored turban. "That we are, my lady. I've double-checked everything. We can be on our way as soon as your cousin gathers the rest of her belongings."

"Diona has all she needs," Avilia replied casually. She glanced at the strapped baggage, letting her eyes linger a moment longer on a small pouch lashed firmly to a trunk. "Do not forget to hand this package personally to Sheik Kahlil," she told him.

Sinbad squinted his eyes from the glaring sun. "No, indeed. Everything you asked shall be carried out to the minutest detail. In six days' time—seven at most—we shall be in Jerusalem. Rest assured Diona is in good hands."

Avilia laughed merrily. "I'm certain of that, Captain Sinbad. That's why I chose you for the task. Ah, but I almost forgot!" She drew inside her robe and took out a small purse laden with coins. "As agreed, here is half your payment in advance. Sheik Kahlil with provide the rest himself upon your arrival."

Sinbad took the purse, tossed it in his palm, and tucked it safely away.

"You can count it if you like . . ."

The mariner grinned. "Not necessary, my lady. We trust each other, do we not?"

At this Avilia unclasped her veil, stood on her toes, and kissed Sinbad lightly on the cheek. "Take care, Captain," she whispered. "And should you decide to return to Damascus . . ."

He kissed her on the lips, unmindful of Argulo's grimace, and held her at arms' length. "Although my heart belongs to another, I shall never forget you, Avilia." And he turned to the attendants, gesturing that he was ready.

"Stay close to the main caravan route," cautioned the skinner. "And be mindful of that rogue Ben Abdul. Danger waits amid those Judean hills—and many an unwary traveler has come to regret his journey."

"I'll be careful," assured Sinbad. He was no hero in these matters, not by any means, but a lifetime of adventure had made his senses as sharp and as cunning as any. If this Ben Abdul had any designs on him or his charge, the bandit would sorely pay for his folly.

"One more thing," said Avilia. She clapped her hands and a servant came running. He kneeled before Sinbad and held out his open hands. Sinbad stared and then laughed. It was the knife—the tiny knife he had agreed to purchase in the bazaar but had completely forgotten about.

"A gift for you, Sinbad," said the smiling Lady Avilia. "Keep it hidden and use it well."

"And now we go," he sighed. He whistled loudly and from the nearby pond Don Giovanni came leaping and bounding, hopping onto Sinbad's shoulder as the sailor arched his body low. "Ha!" he said to the frog. "Thought I'd let you spend the rest of your life sloshing about in mud, eh?"

His merriment was short-lived—he turned abruptly at the sound of an anguished cry and looked on startled to see lovely Diona being dragged toward the camels by two brutish servants.

"Louts! *Animals!*" cried the girl, spitting into the face of the servant twisting her arm. "Oww! Let go will you? Allah, that *hurts!*"

Sinbad grew angry at the sight of the helpless girl. That Diona was spoiled, strong-willed, childish, impudent, and all the other things Avilia had told him might well be true—but the handsome sailor from Baghdad was not about to stand idly by and watch the highborn girl being treated like so much dirt.

"Take your hands off her!" he boomed.

The surprised servants stopped in their tracks, their eyes looking first to Sinbad and then to Avilia.

Avilia stepped closer and nodded. "That won't be necessary," she told them. "My cousin can make it to her camel by herself." Then she glared at the girl, saying: "Can't you, Diona?"

Diona returned the icy stare, rubbing at her pained wrists. "Very well on my own, my lady," she answered. And while everyone looked on, she brushed past Avilia and lifted herself onto the saddle of the kneeling camel, scornfully looking at Sinbad, who offered his hand.

"It would be better if we were on speaking terms," said the sailor. "It's a long ride from here to your husband's camp."

"Go away," replied Diona with unabashed anger. "I can take care of myself well enough. If it's company you seek, look to your frog—and leave me alone!"

Don Giovanni, still pretending to be merely an ordinary frog, sat dumbly on Sinbad's shoulder, but as the sailor turned, in resignation, he whispered: "There is trouble ahead on this little adventure of ours, mark my words."

Sinbad frowned and mounted his camel. He slapped it gently with his whip and the beast grunted, standing upright. At the urging of the skinner, Diona's camel did the same.

Argulo stepped up for the first time to face Sinbad. Written across his features was a mixture of sarcasm and

119

humor. "Better for you to have her hands tied and her mouth gagged," he told the sailor. "Lady Diona is a hellcat personified, Captain. A mutinous crew indeed! You shall regret giving her these freedoms."

Sinbad glared down at the man, well aware of Argulo's desire to be rid of him forever. "I doubt such a measure will be necessary," he replied dryly. Then he swung his beast around, knowing that the camel's hooves would kick up clouds of dirt into Argulo's face. As the outraged lord coughed and sputtered, Sinbad looked to Diona with a smile. Diona, it was plain, was trying to contain a grin of her own.

"Something tells me, my lady," he said, "that you and I shall become good friends before our excursion is done." And he winked at her good-naturedly.

Suddenly Diona's expression turned dour again. Her complexion darkened and a small scowl toyed at the corners of her mouth. "Save your sweet words for another, Sinbad!" she rasped. And, using her whip, she urged her camel forward onto the path that led down to the road.

Sinbad shook his head and sighed, wiping perspiration from his brow as he watched the girl ride quickly away from the estate she loathed. "You know, my friend," he confided to Giovanni, "I suspect your estimation of this matter may be right. I'm afraid we're going to have our hands full." And, with a slap and a whoop, he pressed his own camel on in hot pursuit, tightly holding the reins of the third camel, laden with supplies and luggage. The beast wheezed as he tore down the road after Diona.

"May Allah ride with you, Sinbad!" cried Avilia after him. Then she stood in the middle of the path, smiling as the mariner caught Diona's camel and slowed him down. When they had passed the gates of her home and disappeared from sight, she shrugged, sighed wistfully, and walked slowly back toward the gardens where Argulo stood impatiently waiting.

"He's gone," was all she said.

120

The lord glowered. "Good riddance." His brows slanted and he looked at her intently. "Well, my dear? Do you think our handsome sailor suspects?"

Avilia shook her head, smiling thinly. "Not a chance. I made sure of it."

Argulo laughed. "Then double good riddance. They deserve each other."

Sinbad soon reached the open road. Passing rows of cypress and date trees, he waved to workers in the fields as his small party crossed over well-trodden paths. Lush fields of wheat and barley caught the strong morning sunshine. Far off to his right he saw the high walls of Damascus glistening against a perfect sky, while before him lay only the endless sand of the open desert. A beautiful panorama—but every bit as deadly as it was alluring. Even the best of men had fallen prey to the desert's traps. Once a man was lost in those wastes, he would not take long to die.

The bottom of the huge red ball that was the setting sun brushed softly against the peaks of mountainous dunes, scattering scarlet hues along the length and breadth of the vast sweep, changing the sand from gold to blood-red.

Already the night chill was in the air. Although day was blistering and scorched the sand, nighttime was cold enough to chill to the bone, and a cruel wind bit fiercely through all those who dared face the desert's wrath.

Sinbad glanced at the roughly sketched map given to him by one of the skinners. They had stayed close to the caravan route, he knew, and had now come to a place where the dunes broadened and a valley of sand, like a riverbed, sloped and narrowed as it twisted its way south. The skinner had told of an oasis nearby, one always used by travelers taking this route to the hills of Judea. Yet Sinbad could see no sign of such a welcome haven—only more of the same.

He swung his camel around and looked to Diona. The

girl was shivering at the feel of the gusty wind whirling among the dunes. The bridle jangled as Sinbad leaned over in the saddle. She seemed tired, perhaps, but no worse for wear. All day they had ridden with barely a pause, putting good distance between themselves and Damascus. And in all that time Diona had not spoken a single word to him. She had remained poised and calm, following Sinbad's lead and showing no interest in the journey at all.

"It will be dark soon," said Sinbad, breaking the quiet between them. "We're going to need some kind of shelter over our heads."

Diona nodded.

Sinbad watched the sun slide below the horizon and shivered. There was little point in even trying to find this oasis. He dismounted, offered Diona his hand, and helped her down. Then, using blankets and rope, he carefully constructed a small windbreak so they could rest with their faces turned to the shelter of the blanket. He built a tiny fire from dung and apportioned out some salted meat and dried biscuits from his saddlebags.

Diona ate somberly, still unwilling to speak, and Sinbad respected her desire for solitude, although from the corner of his eye he saw her glancing at him several times.

It was growing colder by the minute. He handed the girl a quilt and made his own place opposite her to lie down. "Best that we should sleep now," he told her. "I hope to be up well before dawn to continued our journey."

Diona chewed slowly on the last of her biscuits and cleaned her hands in the sand. Then, not even bothering to say good night, she wrapped herself in the quilt, turned her back on Sinbad, and went to sleep.

"I do not trust her, Sinbad," whispered Don Giovanni as the mariner made himself comfortable. Sinbad made no reply.

He stared at the flapping blanket and listened to the low

122

howl of the wind. Above, the stars were resplendently aglitter and he fancied himself upon the sea, wishing the dunes were salty waves gently bobbing against the hull.

Ah, Sherry, would that you were with me now, he thought, gazing blankly into the distance. And then, as Don Giovanni nestled between the warmth of his shirt on one side and the blanket on the other, Sinbad closed his eyes, drifting into a peaceful sleep.

He stirred at the feel of a hand nudging his shoulder. His eyes opened to find Diona, her unbound cocoa hair flowing freely in the breeze.

"My lady, what—?" He froze.

Diona smiled thinly and wielded a curved knife before his eyes. A knife she had no doubt secretly hidden within the folds of her garments before they had left Damascus.

Her eyes flicked with uncertainty and she bit at her lip. "I don't want to kill you, Sinbad," she told him in a low, throaty tone. "But I won't hesitate if I have to. Do you understand?"

Sinbad made no move to dissuade her, not knowing if she could really murder a man but unwilling to take undue risks. Experience had taught him much about women, and a woman betrayed was never to be taken lightly.

"What are you going to do?" he asked in a calm voice.

Diona glanced around uneasily, then turned her cold eyes back to the sailor. She pressed the tip of her knife against his jugular and ground her teeth. "I'm going to tie you up and leave you here," she said at last. "No harm will come to you, with luck a caravan may be along in a day or two. . . ."

Sinbad narrowed his eyes, holding her gaze while fully aware that the frog had slipped from sight and was now circling behind her.

"And what about you, my lady? I need not warn how dangerous the desert can be to a novice."

Diona frowned, and then, as though her mood had

changed with the bat of an eye, she laughed. "Ah, good Captain! Do not worry for me. I promise you I'll find safety long before you will."

"Safety where?" he asked speculatively. "Surely not here?" And he lifted his arm to gesture around him.

"Keep still!" snapped the girl. The knife pressed harder against his flesh and Sinbad held his breath. "I warn you, Sinbad! Don't play little games with me. I'm not your beloved Avilia. I'd just as soon gouge out your eyes as let you go."

Sinbad drew a deep breath and exhaled it slowly. Diona, it seemed, was even more determined than he thought. "All right, then. Bind my hands, if you will. But first, hadn't you better give more thought to your circumstances?"

"What do you mean?"

"The wind is rising," said the sailor. "We face a desert storm, a sirocco. You'll be blinded in an hour, drowned within a sea of sand. . . ."

Diona looked around again. The wind was blowing more furiously than before.

"You're trying to frighten me," she said.

Sinbad shook his head. "No, my lady, I'm not. I'm serious. To leave our camp now would insure your death—and that lover of yours will never see you again."

Diona felt confused; she lightened the pressure of her knife and tensely pondered her choices. Sinbad smiled inwardly, realizing his ruse had worked.

"Now, Giovanni!" he barked, and the frog leapt from the side, his webbed feet knocking into her hand and causing the knife to fall.

Diona, caught badly off guard, tried to recover and grab the weapon. But Sinbad was up like a bolt, scooping up the blade and tossing it into the wind. Diona started to go for it, but the mariner caught her arm and swung her around, bringing her to her knees as he twisted her arm behind her back.

Diona squirmed and writhed, swinging her free fist

124

blindly, trying to throw sand in Sinbad's eyes, jab him in the ribs with her elbow, topple him over. But the more she tried, the firmer his hold became, until tears were streaming down her face.

"Had enough?" bellowed the sailor, angrily pushing her face farther and farther down until her lips almost touched the sand.

Diona was determined not to scream or plead. "*Damn you*," she sniveled, her shoulders shaking.

Sinbad let go suddenly and she fell in a heap upon the ground. He leaned over and waved a menacing finger at her. "Don't ever try that again," he warned sternly. "Next time I won't be so lenient."

"Next time you'd better kill me!" Diona cried, holding her injured arm and tending her more-injured pride. "You'll never reach Jerusalem with me! *Never!*"

Sinbad threw up his hands in exasperation. "Maybe Argulo was right," he mumbled. "You *are* a little hellcat. A vixen like you deserves to be tied like a dog."

At this Diona put her hands to her face and began to cry oceans of bitter tears.

Sinbad felt his anger quickly flee. He saw within the girl a trace of Sherry, the way Sherry had looked that night before their attempted escape. Suddenly Sinbad was filled with compassion; he reached out to soothe her and she brushed him away. "Leave me alone," she wept. "The last thing I want is your pity."

Sinbad nodded slowly. "Very well," he said, staring up at the moon and stars. He realized there were hours left before dawn, enough time to sleep again and perhaps put this little episode behind forever.

"You'd better go back to sleep," he told Diona as Don Giovanni hopped back beside him. Then he threw her the blanket.

Diona turned around, looking at him with clear surprise. She held out her arms, wrists crossed and pressed together like a prisoner. "Aren't you going to bind me?" she asked.

125

Sinbad shook his head. "Not if you give me your promise not to try and run away again tonight."

Her almond eyes widened. "And what about tomorrow?"

Sinbad wiped away a tear from her cheek and smiled. "We live our lives one day at a time," he replied philosophically. "If you give me your word not to play any more games tonight, I'll not tie you up."

A tiny smile flickered somewhere deep within her eyes and Diona, exhausted because she hadn't yet slept, readily agreed.

Sinbad grinned, relieved. "Good. Get some rest now. I'll wake you an hour before dawn."

She did as asked without complaint. Sinbad watched while she pulled the quilt around herself and hugged at it tightly. Moments later the weary girl was deep in slumber.

Women, mumbled Sinbad, warming his hands beside the dying fire. And with a long sigh he closed his eyes, confident there would be no more tricks at least until tomorrow.

The camels rambled slowly along the rocky riverbed, grunting as they lurched over ruts and gulleys in the parched terrain.

Scrub weed dotted the landscape in the most peculiar places, jutting from beneath great rocks and over rugged dunes, the only foliage in an otherwise deserted world. It was only early morning, but already the heat had become so oppressive that even lizards and snakes dared not venture from their burrowed nests into the open, and only the sounds of the camels broke the total silence and solitude.

Again and again Sinbad was forced to pause in the journey, allowing Diona to drink her full water ration before noon and part of his own as well. With the girl trailing behind, he led his beast to the height of a windswept dune and peered out across the expanse. His lips were dry and cracked, his tongue beginning to swell. He shaded his eyes and peered intently ahead, straining for a glimpse of the near horizon. The riverbed twisted and coiled until it ended abruptly, and there, where the desert became flat and rocky, he sighted tiny specks swaying darkly in the distance.

A *mirage?* he asked himself, as the forms seemed to take vague shape. Then he smiled.

"Can we rest soon?" asked Diona, bringing her camel beside his own and looking at him hopefully.

"Can you see those trees?" he said.

Diona stared and nodded.

"We've reached the oasis at last. We'll be there in less than an hour, with any luck . . ."

Diona smacked her lips at the prospect of fresh water and a cool shaded place to get out of the sun.

Sinbad rode down from the dune and, with the girl right behind, picked a path along the gulley until they were in full sight of the swaying trees. Shadows of the branches threw dark patches over a wide pool of water close beside the gnarled roots, and deep blue grass formed a circle of protection around the oasis, a patch of life in a desolate wilderness.

Without a word they dismounted and raced for the pool, drinking with frenzy, splashing it over themselves, dunking their heads, and sighing with relief.

"We'll stay through evening," Sinbad said, "then continue under the stars." And while Diona gratefully rested beside the bank, laughing as Don Giovanni pranced at the water's edge, Sinbad gathered dates from the trees. Then they quenched their thirsts again, ate, and stretched out to sleep beneath the lumbering branches of a great cypress.

The sun had begun to set by the time Sinbad awoke to find Diona already up, sitting with her chin on her knees and gazing blankly toward the west. Sinbad stretched lazily, wriggling around to work the stiffness out of his muscles. The girl pushed loose hair from her eyes, looked at him, and smiled. "Did you sleep well?" she asked.

He nodded and sat up. The camels were nibbling at grass along the edge of the oasis, making small noises as they chewed. The murmur of swaying grass drifted peacefully into his ears and he glanced at the still waters of the pool, thinking of the sea and the strange fascination it had always held for him.

"When do we leave?" asked Diona, breaking into his thoughts.

Sinbad frowned. "Soon. After we eat something and refill the waterbags."

"Already done," replied Diona, gesturing to the goatskin pouches left laying beside the bank. "I did it while you were still sleeping."

Sinbad grinned and started to stand. Diona reached out and took hold of his sleeve. "Sinbad," she said, casting down her eyes, "about last night . . . I want you to know that I'm sorry. I never would have harmed you. I want you to know that."

"Forget it. I already have."

She smiled fully and nudged him to sit down beside her. He hesitated. Her tugging became stronger, her hand folded over his. She wet her lips and looked deeply into his eyes, closing her own as she leaned forward and kissed him.

The mariner was taken by surprise. He shared the kiss briefly, enjoying the honeyed taste of her mouth upon his own. But then, as her arms closed around him, he nudged her back, releasing her hold.

Diona pouted. "What's the matter?" she said. "Don't you like me?"

Sinbad laughed. "I like you fine, my lady. You're a beautiful young woman. But how is it that last night you wanted to kill me and tonight you want me to make love to you?"

Diona's eyes betrayed her sense of growing anger. "Am I not good enough for you?" she seethed. "Or has my sweet cousin got you bewitched?"

128

Sinbad laughed again, this time with more gusto, while Diona sat and fumed, rattled at being taken so lightly by the famed mariner. "It is a mistake to mock me, Sinbad," she hissed. "It could prove your undoing."

Sinbad looked at her questioningly. "And what do you mean by that, my lady? More of your tricks?"

"I doubt I shall need them," she rejoined as a sly smile crossed her full lips and she complacently met his gaze. "Ah, Captain," she added with a hint of amusement, "can you not see? Has Avilia blinded you so? Don't you know that she plays us both for fools?"

"Oh?" said Sinbad, slanting his brows.

Diona chuckled to herself, shaking her head at the secret joke. "Tell me, Captain, why do you think this marriage is of such great import to my cousin? Why has she paid you so grandly merely to escort an errant girl she despises on a common sojurn to Jerusalem?"

"Avilia says that the sheik will have no other; that when he saw you in Damascus he fell immediately in love—"

Diona laughed bitterly. "And you believe it?"

The sailor shrugged. "It's none of my affair why he desires you so . . ."

"Nor his motives?"

"As you said, your cousin has paid me handsomely to deliver you. But why you are such a valuable prize I cannot say. His business is his own."

"Then indeed you *are* a fool," snapped the girl. "Kahlil needs me not—his tents are filled with wives. Yet,"—here she sighed—"he *does* have his reasons. . . ." She leaned closer to Sinbad and her voice lowered to little more than a whisper. "He will make of me his hostage."

Sinbad winced. "Hostage? What in the name of the Prophet are you talking about, child?"

"Isn't it obvious? Avilia wants me far and away from Damascus. You see, I know too much of her little games. Avilia must have me out of the way; she would even kill me if she had to."

Sinbad focused his eyes intently upon the girl; he felt a sudden chill. "I don't understand what you're talking about. What harm can you do Lady Avilia? She is every bit her own woman, renowned throughout Damascus. A beloved face at the sultan's court, a woman of charm and fortune, a patroness of the arts . . ."

Diona clenched her hands and glared at the mariner. "How little you know! It is a sham, Sinbad, a sham! My cousin has squandered her wealth for years, and now, despite her show of riches, owns not a fig. She is in debt to virtually every money lender in Damascus—"

"I still don't see what all this has to do with either you or me," he said gruffly. "Fortunes come and fortunes pass. Avilia, if what you say is true, shall somehow regain her wealth."

Diona's eyes flashed. "Aye, Sinbad! At my expense! Listen to me: When my own father died just this past year, Avilia, being my closest relative, made me her ward—"

"A kindness on her part, surely."

Diona sneered. "A kindness to line her own pockets! My father's estate, which amounts to no small sum, was left in trust with her as dowry for the man I marry. Avilia and her former paramour, that pig Kahlil, have plotted between them. Once I am wed, the sheik has agreed to split half the dowry with her—enough wealth to wipe away Avilia's considerable obligations and let her live wantonly again. But I caught wind of this little intrigue long ago, forcing my cousin to make any hasty plan she could to insure that the marriage takes place as scheduled. Were it not for your presence in Damascus, that brute of a worm Argulo would have personally done Avilia's bidding. He, too, plans to share in these illicit profits—profits brought at the expense of my misery." She paused and smiled grimly at the increasingly uncomfortable sailor, then added: "And you, Sinbad, have become her tool. A purse of gold was all it took to bribe the world's most famous mariner into doing her dirty work for her."

130

Sinbad ignored the insult, but he felt uneasy. He puffed his cheeks and blew the air out of his lungs in a slow, steady stream. Could all of this be true? he wondered. Could he indeed have played the pawn in such a filthy game? Or was this entire story merely another of Diona's clever ruses to gain her freedom? A carefully-thought-out concoction of half-truths, innuendos, and sheer lies. . . .

Diona sensed his doubts. "You don't believe me, do you?" she said.

Sinbad drummed his fingers nervously. "Should I? Have you any proof of what you say?"

Diona lifted her chin and gazed at him defiantly. "My true love could prove it to you. He possesses the secret paper upon which my cousin Avilia and the sheik have made their covenant."

"Your *true love?*" said Sinbad.

Diona smiled. "My only love—the man who's going to take me far away—and leave Avilia with an empty purse!"

A tightening knot grew in Sinbad's belly. He didn't quite believe her, but he didn't quite disbelieve. "I don't know what you're talking about. I've been paid to bring you to Jerusalem, and that I intend to do."

"Then you're a fool, Captain Sinbad! But don't take my word for it. Let my lover prove it for you."

"What lover? Who?"

Her smile deepened. "You'll find out," was all she said.

Could it be? Was there someone else in her life? No. Impossible. Avilia had explained it to him. This was just another ruse . . . Or was it?

"Listen to me, Sinbad. You can save yourself; there's still time. Take me to my lover—now."

The bold captain shook his head. "I gave my word to bring you to Jerusalem, and that much I'm going to do. What happens then, whether you wed the sheik or not, is not my affair. If there *is* a secret lover, then this quarrel is with your bridegroom—not with me."

Diona bristled, her temper flaring. "By then it will be

too late! Don't you see? The sheik's agents will be following us long before we reach the city. They'll wrest me away from you, Sinbad, by force—and care all the less if they have to kill you in the process."

Sinbad laughed. "I'll take my chances."

The girl's wet eyes flickered sadly. Diona knew she had pleaded her best case—and lost.

Sinbad abruptly ended the conversation. He stood up, glanced at the setting sun, which by now had all but disappeared behind the distant dunes, and tended the waiting camels.

"Beware, Sinbad!" the crying Diona shouted to him. "The journey is not yet half done—and Jerusalem is still far away. You may yet wake to the cold steel of a knife in your back—remember that this is Ben Abdul's country we are in."

Sinbad turned slowly and faced the trembling girl. "Is it the bandit who might use the knife?" he asked sardonically, "Or you?"

Diona lifted herself from the grass and cleaned off her desert robe. "I am your prisoner," she reminded. "My hands can be bound. But heed my advice, Captain Sinbad of Baghdad: From here to Jerusalem, you had better not close your eyes even once!"

A true sirocco had begun to blow in the early hours before the next dawn. The steady, oppressive wind made their going on impossible. Sands swept with fury, lashing at the beasts of burden, causing them to stumble in blindness. It was all Sinbad could do merely to keep Diona beside him while the wind howled like a tempest upon the sea.

Near a dry bed of a rutted ridge, Sinbad set up an emergency shelter. He pegged the small tent as firmly and deeply as possible, working alone in the terrible storm while Diona stood by idly, gloating at his difficulties. When the work was finally complete, he roughly pushed the girl inside the shelter, secured the nervous camels to posts, and slipped inside himself.

Diona huddled in the far corner, avoiding any contact. Resigned to her hostility, Sinbad wiped the sand from his mouth and eyes and squatted. From inside his tunic he took out Don Giovanni and the frightened frog hopped toward the blanket and furrowed himself within the folds.

The wind was picking up; Sinbad peeked at the swirling storm, hoping that by the time the sirocco had ended they would not find themselves literally buried alive beneath a newly formed dune.

He took out a slab of salted beef from the saddlebag, offered some to Diona, who ignored him, and curled himself up as he ate. Bad weather like this could last for days, he knew. A sirocco was the scourge of the desert, and the wily sailor feared it accordingly.

Time passed slowly. Diona fell asleep. Sinbad tried also, but was unable. Each time he closed his eyes to drift into slumber he was awakened by the sounds outside. But it was more than that, he knew. The things the girl had told him yesterday played around the edges of his consciousness, nagging at him, gnawing at him, filling him with doubt. He wished the storm would end, wished he could be done with this little side journey of his life.

He glanced at the sleeping girl, noting the tiny lines of anguish etched into her gentle features. And again he thought of Sherry, his only true love, and the struggle she had fought for the man she loved.

You're a sentimental fool, Sinbad, he said to himself with a scowl. *The odds are better than even that everything she told you was a lie. She and her lover . . .*

Who was this secret lover? Sinbad wondered for the first time. What youth of Damascus had so captured Diona's heart and imagination? And he thought back to his first night at Avilia's home. The fine supper spread before them, the noble and educated guests. And he recalled the

133

words of the dreamy-eyed young poet Dionatus. *Should perchance this marriage not work out, I know another more than eager to ask for her hand. . . .*

Then came the laughter at his remark, the light banter of not taking him seriously.

Sinbad sat up, his eyes suddenly wide. *Could it be Dionatus she loves? Can he be the youth so foolhardy as to follow the girl into the desert?*

Sinbad thought hard. The pieces did seem to fit into place. When he had first seen Diona she had been running among the shadows, out of breath and nervously glancing about. Clearly she had just come from a brief interlude with her lover. And certainly Dionatus was at hand that very night—by the time Sinbad had come to the supper table the youth had already taken his seat.

Sinbad sighed a forlorn sigh; he reflected upon the foolishness of the young. What if the poet tried to stop them from reaching Jerusalem? Sinbad knew he would have to fight him, stop him in any way he could. Yes, even kill him if the poet were so reckless as to demand honor. The mariner groaned silently and put his head to his hands. A simple journey between two cities was rapidly becoming the most complex one he had ever faced.

The camels began to grunt restlessly, scratching their cloven feet into sand and kicking at the side of the flapping shelter. They carried on even more frantically in the ensuing moments and Sinbad became concerned. He peered outside and was greeted with a rush of flying sand. Clearing his eyes and staring ahead to where the ridge wound along the trail, he caught sight of a dark shadow moving slowly closer toward the tent. Sinbad drew his dagger and pushed his way outside.

In the fierceness of the storm he could hardly see a thing, though dawn was breaking and the night sky was growing light. There was another camel heading this way, he saw to his shock. A single rider, covered from head to toe with protective robes and scarves to cover his face.

The rider saw Sinbad amid the swirls and waved a frantic hand. "Shelter, good traveler," he shouted. "Can you give me shelter?"

Through the blizzard of sand Sinbad could see that he rode alone, and the sailor fought his way forward to reach the rider and help lead the blinded beast toward his camp. The animal was in a bad way, gasping and slightly limping.

Sinbad helped the man down and tied the camel's reins to the post. Then he pushed open the entrance flap and waited as the traveler gratefully hurried into the tiny tent.

Diona sat up startled at the sight of the stranger. The man seemed equally surprised to find a woman inside. Removing his sand-encrusted scarf, he bowed politely to the girl and turned to his host.

"May the Prophet bless you for this kindness," he said humbly, with a voice that wheezed of sand in his throat.

"The courtesy of the desert demands no less," replied the mariner. And he handed the bedraggled traveler his water bag and gestured for him to sit.

At first glance the stranger seemed old, what with his windblown face and wrinkled eyes that told of many years' hard living upon the desert. Yet as the man sat and wiped away dust and grime his features suddenly took on a younger look. He was a rugged fellow, muscular and powerful, well bred for a Bedouin's life. He sported a short beard and brush moustache, with thick, bushy black eyebrows that all but joined above the bridge of his nose. Sinbad caught Diona glancing at him with some fascination, but when she saw Sinbad look her way, her glance quickly turned and she withdrew meekly back into her shell.

The weary traveler took several swallows of water and, after washing out his mouth, stuck his head outside to spit. Then he returned the water bag to Sinbad. "Your kindness has saved my life, my friend," he said hoarsely. "Permit me to introduce myself. I am Assal Karli of the Bedouin, son of Sheik Aluf. While leading our flocks to the well of Jamura, I became lost in the storm. Hopelessly

135

lost, I'm afraid. As you saw, my animal became lame. He fell beside the rocky bed of the *wadi* and, in pain, poor creature, led me to this very tent."

"Then truly Allah has seen fit to find you safety," Sinbad told him.

Assal Karli raised his brows and looked up as though toward heaven. " 'Tis all too true, my kind host." He turned to Diona and smiled. "And finding myself in such pleasant company has made me doubly blessed."

"Allow me to introduce ourselves," said Sinbad, bowing politely in acknowledgement of the gracious praise. "The lady is Diona of Damascus, on her way to be wed in Jerusalem. And I am Sinbad of Baghdad, her escort at the bequest of her family."

"I am *honored*," cried Assal Karli, recognizing the name at once. "Misfortune has turned to fortune indeed. And he bowed his head to both of his companions. "Truly, fate must have ordained this most unexpected turn of events for me."

Outside, the storm had continued to intensify. Sinbad listened uneasily to the shrieking of the wind and felt the tent shake and shudder around them. "I fear that fate has not done with us yet," he said glumly to the Bedouin.

Assal Karli smiled. "Our sirocco has you most concerned," he said. "But rest assured, there is no need for anguish. We of the Bedouin tribes are used to such storms. We understand them, perhaps better than any in Islam. Listen . . ." And he put his hand to his ear. "The wind approaches its greatest force. Can you hear? That means that soon it shall begin to wane. Wane and, ah yes, die. And so the sirocco shall pass. Such is Allah's will."

"I hope you're right," replied Sinbad with an uneasy sigh.

The strange smile of the Bedouin deepened. "I promise it, Sinbad. By nightfall we will all be on our way."

Toward evening the weather did begin to clear. Sinbad

was the first to leave the shelter, half digging to get out of the tent. He stood knee deep in sand and looked on incredulously at the altered landscape. New dunes had arisen where before there had been none, old dunes that had marked the boundries of the ridge were suddenly gone. The face of the desert had been changed, as if the finger of Allah had touched it and redesigned it.

A flaming red ball of sun lowered rapidly to welcome the coming night as Sinbad and Assal Karli inspected the damage to their beasts. Sinbad's camels had weathered the sirocco well, but the Bedouin's stood painfully, drooping its head and softly grunting.

"He'll have to be put out of his pain," said Sinbad.

Assal Karli nodded sadly. "A pity; I had come to love the beast. And it's a long march to my father's tents."

Sinbad began to discard some of the excess supplies loaded on the extra camel. "Where is this camp of yours?" he asked. Assal Karli pointed to the south. "Not very far from here, Captain Sinbad," he replied earnestly. "Will you not come with me to my father's tents? He shall be most appreciative to know his eldest son is safe because of your kindness. And there is no reward he would not grant. . . ."

The proud mariner scoffed at the mention of accepting payment for common desert courtesy.

"Then will you at least accept Bedouin hospitality?" asked Assal Karli. "Spend but this night among us before you continue your journey tomorrow."

As the *wadi* and the tents of Sheik Aluf lay almost directly parallel to the caravan route, Sinbad knew that little would be lost in going with Assal Karli. And a night safely spent, with hot food and good company, would prove a most welcome diversion during this long and arduous journey.

"All right, my friend," said Sinbad with a grin. "We shall be honored to accept your hospitality." He turned over the reins of the pack camel to the Bedouin, and said: "Lead the way."

Assal Karli, whip in hand, expertly nudged the beast into kneeling submissively. Then the two men broke camp, Sinbad giving a hand to the still silent Diona. Their eyes met briefly and Diona quickly cast her glance away. But in that moment of contact Sinbad saw a renewed fire in her eye, and the hint of a cunning smile. Just what it meant, the sailor had no idea—only that he somehow began to feel uneasy again.

"Up you go," he called to the frog, kneeling and putting the girl temporarily from his mind. And Don Giovanni, as was his way, hopped onto Sinbad's shoulder.

The camels grunted as they rose from kneeling positions. Assal Karli kicked lightly into the flanks of his own and led the way, Diona riding close behind and Sinbad bringing up the rear.

When the others were well out of earshot, Sinbad turned to his companion. "What do make of this unexpected company?" he asked.

The frog tapped a webbed foot against Sinbad's collarbone. "Don't ask me why," he replied, "but I don't trust him."

The mariner looked at Giovanni curiously and sighed. "I can't explain it either. But I think you're right."

The night was cool and clear, the wind blowing gently, as they forded the *wadi* and, coming down from the dunes, sighted the dim fires of the Bedouin camp. Above the sky glittered with a universe of stars, all the constellations known to man, and Sinbad again fancied himself upon the sea.

It was not long before the sounds of camp filled the air—the laughter of men, the *baa*ing of herded sheep, the occasional clanging of bells tied around the necks of restless goats.

Veiled women, silent and sandaled, slipped among the men removing plates and cleaning them in sand. It would have seemed a perfectly typical desert camp except for two things which Sinbad observed. First, there was no sign of children; second, there seemed to be too many men standing night watch. Rugged, fierce men, who watched the riders coming down from the heights with scowls masked by the shadows.

Suddenly there was more of a commotion. Men leaped from their places around the campfire, pointing and shouting. From the largest of the tents a heavyset, sweaty man dressed in the heavy robes of the desert appeared. Bearded, with a large mole in his left cheek near his nose, he stood staring as the riders came closer, nervously twirling his many golden finger rings. Then a wide grin broke over his face.

"Assal!" he called with a laugh. "You've come back after all! And what's this? You've brought visitors?"

Assal Karli slipped from his camel and beamed while the sheik grasped him firmly by the shoulders and held him at arms' length. "Many had already given you up for dead," he said with a chuckle and a glint in his cunning eyes. "Your mother despaired and wept all last night, berating me for your death. 'Foolish woman!' I told her. 'Would merciful Allah let such a son die in a mere sirocco?' I knew my son well enough; I knew that Allah, may His name be blessed, would ride with him on his errand and bring him back safely to me." Then the sheik glanced to the strangers upon their camels and furrowed his brows. "All . . . has gone well?" he asked in a whisper.

Assal Karli grinned. "Very well, Father. I could not have hoped for better fortune." He swung his body around to face his companions, the hems of his robe brushing against the sand. "Permit me to introduce my friends whose hospitality saved my life. Lady Diona of Damascus"—the sheik eyed her appreciatively and bowed—"and her noble escort to Jerusalem, the famed Captain Sinbad of Baghdad."

The older man quickly smiled and faced the mariner. "Indeed, fortune is strange, Captain, that my humble tents should have the honor of greeting a man renowned throughout all Araby." And he bowed deeply. "My home is your home. Come. Let the women prepare food while you warm yourself beside the fire."

Minutes later Sinbad found himself comfortably settled, while serving girls filled his cup with thick desert wine and placed before him dripping slabs of goat meat on a skillet. Assal Karli's father proved himself a genial host, eager to cater to Sinbad's every wish, spoken and unspoken. Yet despite the overwhelming conviviality, he still felt uneasy. Diona had been whisked away to the women's quarters to be tended as a woman of her rank deserved, but she had been out of his sight—and protection—for quite some time now and Sinbad didn't like it.

"So," said the sheik, oblivious of Sinbad's concerns, "you undertake this journey to reach Jerusalem. A most provocative city, Captain. I have been there myself many times to pray at the Great Mosque."

"Such is my own desire as well, my lord," replied Sinbad. "But not until my business is done."

The sheik frowned briefly and then laughed, and Assal Karli, at his father's side sipping his wine, shared the old man's mirth.

"You have been most blessed upon this travel of yours," the sheik went on, "not to have run into misfortune on the way. . . ."

Sinbad looked at him questioningly. Don Giovanni, resting meekly at his side, stirred. "What do you mean?" asked the mariner.

The sheik grinned broadly, exposing a mouth full of blackened teeth. His gold earrings glimmered in flamelight. "Why, I speak of the Karmathian bandits, of course. And that fellow—what is his name?—ah yes, Ben Abdul. The rogue. The thief. The butcher of the desert."

"I have heard of him," acknowledged Sinbad. "But he and I have no quarrel. I carry no great fortune to be robbed—"

140

"Ah, but you do," countered the sheik with a sly glint in his eye. "Surely the lady Diona is a prize worth any man's trouble. And Ben Abdul, after all, is but a flesh-and-blood man as we."

Sinbad locked his gaze with the wily desert sheik, sensing something hidden behind his words. "As I've said," he reiterated, "I seek no quarrel. But I will fight him if I must, on any terms."

The sheik laughed grandly, nearly spilling his wine. "Well spoken, Captain Sinbad! I should have known to expect no less than that from a man like you."

Sinbad did not reply. He saw that the sheik seemed to enjoy this game of banter, but that Assal Karli, as the conversation progressed, seemed to become uneasy, drinking more heavily and sulking over his wine.

A cooling wind blew in as a serving girl entered carrying a tray of dates and figs and other treats. She offered them to each of the men and Sinbad accepted only after seeing the sheik take, and taste, something first. The two men exchanged small smiles.

"You must be very tired," said the sheik with a yawn.

"I am. And I must be on my way before dawn. Already this storm has cost me a day's traveling time and I shall have to hasten to make up what I've lost."

"Then sleep, Captain Sinbad," said the sheik suddenly. He held up his goblet and offered a toast. Sinbad put the wine to his lips and sipped. The wine was good, strong and sweet.

Sinbad leaned back against the cushions, suddenly more exhausted than he had realized he was. "Yes," he whispered, "I . . . I do need sleep. But I must be woken. . . ."

The sheik's smile deepened. "And you shall be, good Captain. My word upon it. Before the sun rises you shall be awake—and ready to continue your journey."

Eyelids drooping, Sinbad nodded. His cup fell from his hands and his head slumped onto the cushions. The sheik and Assal Karli looked at each other. Then they stood up and left the tent.

Terrible shadows swam in the dark recesses of Sinbad's subconscious; strange and distorted reflections of his memories of Baghdad and the sea. At times it was as though he were floating above the world, staring down while the play of life unfolded below. Then came the sensation of falling. Falling, falling into some unknown abyss from which there could be no return. Tumbling past hideous monstrosities that were sickening as they were familiar. He could see the face of the caliph, mocking and scorning him as he fell, and laughing demonically at his plight. *No!* cried Sinbad in his dream. *No!* But the laughter only grew louder, magnified a thousand times, and the blackness of the world exploded into a charge of fiery light with dancing flames licking at him and dragging him farther down into the hell of his mind. And Sinbad screamed again in terror.

With open eyes he stared at a half-world of reality. He felt the sensation of being dragged from the tent and left to lie upon the night sands. He tried to sit up, but found himself glued to his place, frozen in time and motion.

Blurry figures stared down at him. Grim, dark figures that smiled among themselves. The sheik was there, he was sure, hands on hips, bellowing commands as his tents were drawn and folded, his entire camp in a frenzy to move as quickly as possible. Out of the grimness came Assal Karli, but now the young man wore robes different from those Sinbad had seen. White, finely woven robes of a desert chief. Burly sentries drew curved swords and placed them at Sinbad's throat. The sheik looked to Assal Karli questioningly, but the younger man hesitated.

And then Diona was there, kneeling beside Sinbad and putting a hand to his fevered brow. "No," she whispered. "Do not harm him. He has been good to me—he wanted to be my friend."

While the sheik grimaced, Assal Karli snapped his fingers and bade his soldiers to put away their weapons. "He is dangerous," Sinbad heard the old sheik protest. But Assal Karli was firm. He took Diona by the hand and the girl drew her body close to his. As Sinbad looked on, unable to communicate, Diona was crushed within Assal's arms and they shared a long and passionate kiss. "My darling, my darling," she panted. "I thought you would never come. And then, in the storm—"

Assal Karli put a finger to her lips, hushing her before he kissed her again. Then he turned to his waiting men, signaling for the camels to move out. To Sinbad's surprise they quickly obeyed his every word, the old sheik even bowing before him. "Thank you for your clever ruse," Assal told Aluf. "You nearly made *me* believe you were my father." To which the older man laughed. "You did me the honor of choosing me, lord. I enjoyed our game immensely." And they all laughed loudly.

Sinbad tried vainly to rise; he fell back and Diona kneeled beside him again. "Forgive me, Sinbad," she told him, the hint of tears in her eyes. "But remember that I tried to warn you. I asked you to take me to my lover of your own will—but you refused."

Sinbad desperately tried to speak; his tongue wobbled helplessly in a dry mouth. The girl smiled. "Shhh. It's all right. The wine you drank was drugged, but not poisoned. The effects shall wear off within hours. But you owe your life to the man whose life you saved. Assal Karli, my lover. Known to the world as Ben Abdul. . . ."

And then they were gone, riding off to the east against a backdrop of crimson sand in the dawn light. Sinbad watched the camels disappear, and with heavy eyes fell asleep again, knowing he had been tricked.

My dear Captain Sinbad,
Do not blame yourself. This marriage would never have taken place anyway. Trust that no one, not

143

*even my loving cousin Avilia, shall be hurt. Everything
I told you was true; upon word of my mysterious
disappearance, you can be sure that Avilia will cleverly
claim my father's fortune for herself. She is welcome
to it, I promise you. I have all I need or shall ever
need. The desert is my home now and I am content.*

*Ben Abdul, despite what they say in Damascus, is
not the devil you believe. He is just and fair. As
proof of this, he has left you your camel and the
purse of gold my cousin paid you. But it would be
better to stay away from Jerusalem. Sheik Kahlil will
be most displeased to learn that his share of the
fortune is not forthcoming.*

May Allah bless your days.

Diona

Sinbad sighed and put aside the hastily scrawled note
he had found attached to the water bag. For a long while
he sat in the sand, shading his eyes from the sun, and
shaking his head from side to side.

"You seem amused," said Don Giovanni, hopping into
his lap.

The mariner shrugged and laughed. "I do find this
episode ironic, yes," he confided. "But Allah is all-wise.
He has fixed the course of our lives long before events
transpire."

The frog nodded sagely. He had tried to warn Sinbad
during the night, tried to arouse him from his forced
slumber. But Ben Abdul's men had caught him and tied
him into a sack until dawn, thus insuring that their plans
went unfoiled.

"Will you go after her?" asked the frog.

Sinbad shook his head. "Diona has found her freedom,
has found everything she wanted. Who am I to try and take
it from her? Not to mention the army of Ben Abdul's men
I'd have to face if I tried." He sighed deeply, tossing the
purse of gold in his palm. "No, good friend and compan-

ion, Diona is right. Avilia shall have what she was seeking, no harm is done after all."

"Then what will we do?"

Sinbad laughed, his eyes dancing merrily. "Why, we'll do what we set out to do! Sail the sea, find the Red Dahlia. My purse is not enough to buy the ship I sought, but with skill and luck we may somehow gain the rest."

"And where do we go?"

"To the sea, of course. Where we belong. Let's put all of this behind forever." He stood up wearily and readied the camel for travel. "We go west, Giovanni," he said as the frog jumped to his shoulder. "West—to the port of Jaffa."

The smoke-filled tavern hushed suddenly when the lamps dimmed and the slow beat of drums began. Sinbad, mulling over his goblet, lifted his gaze from the roughly hewn table top and peered toward the stage. Around him, jamming the other tables, a host of patrons put down their own cups, wiped their mouths, and stared in expectation. Sailors from every port, Alexandria to Tripoli and as far away as Tunis, held their breath as the snake dancer slipped from behind the curtain.

Her body was slim and dark-skinned, Sudanese, with coal-black hair tumbling over her firm breasts. She seemed to float across the stage, the cobra coiled about her shoulders and neck. The music, up until now languid, took on a quicker beat, with low-pitched flutes weaving a staccato African melody.

The dancer's hair flowed with her every movement, teasingly hinting at the perfect body beneath. A provocative smile glimmered upon her full lips as she drew the cobra's head to her breast. The crowd gasped as its venomous tongue lashed, and to everyone's amazement the ebony beauty laughed, seductively shaking her shoulders while the snake slinked its scaly body lower, twisting around her waist and clasping itself around her thighs.

Dark colors from the lamps danced; the girl twirled and sang a wild, savage song, reminiscent to Sinbad of the strange tribes he had encountered along the African coast some years before. The faces of the watching sailors turned hungry with desire as the dancer taunted them with the motions of her hips. Her body shone with perspiration; she ran her fingers up and down the snake's length, stroking and massaging him. And, acting as though crushed beneath the weight of a man, she ended her song with soft moans and delicate spasms of her hips.

She stood motionless for a time, naked except for the silk veil pinned around her womanhood, and panted while the snake again coiled itself around her throat. The audience was transfixed; to a man, Sinbad included, they all wished to possess her there and then.

The dancer's eyes glinted with enjoyment at the sight of the aroused crowd. She bowed stiffly, teasingly letting her breasts shake. Then she was gone, fled from sight back behind the heavy curtains. Amid the murmurs of the frustrated sailors the lamps were lighted to full intensity and the music stopped.

"More, more!" they shouted, clapping and whistling and stamping their feet. The ruckus continued for quite a time, but the mysterious snake dancer did not return, content to let them howl until the next show.

Prostitutes astutely slipped among the frenzied crowd, flashing smiles and offering hours of pleasure for a handful of copper coins. Many of the tables quickly emptied as a score of womanless sailors, wine bottles in hand, followed them out into the streets and alleys to conduct their business.

Sinbad, declining propositions, glumly went back to finishing his drink. He and Giovanni had been in Jaffa nearly a week now, with little prospect of raising enough money to purchase either ship or crew for their voyage. Jaffa was a squalid town, teeming with ships and seamen, merchants from every known land in Araby and beyond, and cargoes to be loaded or delivered to market. It was the perfect place for Sinbad to find everything he needed—if only he had enough money.

He pulled his purse from his belt and poured the contents onto the table. Gold coins glittered in the light—a small fortune, for most purposes, but far short of what was needed to buy a ship. For that heady ambition he would have to triple his wealth.

The sound of raucous laughter caused him to turn, and he looked on with idle curiosity at a crowd of men near the back. They were placing bets, some of which were quite sizable.

"Two to one!" cried a furtive little man in the center of the group, a serious expression upon his cherubic face. "Two to one I'll pay. Who can do better than that?"

Most of the sailors laughed again, shaking their heads. "Against your man? Against the Bruiser?" derided one stout fellow. "You must be mad!"

"Why, the last man to fight the Bruiser died in the ring!" called a shipmate. "We'd be fools to take your offer!"

The small man grinned, and his beady eyes glinted as he scratched his turbaned head. "All right, all right. Two and a half to one—it's the best I can do. What say you to that?"

The sailors glanced at one another, becoming tempted at the offer. Then, downing more wine, they began to agree.

"Name your fighter," said the little man, relieved. "And be at the wharf at midnight. All will be ready." He turned to leave, then hesitated, saying: "Three rounds—after that my man will take on any other offers."

"At two and a half to one, there'll be plenty more, Feisal! Bring your money!" And they laughed again, obviously pleased at the bargain they had struck.

Sinbad placed the frog back on his shoulder and got up. At the next table sat an aging man, a veteran of the sea, if

147

his windblown and craggy face told anything. Sinbad approached the mute fellow and cleared his throat.

"Pardon me for interrupting you," he said apologetically, "but could tell me what that's all about?"

The old sailor pushed aside his cup and stared up at Sinbad, screwing his eyes, looking the man and the frog over with care. "Don't you know?" was all he replied.

Sinbad shook his head. "Forgive me if I seem foolish, but I'm a stranger to Jaffa—"

The sailor chuckled. "Feisal is putting his man up for a match again, that's all."

"Feisal?"

The sailor tickled his fintertips at his stubby chin. "*Hmmm.* Then you *are* a stranger, aren't you?" He gestured for Sinbad to take the chair opposite. When the mariner had seated himself, the man leaned halfway over the table and continued. "Feisal is a promoter," he said. "Perhaps the best-known in Jaffa. And whenever new ships dock for a day or two, he likes to give them the chance to take away his money." Here he chuckled again. "Of course Feisal's too crafty to just *give* his fortune away. Oh, yes. You have to earn it."

Sinbad frowned. "Earn it how?"

"By spending three rounds in the ring with his man." His breath was hot upon Sinbad's face, and he grinned. "Three rounds at the best odds anyone will give. Why, an enterprising fellow could wind up rich, what with side bets and all."

Sinbad became more than interested when he heard this. "Are we speaking of a wrestling event?" he asked. "Or boxing?"

The old sailor shook his head. "Both. Fighting against the one called the Bruiser. A dim-witted fellow brought here as a slave from the Libyan desert before winning his freedom. Now he fights for Feisal exclusively."

"And this promoter, Feisal, he'll match any bet?" Sinbad wet his lips.

His companion laughed heartily. "But of course! Feisal's good to his word. He has to be—otherwise no one would enter any contest with him."

"And any man can enter?" wondered Sinbad.

At this the old sailor broke into an expansive grin. "The Bruiser fears no man. *No man*. He's had—oh, about thirty fights this past year and won them all. Seven of his opponents died in the ring, their heads smashed open like melons; another six or so lived a few days before dying of their injuries. Those that survived thank Allah for their fortune. . . ."

Sinbad gulped. "He sounds menacing."

"Oh, he is. He is. Once you lay eyes upon him, you'll never forget. Never. The Bruiser can break a man's back the way you or I would snap a twig. Does that answer your question?"

Sinbad leaned back in the chair and thought long and hard. "I'd like to get a look at this fellow," he admitted after a while. "What must I do?"

"Do? *Do?*" The sailor chuckled again. "Have ye a mind to meeting him in the ring, eh?"

Sinbad put out his palms and smiled. "Well, I didn't quite say *that* . . . ."

"I know, I know," replied his companion. "You just want to see him, right? Have a quick glance at the man all of Jaffa fears? And maybe study his tactics, seeking a way to beat him—and gain yourself some extra money."

"You are very wise, my friend," said Sinbad. "I won't lie to you: I need to raise some cash. And I don't mind telling that I'm at my wits' end on how to do it."

Here the old sailor's face darkened. He studied Sinbad more intently than before. "Can ye fight, then? Eh, son?"

Sinbad frowned. "I was tutored in the art, yes. And during my youth I was acclaimed a champion."

"Hmmmm." The sailor tugged a finger at his earlobe. "It should take more than that to stand up against the Bruiser, I think."

"But others do—"

The sailor scoffed. "Foolhardy souls at best. The glitter of Feisal's gold makes them willing to throw away their lives. No man with good sense asks for such a fight."

"Perhaps not," Sinbad rejoined swiftly. "But I've never been one to run from one either."

The sailor furrowed his brows. "Then you're serious?"

"At least as far as getting a good look at the fellow, yes. Why not? What have I to lose? Just tell me where this fight will take place."

The old man heaved a sigh as he rose from his seat. "It's not very far from here," he said. "There's an old warehouse beyond the North Pier. Deserted for many years, now used by Feisal for his matches. Do you know it?"

"I don't think so. As I said, I'm a stranger here in Jaffa. . . ."

The sailor pursed his cracked lips and smiled as he shrugged. "Very well, then. I'll take you there if you like. But mind you—you put your life in your hands by challenging the Bruiser."

Sinbad laughed and winked at his companion. "Your warning is well taken," he replied. Then they crossed the dusty floor of the tavern and came out into the quiet street. The aging sailor led Sinbad past the old quarter, marked by twisting alleys and silent bazaars long since shut for the night. A brilliant crescent moon hung low in the sky and reflected its light off the waters of the harbor. Silhouettes of hulking ships lay still along the wharves, sails furled and banners aflutter. The very sight of the sea exhilarated Sinbad and he felt his heartbeat quicken with excitement.

Sinbad paused at the roadside and peered out at the majesty of the ocean before him. "There she lies," he said proudly to the frog. "The Mediterranean, jewel of seas."

Don Giovanni stared dumbstruck; he had never seen so much open water in his life. Greater than the greatest river, sweeping away to the horizon. It was a humbling sight to the frog.

"Then you are a sailor, too?" the old man asked Sinbad.

With the smell of salt water swelling his lungs, Sinbad nodded. "The sea is my wife and my mother; I've known no other."

A faraway blast from the horn of an approaching ship broke the quiet, and the old man sighed, wistfully searching for the nearing vessel. "I also love the sea," he said, a sad expression crossing his features. "But alas, no ship has room for me now. . . ." He hung his head and stepped into a shadow so that Sinbad could not see the tears in his eyes.

"But surely you're still an able seaman," protested Sinbad.

The old man shook his head. "My body can no longer do the work of a young man. Why should any venturesome captain hire me when he can have a man half my age for the same pay?"

"An experienced sailor is hard to find," Sinbad said.

"Aye. But few seem to care these days. Believe me, I've tried. To sail again I would serve in any capacity. Cabin boy, cook, anything. . . ."

Sinbad and Don Giovanni were touched by his plight. They exchanged quick glances and the frog nodded. Sinbad smiled. "*I* am in search of a crew," the mariner said to the old man.

The crusty sailor turned from his darkened place and stared at him. "You? Are you a captain?"

"I am. And I seek good men to join me on an adventure across the Pillars of Hercules. *Experienced* men, who are willing to risk all. Although"—and here he frowned—"I can't promise much in wages. . . ."

The old man's eyes brightened; his lip quivered. "You," he stammered, "you would sign *me* on board your ship?"

"I have need of a ship's cook, if you're interested. . . ."

Sinbad's companion narrowed his eyes and looked at him questioningly. "Who are you?" he asked.

The bow was deep and gracious. "Captain Sinbad of Baghdad at your service."

The startled sailor acted as though the air had been knocked from his lungs. He had never dared to dream of meeting the fabled mariner, let alone of sailing with him.

"Well?" said Sinbad, feigning impatience. "Do you accept my offer?" And he stuck out his hand.

The two men shook firmly to seal the bargain, and Sinbad was pleasantly surprised to feel the strength in the old man's grasp.

"I am called Milo," the sailor told him. "Milo of Tyre. And I've sailed the seas for forty years. You won't regret taking me on, I promise you."

Sinbad clasped his shoulder and laughed. "I'm sure I won't. But as I've said, I am sorely in need of raising some more money. Without a bit of Feisal's gold I won't have a ship—and neither of us can cross the Mediterranean without wood beneath our feet."

"Well, why didn't you say so before!" said Milo, and he laughed in unison with his captain. "Come. The hour is close to midnight and everyone will have already gathered. . . ."

"You think I might have a chance against this Bruiser?" asked Sinbad as they briskly made their way down to the docks.

Milo frowned, but there was an unmistakable glint in his eyes. "The Bruiser can be taken—but you'll need some clever tricks to do it."

"There's more to prizefighting than mere brawn," Sinbad observed. "If my guess is right, this fellow wrestles on strength alone. Perhaps he has the advantage in that category, but skill and wits, I trust, shall belong to me."

The doors of the rickety warehouse had been flung open. Small lanterns hung from posts to guide the bettors along their way down the darkened wharf. A fair-sized crowd had already assembled both inside and out, with bookmakers frantically trying to outbid each other as they shouted the latest odds.

There were all manner of men to be seen, Sinbad noted as he and Milo reached the broad wharf. Pickpockets and derelicts mingled among sailors from every land. Sinbad recognized the colorful tunics of the seamen of Sidon; the dark, heavy garments of the shipmates from Tarsus in the Byzantine Empire; there were those from Gaza and those from Crete as well. Libyans from the land of the Zeirids, swarthy adventurers of the Maghreb. A microcosm of all nations gathered here upon this pier to wager on the outcome of tonight's fights.

"This way," said Milo, taking Sinbad by the arm and leading him past the murmuring groups.

Inside the warehouse Sinbad blinked from the light of a dozen huge torches set at random along the splitting wooden walls. The floor was smothered in sawdust that rose with every step. Slab benches, hard and uncomfortable, had been set around the raised platform that served as a ring. Sweaty and odorous men, unshirted, were already wrestling, grunting and groaning, in the preliminary matches.

Sinbad and Milo took good seats near the front. Hoots and boos rose all around as impatient onlookers demanded the appearance of the Bruiser—the man they had come to see.

"A rowdy lot," mumbled Sinbad, frowning at the terrible stench which permeated the air.

"Aye," agreed Milo somberly. "And it will get worse as the evening wears on. They're here to see blood, maybe even death. . . ."

Sinbad shuddered involuntarily. "Not mine, I hope," was all he mumbled in response.

The two wrestlers on the stage wheezed as they grappled. Then one, with a sudden jerk, wrenched the arm of the other and sent him flying. The second werestler banged his head against the wooden floor and lay in a semi-daze while his adversary kicked him savagely in the face.

More hoots from the crowd. "Take those clowns off!" they shouted. "Bring on some men!" and "We're not here to watch eunuchs!"

The dazed wrestler coughed blood and went into a stupor. His seconds lifted him up and carried him out while the winner of the match held up his hands in victory. A smattering of copper coins were tossed onto the platform and he eagerly gathered them up before leaving.

"Bring us the Bruiser!" someone bellowed. And again and again the cry was repeated. *The Bruiser! The Bruiser!*" Foot-stomping and whistles drowned out the shouts of the bookmakers. The din became so furious that the promoters of the matches were unable to restore even a semblance of order.

But then, from some hazy room in the back, came Feisal. At the sight of the wily man the crowd grew silent. His reptilian grin split his face from ear to ear. He climbed onto the platform, avoided a small pool of blood near the center, and faced the audience. By now the warehouse was jammed. Sailors and varied followers stood lined up outside the doors, straining to get a glimpse over the standing-room-only crowd.

Feisal the promoter signaled for the doors to be shut. The last of the sailors forced their way inside, and when the arena became quiet he said: "Tonight Mongo the Bruiser, champion of all Islam, has agreed to face all comers, not just the customary three . . ."

Great cheers arose from the benches.

"And having given you all my word," Feisal went on, "I shall take all bets against Mongo at two and a half to one—for any man who can spend only three rounds in the ring!"

Again came the cheers, even louder than before. Milo turned to Sinbad. "These matches have always been four rounds," he confided. "But, as no man has ever lasted, Feisal's lowered the time limit."

Sinbad chewed tensely at his lip. "And how long is each of these rounds?"

"Four minutes. Few have ever made it past the first. Only one that I know of made it into the third."

"And what happened to him?"

"The bruiser cracked his skull. He was fortunate the match ended before Mongo killed him."

Sinbad groaned. The idea of getting into the ring with such an animal was becoming less and less appealing with every passing moment.

"Shhh," said Milo, a finger to his lips, as Sinbad was about to ask another question.

From the stage Feisal was calling for order again. The audience quieted. "The first contestant," he said, "shall be Ororex of the Fatimite Caliphate. The champion of Cairo. Now, who will place their bets?"

Milo raised his brows drmatically. "I have heard of this Ororex," he whispered to Sinbad. "An ape of a man, they say. If anyone has a chance of beating the Bruiser, it's him."

The bookmakers were kept more than busy with the first challenge. Tens of dozens of Egyptian sailors, more than eager to wager their hard-earned gold on their compatriot, clamored to get in as many bets as possible. They knew their man, knew just how awesome Ororex truly was. What they didn't know, or seem to care about, was how awesome Mongo the Bruiser was. And tales of the champion of all Islam did not seem to faze them.

Sinbad waited anxiously for the betting to be done and the fight to get under way. Slowly the bettors returned to their seats, and a new silence prevailed.

Then came the cheers. From the back rooms came a man the like of which Sinbad had never seen. A brute—an enormous fellow with biceps twice the size of his own, shoulders as wide as a broadsword, callused hands capable of lifting a horse. His face was scarred and mean, and his

155

scowl sent shivers crawling up Sinbad's spine. Wearing only the briefest covering at his loins, the fighter climbed onto the platform, sneering as he flexed his muscles, veins popping from his neck and arms. The crowd went wild.

"Merciful Allah!" cried Sinbad. "No wonder he's a champion!"

"Aye," agreed Milo. "Ororex is a hefty fellow."

"Ororex?" Sinbad peered at his new friend with astonishment. "That's *Ororex?* I thought it was Mongo!"

Milo chuckled. "Not quite. Here comes the Bruiser now."

And this time the roars were deafening. Sinbad turned and strained his eyes to get a glimpse of the fighter making his way to the platform from the other direction.

Easily seven feet tall, taking strides twice as long as his accompanying trainers, the champion of Islam seemed like a giant. White teeth glinted with his smile; his rugged features were virtually unmarked despite his many fights in the ring. His dark complexion was set off by a chest covered with black hair. The muscles of his stomach were taut and supple; you could hit him with a hammer and still he wouldn't feel it.

As the audience shouted his name at the top of their lungs, Mongo the Bruiser grinned, acknowledging their cries by clasping his hands above his head and bowing before them. Small round gold rings glittered in his earlobes, and his eyes smoldered at the sight of his waiting opponent. The nostrils of his hooked nose flared as he climbed onto the stage, and by comparison the mighty Ororex seemed a dwarf. Sinbad's eyes widened when he balled his hands into fists—fists the size of vases.

Mongo set his jaw in grim determination. Ororex sneered. Feisal scrambled off the platform, a bell rang, and the fight began.

The Bruiser moved gracefully for a man his size, Sinbad observed. Forever on his toes, Mongo half danced his way

156

across the ring, chest bulging and glistening with sweat, bare fists up in a defiant stance. Ororex bravely came on and jabbed. The giant stepped to the side, laughing as the blows barely glanced off his arms. Then he let loose a blow of his own—a hard left fist that crashed into Ororex's belly. The smaller man grimaced with the sting but adroitly maneuvered away in time to avoid the next oncoming blow.

They danced again. Ororex kicked high, a solid kick in the groin that would have staggered another man and sent him sprawling. But Mongo didn't even budge from his place. He glared at his adversary and grinned. Then smash, smash went his fists, a left and a right connecting with Ororex's jaw. The champion of Cairo reeled back, ducking instinctively and shielding himself against further jabs. But he had been hurt, no question of it. Blue welts were rising on the side of his face.

The Egyptian sailors began to jeer. Their man was being trounced and the first round was hardly half over. But from the galleries in the back, where the local seamen had gathered, came the ecstatic cries of: "Mongo! Mongo! Kill him, Mongo!"

Spurred on, the giant gave up all pretense of classical Greek boxing. Now it became a free-for-all, no holds barred, anything goes. Mongo jumped on the injured Ororex, knocking him over like a bowling pin, wrenching his arm and nearly shoving him off the platform. The smaller man wheezed in pain and somehow gained enough strength to push the Bruiser away. Ororex's fists did a terrific one-two combination, landing solidly on the giant's face. Again the Bruiser was not perturbed. He drew back his own fist and pounded the fellow with a blow so fierce that when Ororex's nose broke you could hear the crunch of cartilage across the arena. Dizzily Ororex tumbled, his face spouting blood like a fountain. Mongo prepared to leap on top of him, hoping to crack his ribs with the crush

157

of his weight. Just then, though, the bell rang. The first round was over.

Ororex's trainers half dragged the dazed fighter to the far corner, gasping at the sight of the bloody pulp that had been his face. While Mongo flexed his muscles and stood proudly in his own corner, the trainers did all they could to revive Ororex.

The bell for the second round rang. Ororex leaped to his feet, displaying more energy and courage than any had given him credit for. But to go on was really useless. Mongo, incensed at the fact that his opponent had even dared come out for the second round, decided to end it quickly. He grabbed Ororex by his hair, yanked him to the mat, and stomped on his throat with his callused foot. Ororex gasped for air. His hands flayed about helplessly. He began to gurgle and groan, his eyes now glassy and unseeing.

Mongo jabbed him in the ribs with his big toe. Ororex rolled over, flat out, his face twisted in torment. And then he collapsed in a heap, thankful for the oblivion that soon came.

The crowd screamed for more, but Mongo shook his head. Ororex had fought cleanly and well. Mongo would not punish him further.

It did not take long for the unconscious champion of Cairo to be pulled off the platform and carried to the dressing room. In the next moments, a beaming Feisal came back onto the stage and announced the next contender. Mongo took a sip from a water bottle and wiped his mouth with the back of his arm. His next opponent was from the Sudan of Africa. A black man, once a slave, also renowned in his own land as the best.

"Well?" said Milo with a small smile of satisfaction. "What do you think of the Bruiser now? Are you still so eager to make a match?"

Sinbad drew a long breath and let it out slowly. "Mongo's the most powerful man I've ever seen," he admitted. "But he lacks finesse. He has no class, just strength."

Milo looked at Sinbad sharply. "Strength is all he needs."

A minute or two later the African appeared. Because of the din, Sinbad could not catch his name. Not that it mattered, though. The African was a fine specimen of manhood—but no match against Mongo. He began well enough in the opening seconds, what with his agility and ability to slip out of reach of the Bruiser's terrible blows, but by the time the round was over the poor fellow was lying prostrate upon the stage, not as bloodied as Ororex had been, but with a broken collarbone, swollen lumps for eyes, and a mangled leg, crushed when Mongo had pounced on him.

In short order it was time for the next bout. A tall, fearful Moor came onto the stage, but this third match became only a parody of the others. The Moor knew full well he had no chance; he only hoped to dance around and keep out of Mongo's way long enough to finish the three rounds and collect the prize. Mongo, though, was having none of these games. He caught hold of the Moor, broke his arm, heaved him up into the air, and sent him flying onto the first row of spectators.

The losing bettors became quiet and sullen. Feisal, grinning from ear to ear at this especially profitable night, came back to announce the fourth fight. There was little enthusiasm, particularly when the audience heard that the fighter had had almost no experience at all. With a minimum of bets, in spite of Feisal having raised the odds to four-to-one, they all saw the youth from Tarsus literally run off the stage before any real damage was done.

"Is there anyone else?" called Feisal, trying to keep his audience as long as possible. "Who among you will climb into the ring with the Bruiser?" There were no takers and Feisal frowned. He looked at Mongo, who was standing patiently in his corner, oblivious of the crowd. "Surely there must be someone," cried Feisal, "someone not afraid to meet the greatest fighter in the world. . . ."

Still no takers. Sinbad stirred and looked at Milo. The old sailor shrugged.

"Four to one," went on Feisal. "Four to one, and only two rounds in the ring to win the prize. What say you all? Is there none among you with a sporting heart?"

"I'll take that offer," said Sinbad, standing with his hands on his hips and glaring down at Feisal.

"And who are you?" asked the promoter.

"Captain Sinbad of Baghdad."

At the name, all eyes turned. Feisal nodded in appreciation of the famed mariner and his known skills. Here was a chance to clean up again, one last really good fight before the night was done.

"Then so be it, Captain Sinbad. You may retire to the dressing room and prepare. You have ten minutes. . . ."

Suddenly there was great interest in the match. Sinbad's presence in the ring came as quite a surprise to the gathered sailors from every corner of the globe, but he was one of their own. A man of the sea, a man of courage and skill and wits. Oh, how they would like to see him win!

And the betting began, every man willing to put his last coins up against the hated Feisal. Sinbad handed Milo his purse. "Here, my friend. Bet it all."

Milo stared at him and gulped. "Are . . . are you sure you know what you're doing?"

"I don't want to think about it," replied Sinbad as he turned to leave for the dressing room. "It would only make me change my mind."

Sinbad stripped out of his clothes slowly. While Don Giovanni looked on from the dressing table, the mariner rubbed himself down with oil. Then he sat at the edge of the table and patted the frog gently. "I fear I've made a bad mistake," he ruminated, shivering at the thought of what might come if he were not careful. One good, solid blow from Mongo's hammerlike fists was all it would take for him to share Ororex's fate.

"Perhaps you were hasty in accepting the contest," replied the frog, "but your instincts were right: This brute can be beaten."

Sinbad smiled kindly. "And what do you know of prizefighting? Have you a secret weapon I can use against him?"

Don Giovanni narrowed his eyes. "I may only be a bullfrog, but I'm not blind. Like every Achilles, even Mongo has a flaw. . . ."

Sinbad peered at his friend questioningly. "What are you talking about?"

"Pay attention to him in the ring," advised the frog. "The Bruiser leads with his right leg."

Sinbad nodded. "I noticed that, too. What of it?"

"He's vulnerable. He leaves himself open for a second— a split second—enough time for you to get inside and hit him. And watch, his face twitches when you pass to the right. I've seen him swing and miss time and time again."

"He's a brawler, not a fighter. That's why."

Don Giovanni smiled enigmatically. "Perhaps. . . . But I have another guess. The sight in his left eye is bad. Keep moving to the right and you'll see."

Sinbad's face suddenly was aglow. "He can be blindsided!"

"Exactly," said the frog soberly.

The mariner pounded a fist into his open palm. "If that's true, then I know just the way to bring this giant down."

Don Giovanni sighed. "I hope you're right."

The cheering began again outside as Feisal called for the challenger to come to the ring. Sinbad put the frog back onto his shoulder and walked outside boldly, his eyes straight ahead, not paying any attention to the jeers and foot-stomping of the Mongo partisans. Milo was waiting for him at ringside, a water bottle and a towel in his hands. He gave Sinbad a small victory sign as he climbed onto the stage, then let the frog sit on his own shoulder while the fighters waited for the bell.

A loud cry went up from the crowd when it clanged.

Mongo, seeming more bored than awed by this latest adversary, came out in his usual stance, right foot forward, left fist ready to jab. Sinbad went into his own classical stance as taught to him by the Greeks. He paced around the Bruiser, missing no opportunity to taunt the man with soft jabs into his fleshy midriff. As Giovanni had said, each time Sinbad moved to the right, the Bruiser's face twitched, his left eye blinked, and he was unable to land a blow. But it was only seconds into the match, and Sinbad knew he still had a long way to go.

As a test, Sinbad purposely left himself open on the Bruiser's right, half a pace in front. It was a mistake. The champion of Islam, ill-sighted or not, knew where to deliver, and his right hand came full around, catching the sailor squarely in the solar plexus.

"Ooof!" groaned Sinbad as he staggered back, gasping for breath. The crowd hooted and howled while he made a desperate effort to hold himself erect and dodge the menacing succession of quick lefts and rights that came whizzing by his ears.

I'll not make that mistake again, he vowed to himself as he sidestepped the flashing fists and managed to catch his breath. And, weaving his way inside, always to the right, he somehow held the feared Bruiser at bay, delivering a few well-placed blows of his own at Mongo's steel jaw.

The brute grunted, his eyes glaring at the pesky adversary. He let his guard down and grabbed for Sinbad. The mariner landed a fast uppercut solidly upon Mongo's chin, and for the first time tonight the champion of Islam seemed momentarily dazed.

Sinbad backstepped, hunching his shoulders, blocking fierce punches and scoring a few glancing blows of his own. The fervor of the crowd rose to new heights as the combatants began to go at it with everything they had.

"Get him, Sinbad!" cried Milo, excitedly pounding a fist into his hand. Don Giovanni hopped up and down upon the sailor's shoulder, unable to constrain himself.

A left, another left and a right, all landed well. Sinbad, well pleased with his effort, had started to outclass his opponent. But Mongo was having none of this. With a terrible cry that frightened the mariner almost witless, he lunged forward, grabbed Sinbad by the arm and flung him to the floor. Sinbad rolled over just in time as a huge foot came crashing onto the mat, splintering the wood. Then he swung his arms low like an ape and, with a one-two combination, nearly lifted Sinbad into the air. Sinbad pitched forward, his head dizzy and a sickening knot tying in his gut. He saw the brute winding up again but he was too weakened to run. One more good blow would do it, one more solid punch would take him out of the match.

The bell sound. The first round was done.

Amid roars from the eager crowd, Milo pulled Sinbad to the safety of his corner and sopped water over his head to revive him. Sinbad stared at his friend groggy-eyed. "What . . . what happened?" he mumbled.

"You let him get too close," replied Milo, sponging the mariner down.

Sinbad panted, sweat poured from his body. He stared across the platform to where Mongo stood calmly, waiting for the second round to start. It didn't take much to see that the Bruiser was mad, enraged that such a piddling foe had lasted even this long. And that he might endure through round two was inconceivable. Captain Sinbad would have to be dispatched quickly.

"Remember the strategy," whispered the frog as Sinbad flexed his muscles at the sound of the warning bell. "Stay to the right, work your way around him!"

"That's easy for you to say," Sinbad replied dourly. "You're not in the ring with him."

And just then the bell rang, signaling the beginning of the second and last round of the match.

It was do or die. Four minutes to conclusion. Mongo came on like all hellfire, forgetting any pretense of classical boxing and concentrating all his efforts on eliminating Sinbad in the opening seconds by any means.

Sinbad opened up with all he had, but like a tree trunk, Mongo stood, almost grinning while the hard punches made no impression. Then with a mighty roar the giant of a man lunged. Sinbad twisted and dodged out of the way, feeling the rush of wind by his face as the burly hands came slashing by.

"Look out, Sinbad!" cried Milo.

The mariner pivoted back. Mongo came rushing in a half dive. Sinbad adroitly arched himself from range and stuck out his foot. There was too much impetus for the Bruiser to slow down in time to avoid it. His legs tangled and he went sprawling over the mat, hitting the floor with such violence and force that the whole platform shook.

The crowd went wild with laughter. Mongo, the feared Bruiser, champion of all Islam, lay stretched before them like a clown, brought down by a man half his own weight.

Livid with rage, Mongo picked himself up. He wiped his mouth with his hand and glared at Sinbad, who stood waiting with both fists at his side. "I'll kill you for that," growled the incensed fighter. "Better say your prayers." And on again he came, his stride cracking the boards underfoot.

Sinbad could hear Feisal calling from the sidelines for Mongo to kill him. The promoter, eager to protect the good name of his investment, was bent on Sinbad's demise.

Mongo opened his arms umbrellalike and grabbed Sinbad before he could pull away. The Bruiser began to squeeze, holding Sinbad in a terrible hug that almost cracked his ribs. And the more Sinbad struggled the worse the hold became. Mongo started to strain all the harder, squeezing the very air out of Sinbad's lungs. The crowd was in a frenzy, whooping and screaming. With all his effort, Sinbad gouged open the Bruiser's left eye and poked a finger into it. Mongo cried in pain, loosening his hold just long enough for Sinbad to wriggle out of the grip and slide to the floor.

The sinewy giant leaped, hoping to crush Sinbad beneath his weight. The sailor from Baghdad scrambled and just slipped from under in time. Then onto his feet he jumped. A second time Mongo appeared the buffoon, bumbling and useless, against this agile adversary from the east.

The crowd began to boo him as he rose. Mongo waved a menacing fist of defiance at them all and came on again, this time with his mouth foaming and his eyes flaming balls of anger. He smashed at Sinbad, hitting him in the belly, and, while the sailor doubled up, he took his head between his massive hands and began to squeeze. The pressure was excruciating. Sinbad's face started to turn colors, first to pink, then to scarlet, then to purple.

"He's killing him!" cried Milo. "Stop the fight! We concede! Stop the fight!"

The Bruiser looked to Feisal but the sneaky promoter shook his head. There would be no mercy tonight.

Sinbad tore his fingers into Mongo's belly, desperate to make the brute desist before his skull cracked. If only he could twist himself to the Bruiser's blind side. If only . . .

With his last strength, Sinbad managed to turn to the left and free one of his pinned arms. Then he delivered a side-handed Chinese chop to Mongo's throat, well placed so that raw nerves were battered. Mongo yelped like a stuck pig. Sinbad pushed himself free and charged at him, issuing chop after Chinese chop, each numbing the giant and taking a terrible toll on his nervous system.

The crowd quieted. Something was happening, something never witnessed before. These strange blows of Captain Sinbad's were stopping the champion of Islam in his place, causing him to stand dumb and witless, to poke harmless fists into the air, to stare into space like an idle idiot.

Feisal screamed with bulging eyes for his fighter to do something, to hit Sinbad. But Mongo could not hear. The growling giant tottered, knuckle punches and hammerblows, finger jabs and knife hands pouring over the most vulnerable areas of his body. Kidneys, neck, face, solar plexus. Suddenly he pirouetted, reeling across the platform in a stupor, his mouth hanging wide open and his tongue lolling helplessly.

And then he fell. The astounded audience gasped. The Bruiser had fallen, come crashing to the mat like a mighty house in an earthquake. His glazed eyes peered up at the ceiling. For a full minute the silence prevailed, no one as much as moving a muscle. Sinbad drooped his fatigued body and looked to Milo and Don Giovanni. The frog smiled.

"The Bruiser is defeated!" somebody suddenly yelled. And the cry was picked up a hundredfold. "We've won! We've won!" By the score they jumped from the benches and converged upon the hapless promoter, demanding their money at four-to-one-odds.

In all of Jaffa's prizefight history there had never been such a ruckus as happened on that night. Within minutes the word had spread throughout the city, carried into every tavern and brothel, been taken aboard every ship flying every flag. Mongo had lost his fight! Jaffa had a new champion—Sinbad of Baghdad!

"Allah above!" cried Milo gleefully, throwing a towel around Sinbad's shoulders, leading him from the platform. "I've never seen anything like that in all my days. How did you beat him? What sort of tricks were those?"

"Taught to me in Cathay," replied the exhausted mariner. "An Oriental form of fighting employed by the best warriors of Peking. But best never used except when necessary. This art form is deadly."

Milo shook his head in wonder and glanced at the still-prostrate Mongo lying near the far edge of the ring.

"Go collect our winnings before Feisal reneges," said Sinbad. "I'll be all right. I just want to have a look at *him*." And he turned toward the moaning Mongo.

Feisal dispatched his bookmakers to pay off all debts.

He stepped onto the stage and glared down at his fallen fighter. The Bruiser struggled to his knees and looked pitifully at his patron. "I . . . I'm sorry, Feisal," he wheezed. "I've never faced anyone . . . like that. . . ."

Feisal glowered. "Sorry? Sorry, you say? You *fool!* You *clown!* Do you know how much this fight has cost me? Four-to-one odds I have to pay. Four to one! I'm ruined! Do you hear? *Ruined!*" His lips were quivering and his hands were shaking. There had been hundreds of bets placed, amounting up to a tidy sum indeed. It would take months to recoup from tonight's disaster.

"Forgive me, Feisal," whimpered the Bruiser. "Take my share of the purse, if you like. . . ."

"Your share? Why, you crawling flotsam! You sewer rat with a swine for a mother! You have no share! You have nothing. And I'll see to it that you never fight in Jaffa again! In fact, I'll see to it that you never fight anywhere again! Go, get out of my sight! And be glad I don't have you sold back into slavery!" Then, to add insult to injury, Feisal nastily kicked Mongo in his already bruised and sore ribs.

Sinbad turned green with anger as he observed the scene. "Why, you ungrateful cockroach," he hissed between clenched teeth. And he grabbed the promoter by the collar of his tunic, lifted him up, and threw him from the platform, heaving him upon the group of bookmakers. Then, while the bettors roared with laughter at the sight of the despised Feisal finally getting his comeuppance, Sinbad gave Mongo a helping hand. Meekly the giant stood to his feet and rubbed at his numbed muscles. "You could have killed me," he said to Sinbad. "Why didn't you? Had Feisal had his way, I certainly would have killed you."

Sinbad shrugged. "Prizefighting is a sport. I would never enter any contest with the thought of taking a man's life."

Milo was waving for Sinbad's attention. Laughingly he held up the bulging purse of gold, more than enough to purchase the ship the mariner had been seeking. More than enough to hire a crew of Jaffa's best seamen.

"Have you someplace to go?" Sinbad asked Mongo as the defeated fighter dejectedly walked from the platform.

Mongo shook his head. "Now that Feisal's turned against me, I have nothing. They'll never let me fight again. The best I can hope for is to find some work on the docks. My back is still strong, I can carry crates off the ships. . . ."

Sinbad looked at him with a growing sense of pity. Out of the ring, it seemed that Mongo was really a gentle fellow, not at all like the monster Feisal had made him out to be. Powerful as an ox, but meek as a lamb.

"Hold on," said Sinbad, jumping off the stage after him. "Perhaps you'd like to come with me instead. I'm looking for a crew of able men. Men with no fear and a thirst for risk and adventure. I can't make bold promises, but our voyage holds great opportunity . . ." He looked up at the giant and grinned. "And I don't mind saying someone with your strength would be a fine asset on a perilous voyage to the Pillars of Hercules."

"Then I'm your man," laughed Mongo. He clasped Sinbad's hand so hard that he almost broke it. "Besides, I was getting tired of prizefighting anyway."

Don Giovanni hopped onto Sinbad's shoulder as Milo came over with their winnings. With a little bit more luck, both ship and crew would be his within a week, and then they would be off, across the Mediterranean in search of the mysterious Red Dahlia.

Milo, Mongo, and Sinbad, with the frog on his shoulder, walked briskly from the old warehouse and out into the night air. The mariner from Baghdad, hastily dressed in his desert clothes, thought only of donning a captain's garb again and getting a ship under his feet. Milo began to sing an old sea chantey and Mongo joined in, keeping harmony while Don Giovanni tapped his webbed foot in time. Soon even Sinbad joined in the tune, looking to each of his friends and beaming. It was a small crew who stood beside him now, but as loyal and steadfast as any he had ever had. A good beginning for the adventures ahead. Yes, a very good beginning.

PART FOUR:

A CHAMPION OF ARABY UNDER-
TAKES HIS VOYAGE AND MEETS
THE SCOURGE OF THE MEDI-
TERRANEAN.

Captain Sinbad stirred from his thoughts at the sound of the harsh voice of his new first mate calling above the wind. He turned from his post at the bridge and gazed forward to the tall masts, the maze of taut shrouds and rigging and the golden-swelled canvas. Cotton clouds rolled slowly by in a perfect blue sky. He filled his lungs with the invigorating salty air, feeling the gentle rocking of the deck, hearing the soft creaking of aged wood as his ship slashed through the swells. A fine ship, stout and sturdy, worthy of any voyage.

Less than a dozen years old, she'd been built in Acco by the best craftsmen west of Basra. Sleek, double-masted, and constructed with the finest hardwoods imported from the forests of Byzantium, she was as seasoned as she was sturdy. Thirty-one meters long from bowsprit to stern, she carried a crew of twenty-three. Sinbad knew he had been lucky to get her. Her price had been high; the cost of refitting her for long-distance duty had taken every coin left over. Still, Sinbad did not complain. He renamed the ship *Scheherazade* and eagerly signed on his crew.

It only took a couple of days until his complement was complete, many of his sailors gladly forgoing better wages on other merchant ships for the opportunity of sailing with Baghdad's most famed captain. And much to Sinbad's delight, he was even able to find several available seamen who had sailed with him before, including crusty Abu the Persian whom he immediately made his first mate. Thus, with Mongo as boatswain and Milo his trusty cook and servant, not to mention the constant companionship of Don Giovanni, Sinbad sailed from Jaffa's harbor in good company.

He had contracted with Jaffa merchants to carry a cargo of silks and spice to the isle of Crete, some eight hundred kilometers to the west. There, with any luck, he hoped to load another cargo to carry farther west, and thus to make his way to the Pillars of Hercules, where he hoped to find the elusive prize that might change his life. But at times he completely forgot the quest for the strange flower, thinking that once back upon the sea he would never return to Baghdad again. But fate was to intervene in all these matters, and when they were four days out of Jaffa, an entire new set of circumstances began to alter his life.

The waters had been calm, the winds brisk. It had been a perfect voyage, and the isle of Crete grew closer by the hour. The *Scheherazade* had completed half her voyage and her crew, Sinbad included, were eagerly looking forward to port. But on the morn of the fifth day, the first mate, Abu, sighted another ship on the horizon, a cumbersome vessel that kept a constant distance behind. Ships passing upon their respective voyages were a common enough occurrence, but this one didn't seem to go away. It was almost as if these strangers were following the *Scheherazade*—and Sinbad wanted to know why.

He was standing in his familiar captain's stance, his hands clenched behind his back, his face an expressionless mask, his body erect. He watched Abu keenly as the first mate squinted and put the spyglass to his eye. For a long moment the Persian fixed his gaze at the distant ship, finally frowning as he handed the glass to his captain.

Sinbad didn't take it. "Can you see her flags?" he asked.

The burly, thick-necked first mate shook his head. These waters, it was well known, were infested with Barbary pirates who preyed like vultures on harmless and un-

174

suspecting merchant vessels. Attack was a constant threat for every ship.

"What do you make of her?" asked Sinbad at last.

Abu scratched his graying whiskers and scowled, spitting across the rail before he answered. "Not pirates, Capt'n. She's moving too slow, not gaining on us, not losing."

Sinbad balled his hands into fists and edgily stared out at the faraway ship. Crimson sails glinting fully unfurled in the sunlight, the ship maintained an identical course to that of the *Scheherazade*.

"Slacken our sails, Abu," the captain said at length.

"Sir?" The first mate furrowed his bushy brow and looked for a moment to the equally perplexed Milo, who stood several paces behind at the railing.

"It's the only way we can get a better look at her," Sinbad confided. "I want to know who she is."

Abu saluted smartly, ready to carry out the command. An experienced sailor like Sinbad was never to be questioned, no matter how unusual his request might seem.

Long hours passed tensely. It was nearly evening, but the cloudless sky still spread its relentless glare. The bow of the *Scheherazade* dipped and rose gracefully while the busy crew stood quietly at their posts, every man suddenly more aware than ever of the nearby ship. Sinbad's ploy had worked well. Without realizing it, the other vessel had almost cut in half the distance between itself and the *Scheherazade*.

With Don Giovanni perched on his shoulder and Milo and Mongo flanking him, Sinbad came again onto the bridge where a dour and somber Abu stood waiting. "I think you had better see this for yourself," he said, giving over the glass.

Sinbad shaded his vision from the sun and stared long and hard into the spyglass. The approaching ship was Arabic in design. Jason had no trouble in recognizing the familiar smoothed lines and sails of the craft. But she was

175

no ordinary merchant ship. With her broad bulwalks and imposing bulk, she could only be a warship. But why would such a vessel be here, halfway to Crete?

The answer was not long in coming. Sinbad lifted the glass higher, he could clearly see the banners she flew: the flags of Baghdad—each emblazoned with the caliph's imperial crest.

It's not possible! Sinbad thought.

Suddenly the warship's signal flags had been raised, demanding that the *Scheherazade* furl sail and wait to be boarded. Abu and the others looked on astounded.

"What do you think she's after?" said Mongo, leaning hard against the railing, staring incredulously over the dark blue water as the larger ship, knowing it had been identified, no longer made any pretense of keeping at a distance.

Sinbad had not lied to his friends or crew—he had honestly told them of the misadventures which had culminated in his forced departure from Baghdad as a fugitive. But he had never believed that the caliph would be so vengeful as to send a ship across the sea to capture him and haul him back for punishment.

"I fear it can only be myself the galley is after," he said at last in response to Mongo's question. "Schahriar will not rest until he has me back."

Mongo shook a menacing fist at the ship. "And we should allow them to bring you back in chains? *Never!*" And Milo and Abu expressed their agreement.

The galley slashed through the water with full sails swelling, pressing forward now at its best speed to reach the hapless merchant vessel. Despite Mongo's bravery, Sinbad knew full well that his own crew would stand little chance in a fight against an enemy of such overwhelming force. There would be little choice—either give himself up or stand by and watch his friends be captured, and likely sent into slavery.

"Are you certain it's you this galley seeks?" said Milo

with hope in his voice. "Perhaps you're wrong. Perhaps they want to stop us for another reason."

Sinbad laughed a bitter laugh. Shaking his head, he said: "No, this is the caliph's doing. I'm certain of it." He raised the glass again to his eye and this time focused on the small gathering of robed men standing together upon the galley's bridge. His gaze swept among them and he gasped. Standing apart and aloof from the rest was Dormo. The old Greek seemed weary as his bony hands grasped at the rail and he peered blankly out toward the *Scheherazade*. If there had been any lingering doubts in Sinbad's mind as to the purpose of this ship's presence, they were gone now. His old friend and future father-in-law had clearly been commanded by the caliph to personally bring him back for justice. Sinbad gritted his teeth angrily. Most likely the vindictive Schahriar now kept Sherry as hostage to insure Dormo's loyalty.

The lookout called from the crow's nest above. "She's signaling us again, Capt'n! Ordering us to come alongside—"

"In a pig's eye!" rattled Abu. "Full sails!" he barked to the crew before Sinbad could stop him. "We may not be able to fight her, but she'll have to catch us if she wants our captain!"

Shirtless and sweaty, the crew raced across the deck, grappling the halliards and tackling the yards. Moments later the sails *whooshed!* with a full wind; the *Scheherazade* slipped into a new tack and began to outrun the cumbersome galley.

"I appreciate what you want to do," said Sinbad to his companions, "but you know what will happen if we're caught. . . ."

Abu laughed grandly. "Caught?" He screwed his eyes and glared at the captain. "Is this the same Sinbad who led me halfway around the world?" And he spit into the wind. "We signed on together and we'll stand together!"

The crew cheered in response, and Sinbad, having little time to thank them, spun to the helmsman and issued new orders. They were going to outrun the galley if it took a week.

A magnificent sun splaying scarlet rays dipped gently in the west as a velvet-black night inched up against the sky from the east. Spray foamed across the deck as the *Scheherazade* cut through the waves and hastened in the direction of waning daylight. The air crackled with excitement. Sinbad worked beside his adventurous crew, sharing in the labors, exulting in the feel of salt and wind against his flesh.

The galley also drew every stitch and its signal flags continued to call for the smaller ship to stop. Slowly, as the sun all but slid from sight, the pursuing galley was lost in the shadows of night. Sinbad turned to Abu and both men grinned. For the caliph's men night was a bane, a hindrance in the already difficult task of catching a smaller and fitter vessel. But for Sinbad it was a blessing. Under the blanket of darkness, he hoped to elude the galley once and for all, changing his course where necessary and losing the Baghdad ship in the vastness of open sea.

A plethora of stars shone across the heavens. Following the guidance of the Big Dipper, the *Scheherazade* slipped away. The galley could still be seen giving chase, but at each bell's sounding she was farther away than the hour before.

"With luck, we'll lose her by dawn," a buoyant Abu said to the captain. And Sinbad grinned. Going below to his cramped quarters, he said: "Rest the men in shifts and wake me if there's any change."

He slept restlessly, as he often had these past weeks. When Abu's strong knock on the door woke him, he jumped up with a start, the images of an ill-remembered nightmare shattering like broken glass. Sinbad pushed back his hair and wiped the sleep from his eyes. It was still dark. He glanced from the porthole and observed the faint glimmer of approaching dawn fanning in an arc across the east. The sun would be rising soon.

"Excuse me, Capt'n," said Abu as he opened the unlocked door and stepped inside. "You said I should wake you if—"

Sinbad sifled a yawn and slipped off the bed. "What is it? Has anything happened?"

The first mate frowned in the shadows. "About the galley, Capt'n . . ."

"Is she closing in?"

"No, Capt'n. But she's . . . perhaps you should come and see for yourself."

By the time Sinbad reached the bridge, the sky had grown a shade brighter. All of his crew were already awake, all of them standing silent and grim as they stared out over the starboard side. The galley was stationary, beseiged on all sides by a handful of smaller ships. Fire arrows were racing across the sky, one sail was ablaze, great tongues of flame licking at the clouds while billows of thick smoke rose above them.

Sinbad's eyes widened in shock.

"Barbary pirates," said Milo, drawing to the captain's side. "Look closely, you can see them converge. They've got the galley pinned."

"They must have been trailing the galley in the same way she followed us," added Abu. "They waited until the hours before dawn and struck. The galley hasn't got a chance." And, as if to add credence to his words, the second mast burst into flame, wind fanning the fire virtually out of control.

Sinbad turned away from the terrible sight. True, he had sought to evade the galley and would have fought her himself if he had to, but that was different. To stand by and watch her being cut down like this, plundered and burned by scavengers who cared little for the value of human life, was more than he could bear. He thought of

179

Dormo and wondered if at this very moment the aging Greek were lying dead with an arrow plunged in his breast, or worse, being dragged in chains to the hold of the pirate ship.

Poor Dormo! The vizier was not his enemy, nor were the other sailors aboard the galley, who were only doing their duty to the caliph. All were seamen, like Sinbad, and brothers as well, be they men of Baghdad or not—and for that reason every man on the *Scheherazade* looked on with pity and grief while their recent adversaries valiantly fought off the grim freebooters who attacked them.

"We must come to their rescue," said Sinbad, setting his jaw in determination.

Milo stayed his arm before he could give the signal. "What good can we be?" he said sadly. "By the time we reached the ship there'd be little left besides ashes and corpses."

"Aye," chimed a disconsolate Mongo. The giant stared glumly at the pitched fight across the water and sighed. "Once they've dispatched the galley, the pirates will turn on us. And what chance do we have against those ships when even the galley fell?"

"But the galley was caught by surprise," protested Sinbad. "Maybe we can—"

"Ship ahead, sir!" cried the lookout, taking Sinbad by surprise.

"Where away, mister?" he called.

"Five points off the port bow!"

The *Scheherazade*'s captain dashed to the rail, Abu at his heels. Beneath the brilliant morning sunlight they indeed did see another ship approaching, from south this time. She was a single-masted ship, a cog from first appearance, sweeping down upon them at a fierce clip. Sinbad glanced to Abu in trepidation. The first mate lifted the spyglass and peered. "She flies a black flag, Capt'n. . . ."

No more needed to be said. The *Scheherazade* itself was being chased by Barbary pirates.

"By Allah, where did *they* come from?" cried Milo.

"Who knows? These waters are dotted with tiny islands—each a perfect haven for cutthroats."

"Then they're not the same pirates who attacked the galley?" asked an astounded Milo.

Sinbad shook his head. "Those ships came from the opposite direction. Besides, if they were part of the other group, they'd still be too preoccupied pillaging and gathering their spoils." He spun around and faced his officers sharply. "But I do know this: If we don't act fast, we'll surely share the same fate."

"Sound battle stations!" shouted Abu. "Break open the stores!"

The full compliment of twenty-three acted swiftly, without panic. There was nary a man among them who had not faced freebooters upon the high seas before, and none were afraid to fight. As the *Scheherazade*'s sails slacked and spilled some of their wind, bows were drawn, swords unsheathed, and knives glinted in the sunlight. Meanwhile, the crimson sails of the enemy were drawing steadily closer.

The pirates were well in sight. Sinbad watched tensely as the enemy crew took up strong positions along the starboard side. The corsairs, aiming snub-nosed arrows, formed a double line of archers while others among them lit torches from strategically placed canisters of burning oil. Helmeted and breastplated, they brandished curved scimitars above their heads, whooping war cries and preparing to toss their grappling hooks.

Sinbad stared at a fiery figure upon the enemy bridge—the pirate captain, he was certain. Tall, lean, with flowing red hair and a trimmed crimson cloak. Sinbad winced. The captain had curved hips, and beneath the armor, firm and supple breasts. . . .

"*By the Prophet!*" he thundered. "Their captain is a *woman!*"

Hurtling darts cracked against timber on all sides. Sinbad

181

and his men ducked from the barrage. "Look again, Captain!" rejoined an equally stunned Milo as he raised his head and peeked over the railing, his keen eyes not missing a single trick. "They're *all* women!"

As arrows and spears flew, the crew of the *Scheherazade* looked on in wonder, hardly believing their own eyes as they watched the Amazon women boldly preparing to board.

"Are we to fight these women?" called Mongo, unafraid to crack as many heads as need be but quite disturbed over splitting female skulls.

More arrows came whistling. "We'd damn well better!" called back Abu. He wielded a knife in one hand and a club in the other, ready to match the attackers blow for blow. "Unless you've a taste for a slave's chains!"

The hostile ship had slackened its huge sail and drawn in its oars. Its side grated against the *Scheherazade* and the pirate girls whooped and hollered. A dozen grappling hooks of steel were thrown and secured, and then the melee began.

The brave crew of Sinbad's ship fought desperately to free the firmly placed hooks and chains, but already they were beginning to fall under the onslaught of javelins and flying pins. Oil-soaked arrows sputtered into pine and tiny fires sparked across the main deck. Sinbad leaped from the bridge, Mongo and Milo at his side, and the three men stood steadfast while the first wave of screaming freebooters clambored onto the *Scheherazade*.

Steel-pointed missiles slammed into the bulwark, and smoke rose sickeningly all around. And on came the Barbary pirates, tall, powerful women, knives clenched between their teeth, long sabers in their hands.

Lips drawn back from his teeth in anger, Sinbad blocked the main thrust of the assault. Without a thought he drew his knife and swiped with his sword. Steel clanged against steel; a pirate lunged and parried, matching Sinbad thrust for thrust. Amid the tumult from behind, Sinbad caught a fleeting glimpse of Mongo lifting a pirate off her feet and hurling her into a group of charging companions. Caught off guard, the women fell back, cracking the rail and falling into the water with foul oaths upon their lips.

Suddenly Mongo was being attacked from the side. Both Sinbad and Milo valiantly tried to reach him, but to no avail. The mobs of rampaging women pushed both sailors back, cornering them beside the steps to the bridge. In a split second's time Mongo was down, struck by a pin on the back of his head. The giant groaned and fell back. He dizzily reached out to choke his closest adversary, then crumpled to his knees. A great cheer went up from the women.

All along the deck the outnumbered men of the *Scheherazade* were one by one being disarmed and pushed to the floor, tips of swords at their throats. The jubilation of the pirates increased, and raucous laughter filled Sinbad's ears. Then came a deafening roar, and even as he fought off the Amazon pressing him, Sinbad saw the red-haired captain of the pirate vessel sweep on a rope from her own ship onto the *Scheherazade*.

The fiery beauty discarded her helmet and eagerly joined the fray. Her long hair tossed in the wind as she single-handedly wounded two of Sinbad's best men, then laughed at the sight of them at her feet.

"Don't harm them!" Sinbad heard her bark to her subordinates. "I want these men alive—all of them!"

To make slaves of us? thought an anguished Sinbad. And with renewed strength he fended off the brutish Amazon before him, grabbed hold of a line, and adroitly swung himself toward the scarlet pirate.

The captain of the women grinned. "He's mine!" she warned her companions, who had sought to block Sinbad from reaching her.

By this time all of Sinbad's crew had been subdued one way or another, but Sinbad showed no fear of being alone. The pirate hordes looked on with smiles as he lunged. The redheaded captain stepped back, parried with her saber, then led a charge of her own, upstrokes and downstrokes keeping Sinbad on his toes every second. The onlookers stepped aside and cleared a large section of deck, allowing the two combatants complete freedom. If any of the women were concerned for their leader's life, none showed it. Contentedly they watched, as certain of the outcome as if it were a foregone conclusion.

Sinbad's blood began to boil. He fought his best fight against this woman, but found that he was only managing to hold her to a draw. This girl showed more skill and courage than he would have thought possible, as she fearlessly pressed the attack. It even seemed as if she were toying with him. All very frustrating to Baghdad's most revered mariner!

The air became a bedlam of hoots and jeers. Sinbad's crew stood by sullenly while the women cajoled their leader into action, shouting phrases like: "Make him a eunuch, Melissa!" and "Cut off his balls!"

Their merriment only increased Sinbad's fury. Like a tiger unleashed he began to thrust again—and this time clearly gained the upper hand as Melissa was forced to protect herself against his fierce onslaught.

"You fight well, sailor!" cried the pirate girl with honest admiration in her voice. Sparks flew as their weapons crossed.

"And so do you," admitted Sinbad, not letting down his guard for a moment. Then they grappled briefly, only to pull apart and begin their thrust and parry all over again.

"We could fight like this all day, I think," said Melissa after a time. Her cheeks were flushed and she was panting for air.

"I don't mind," rejoined Sinbad, his own face drenched in perspiration. "I have plenty of time. . . ."

Melissa grinned, then slashed wildly. Sinbad sidestepped and chuckled. "Are you getting tired?"

Melissa shook her head. Her blue eyes flashed and she

184

threw back her hair. "Not at all. I'm enjoying every moment of it."

And back to the fight they went, the crowd at times gasping when Sinbad's blows came too close for comfort, and rallying when Melissa's jabs and stabs came close to their mark.

"This fight of yours, as brave as it may be, is really useless," Melissa said to him a few moments later.

Sinbad shrugged as he regained a defensive posture. "I have very little to lose," he confided. "You already have both my ship and my crew at your mercy, and no doubt you'll be claiming all my cargo as well."

The pirate captain's eyes narrowed. "And what of your own life, Captain?" she asked. "Have you no care for that precious commodity?"

"Great care, my lady," replied the mariner. "But you keep me at a disadvantage. Even should I win this little match of ours"—his eyes glanced briefly to Melissa's crew,—"I fear my life will be worthless—unless you call off your dogs."

Melissa laughed grandly. "You have a point, sir. Perhaps it might then be in both our interests to call the fight to a halt. Maybe we can say it was a draw—"

Then unexpectedly she lunged again, and once more their blades crossed. Sinbad grabbed hold of her free wrist, she grabbed his own, and as they grappled they stared long and deep into each others eyes.

"You are far too couragous to kill, sir," said Melissa. "And far too handsome as well. Surely you could be put to far better use than being served as supper to the sharks."

Sinbad grinned. "Thank you, my lady. I would be pleased to say the same about you—were it not for your unfortunate tactics in robbing me of my ship. Better to repay you if I can—and let the devil claim your soul."

Here the fiery girl's eyes darkened and the smile vanished from her face. A fleeting shadow crossed her feminine features. "Surrender to me now, sir," she commanded.

185

"You have irked me long enough, and I don't want to see you dead unless it becomes absolutely necessary."

Noting her rising anger, it was Sinbad's turn to laugh. Taunting her was the only way he might possibly loosen her defenses and catch her off guard.

"Surrender to you?" he asked. "For whatever reason? Unless you have a mind to meet my own terms."

"Insolent sod!" snapped the girl. And breaking his grip, she drew back, then thrust and thrust again, desperate to bring him down. Sinbad circumvented her attacks with an endless variety of parries, causing her to use her blade more wildly than before.

At length Melissa grew weary and began to stalk again. "You are a fine specimen of swordsmanship, sir," she told him. "Although I am not disposed to meet any terms you may ask, I am willing to hear what you have to say."

"Most gracious of you, my lady. I can see that you are something of a gentlewoman, although your occupation leaves doubts in my mind. But be that as it may. My terms are simple: Take whatever cargo you desire. Any or all of it—but give me your word to release my crew unharmed and return to me my ship. We shall go on our way and this incident of piracy shall be forgotten."

Melissa smirked. "To the victor go the spoils," she reminded. "Look about you and refresh your memory that both crew and ship are already mine—to do with as I choose. As for you, well,"—she shrugged—"as I said, I would rather not kill you, but if I must . . ."

Sinbad gritted his teeth and pressed in again. "Then we have nothing to discuss."

"Here me out!" countered Melissa as she parried. "I will give my word that no harm shall come to you or your men if you put down your sword and submit willingly."

"A one-sided bargain, my lady. You'll have to do better."

The pirate growled at his insolence and charged once

186

again. "Arrogant brat!" she hissed. "Who do you think you are?"

"Captain Sinbad of Baghdad at your service," replied the sailor, smiling as he dodged her rapid series of thrusts.

"*Really?*" Melissa's eyes visibly brightened at mention of the name. "You do me an honor, sir! I shall be proud to be known as the woman who killed you. Perhaps it will make my name as famous as your own."

"I'm not dead yet, my lady," observed Sinbad, carrying on the banter. "And who knows? Maybe I'll get lucky and have the honor of killing *you*. Perchance you are well known in these parts?"

"All the Mediterranean is my domain," she snapped. "From Tripoli to Sardinia to the Barbary coasts. My reputation is unmatched—in three years upon the sea I've captured nearly a hundred ships. And no one hears my name without fear. No woman, no *man*. These are my home grounds on which we fight, Captain Sinbad of Baghdad. My waters and my terms."

"You leave little room to negotiate, my lady."

Melissa's flaming hair bounced as she threw back her head and glared at Sinbad with a mixture of contempt and admiration. "So do you, sir. And I am becoming bored with this conflict of ours. I have better ways to pass the day."

The fight picked up in its ferocity. As before, though, their skills were evenly matched and neither could gain the upper hand. The pirate crew was growing restless, wishing to have done with this, to sack the ship and be on their way to count the booty.

"I can force you into giving up, you know," she said, after their fierce exchange had briefly tapered down to a slower pace.

Sinbad shook his head. "I don't think so, my lady. . . ."

"No? Then I'll show you." She snapped her fingers and her crew drew the tips of their blades against the throats of Sinbad's men, leaving them shivering with the knowledge that these women would kill them without a second thought if commanded by their leader.

Sinbad watched this new maneuver with growing anxiety. "You're bluffing," he said.

Melissa's brows rose and she smiled catlike. "Am I? Do you care to test me?" She signaled for Abu to be brought to the fore and looked on as Sinbad watched his first mate humbled to his knees. Then a huge Amazon stood over him and lifted her sword, ready to lop off Abu's head at Melissa's instruction.

A grim silence prevailed across the deck of the ship. The swordplay between the captains had now ceased completely, and Sinbad tensely studied his foe. Her threat was real, he decided, noting the hard and steely look in her eyes. This pirate meant every word she had said. And Abu's life—indeed, the lives of all his men— were worth more to him than either his ship or his wounded pride.

"Well, Captain Sinbad?" asked Melissa, folding her arms and tapping her foot impatiently. "What is it to be? This man's life is in your hands. Do you yield and turn yourself over? Or . . ."

Sinbad hesitated. He looked to Abu, and the first mate returned the glance with pleading eyes.

"You have fought me to a draw, sir," Melissa went on in a soft voice. "Far better than many others have fared, I assure you. There is no shame for you."

Sinbad sighed. The fight was lost; being stubborn was not going to help. "You'll honor that promise about not harming any of my men?"

"Certainly, Captain. I am always good to my word. It's the code of Barbary."

With downcast eyes Sinbad flung his weapon to the floor, frowning as a slim-waisted pirate scooped it up as part of her spoils. "You win, Melissa," Sinbad told the captain. "Do as you will. The *Scheherazade* is yours."

The women cheered; the battle was finished at a minimum of bloodshed. Melissa, gloating over this victory, loked at the sullen mariner and beamed. Then she addressed her officers: "We've lost enough time already. Bring the prisoners on board our ship and lock them in the hold. We'll commandeer the *Scheherazade* as well and sail her home to Phalus. Then I'll consider what to do."

"What do you suppose this place called 'Phalus' is?" wondered Milo, idly toying with the links of his ankle bracelets.

Sinbad endeavored to lift himself up from the dirty spot he had been occupying and strained to peek between two creaking slats in the wall. He had an unobstructed view of endless blue ocean. "There must be—oh, a thousand tiny islets in these waters," he replied. "Strung out like a pearl necklace all the way to Crete. My guess is that Phalus is the hideaway for Melissa and her crew. Most likely some deserted spot rarely touched by any ship, far away from the common sea lanes and warships searching for pirates."

"A hideaway where they can count their spoils in seclusion," mumbled Mongo, rattling his own chains and staring disconsolately down at the flea-and-roach-infested floor. "*Prisoners!* Merciful Allah, what a sad fate!"

"Slaves is more like it," broke in Abu, shoulders sagging and eyes dull in the half-dark of the damp, miserable hold. "These women won't lose much time selling us off. Mark my words: They'll have us all galley slaves before we know it." And he glumly fell into a melancholy silence, a silence that doomed men the world over have always shared.

Sinbad of course did not sanction the gloom of his shipmates, but under the circumstances it was difficult to take heart. He sat down again in the shadows of the swaying overhead lantern and surveyed his new domain. Bugs of every sort were brazenly crawling along the cracked planks, weaving in and out of smelly pools of stagnant water, climbing up the sodden beams, darting among the tightly clustered manacled men. Here and there along the walls he saw names notched into the wood, names of other poor seamen captured by Crimson Melissa and her band, thrown into this very hold and left to languish while the gleeful pirates celebrated on the decks above, then sailed off for Phalus with their booty.

"Bah," grumped Milo. "What's the use in complaining about our destiny?" He smiled wanly at his companions, desirous of instilling at least a glimmer of hope where there was none. "At least when we reach Phalus we'll be taken out of this hole and allowed to breathe."

"Aye," chimed Sinbad. "Better to be upon land than here. And maybe we can devise some way to escape . . ."

Before his thought had been completed, the sound of a scraping boot rose from the dimness of the outside passage and then the door creaked open. A gentle, elfin face appeared from the shadows and surveyed the hold before its possessor stepped inside. Every sailor turned abruptly to face her. Her features, dark-complexioned and pretty, were those of a girl barely out of her teens, fresh with vitality. But the garments she wore told a different tale; dressed in the same armored breastplate over her tunic as the others, a long, curved carving knife strapped to her petite waist, she would clearly prove no delicate virgin unnerved among this sudden world of men.

Her eyes scanned the prisoners, and, secure that they planned no tricks, she gestured to two women outside to bring in the buckets of slop. Bowls were passed around, each man holding his in both hands while the greasy, cold stew was apportioned. Then, when the bowls were all filled, everyone was handed a small cup of fresh water.

"Eat," said the guard.

The crew of the *Scheherazade* exchanged glances. Sinbad nodded. It wasn't a very appealing meal, but most lost no time dipping their fingers into their bowls, gulping down the stale chunks of meat and slurping up the watery sauce. All except Sinbad, who sipped at his water and pushed his bowl away.

The dark-eyed guard frowned and considered him

reproachfully. Her mein was serious as she came and stood over him. "And what's the matter with you?" she inquired. "Isn't our cuisine to your liking?" Her companions snickered.

Sinbad returned her look with a bored expression. "I'm not very hungry."

The guard scowled. "Don't make me waste my time, Captain. It's some days' journey to our island, and my orders are to see to it that all of you reach Phalus alive and healthy. Now eat."

"I'm still not hungry," replied Sinbad with defiance.

She made to draw her knife, then paused to regard him more thoughtfully. Melissa would be most displeased, she knew, if any of the crew were lost before sighting shore—especially this mariner from Baghdad who had for some reason captured the pirate captain's interest.

"Don't make trouble for yourself, Captain Sinbad," she advised. "Just do as you're told. Or perhaps you'd rather I inform Melissa of your brazen attitude?"

If that was intended as a threat, Sinbad certainly was not intimidated by it. "You may inform your captain whatever you like," he dryly replied. "But make certain to assure her that all our attitudes would improve both remarkably and instantaneously—*if* we weren't degraded like this." And he pushed away his bowl of slop, purposely letting it spill over the brim. Within seconds a host of roaches were rushing to feed.

The guard's features hardened and her stare became more menacing. "How dare you!" she seethed, long hair falling lightly about her face. "Who are you to make such demands!"

Sinbad looked at her blankly. "We are not animals, my lady—"

Her hand swept the knife from its sheath in the bat of an eye; the girl weilded it expertly, bringing the razor-sharp edge only a hairsbreadth from Sinbad's throat. "I am *not* a lady!" she hissed, obviously touchy at being called

191

anything but a pirate. "I am the first lieutenant of this vessel, second in command to our captain." She smiled thinly at Sinbad, adding: "And soon to be captain of your own ship."

The mariner felt his blood stir. It was all he could do to restrain himself from wrenching the knife out of her hand, throwing her over his knee, and giving her a well deserved spanking. Exactly what she needed, if he were any judge of pirates.

"Now," went on the guard, "do you eat or not?"

Sinbad's face had defiance written all over it. "Not," was all he answered.

The girl turned in a huff, the knife still aimed for his throat. Looking over her shoulder, she called for more guards to come at once and subdue the unruly prisoner. As loud sounds of racing boots clattered outside in the corridor, the girl ordered Sinbad to stand. He did so feebly, signaling for his worried men to keep their places and not provoke an incident. Don Giovanni, curled beneath a blanket, poked his head out and stared at the proceedings. The captain was going to get them all into a heap of trouble, he was sure—the pirates seemed ready to have him keelhauled.

Sinbad, though, was unperturbed. Through the mixture of dim torchlight and shadows from without, he perceived the two figures advancing at the guard's call. He stared with surprise as they came into the hold. They were men—the first yet seen aboard this curious ship. Tall, broad-shouldered, with thick necks and sinewy limbs, shirtless and muscular. They held shortswords in their hands, and with threatening gestures backed Sinbad up against the wall.

"Mistress?" said the first as he looked to the angered lieutenant. And he waited submissively for her instruction. But missing from his stare, Sinbad noted, was any sign of appreciation for the woman he addressed. Certainly this young pirate girl was a fine specimen of

192

womanhood, turning every head including his own. But to these powerful guards she held no interest, almost as though she were sexless, almost as though the firmness of her breasts or the curve of her hips were of no appeal. Most peculiar for men at sea. . . .

The girl regarded the waiting guards with smoldering eyes. "This one," she said, pointing to Sinbad, "refuses to follow my orders. Teach him a lesson."

The burly men looked at each other and grinned. "Yes, mistress," the first replied with a touch of sadistic pleasure in his voice. And he stripped Sinbad's shirt with his bare hands and made ready to flog him with the flat of his weapon.

Mongo growled and leaped to his feet, straining to break free of his shackles. Abu and Milo, followed by a handful of others, tried to reach and constrain him. The pirate girl scanned the ill-lighted hold, realizing she had a near-mutiny on her hands.

"Bring the prisoner on deck!" she commanded. "We'll give the punishment there—"

Sinbad tried to break free. The guards toppled him to the floor. All at once every man in the hold was up in arms, Mongo in the forefront, veins bulging in a powerful attempt to save his captain from harm. The guards brandished their swords and held the manacled crew of the *Scheherazade* at bay while the girl struggled to get Sinbad out of the door.

"What's going on here?" came a booming voice of authority.

A roomful of shouts and near-melee returned to silence as Melissa, Scarlet Pirate of the Mediterranean, strode into the hold, her icy glare shooting from face to face. The sailors of the *Scheherazade* stood meekly in their places, casting their gazes away.

Melissa's lieutenant sighed with relief. "These dogs tried to riot," she panted, looking furtively at her commander.

Melissa frowned. "I thought I ordered you not to harm any of them. . . ."

"I was only doing my duty, Captain. This one's been causing us difficulties."

"Men in chains give you problems, Felicia?" asked the pirate leader with a sneer. Then she turned sharply to Sinbad, glaring at the mariner held firmly in check by her two goons. "I thought we made a bargain, you and I?"

Sinbad lifted his head and brusquely pushed off the hands constraining him. "The bargain was to treat us as men, not animals—pigs in a pen receive better treatment than this." And in protest and agreement his crew rattled their chains and growled.

"Why you *scum!*" bristled Felicia. She made to strike the mariner with an open hand, but Melissa stayed her arm. " I can take care of this," she said.

The younger woman objected hotly. "But Captain! This man has openly defied you! Scorned you, tried to make fools of us all. Give him to me. I'll see to it he begs for mercy, crawls on his knees to you for this outrage. . . ."

Melissa's eyes flashed. "I said that *I'd* handle the matter, Lieutenant. You may leave—is that understood?" The harshness of her command left little room for her subordinate to argue.

"Aye, aye, Captain." Felicia saluted smartly, spun on her toes, and walked briskly from the hold.

Melissa waited until her footsteps could be heard upon the hatchway steps and then confronted Sinbad with her hands on her hips and a smoldering in her eyes. "I'll have no more of these little games, Captain Sinbad," she warned roughly. "Remember, your life is still in my hands. This time I'll let your exercise in futility pass—but not again." Then she snapped her fingers, ordering her loathsome guards to release their hold. Sinbad got up slowly, rubbing at his bruised arms. He ignored the half-grins of Melissa's goons. The fiery pirate folded her arms and smiled.

"They're eunuchs," she told him proudly. "Runaways from the court of Persia. Not much use in anyone's bed—but fiercely loyal and trustworthy to me. At a clap of my hands

194

they would obey any command I give them. *Any command*." Her smile became sardonic. "I'm sure they would be eager to turn you into one of them. . . ."

Sinbad frowned distastefully, thinking the life of a eunuch not one to be admired.

"Now then," Melissa went on. "I trust there won't be any more trouble from you?"

Sinbad glanced at the hulking eunuchs, both still grinning stupidly at the possibility of performing a quick castration upon the *Scheherazade*'s famed captain.

"Your bowl is yet untouched, Captain Sinbad," Melissa said as she focused on his supper. "Eat it."

Forced to swallow his pride, Sinbad sat crosslegged and picked up the bowl. Melissa laughed grandly; for the second time she had matched wits with her famous prisoner, and for the second time humbled him. As the eunuchs followed her out and locked the door, Sinbad spit the food out of his mouth and hurled his bowl against the wall. There and then, while his crew sullenly returned to their places, he vowed that the next match of wits between himself and Melissa would end with the Scarlet Pirate in humiliation. But for now he could do nothing—nothing except wait until the voyage was done and the island of Phalus safely reached.

Time dragged ever so slowly, the pirate ship sailing in the lead and the commandeered *Scheherazade* in tow behind it. As the sun set, the sky's crimson glow seeped through cracks in the aging boards. One day, two days. A third. Always the same routine. At sunup Felicia would have bowls of slop brought and withdrawn, and the procedure would be repeated before sunset. The foul mess concocted by the ship's cook remained far more suitable for the roaches who shared their cramped quarters than for the men who were forced to live in them. Still, the slop kept them alive—kept them going until they reached their destination. That was all that mattered. Staying alive.

* * *

"Land ahoy!" cried the lookout.

The pirate vessel lurched in strong winds, tilting hard to port as the ship cut through increasingly choppy waters and made its way north.

From the holes in the slats Sinbad watched the isle of Phalus appear with the bright sunshine of a new day. It was a small island, golden sandy beaches on one side with swaying palms behind them, a deep-water cove on the other, sided by long reefs and dangerous shoals. The cove was well hidden from sight, surrounded as it was by tall, thickly grassed hills that provided a natural protection both from the elements and passing ships. It took good knowledge to clear the shoals safely, Sinbad could tell; the pirate ship would have to do some very fancy maneuvering to slip between the reefs into harbor. A ship unfamiliar with these environs was certain to smash against the reefs long before it could negotiate its way to the cove. All the more reason for Melissa to have picked this island for a hideout.

As the vessel neared its berth, Sinbad saw a small gathering of women—also pirates, by their dress—come out to the pier and wave happily as their companions came home at last.

"Good fishing this trip, Rebecca!" Sinbad heard Melissa yell out to the woman in the forefront of the waiting pirates, a heavyset woman, nearing middle age, with barrel-shaped arms, three chins, and what seemed to be a permanent scowl etched deeply into her craggy face.

Lines were thrown and the anchor dropped, and the pirate ship came to rest in the harbor. Then, before Sinbad could see or hear anything else of what was going on outside, the doors of the hold abruptly opened and in walked Felicia, escorted by several of her largest Amazons and followed by both somber eunuchs, who thumbed their swords as they stood at either side of the door. The shackles were unlocked from their legs and Sinbad and his crew lined up and filed out along the corridor. Up the steps they were led and out from the forward hatch onto the main deck, where they were greeted with the first sunlight they had seen in nearly five days. The sea breeze was strong and salty, rushing against the weary crew like a balm, soothing them, filling their lungs with clean air.

"This way," said Felicia, prodding Sinbad with her knife.

He stepped slowly down the gangway, glancing at the rows of staring women at either side. A fine-looking bunch of women, he thought, taking note of their supple bodies and bronzed complexions.

Abu, feeling a stirring in his loins, whispered to Sinbad: "By the Prophet! There must be a hundred women on this island! And not a man among them!" He shook his head sadly and sighed. "A pity that we are chained like this. Otherwise Phalus could prove to be a paradise."

"Don't get your hopes up," grumbled the captain. "Women they may be, but they're still our jailors. Or have you forgotten?"

"Keep moving!" barked Felicia. She jabbed Sinbad lightly in the ribs, and the mariners hurried down onto the dock where a beaming Melissa already stood waiting.

"A good catch this time, eh, Rebecca?" she said with a gleam in her eyes. "Twenty-three men. Twenty-three!"

The larger, older woman narrowed her eyes and inspected the prisoners one by one as they came down and were lined up along the grassy walk. She pursed her lips and paced up and down the line, hesitating here and there, selecting one crewman or another for closer inspection. At times she seemed pleased, at others disappointed. But when she paused in front of Mongo her eyes lit up like stars. "Who is this one?" she asked.

Melissa shrugged. "Just a brute. Of no particular intelligence; I interrogated him myself."

The woman called Rebecca ran her fingers across Mongo's biceps, looked at his eyes, examined his teeth. "He'll bring a fine price, Melissa. Cull him from the others. A shame he'll only be with us for a short while."

The pirate captain smiled. "You may keep him if you like," she said. "As a present from me. A personal slave."

"Bah!" Rebecca scowled, but her cheeks flushed with a hint of embarrassment. "Any others of note?" she asked.

"Only this one." She lifted her hand and pointed to Sinbad, who stood defiantly at the beginning of the line.

Rebecca curled her lip, tapped her fingertips at the side of her face. "What about him? He doesn't seem very special to me. Except for that stupid frog sitting on his shoulder."

A mischievous smile crossed Melissa's lips; her scarlet hair glowed in morning sunlight as she tilted her head. "Perhaps you're right, perhaps not. But he tells me that he's Captain Sinbad from Baghdad."

Rebecca seemed startled. "Sinbad? Are you certain?"

Melissa laughed. She clapped her hands and lifted her gaze toward the sky. "Oh, lucky day! Can you imagine the price he might bring on the open market of Tangier? Why, I'll wager that a hundred bidders would pay any price—*any price*—just to make him their own! The world's most renowned mariner, Rebecca! Can you imagine! And I caught him with hardly a fight!"

The older pirate moved closer to Sinbad and studied him anew. "I've heard many tales of your exploits, Captain," she said at length. "Your—er—visit to Phalus is truly an honor."

Sinbad bowed his head politely. "I wish I could say the same, dear lady. Phalus seems most inviting to me and my crew"—he briefly scanned the groups of alluring young women—"but alas, not as your prisoners."

There was an unmistakable twinkle in Rebecca's dark eyes. "Yes, it is a shame, I agree. But such are the fortunes of life. Still, good Captain, it could be worse. At Phalus we take good care of our men before shipping them to the slave markets. Don't we, girls?"

Giggles rose from the onlookers, but Felicia, dourly standing behind her leader, frowned. "This one's more trouble than you realize, Rebecca. He's shrewd—I know his games. He hopes to win us over with his charms."

Melissa's angry glance at her lieutenant was not missed by either Sinbad or the observant frog. "Enough of this," snapped the fiery captain. "Rebecca, have them all taken to the guardhouse. I want them watched twenty-four hours a day until our preparations are done."

"Aye, Melissa. And him too?" She looked to Sinbad.

Melissa ran a fingertip over her lip, lost in concentration. "No," she replied between breaths. "Isolate him. Put him with the Athenian."

Rebecca clapped her hands and the pirate crew snapped to attention. Then, with weapons drawn, they marched the men of the *Scheherazade* in quickstep away from the harbor to a large stone fortification set beyond the small cluster of huts that served as the island village. With downcast eyes the men obeyed the lash of whips and prodding of knives until they were behind the massive walls and locked away in a subterranean dormitory.

Rebecca and her chief strode to their own abode, the largest hut of all, atop a sandy hillock dotted with leafy palms. Sinbad watched as they left, finding himself now alone on the wharf except for Felicia and the two eunuch goons.

"All right, march!" she barked.

"Where are we going?" he asked casually as he was led toward the beach.

"You'll see," growled Felicia. "But you can count yourself lucky. By comparison, your stay here on Phalus will be in luxury. And I'm sure the Athenian shall be glad for the company. Now move! You may have intrigued Melissa— but you haven't fooled me! And my patience is wearing thin."

To Sinbad's surprise, he was led to a shaded grotto and then down a winding black stone staircase. When they reached the bottom he found himself upon a flat, well-lighted landing. It seemed to be a secret stronghold, perhaps where the pirate booty was stored.

Sinbad stepped away from the torchlight and bathed in the shadows. "Why are you bringing me here?" he asked.

Before the question could be answered, he spun around at the sound of a fearsome growl. "By the beard of the Prophet!" He jumped back at the presence of a sleek black panther with fangs bared, scratching for him. The animal's eyes glowed like fire in the dull light, and the cat hissed, humping its back as if preparing to leap. Only the linked iron chain set into the stone wall on one end and hooked to his collar at the other prevented him from tearing at Sinbad's throat.

Felicia smiled—a wicked sadistic smile that made Sinbad shiver. "Only a pet, Captain," she told him in mock assurance. "We keep him down here to protect our stores from those who might be tempted to take more than their share. But you won't have to worry, not where you'll be." And she signaled for the eunuchs to unlock the thick gate behind him. Iron moaned as the gate swung wide. Sinbad was taken inside another chamber, this one more like a prison cell. Large and dark, it was lit by a single oil lamp that burned upon a shelf in the corner. There were a few pieces of furniture—mats for sleeping, a tiny table with broken legs, water jugs and the like.

"Make yourself comfortable, Captain," sneered Felicia as Sinbad glanced around. Then, before he could protest, she and the eunuchs were gone, slamming the barred gate shut, locking it and hurrying back to the entrance of the grotto.

Sinbad grasped at the bars and tried to shake them loose. "Let me out of here!" he boomed. "I want to be with my men! At least give me that much!"

But there was no reply, save for the distant gleeful laughter of Felicia, who had heard his baleful cries.

"It's no use, Sinbad," mumbled Don Giovanni as the sailor tried again to open the gate. "We're trapped. We can't escape."

Sinbad looked up at the iron hinges firmly in place and

saw that the bars from ceiling to floor could not be budged by ten men of twice his own weight. As painful to admit as it was, he knew the frog was right. Here they were and here they would stay until Melissa saw fit to decide otherwise.

"*Bitch!*" he bellowed, shaking a fist. The only answer was a ferocious growl from the watchful panther opposite. The great cat curled its tail and paced to the end of its leash, all the while glaring at Sinbad, no doubt contemplating what he would taste like for supper.

"I wouldn't agitate him if I were you," came a voice from behind. A dark figure came forth from the shadows, a frail, bent, aging man with watery eyes and a sad smile on his cracked lips. "The cat is never properly fed," he went on. "Felicia does that on purpose, you know. Keeps him more on his toes . . ."

With his hands on his hips, Sinbad stared. "And who are *you?* I didn't see you when they brought me here."

The smile expanded slightly. "I occupy the adjoining cell; the wall is open between us."

"Then you are also a prisoner?"

The old man sighed. "Alas, yes. Lo, these past eight months, if my reckong is still sound. But it's difficult to keep track of such matters, you see." He glanced at the forboding walls that surrounded them. "No sunlight, no stars. It tends to make you claustrophobic. I daresay that some men have even gone mad. After all, when you're alone so long . . ." He shrugged. "Ah, well. It could be worse, you know. At least these women pirates feed me. Oh, yes. Twice a day. Once in a while three. And you know, occasionally they even put a bit of meat into their soups. Real meat! Ah, 'tis a treasure worth more than I can say. Yes, indeed it is. I never—"

As Sinbad listened in astonishment, the peculiar fellow went on and on and on, hardly pausing to catch his breath, speaking of this and that, and a hundred items of trivia that hardly bore saying. It was clear to Sinbad that his companion had not had a living soul to speak to in so long that now he was unable to restrain himself even if he had wanted to.

". . . It was just last week that I was thinking,"—the odd stranger furrowed his brow and tapped a finger against his cheek—"or was it the week before? Well, never mind. Anyway, as I was saying—"

Sinbad put out his palms. "Hold on please! Just a second. Slow down a moment, will you? I'm confused enough as it is? Who are you, my friend? And what are you doing here on Phalus?"

A broad smile came to the man's face and he nodded slowly, as if realizing how foolish he must seem. "Forgive me, sailor, but it has been a very long time since I had company. . . ."

Company, thought Sinbad. "Why, you must be the Athenian!"

The old man's eyes glittered. "Why yes! Do you know me, then?"

"Only what the pirates muttered before I got here."

"Then welcome, my friend." He bowed expansively. "These quarters are humble, but I'm sure we'll spend the time merrily while we wait to be taken."

Sinbad leaned uncomfortably against the wall. "Taken where?"

His companion scratched at his straggly gray beard. "Any of a number of places, but the last batch of prisoners were taken to Tangier."

Slaves, Sinbad told himself, reminded of the fate that awaited. "Why were you not taken with them?" wondered the mariner.

"Me? Oh, they wouldn't take me away. Not in a hundred years. Not while I hold the key . . ."

"What key?"

The Athenian grinned and pointed to his head. "It's all locked away up here. They've been trying for ages to get it out of me. Damn clever, that Melissa. Why, she's tried every trick in the book. They've seduced me, got me drunk, beat me, threatened my life, vowed to sell my daughter into slavery . . ."

"Stop, stop," pleaded Sinbad. "You're losing me again. Start from the beginning and explain all of this."

With a deep sigh the old man seated himself on the floor. Dejectedly he closed his eyes and nodded. "It's a strange tale, my friend. Yes, indeed. I only hope you won't think me too demented."

"I've heard many strange tales in my day, old-timer. Let me hear yours."

"Ah, well. All right. But where shall I start? My name is Methelese. I am a scholar and philospher of Athens. With my lovely daughter Clair, I sailed upon a merchant ship, set for Rhodes, where I hoped to complete my work. But along the way, much as yourself, I should think, my ship was accosted by these brigands of the sea and those of us who survived the bloody battle were taken prisoner and brought here to Phalus. That was nearly eight months ago, as I mentioned. During that time I've seen other prisoners come and go like the tides. Egyptians, Cypriots, Hebrews. All sharing the same fate. The Scarlet Pirate, you see, rarely kills her victims. She shrewdly uses them, first here on Phalus to keep her mates happy, and—"

Sinbad leaned forward inquisitively. "Keep them happy how?"

Methelese chuckled. "You'll learn that for yourself, my friend. But the rigors of satisfying a hundred women and more can be quite taxing, I assure you. How many are there among your party?"

"Twenty-three."

The Athenian's brows rose in speculation. "Then you are most fortunate! One man for nearly five women! The last group of prisoners only numbered nine. Each man was forced to please a dozen! Ofttimes in the same night!" Methelse shivered. "Poor fellows. Some nearly died from the strain."

Sinbad was incredulous. "And . . . and what of yourself?" he managed to ask after a pause of silence.

"I am old," conceded Methelese. "Not of very much use. So I am kept here, apart from the others and their debauches, allowed to waste my life away."

"And pray tell, good philosopher, what makes you so special that Melissa has seen fit to keep you alive all this time? As you've already admitted, your services to her are—er—minimal."

"Ah, but are they?" Methelese clapped his hands and laughed. "But have you forgotten? They believe me to hold the key—the key, man! In my head, I hold the key to many of the world's secrets. Lost arts, treasures, potions. In fact, the purpose for my visit to Rhodes was to search the temples for the Book of Knowledge. There it was my intent and purpose to learn the meaning of this shallow life in which we live, and share this wisdom with all. No, my youthful friend, I have many secrets to unlock for Melissa and her renegades. I am a storehouse of the places where gold, pearls, the wealth of man, have been buried and lost over the centuries. These pirates would be foolish indeed to kill me. They thirst for what I could tell, and would gladly sail beyond the Pillars of Hercules to find such lost riches."

Sinbad's shoulders sagged and he frowned. His friend did indeed have an interesting story to tell, but one of little use in their current predicament.

"Thus," went on Methelese sadly, "they hold my darling child apart from me in another dungeon and vow never to set either of us free until I tell them everything they want to know."

"So why not tell them?" said Sinbad. "What good are these secrets of yours when no one can solve them? At least Melissa would reward you with freedom—"

The Athenian flushed with anger. "I can see you are not a man to think of others! Are you so selfish that you would unravel the world's mysteries for your own life? You would give to pirates the enigmas of the universe in exchange for a single petty life? Selfish man! Bite your tongue! Never! Never will I reveal all that I know, even should my bones rot for eternity within this foul and miserable abode. Let men quest, if they will, but I, Methelese of Athens, am unbending. Like a rock I stand, like the Pillars of Hercules themselves, steadfast in the knowledge that what I do is right!"

"That doesn't help us any, does it?" rasped Don Giovanni, annoyed at his self-rightiousness.

Methelese's tongue wobbled in his mouth. He stared at the frog, doubting his ears and his sanity. "He speaks! By the gods of old, the creature speaks!"

Sinbad grinned. "Well, it seems that you don't know *all* of the world's secrets after all," he said dryly.

The Athenian blinked his eyes and turned to Sinbad. "This must be a trick. You are a ventriloquist. . . ."

Sinbad shook his head. "I promise you I'm not. Allow me to introduce you to Baghdad's most well-traveled bull-frog, Don Giovanni."

Don Giovanni bowed politely on Sinbad's shoulders. "An honor to meet you, Methelese."

The Athenian hunched forward and examined the frog more closely, touching him lightly with his fingertips.

"Ouch, that tickles!"

Methelese quickly withdrew his hand from Don Giovanni's belly. "Excuse me—er—my friend. I didn't mean to offend you. . . ."

Sinbad roared with laughter and slapped the confused philosopher on the shoulder. "Take heart, Methelese. He's not a wizard, nor am I. But you see, we have traveled many a long road together, and have our own interesting tale to tell."

"Then by all means tell it!" cried the philosopher, with a scholar's eagerness to learn wonders.

Sinbad nodded gravely. "All right, I suppose I should. But," he cautioned, "I have to have your word never to speak of it with anyone. You see, save for my most trusted crewmen, Abu, Milo and Mongo the Giant, no one in the world knows of Don Giovanni's plight. It is our own little secret, carefully guarded, and must remain so."

"I understand. You have my solemn oath." And Methelese held out his hand to shake on it. "Never a word shall I utter, not even to my dear child Clair, should I ever have the fortune to gaze upon her lovely face again."

And so, sitting in the shadows, Sinbad told his sorrowful story from its beginning, how after so long a time and so many shared adventures he and the frog had wound up here on Phalus as the Scarlet Pirate's most prized prisoners. It was a woeful tale, and it brought a tear to Methelese's tired eyes when he had done.

Somber and grim-faced, the Athenian said, "Then escape for you is most important."

"Imperative, my scholarly friend. Not just for me and my crew, but also for my beloved Sherry, who languishes in the palace of a man she loathes. For that reason alone I must continue my voyage and find the Red Dahlia."

Methelese sucked in a lungful of the damp air and held it a long time before slowly letting it out. He shut his eyes wearily and began to gently rock back and forth in his place, sighing on several occasions, rubbing a bony finger alongside his nose. At length his eyes opened and he looked long and hard at the sullen mariner. "*Perhaps* there is a way to help you," he confided.

Sinbad stared. "How? Tell me! I'll do anything!"

Methelese grunted. "We must not be hasty, Captain, lest we be foiled before we start. *But* . . ." His eyes scanned the darkened cell as if seeking out unwanted listeners, and he rubbed his hands together in a slow deliberate motion. "There is a tunnel leading to the dock," he said quickly, in a secretive whisper. "I came upon it once months ago, but as I have no ship"—he shrugged—"it was of little use . . ."

"But *I* have a ship," cried Sinbad gleefully. "The

Scheherazade, fit and trimmed and sitting idly in Phalus's harbor! Where is this tunnel, old-timer? How do I find it?"

"Ah, the impatience of youth," mumbled Methelese beneath his sour breath. "Even if I show it to you, you'll still have to devise a way to free your crew . . ."

"I'll think of something, don't worry."

The Athenian frowned. "And there is one other condition for my help . . ."

Sinbad held firmly at both his shoulders. "Name it!"

"My own release—and Clair's as well. She is kept in quarters close to Melissa's own, so the way will be dangerous. You must take us both far from Phalus—I care not where—but the Scarlet Pirate's wrath is not to be toyed with."

Sinbad laughed, buoyed at the thought of at last turning the tables on his fiery adversary. What wouldn't he give!

"All you ask is freely given, friend Methelese. Now all we need is a plan."

The Athenian smiled. "We shall have to bide our time and wait for the pirate banquet to commence. All your crew, including yourself I should think, shall be brought forth from their cells for these buccaneers' pleasure. And then, amid this party and debauchery, shall be our only chance. There won't be much time and the risks are high. Have no doubts, if we are caught in our scheme, Felicia will have no qualms at serving us one at a time to her hungry pet." And as if giving credence to his words, the sleek black panther growled and bared its sharpened fangs.

Sinbad shivered. "We'll have to chance it, old-timer. One way or another we must get off Phalus—and if it takes my killing the Scarlet Pirate myself, then I'll have to do it."

PART FIVE:

FROM ONE FRYING PAN RIGHT
INTO ANOTHER.

Sinbad woke to the sound of keys fumbling in the lock and the groan of the iron door. Felicia, a eunuch holding a torch beside her, walked calmly into the cell. Sinbad roused himself slowly, letting his sleepy eyes wander about his confining quarters. Shadows danced across the ceiling; he could see tiny insects dashing for shade from the flickering torchlight.

What time was it? He cursed softly under his breath. In this black hole there was no way of knowing if those outside beheld a star-dazzled midnight or a bright noon sun.

"On your feet," growled Felicia, glaring down at him, a small whip clutched tightly in her hand.

He looked up at her in confusion. "What—what's going on?"

Felicia sneered coldly. "I'm taking you out of here. The captain has sent for you. Now up—before I have to get rough."

Sinbad flexed aching muscles and recalled his discomfort upon the thin mat that served as a bed. Pebbles and rocks had dug at him ceaselessly, forcing him to toss and turn in a constant effort to find a less-punishing position. "Why am I being sent for?" he asked while he stood.

The pirate girl snapped her fingers restlessly. "Come on, come on. I've no time for your questions. Just follow me and keep your mouth shut."

He nodded and bent over to pick up the sleeping frog from beneath his blanket.

"Never mind your pet," snapped Felicia. "You can leave him here."

He shot her an angry glance. "Where I go, he goes. Otherwise you can inform your scarlet-haired leader that I refuse."

The young pirate groaned, knowing from past experience that the cocky mariner meant what he said. "All right, all right. Wake him and take him. See if I care. But hurry up."

Sinbad stuffed the yawning frog inside his shirt and followed the eunuch out the door. Moments later, after passing the panther's watchful eyes, they had reached the stairs and come out of the grotto. Sinbad gazed up at the sky; it was a brilliant night with thousands upon thousands of twinkling stars thickly clustered above his head. A perfect, cool evening with a lazy half-moon hanging above the treetops.

"This way," muttered Felicia wearily, directing him to the path that led away from the village and to the thatched-roof villa that served as Melissa's house.

Palms were swaying in the breeze, and there was no noise to be heard, save for the surf crashing against the white beach and the occasional hoot of an owl. Few lamps were lit in the cottages, and, apart from his guards, the only other signs of life that Sinbad could see were the sentries, three fierce Amazons, hands to the hilts of their swords as they marched up and down the nearby dock, keeping a careful eye on the two berthed ships and the ocean beyond.

They walked the path to the villa, Felicia in the lead. "Wait here," she commanded, leaving him to stand with the eunuch beside the leafy trees. Then the girl strode briskly around the side of the whitewashed stone edifice and gently rapped on the door. The shutters were tightly closed but Sinbad could make out a dull orange glow of lamplight behind the window. He strained to hear what the pirate was saying when Melissa finally opened the door, but with the surf so close and the leaves rustling from the wind, he could not eavesdrop.

"Getting chilly, isn't it?" he remarked with a smile to the grim eunuch.

The castrated brute grunted in reply. They waited for what seemed to be a long time before Felicia came back and told Sinbad to go inside.

"Alone?" he asked.

Felicia smirked, her hair tossing freely in the breeze, her young features bathed in moonlight. "Alone," she replied.

"Aren't you afraid I might do some harm to your boss?"

There was a girlish glint in Felicia's eyes when he said that, the first hint of femininity Sinbad had seen in the fierce second-in-command. "Melissa can take care of herself. Now do as you're told." And she played with her whip as a warning. Sinbad shrugged, finished his walk to the end of the path, and rapped upon the door.

"Enter," came a reply.

He unhooked the simple outside latch and entered the room. Glaring light from randomly placed candles and oil lamps made him shade his eyes. After a second or two of adjustment he looked around with surprise. The cottage was more finely furnished than he could have imagined, with all manner of rare and exotic artifacts hanging from the walls and placed around the room. There were curious statues of ivory set upon glass tables. Images of elephants, swans in a pond, tusks on the wall, and a fine bear-pelt complete with head resting on the floor in the center of the room. Velvet cushions were spread everywhere, alongside them brass braziers where incense burned and sent tiny whiffs of dark smoke up toward the ceiling. Golden goblets adorned rows of mahogany shelves, interspersed with tiny hand-painted figurines of oven-blasted clay. Miniature soldiers and courtesans, ladies-in-waiting, kings, queens, knights in armor. Sinbad knew that the value of these items was incalculable. But when such spoils are taken without payment, the new owner need never calculate their worth.

"Welcome, Captain Sinbad," the pirate said.

Sinbad turned to find her stretched out upon a divan of deep blue velvet, dressed in a fabulous Eastern robe of Cathay, inlaid with threads of pure gold at the collar and hems, which offset magnificently the fine black silk of the garment. Bejeweled with golden rings studded with rubies and sapphires, a pearly necklace dangling from her throat, Melissa held in her hand a silver goblet filled to the brim with sweet dark wine. Her scarlet hair fell in curls almost to her luscious hips. She looked at the startled mariner and smiled spicily.

"You sent for me, madam?"

Melissa softly drummed her fingernails along the side of the inlaid silver goblet. "I did."

"Why?"

The Scarlet Pirate laughed lustily. "To talk, Captain." She shifted her weight and crossed her legs, noticing as Sinbad's quick eye caught the curve of her exposed thigh.

"To talk about what? Where I am to be sold as a slave?"

Melissa laughed again, this time with more abandon. "Come, Captain. Sit beside me. Pour yourself a cup of wine. It's the finest I own, and I promise you'll be pleased. Roman brew, a heady stuff guaranteed to make your dour face less forbidding." She giggled and took a sip.

He reached for the empty cup on the side table and poured from the Greek urn. Melissa watched with a pleased expression as he drank. Then she moved over, giving him plenty of room to sit. One swallow and he could feel the fire burning through his veins. "It *is* good," he admitted, seating himself comfortably. "Where did you steal it?"

She ignored the sarcasm in his tone and answered simply, "from a merchant ship headed for Constantinople. Ten barrels being sent to the devout priests; a shame it never reached them. But then, Christians wouldn't have appreciated it, anyway."

Sinbad rubbed the toe of his boot into the thick rug and leaned back. He shut his eyes and pinched the bridge of his nose. Melissa stretched out her hand and brushed a shock of unruly hair from his brow. Sinbad looked at her, grudgingly admiring her well-developed shape.

Sensing his interest, Melissa smiled seductively. "You know, you and I don't have to be enemies," she told him.

He laughed caustically. "Since when does a prisoner become anything less to his jailor?"

Melissa pouted; she ran a slow finger over the rim of her goblet, eyes focused on the rich wine. "Perhaps you need not be a prisoner," she said. "Perhaps you and I can come to—er—another agreement. . . ."

A harsh wind had begun to blow outside, and it whistled as it crept through the locked shutters. From the far distance came a low rumble of thunder, signalling an approaching storm.

"I'll get to the point," Melissa went on, now looking at Sinbad once more. Her eyes were wide as she said, "I have need of a man like you, Sinbad. You're strong, virile, intelligent: exactly the qualities I need. The Mediterranean is filled with freebooters—thousands of them. But I'd trade them all for one like you . . ."

Sinbad stirred restlessly. "What are you proposing?" he asked, taking her goblet from her hand and putting it down on the table.

Melissa sighed. She threw back her hair, spilling it freely over her shoulders, and shut her eyes. "I've been thinking, Captain. This life I lead, as rewarding as it may be, is a lonely one. I have need of companionship—real companionship, not eunuchs or drunken buccaneers who court me like I was a sow. When I met you, I knew you were different; gods yes! A man I could trust, a man I could admire." She looked at him girlishly. "And yes, even one I might love."

A brief silence passed between them, with Sinbad studying the face of his erstwhile adversary. Behind her mask of bravado lay a still young, lovely but lonely woman. A woman desperately in search of someone to share her solitude, for even a pirate grows frightened as the nights become long and bitter and the shallowness of her empty years cannot be hidden away in a roomful of treasure.

"What do you want of me?" he said at last.

The rain clouds were almost overhead now, flashes of lightning fiercely brightening the sky. Melissa lifted her gaze heavenward, then after a while, said, "I've decided to offer you a partnership, Captain. Stand by my side, sail with me upon my ventures, command your own ship beside mine. Together we could hold the sea in our very hands. There is nothing we couldn't accomplish, no foe we couldn't match, no ship we—"

"We couldn't plunder?"

She looked at him sharply. "Yes, plunder!" She laughed bitterly. "And why not? What have these princes and kings to do with us? Their wealth has been stolen from others, has it not? From weaker kingdoms forced to pay tribute, from land torn asunder by armies who kill and loot the same as I? Who is to say they are more deserving than you or I? Who is to say their theft is more noble than my own? While the peoples starve, they fill their bellies like gluttons. But here, on Phalus, all share in the bounty, from the lowest sailor to my most trusted lieutenants like Felicia and Rebecca. I offer a good life, Sinbad. One filled with adventure, one that a merchant seaman can only dream of and admire. Share this with me, Captain. I give my pledge you won't be sorry."

Sinbad leaned back, considering what she had said. Much had been true—there were many people forced to suffer because of the greed of their kings. Yet even this wanton behavior did not justify the cruelties of piracy, where innocent men and women lost their lives or were pressed into slavery over the capture of trinkets. Sinbad knew his conscience could never allow him to accept her offer, as generous as it might be. Melissa would have to

216

pay a price for her high piracy, as do all who flout the laws of men and God. Still, her weakness did give him an opening, an opening to save his crew and himself. . . .

"Have you discussed this with your lieutenants?" he asked.

Melissa waved an imperious hand and scoffed. "I am in command of Phalus, not they. I make the laws. They have no choice but to accept what I dictate. Now, what do you say, Captain? I need an answer."

"If I do accept your offer, what happens?"

Melissa smiled coyly. "Then you are a free man, again the skipper of your ship, only this time with two dozen of my best Amazons to serve you."

He frowned. "And what of my own crew? What happens to them?"

"There is no room on Phalus for them; they will still have to be taken off the island."

"I won't permit you to make slaves of them," he warned.

The Scarlet Pirate shrugged. "We can discuss these details at another time. Perhaps they can be taken to some remote place and put ashore, there to await rescue by a passing ship—"

"And what about your other prisoners, Methelese and his daughter?"

Here Melissa's eyes darkened and she looked at him with her familiar icy stare. "With the Athenian I will not bargain. He can be of too much value to me." Then she smiled, reached out and took Sinbad's hand. "Or shall I say to *us?*"

The mariner from Baghdad nodded. "Well enough—if you don't harm him, and if you'll reunite him with Clair. . . ."

Melissa frowned, then relented. "All right. They can share a cell together, it won't matter much either way. If you like, I'll even free them tomorrow for the banquet."

"Are we having a party?"

She laughed. "Something like that. You see, we have

our own customs on Phalus. You may find them peculiar, but—er—my Amazons have need of your crew."

A full smile came to Sinbad's face and he thought of what Methelese had told him. It was amusing, this idea of his men being forced to service the Scarlet Pirate's hungry crew. His men might have a few hungers of their own in that respect. In any case, the crew would have to be temporarily freed while the banquet progressed, and what better time would there be for putting his escape plan into action?

"You win, Melissa," he said, his head lowered and his hand gently turning her chin toward him. And then he kissed her, sweetly and tenderly, unbuttoning his shirt and allowing Don Giovanni to hop to the floor.

Melissa stiffened at his touch and moaned softly. Don Giovanni hopped to a cuddly place upon the bearskin rug and gazed up in wonder at the sight of their raising passions.

Sinbad's kisses became many, covering her eyes, her cheeks, the curve of her long neck, returning after a time to her full and parted lips, tantalizing her, tasting the wine with his tongue as he ran small circles around her mouth. As she responded with kisses of her own, he realized that he was suddenly in need of her as much as she was of him. This wild pirate was more woman than she would ever admit, and her hot blood only intensified his want.

She pressed herself willingly against his hard body and squealed as they slid to the floor. His hands worked the back of her Cathay robe, unfastening the gold pin, slipping the garment over her shoulders and down below her breasts. Melissa trembled with delight; his eyes poured over her shapely form, amazed at the lushness of her breasts, the fullness of her hips, the beauty of her gently swaying body.

"Love me, Sinbad," she whispered throatily as his hands caressed her, slowly working their way down. He lingered over the curves teasingly, content with the sensations they aroused in them both. Then he let his fingertips wander over her thighs, ever creeping toward the fullness of her fiery womanhood. Melissa arched herself closer, ripe for the taking, shivering with passions she had rarely experienced before. And as her legs gently separated he buried his face in her breasts, his mouth burning her hard, dark nipples with frenzied kisses.

Her urgency was too much to bear; she unbuckled his belt and pulled down his pants. Then, contorting her body, she took him to her, easing him inside to the limits of her very being, her very soul, her very existence.

With mutual fires their bodies pitched in intoxicating rhythm, as they groaned in the blissful enjoyment of each other's treasure. "Never leave me, Sinbad," she whispered in the heat of her passion, and with a steadily mounting fever born of lust and need they both became engulfed within their lovemaking. All the world blacked out around them; they knew only the intensity of the urge and its explosive fulfillment.

For long moments their sweaty bodies continued to writhe as they tumbled from the sweet pain of ecstasy, back into the realm of consciousness. Panting for air, they lay still in each other's arms. After a time Melissa opened her eyes and, seeing Sinbad's fixed on her, smiled. Then she rolled to the side, contentedly purring like a cat.

Don Giovanni, staring bug-eyed from his cozy nook in the rug, hopped closer to Sinbad and made himself comfortable while the mariner stroked him gently. Outside, the rain had stopped; Sinbad could hear the soft patter of drops falling from the leaves and splashing onto the portico.

"*Mmmm,*" sighed Melissa with a yawn. "That was good. I must compliment you, Captain. You'll have to show me again."

"The pleasure is mine, I assure you," he replied with a grin.

The Scarlet Pirate nestled herself in the crook of his arm and shut her eyes. "I'm tired; let's go to sleep . . ."

Sinbad kissed her forehead. "Sleep well, my fiery love. I'll wake you at dawn." And as she nodded and dropped off into contented slumber, Sinbad looked to the frog and smiled. "Ah me," he ruminated. "What would Sherry say if she could see me now?"

And then, he, too, fell asleep, but not before his plan for escape was set a little clearer in his mind.

Early evening of the next day saw Felicia march the crew out of their prison, unshackled for the first time but still carefully watched by the eunuchs and Amazons, and brought to the largest hut on the island. Circular, with a thatched roof and multiple exposures to allow the maximum of sunlight and breeze, it usually served Phalus as a meeting hall, a place where Melissa and her followers met to divide their loot and plan for their next voyage. Today, though, was different. It was a night of celebration, a night of revelry, when each pirate could choose from the prisoners and spend long hours beneath the stars seeking gratification.

The hut had been carpeted and lined with pillows. It reeked with incense, a rare variety known only among the monks of India; its fumes heightened the senses and would cause even the most reluctant participant to lavishly partake of the night's offering, although in truth it must be admitted that womanless sailors, be they prisoners or no, usually needed little prompting to enjoy themselves. At least on the first night, for a hundred women living without men had grown insatiable appetites.

Under the watchful eyes of the armed eunuchs, who, needless to say, had scant interest in the coming orgy, Sinbad's dumbfounded men were seated upon the pillows and served exotic wines and foods by scantily dressed serving girls sent to cater their every whim. Then, while a flute played and an African drum beat a slow, pulsating rhythm, a dancing slave, adorned with finger bells and ankle bells, began her seductive ballet. Flesh like ivory, lips lightly painted and eyes of coal, she enticed the sailors with her charms, smiling a secret smile and hinting at the pleasures to come.

Abu, seated near the center and flanked by Milo and Mingo, grew restless. Already most of the men had fallen helplessly into the incense-created atmosphere, eagerly following the dancer's movements and anticipating the arrival of the pirates. With slow gulps they swallowed the spicy tidbits laid before them, drank of the sweet wine, and forgot all about their situation. They needed little provocation to serve the manless women, and indeed many were already grumbling about the delay. Every man was accounted for, Abu saw—every man, that is, except Captain Sinbad, and both Abu and Milo became concerned, wondering if the skillful mariner had purposely been kept from the scene.

The sun set dramatically with brilliant washes of crimson pouring into the banquet hall. At the snap of a finger more wine was being served, more food, more incense lighted in the hanging braziers. It did not take much for Abu and Milo to understand that this night of debauchery, although pleasurable for the moment, bore only ill. For when the pirates were done with their pleasures, the drugged crew of the *Scheherazade* would then be at their mercy, to be bound and gagged, dumped into the hold of the waiting ships, and brought without delay to the slave market.

"I like this not," grumbled Milo, sitting crosslegged and refusing to have his silver goblet refilled.

"Nor I," admitted Abu anxiously. He beat a fist against the tray placed beside him and grimaced. "If only we knew where Sinbad is!"

A calm breeze was blowing when the dancer finished. As she lowered her head and bowed before the guests, the wide door opened and in came the pirates. All eyes gazed in astoundment; these were not the fierce, muscled Amazons they had fought upon the decks of their ship, but delectable young women, without armor or weapons, dressed in flimsy shifts woven of the finest silks, with taunting bodies that swayed as they walked, full bosoms and dark nipples, long legs, and perfect hips and buttocks that turned every eye.

Milo gulped as a particularly charming chestnut-haired beauty stood before him and took him by the hand. She knelt with a laugh, bringing the cup of wine to his lips. "Drink," she whispered in a voice that conjured up images of love. And her luminescent eyes transfixed his own, rendering him helpless to disobey. Then, when the last drop was drained, she leaned him back against the cushions and stroked his brow.

The scene was repeated again and again throughout the hut, the temptresses choosing their men at random and inviting their partners to take what they wanted. It was dark out now, the only light a crescent moon peaking from above the hills. The music continued to play but with a new blandishment that heralded the needs of the flesh.

An exceptionally well-endowed woman came to Mongo and gazed with admiration at his powerful frame. The giant stirred, clearing his throat. Since resistance was futile, he did the only thing he could and let the girl have her way, her wiles beyond his power.

"That one is *mine!*" came a rasping voice that forced him to open his eyes. The beauty took her hand from his crotch and looked up with icy eyes to the darkened figure standing over them.

"He's mine!" the blustery Rebecca barked again. And she glowered at the pirate at her feet.

"But I saw him first!" the golden-haired pirate protested.

Hefty Rebecca was undaunted. Her eyes narrowed, and she closed her hands into fists. "Now what about it, Donna?"

Mongo groaned. Of all the women on Phalus, Rebecca was without doubt the most ugly and abrasive. Feeling like a child, he looked up at her. "Donna's right, you know. She was here first and—"

"Shut up!" snapped Rebecca, seething. "Do you do as you're told—or do I have to get tough?"

Now Donna seemed perfectly able to take care of herself, having been a pirate since the age of thirteen when she murdered her husband with a butcher knife for taking a lover and then ran off to sea to join the Scarlet Pirate. But, as rugged as she was, she was still no match for the strong-willed Rebecca. With a long sigh she stared down to the floor and nodded. "All right. You can have him," then she looked up again, "but I want him back when you're through. A man like this should be shared."

Rebecca cackled with triumph. "You can have him when I'm done," she chuckled. "That is, if he's still able." And with hands on hips she roared with laughter.

Donna scurried from her cushioned spot next to the giant and, realizing that all the men were already accounted for, sadly walked outside to wait with the others until the first group was through.

"That was very unfair," said Mongo as Melissa's lieutenant rested beside him.

Staring at his oversized genitals bulging through his pants, Rebecca smiled. "I told you to be quiet. *I'm* all the woman you're ever going to need. And if you're good, I'll have you kept here with me forever—as a personal slave. Would you like that?"

Mongo lay back at her urging and felt a horrible shudder; never before as boxer or sailor had he faced such a terrible fate.

Abu buried his head between the breasts of his own mate, thankful that if nothing else he had not been placed in poor Mongo's predicament. Then as the pirate took him in hand and guided him to her, even he, this last stalwart of Sinbad's crew, succumbed to the need of the moment. It was going to be a long night. A very long night. All he could do was save as much strength as possible—and hope that with the morning he'd be able to explain to Sinbad his own rash actions. Meanwhile the hut became quiet, save for the rustlings of thrusting bodies and occasional gasps and groans.

And more than eighty more pirates stood outside with eager anticipation as they waited their turns.

"You're free to leave the cell," a smiling Sinbad said to the perplexed Athenian.

Old Methelese put down the worn volume he had been reading by candlelight and got up from his stool. Sinbad stood before him beaming, the keys to their prison jingling in his hand.

"But how? What?—"

Sinbad laughed. "No time for all your questions now. Let's just say that I came to—er—something of an agreement with our friend Melissa, and she's agreed to let you out, for now at least." He pointed to the open door, beyond which the panther sat more tamely than usual, feeding on a meaty bone that Sinbad had cleverly given him.

"Oh, by the way," Sinbad went on as the confused Methelese started to leave, "your daughter is waiting for you."

Happiness swelled in the old man's tired face. "*Clair!*" he cried. "Clair! It's too good to be true!"

"That was part of our bargain. I haven't seen her yet myself, but Melissa's promised that your little girl is safe and sound. Go to her now."

Methelese nodded happily. There were two armed guards at the door, Felicia and another Amazon. Methelese began to follow the Amazon out, shading his eyes from the bright torchlight, but then he turned back to Sinbad. "And what about that—er—other matter we spoke about?"

Sinbad winked, carefully making sure Felicia didn't see. "I'm the Scarlet Pirate's partner now," he told him. "I don't have time for such silly games. But if I have the chance, I'll come and see you before dawn. . . ."

"*Melissa's partner?*" Methelese was both shocked and outraged. But then, as comprehension dawned, he smiled. "Very well, Captain. I'm at your mercy." And he left.

Sinbad heaved a long sigh and sat down at the edge of his mat, relieved that the first part of his plan had gone so well. Felicia looked at him uneasily. "Get up," she snapped. "Your business down here is finished."

Sinbad returned the stare and laughed. "I'm your superior now, remember? You can't give me orders."

Felicia's eyes fixed upon the mariner. "Melissa is a fool," she rattled. "She thinks she can trust you, she thinks that you meant what you told her."

"And you know better?" His smile was sly.

"Yes! You're a dog, Captain! A scoundrel and a cunning devil. Melissa is getting older. She's lost her purpose, her will to maintain the spirit of Phalus we all swore to uphold."

Sinbad nodded, studying the girl carefully. "Dangerous words, Felicia. If I reported you to Melissa she'd—"

"*Ha!* That's a laugh. You'll never report me." She came closer, so close that Sinbad could feel her hot breath upon his face. "*Just try it!* I'll expose you from here to kingdom come! I'll twist your words around and make every woman on the island see your clever tricks."

"*Tsk! Tsk!* I doubt Melissa would take your word over mine. . . ."

Felicia straightened her shoulders and smiled, her hair falling before her eyes. "Then we won't need her," she answered simply.

Sinbad scratched at his chin. "I see. Maybe Phalus needs a new leader. Another woman to bring back her old days of glory?"

"Maybe so, Captain."

"And maybe that new leader should be . . . you?"

Here a gleam came to Felicia's eyes. "And why not? I'm capable. Already half the girls have secretly sworn allegience to me. I can take over this place any time I choose—and I don't need the strength of a man's arm to give me comfort!"

225

Unperturbed, Sinbad made himself more comfortable. "Every woman needs a man," he said evenly, tapping his fingertips lightly against each other. "Even *you*. . . ."

Felicia sneered. "Then why am I here now? I could be at the banquet, taking my choice of any of you men. *Men!* What a laugh! Sometimes I prefer the company of eunuchs! At least they won't lie to you, make false promises. . . ."

Sinbad had hit home, he discovered, unlocking what he was sure was this fiery young woman's secret. "What made you become a pirate?" he asked at last.

"What business is it of yours?"

"I'm still your superior," he reprimanded. "Don't forget that. You haven't taken over Phalus yet. Now I ask you again. . . ."

Felicia shrugged; she turned her face and avoided his eyes. "I was once like the others," she admitted in a whisper. "Oh, yes! Foolish and gullible. Believing when I was told I was loved. But I learned the hard way. It cost me much in pride and self-esteem—but, oh, how I learned!"

"What happened?"

There were hints of tears in her eyes, Sinbad saw to his surprise, and the girl turned to him again, not trying to hide them. "I was betrothed at the age of fifteen to a man the envy of every girl in my land. Rich, handsome, strong. . . . He vowed his love was eternal, that we'd spend our lives together in love, without shame or fear, that our happiness was unequaled. But then one day I found out the lies in his viper's words. While away in Damascus he met another, and when his caravan returned home he brought with him a wife. A woman already with child—*his child!* I could not believe my eyes; my world was spinning, I wanted to die, and I almost did by my own hand. But then"—she wiped her eyes and sniffed—"I decided that I would live. I was blameless in this episode. The victim. While he and his new lover lived like a sultan and sultana in his palace."

Sinbad sat back disquieted. "So what did you do?"

A cunning smile crossed Felicia's parted lips. "I took my revenge. One night, very late, I stole over the wall and found my former betrothed sitting alone in his garden, musing and comtemplating his happy life. He was startled to see me, but not displeased. He told me that he still did love me, in his way, and would certainly be pleased if I were to become his concubine. I let him believe in my interest. Then, as his hands slipped my garments off, I lay beside him beneath the trees and allowed him to make love to me again, all the while pretending to enjoy his filthy pleasure. At the moment of his heightened release, when his shoulders shook and he moaned with ecstasy, I drew my hidden knife and I—"

"You killed him?"

Felicia laughed coldly. "No, good Captain. Death would be far too good for the likes of him. No, I did something that he would never forget, something that would insure he'd never dethrone another innocent virgin again. With a single slash of my blade I made him less than a man forever! Now do you understand?"

Sinbad shuddered as he nodded, shocked at what she had done, yet understanding the painful circumstances that led her to it.

"While he cried and bled I ran away," she continued. "Far from my home until I came to the sea. It was then that I met Melissa and joined with her band of women, happy to be away from the world of men for all time. And I've never had another man touch me since."

Sinbad stood and faced Felicia squarely. Don Giovanni hopped from his shoulder and looked on what happened next with growing interest.

"That was all a very long time ago," the mariner from Baghdad told the girl. "For your own sake you should forget—and live your life once more. Not here on Phalus, as a pirate. But out in the world, as a woman . . ."

Felicia shook her head, locks tumbling. "No, never. . . . I don't need men. I don't—"

227

She trembled visibly as he took the small torch out of her hand and threw it to the floor. "What . . . what are you *doing?*" she gasped. She made to draw her knife, but Sinbad reached out quickly and held her hand. Then, to her total amazement, he pulled her to him, crushing her in his arms.

Felicia squirmed and wriggled and tried to break free. "No, *don't!*" she cried when he kissed her. "Let me go or I'll do the same to you! Let me go or I'll . . ." Like butter her hate suddenly melted, as his mouth caused fires to ripple through her quivering body. And she ceased her protest, returning the kiss, enfolding her own arms around him, clutching wildly in an empassioned embrace.

Don Giovanni, by now used to his captain's amorous behavior, hardly gave a second glance when the couple dropped upon the hard mat entwined as though they were one.

The most frigid pirate of Melissa's crew took her hated adversary with urgency, panting and scratching as long subdued sensations rushed to the surface like a tidal wave. She bit and screamed and pulled him harder against her, hating him and loving him at the same moment.

Her climax was a vortex of emotion which drove her dizzily higher and finally exploded, every fiber in her body contracting with crazed and uncontrolled fury. And in this vortex she spun until the last vestiges of pleasure and excitement had faded.

Catching her breath, she said, "You shouldn't have done that, Captain. I told you I'm not like Melissa; you'll not turn my head with your charms. . . ."

"Nor would I wish to," Sinbad replied, thoroughly exhausted. His eyes wandered and focused on the panther chained beyond the iron gate. The woman who lay in his arms was every bit as untamed. Felicia yawned; he kissed her mouth tenderly. "You mustn't tell anyone about this," she cautioned. "Especially Melissa."

"Believe me, I won't," he answered with a relaxed grin. He kissed her again, then stroked her hair and the sides of her face. Felicia purred in his embrace. Slowly, her lids closed over her luminous eyes and she fell into a contented slumber. Sinbad watched her and for a fleeting moment wished he were not forever bound to his beloved Sherry. He sighed, then signalled to the watching frog. "Come on, Giovanni!" he said. The frog obeyed immediately, and when Sinbad was assured Felicia was soundly asleep, he stood up and tiptoed out the open door, locking it behind. "Rest well, Felicia," he muttered to himself. "I'm sorry to have to leave you like this but I don't have any choice. Trust that I'll come back for you as fast as I can."

In the shadows Felicia stirred and rolled over.

Losing no time, Sinbad passed a waiting sentry, returned her salute, and sent her on a fool's errand halfway across the island. Then, slipping through shadows with Felicia's knife in his hand, he made his way to where Methelese was now being kept with his daughter. He unlocked the door of the spare cabin and woke the aging Athenian from his slumber.

Methelese stared with sleepy eyes.

"Shh," said Sinbad, a finger to his lips. A second cot lay across the room with a sleeping figure tucked beneath the blanket. Sinbad glanced at Clair, unable to see more than a silhouette, and turned back to the startled philosopher. "Don't make any noise, just listen. Wake your daughter five minutes after I leave. Then wait for me to come back. I want you to lead us all down through the tunnel you told me about—"

"When? Tonight?"

Sinbad nodded. "As soon as we can."

"But what about the banquet?" He looked from the barred window to the meeting hall where the revelry continued as before.

"Let me handle that. By now most of the Amazons are off in their drugged slumber. I'm going to create a diversion, rouse my men, and slip right through their lines to the *Scheherazade*."

"And what of Melissa?"

Sinbad smiled. "It's all under control; she's waiting for me at her villa. By the time she gets restless and comes to have a look it will all be too late. Now, are you with me?"

Methelese lifted himself and nodded dumbly. The risks were great, he knew, but there might never be another opportunity like this.

Silently Sinbad took his leave and crossed between the palms to the broad grassy knoll in front of the banquet hall. There he was greeted by a few pirates drunk on wine and dizzied by the potent incense.

"Spend some time with *me!*" one pouted, trying to lift herself as he passed. "Don't let Melissa have it *all*," grumbled another.

Sinbad laughed. "You'd better not let your commander hear you say that," he chided.

"We'd rather have *you* to lead us," said a third girl, frowning. "Melissa has *all* the fun."

"There are plenty of good men inside," he assured those awake. "Get some rest and take your turns again." And he left them to wearily lay their heads back on the grass. A burly eunuch, hands on hips and a scowl on his face, stopped him at the entrance.

"What are you doing here?" he growled.

"Stand aside," said Sinbad impatiently. "I'm second in command on Phalus now—or hadn't you been told?"

The eunuch grimaced. "Aye, I know that. But Captain Melissa gave orders for no one else to enter. Including you."

Sinbad replied boldly. "Don't be silly, man. I'm here on business—official business. Melissa herself ordered me to find Rebecca and speak to her."

The eunuch seemed dubious; he glanced over toward the shady villa where the lamps still burned brightly in the window. "Perhaps I should speak with the captain first myself. . . ."

Sinbad nodded. "Certainly. Go ahead. I'll wait here. But make it quick, I've a lot to do." Then, as the eunuch grunted and turned toward the path, Sinbad delivered one of his Chinese chops to a strategic spot at the back of the brute's head. The oaf staggered momentarily and silently crumpled to the ground. He would be unconscious, Sinbad knew, for the better part of an hour.

He dragged the hefty body beneath the shade of a thick palm and then cautiously opened the door to the hall. Once inside, his eyes burned with the sting of the powerful incense permeating the air. Everything was quiet, the orgy having worn itself down, and the only sounds to be heard were the snoring of some of his men and the occasional moans from sleeping pirates.

"Allah's mercy," Sinbad murmured to himself, fighting his way between and over the bodies of his men, who lay scattered across the room, each with two or more Amazons resting beside him. "What's been going on here?" It would have been an amusing sight to behold, were not this matter so serious.

"*Milo!*" Sinbad called in a loud whisper, frantically seeking out his trusted aide. "Milo, where are you, man?"

Groggily, from halfway across the darkened chamber, the crusty old salt managed to raise his head from between the melonlike breasts of a finely proportioned naked pirate. He squinted his eyes at the approaching silhouette and stared in disbelief. "Sinbad? Captain Sinbad, is that really you?"

The mariner from Baghdad slipped over to his friend and cautioned him not to stir. "What's happened here?" he whispered.

Milo's tongue drooped from his mouth; his fatigued features sagged like an old hound dog's. "Allah be praised, am I glad to see you," he wheezed, rolling his eyes. Then he anxiously tugged at Sinbad's collar. "You . . . you have no idea, no idea what tonight's been like for us." He put his hands to his face and moaned softly. "By the holy beard of the Prophet, these women never have enough! I ache as I never thought possible for a man to ache. Why, just by myself I was forced to service three of the fieriest hellcats on the face of the earth!" And as he spoke, one of the girls rolled over in her slumber, eyes closed and smiling. "Milo," she croaked, *"Milooooo. . . .* come back . . . do it again. . . ." And she sighed pleasurably.

The old sailor pulled a face. "See what I mean?"

Sinbad shuddered. "How about the others?"

Milo looked over his shoulder to where a snoring Mongo lay in the arms of snoring Rebecca. "Poor Mongo," he wheezed. "You should have *seen* the things that woman made him do! In all my days I've never even dreamed there were so many different ways—" Then he looked over the other shoulder toward Abu. The first mate lay entangled amid a mass of limbs and torsos, virtually buried under the pile. "And pity Abu," he went on. "They made him take care of five of them—single-handedly! Surely I could never have accomplished that at half my current age."

Sinbad frowned. "Well, never mind about that now." His eyes darted to and fro and, certain that none of the women had stirred or woken, he said to Milo in a low voice, "We're getting off Phalus. Tonight. Within the hour, if possible. Everyone has to be quietly roused."

Milo seemed incredulous. "But how, Sinbad? We can't even move after what we've been through! We're dying, Captain, *dying!"*

"You really will be if you don't get cracking," Sinbad snapped. "I've heard that these banquets often last for a week—imagine how you're going to feel after six more nights of this."

Milo's shoulders trembled with the very thought. "All right," he agreed at last. "What do I have to do?"

232

"We haven't any time to waste. As quickly and quietly as you can, wake the others and tell them wait for my signal. Be sure Abu and Mongo get their pants back on in a hurry—I'll need the three of you to guide the others. . . ."

Milo gulped. "Are you sure your plan is sound? What are you going to do now?"

Sinbad chuckled. "Me? I'm going to end this little bash with a flurry like Phalus has never seen. Now just do as I've said. You have about fifteen minutes to be ready for it. And when I tell you to run, you *run*. Is that understood?"

"Aye, aye, Captain." He saluted feebly and started to put his pants back on, ever-mindful not to disturb the women on either side.

Leaving the perplexed sailor, Sinbad dashed back outside into the starry night, smiling as he took a quick glance back and saw Milo rousing the dazed crew one by one.

He hid behind a row of bushes at first sight of two sentries patrolling the silent walkway to the dock. Angered at their ill-luck in being chosen by lot not to partake in tonight's festivities, the Amazons seemed angry indeed. With hands firmly clutching at the hilts of their strapped daggers, they looked scornfully over at the banquet hall, sneering and exchanging a few bitter jokes about their fellow Amazons.

Sinbad let them pass by, and when a low cloud covered the moon, he crossed among the shadows in the direction of the storage sheds set along the perimeter of the village compound. Once assured that he hadn't been seen, he took out Don Giovanni from inside his shirt and placed the frog beside him on the ground. Then, kneeling, he took out his flints and the oil-soaked cloths he had hidden away.

"It's now or never," he mumbled to the frog. "Keep a lookout while I begin."

Don Giovanni nodded grimly and hopped away, finding a quiet place in the deep grass and scaring away a handful of dancing fireflies. There he waited in position, ever combing the environs for other sentries.

It did not take very long for billows of thick smoke and then the first flames to emerge through the thatched roof.

One sentry nudged the other; they both looked on in wonder. Then, "Fire! Fire! The supply huts are burning!"

Bells began to clang from the tiny lookout tower at the wharf, pirate girls scampered to their feet, doing their best to collect their wits while mayhem reigned all around.

The fields behind the sheds broke into a glorious blaze; from every side new fires were fanning out, fueled by the strong breeze coming in from the water.

In a frenzy, Melissa bounded from her villa to take command of her Amazons. Likewise, Sinbad suddenly appeared. "Over there!" he cried, sending a squad of half-naked women to the most distant flames. "And there, too!" he shouted, commanding others to run the other way. Struggling with water buckets, the drugged girls, sore and hurting, ran mindlessly to douse the fires, while Sinbad made his way to the banquet hall itself.

"Let's go!" he yelled. And with whoops and hollers, his own recently aroused men came flying out the door, charging toward the distant grotto and the nearby cabin where Methelese and his daughter waited to guide them safely away.

"*Stop them!*" screeched Melissa at the top of her lungs.

Men were racing everywhere, knocking over pirates, trampling any and all who got in the way. Before any weapons could be drawn, Mongo crashed the heads of the sentries together and hurled them to the ground. Sinbad and Abu scooped up their knives.

The clang of combat filled the air as the eunuchs tried to halt the advance. Sinbad fought off the first, leaving the second for an enraged Mongo to deal with. The brute backed off in fear of the enraged giant eager to pay him back for indignities suffered. And the fellow howled for mercy when Mongo squeezed him in his arms, in a gruesome bear hug, and cracked every single rib in his body.

"Sinbad, this way!" called out Methelese, waving frantically.

Most of the men had almost reached the grotto. Sinbad could see Melissa and a small band of Amazons come tearing over the blazing knoll after them, but there was no time to fend them off. Not if the treasure rooms were to be ransacked and the ship to be safely reached in time.

"Lead on, Athenian!" And the mariner from Baghdad stood at the grotto entrance, letting his men pour through first, running two and three at a time down the dark steps. Then he threw a torch into the grass before him, purposely lighting another blaze to slow down the advance of the furious Melissa.

Sinbad leaped down to the bottom landing. "Where's the tunnel?" he panted to the waiting Methelese who had stopped at the end of the corridor.

"Straight ahead," the Athenian replied with much pleasure.

"And the treasure rooms?"

"By the cat. . . ."

Sinbad frowned. He had almost forgotten about the chained panther. "All right, then," he said, gathering his still-dazed men. "You and you," he picked them at random, "sack the room to the left. You and you, take the one at the right. Steal everything you can carry. The rest of you follow Methelese, he'll lead you to the dock. Retake our ship as fast as you can—but don't kill anyone unless you have to."

With eager nods at the thought of revenge, Sinbad's men set to the task without any questions.

"But what about you?" asked a concerned Methelese.

Sinbad placed a gentle hand on the old Athenian's shoulder. "I'll be fine," he assured him. "My—er—business will only take a minute or two and then I'll be right along. But right now there's a promise I have to keep."

Then off everyone ran, following the lead of Methelese,

who held a torch and led the band down and away, ever lower into the shaft that would take them to freedom. Knowing exactly what to do, those still with Sinbad, Abu among them, slipped by the hissing panther and broke into the treasure rooms, gasping with astonishment at the incredible wealth. The chambers were thick with captured booty—fine statues of ivory and gold; golden headdresses, inlaid with cornelian and cut glass, studded with emeralds and rubies; bracelets, necklaces, rare diadems from Ceylon, stolen from savage and cunning tribes; tusks from Africa; white-golden images of Oriental gods and goddesses from the temples at the Forbidden City. It was so much; it dazzled and dazed the eye as Abu's slim torch lighted the dank chamber.

The sailors looked at the prizes and each other in total wonder.

"Find some sacks," said Sinbad, his breath swept away. "Load up as much as you can, and wait for me."

They knew precisely what had to be done. And while his men buoyantly chose from among the plethora of stolen wealth, Sinbad fumbled with the keys and deftly opened the lock of his former cell. A wild and frantic Felicia greeted him, slashing at his face with her long nails.

Sinbad fought her off, shifting when she tried to kick him in the groin with the toe of her boot, fending off her small pounding fists striking his chest.

"You *swine!*" she flared. "You son of a whore!" She flailed her arms and wailed; Sinbad tripped her and wrestled her to the ground. "Don't come near me! I'll tear out your—"

"Calm down!" said the mariner, pinning her shoulders.

She spit in his face and he winced. "*Scum!* Camel dung!" Sinbad reddened. "Baghdad trash from the sewer!" And her throaty rasps showed no sign of ceasing.

Sinbad sighed. "I'm sorry to do this," he told her, drawing back his fist, "but you're not giving me much choice. . . ." He hit her squarely in the jaw, knocking her out. Felicia groaned and slumped in his arms.

The clamor of approaching Melissa and her cohorts could plainly be heard as they raced down the stone steps into the corridor.

"*Damn!*" Sinbad gritted his teeth, picked up the unconscious girl, and threw her over his shoulder. Then he ran from the cell, clinging close to the wall to keep away from the clawing panther, and shouted to his lingering men. "Move it, move it!" he urged. "They're almost here!"

All smiles, Abu and the others came rushing out with cloth sacks weighted with gold.

"We're still leaving a fortune behind," said Abu despairingly. "There's enough wealth in there to make every one of us a king!" He pointed behind with his thumb, adding, "we never even had a chance to look in the other chamber. . . ."

Sinbad shook his head ruefully. "A pity, I know, but there's nothing to be done. Now let's keep moving."

Abu held high the torch and together they made all haste to follow where Methelese had taken the others. From behind, Sinbad could hear the loud shrieks of the Scarlet Pirate herself as she came upon her ransacked treasure room and realized that so many of her precious prizes had been stolen—treasures it had taken her years to collect.

"*Catch those devils!*" she bellowed, foaming at the mouth with rage.

And then came the rattling of a chain, the snapping of springs. Sinbad paused and listened with growing trepidation—the panther had been unleashed!

Like lizards fleeing to safe cracks in the wall, the men of the *Scheherazade* hastened through the rabbit warren of dark, secret passages. From behind them came the cat, muted pads dashing on stone, leaping and bounding in pursuit of the intruders.

Felicia began to come out of her daze. Groaning, she opened her eyes. As awareness crept into consciousness she screamed, clawing and biting at her abductor. Sinbad swung her down onto the ground, constrained her and shouted for Abu.

"Take her," he ordered his first mate. "Get her safely aboard the ship. I'll hold our rear."

"But, Capt'n! One man alone against—"

Sinbad gnashed his teeth. "This is no time for arguments! Just do as I say!"

Picking up Felicia and throwing her over his aching shoulder, Abu scampered away down the narrowing tunnel, searching for the ray of light at the end of the shaft. Once he was gone, Sinbad clung like glue to the dark wall; he drew his knife and panted tensely, waiting for the panther.

Eyes aglow in the black of the grotto, the thick-furred female came charging. Its keen senses picked up Sinbad's closeness at once. Then, catching a fleeting glimpse of his silhouette covered in shadows, it hunched back and hissed, then struck out like a rattlesnake.

Sinbad swung around to the center of the tunnel, dodging the wild slashes of its paws. Up went his knife hand. It cut through the soft flesh of the panther's underbelly, weaving toward its heart. The wounded animal roared in pain and brought its full weight to bear against its foe. Sinbad tottered and tumbled back, slamming hard against the jagged wall.

Huge fangs tore for his throat; Sinbad wrenched the cat by the throat and began to squeeze. Into a pool of blood they slipped together, the screaming panther flailing wildly, cavorting on top of its enemy. With all his effort, Sinbad ignored the sting of slashes across his chest, drew the knife from the cat's belly, and plunged again—this time straight into its heart. The panther writhed, coiled its tail, hissed again. But life was draining. Slowly it shut its eyes and collapsed, spasmodically jerking.

Sinbad slipped out from under. Wincing with pain, he looked at the dark blood over his hands and shuddered. The cat had slashed him deeply near his right shoulder, where now crimson stains spread slowly over his shirt. He staggered to his feet, nauseous, wanting to faint, but that was a luxury he could afford. Not yet. Not while escape was so close.

Mindlessly he continued to run. The footsteps of Melissa and her Amazons were still too close behind for comfort. His feet found strength where there was none, carrying him forward, stumbling and tripping, searching for the exit.

How long he had been running he didn't know; it felt like hours. But suddenly his name was being called. From ahead he could see the tiny figures of his men, Abu, Milo, a jumping frog bouncing off Methelese's shoulder. Beyond them a circle of bright daylight blinded his eyes.

Mongo and Abu were helping him to run. Events all around were dizzying. There were two ships berthed at the dock, Melissa's swift craft and the *Scheherazade* moored directly behind it. His own men had begun to clamor aboard the *Sherry;* he could see the few sentries being heaved over the side into the sea. Gangplanks were lowered, as Milo directed defenses against a barrage of whistling arrows which sailed from a large group of pirates who had gathered at the village.

"Set fire to the dock," Sinbad said to Abu. "They mustn't have a chance to follow. . . ."

Abu lost no time obeying. Torches were hurled from one end to the other, and blazing flames instantly ignited the aging planks. Balls of fire spread in every direction. As Sinbad made it to the deck of his ship, he could see Melissa and her Amazons stopped in their chase at the opening of the tunnel, unable to take a single step farther without running into the fire.

Melissa's eyes found Sinbad and she shook her fists. "You haven't seen the last of me yet!" she vowed with all the venom of a woman scorned. "Beware, Captain Sinbad! *Beware!*"

Sinbad, still in pain, refused assistance and turned to his crew. "Hoist the anchor!" he called. "Unfurl sails!"

And the men, weary as they were from the previous night's escapades, looked to the new day's growing brightness and scampered to carry out the orders.

Sinbad stood at the rail, his white knuckles clenched. The mainsail swelled with the wind, sprays of salt water flaying over the deck, as the *Scheherazade* tipped slightly to starboard and began its careful escape between the shoals.

Black smoke was rising above the tiny isle of Phalus; he could still see the fires raging out of control in the village and on the wharf, where a few Amazons aboard their own ship desperately made all effort to lift anchor and pull away before the fire engulfed it as well. But it was too late, Sinbad saw. Already popping fires were breaking out along the hull and bulwark. It would take weeks to repair the damage.

"You taught them a lesson or two they won't quickly forget," chuckled Milo, drawing close to his captain's side. "Phalus shall never be the same." He looked at the burning ship and glowered. "Serves them right if they can't leave the island for a year. That'll teach the Scarlet Pirate a few things about us."

Sinbad nodded, glad the ordeal was over. "What about Methelese and his small daughter? Are they safely aboard?"

There was a twinkle in Milo's eyes as he said they were.

"And Felicia? You have her as well?"

Milo laughed heartily. "Bound and gagged below—kicking like a wildcat, but safe and sound as you instructed."

"Good, good. Then we can get on with our business. We're too far behind schedule as it is."

Sinbad gritted his teeth and subdued the rising pain. A worried Milo took a closer look at his wounds and gasped.

"Captain, you'd better get below, have Methelese look at that—"

"I'll be all right," the mariner replied.

"But Sinbad, you need someone to tend those cuts!"

Sinbad smiled. "Soon. Just as soon as we're away from

Phalus. Just as soon as I know we're . . ." He looked at Milo with a strange stare, rolled his eyes, and felt the blood drain from his face. And then he passed out.

In the dream he could see Sherry, her gentle features marred by tears as she sat in the garden of the caliph's palace and pulled petals off a wilting flower. Sinbad was there beside her, but she couldn't see him. He reached out, touched her cheek, kissed her lips. Still she couldn't see him. To her he was less than a ghost, merely the faintest wind, and she shivered, pulling her shawl more tightly about her as he pulled away in frustration.

Can't you see me, dearest? he wept. *Can't you tell I'm here? Back home, together with you where I belong, never to leave your side again.*

But Scheherazade did not hear. With eyes swollen from crying and features hollow from grief, she lifted her gaze and stared right through him to the distant setting sun. "Come back to me, Sinbad," he heard her whisper. "Come back to me. . . ."

"But I'm here now! Look at me! I'm here!" He took her hand and sobbed with the realization that she couldn't feel his touch.

"I love you, Sinbad," she said to the wind. "But I don't know how much longer I can live in waiting. Please, hear me, wherever you are; and come back, come back as swiftly as you can before I die of a broken heart."

And then she put her hands to her face and sobbed, leaving him cold, miserable, and alone. Sinbad shuddered as the pieces of his nightmare began to shatter. Soon he was alone in a void, a world with no color, where the cold only grew worse.

He opened his eyes slowly, then quickly shut them against the streams of sunlight pouring in through the porthole of his cabin. A hand was reaching out across his forehead, soothing his brow gently, while a soft voice whispered for him to go back to sleep.

Dreamily, Sinbad forced his eyes open slowly, this time letting his pupils adjust to the sun. He was on his own bed, he realized, carefully bandaged, wrapped in blankets. His injured shoulder throbbed terribly, and he remembered everything that had happened. But he did not remember the girl who sat in a chair beside him, her hand touching his face.

She was a pretty young thing, braided golden hair falling over her breasts, brown low lashes half hiding the palest of blue eyes. A petite nose, slight chin. Ruddy cheeks and the hint of laughter in her smile.

"You fever's gone," she said simply, leaning back now in her chair. "You were very lucky; those cuts could have been much deeper. In which case—"

"In which case I'd probably be lying dead in that tunnel on Phalus."

His mysterious companion grinned. "Quite so. You must be charmed, Captain Sinbad, with nine lives like a cat."

Sinbad groaned. "Please, don't ever speak to me of cats again. I hope I never see another as long as I live."

There was warmth in her dancing eyes as she laughed.

He tried to raise himself on an elbow and grimaced as pains shot through him like thunderbolts.

"You mustn't move," cautioned the girl, growing stern. "At least not today. Not until you've had some hot food to give you strength." Then she stood up, walked to the door, and called for the crewman waiting outside the cabin. "Fetch some broth," she commanded. "Bread, butter, perhaps a little wine to wash it down."

Sinbad looked on with curiosity as his crewman hardly glanced over at him, seeming more than content to take orders from her.

She came back to the chair, sat down, and patted his hand. "Don't worry about a thing," she told him. "Everything's well in order. Abu's doing a fine job until you're well enough to resume command. And we should reach

Crete in a day or two. There we'll load up with new supplies and—"

"And set our course for the Pillars of Hercules?"

She nodded her head happily. "Just as you wanted. As I said, you don't have to worry about a thing."

Sinbad scratched his head. "You seem to know quite a bit about me and this voyage . . ."

"Oh, I do, Captain. I do! I know *everything!*"

The glint of mischief in her smile was not missed. "And—er—may I ask who *you* are?"

The girl looked at him oddly. "You don't know?"

He shrugged.

"But my father assured me that you were told all about me. He—"

"Your father?"

"Methelese."

Sinbad's eyes grew big as chestnuts. "You? You're *Clair?*" She laughed grandly. "I am," she replied with a polite nod.

Is it possible? thought Sinbad, wondering if he might still be delerious after all. "But your father told me you were just a child."

"Then you must be pleasantly surprised . . ."

Sinbad scratched his beard. "Umm. I am. But—er—not displeased."

Clair blushed at his admiring eyes, pleased to be so well thought of in the mind of the world's most famous mariner.

"My father likes to think of me that way," she sighed, lips slightly turned down in a girlish pout. "But as you can see"—here she laughed again—"he didn't quite tell you the whole story. . . ."

And he shared her mirth, happy that he found himself being tended by her and not by her capable but stodgy father.

He wanted to continue the conversation, find out more about her and the strange work on Rhodes that Methelese had begun, but before he had the chance, in came the sailor carrying his food. Clair tasted the soup, smacked her lips in approval, and told the man to go. Then, propping Sinbad up on his pillows, she spoon-fed him until he'd eaten everything.

"Now you should get some more rest," she advised, and a spinning head assured him she was right. He lay back as she took away the bowl and left him alone, promising to be back with supper.

"A fair wind all the way," chortled Abu when Sinbad came to the helm for the first time.

Feeling the spray and the breeze, Sinbad nodded. It was good to be up and around again, good to feel the deck beneath his feet and to watch the rolling swells. Clair had been a good nurse, but even her company had been no replacement for the sea, the best cure any sailor could possibly have.

Abu pointed to a dim jut of land on the starboard horizon. "That's Crete," he said with a note of triumph. "With luck we should berth at Chandrax about dawn tomorrow." He looked at Sinbad and winked. "Maybe even give the crew a bit of shore leave. After all, they've not had any since leaving Jaffa."

Sinbad readily agreed. His men, despite all the adversity, had done a good job, and he was very proud of them. They were well deserving of double their promised share of the profits once this long voyage was done.

"Is the cargo ready to be unloaded?"

"Aye, aye, Capt'n. Safe and sound. It was fortunate for us that Melissa saw fit to leave it in our holds when she commandeered the ship."

Sinbad flinched at the reminder of his experiences on Phalus. "And what about our extra passenger?" he asked.

Crafty Abu twirled at his moustache and chuckled. "She's given us some trouble, but she's well enough. If you ask me, it was foolish to bring her with us. She'll only try and run back to her beloved pirates."

"Where is she now?"

"We had to keep her locked in the forward hold. She's a hellcat, that one." And he shuddered in mock fear.

Sinbad laughed knowingly. He made a quick inspection of the ship, reminding himself to get busy on his charts before they reached Crete. Their little escapade had cost them much time and he was eager to make up for the delay. Still, even that could wait for a little while. Having seen that everything was in order, he went back down below.

Felicia, sitting with her arms wrapped around her knees and staring out the small porthole, hardly turned her head as Sinbad unlocked her cabin door and stepped inside.

"What do you want?" she asked with a sneer. Her elfin features were scuffed with dirt and her tunic ripped and tattered, testifying to her struggles with crewmen whenever one of them brought her food or tried to speak to her.

"I came to see how you are," Sinbad replied coolly.

She glared at him. "Go to Hades." Then she turned again to the porthole. She gazed at the sky for a long while, finally saying, "May I ask what you intend to do with me?"

"I haven't given it very much thought," Sinbad admitted truthfully. "But I wanted to get you off that island of yours, take you somewhere where you could begin a new life."

Her voice was thick with bitterness. "To sell me as a slave?"

"No, Felicia. Maybe to find you a home . . ."

"I don't need your help. Put me ashore anywhere. I can find my own way in the world. I don't need you or anybody."

Sinbad sighed. "That may be so, but I'm afraid you'll have to put up with me until this voyage is over."

This time she turned fully around and stared at him intently. "What do you mean?"

"Just what I've said: You're here to stay aboard the *Scheherazade* until this voyage is finished. And let me assure you, it's barely begun. So, until then, you can either sit and sulk alone in your jail, or . . ."

"Or what?" she asked.

"Or become a member of my crew."

Felicia, stunned as she was, made no effort to reply. She sat for a time studying him, wondering if he were really mad enough to give her the chance at freedom.

"It's an honest offer," Sinbad told her.

The young pirate smiled. "You must be joking. I think I'd rather be dead."

Sinbad came closer and stood over her, his arm leaning against the porthole. "That option is available also. Hang yourself, if you like—but it would be a waste for us both. I know you to be a good sailor, Felicia. You can give orders and you can take them. Aboard Melissa's ship you made an excellent lieutenant. My ship needs a second mate, and the job can be yours—that is, if you're interested in some honest adventure this time. You have my word on a full share of the profits."

Leaning backward against an empty barrel, Felicia snickered. "What makes you sure you can trust me? I might jump ship. I might accept your offer now and then kill you during the night. I have ways, you know. And I wouldn't be afraid."

"I know you wouldn't," replied Sinbad with a distasteful frown. There were two sides of Felicia, he knew. One the jilted lover, still looking for revenge upon a world of men that had cheated her; the other a smart, young woman, sensitive and loving on the inside despite a façade of thorns. Sinbad wouldn't give a copper coin for the first; he was counting only on the second.

"I still want you," he said at length. "What about it? Maybe you should languish here a while longer, think it over. . . ."

She sat up straighter, large eyes weary. "Melissa will come after you, you know. And you can count on it. When she finds you, you'll be sorry you lived *this* long. She'll make you squirm, Captain Sinbad. All of you. She'll let you die slowly, bit by bit . . ."

Her words did not frighten Sinbad. "I'll take my chances," he answered with a small smile. "Of course, Melissa won't be too pleased with you either. Not when she learns of your clever little scheme to depose her on Phalus."

Felicia stared, eyes burning. "You wouldn't tell her!"

The mariner grinned. "No? Try me. You see, my little lamb, your fate is unalterably bound with mine and my ship's."

"*You can rot!*" she flared.

Sinbad jingled the keys in front of her face. "All right. And you can stay here. Remember, this is a long voyage and your quarters will feel pretty cramped in a month or two. Let me know if you change your mind." Then he left her alone, shutting the door and locking it.

Felicia picked up her water mug and hurled it against the door. By Allah, she vowed, she wouldn't suffer any more of his indignities! By Allah, he'd pay one day! But then, as she looked at the walls around her, she began to tremble. Months, Sinbad had said. *Months* to be spent here as a prisoner.

With tears in her eyes she bolted to the door and banged on it as hard as she could. "Let me out! Do you hear, Sinbad? Let me out!"

Outside in the corridor Sinbad listened.

"I've changed my mind!" she shouted, her fingernails scratching at the pine. "Let me out . . . *please!*"

"Then I can trust you?"

"My word on it, Captain! Only, please, let me feel the wind, the deck under my feet . . ."

Under his breath, Sinbad chuckled. Oh, Abu, Milo, and the others would certainly call him a fool for freeing such a hellcat merely on her word. Yet Sinbad believed it was the right decision, that Felicia would more than prove her worth as an officer at a time when the *Scheherazade* would need her most.

Crete soon came into full view, and the crew of Sinbad's ship hailed the sight with loud cheers and thoughts of well-deserved shore leave. The island, once famed for its Minoan civilization, still flourished now, two thousand years after the poet Homer first spoke of it in his tales. Since that time it had become a civilization where Greek, Roman, and Saracen cultures flourished, and which served, under the rule of Byzantium, as a stopover for ships of all flags.

As the *Scheherazade* made its way to the port of Chandrax, Sinbad stared in awe at the splendor before him. The mountainous terrain swept into the distance as far as the eye could see, rising high into the cloudless sky. Among these peaks lay the secret cave where Zeus himself was born, a fact that Methelese was pleased to point out to Sinbad. And then the Athenian went on to tell of all Crete's wonders: the architecture of Knossos, the Minoan and Mycenaean civilizations, their arts and culture.

Sinbad listened in fascination, recalling his own tutors, who had also reveled in the pre-Hellenic splendors. But more history lessons would have to wait. There was too much work to be done, and when at last the sleepy harbor of Chandrax came into view he left the dazzled Methelese and carried on with prepartions for unloading the cargo.

The *Scheherazade* plowed a steady course through the turquoise waters, the banner of Baghdad flying high and proud atop the mast. Slowly the ship eased past breakers, heading for its berth at the foot of the hilly city. A dozen or so other vessels from various nations stood peacefully at the quays, while hundreds of squawking gulls flew overhead. Hands on hips, Sinbad thanked Allah for his fortune.

"Will ye look at that," mumbled Milo at the bridge, staring at the harbor. He nudged at Sinbad's elbow and pointed toward two identical long ships of foreign design berthed well away from the rest. The prows were swan-necked and curled at the tips, each at least twenty-five meters long, with oversized steering paddles near the stern on the starboard side. Although they seemed able to carry cargoes of many tons, the ships drew only about a meter of water. Strange dark banners fluttered from the stocky single masts of each, and although Sinbad couldn't place them, he was positive he'd seen them before.

While he marveled at these sleek examples of advanced shipbuilding, Felicia quickly provided an answer.

"I think they're Norse," she told him. "I've seen others like them in the past."

Sinbad regarded her with a measure of surprise. "Are you sure? Those aren't Mediterranean vessels, I know, but what would Norsemen be doing here at Crete?"

She shrugged. "I don't know—but I'm not mistaken. Norse ships have passed through the Pillars of Hercules before, usually to plunder the settlements of Iberia and the Moorish coasts. But these . . ." She found herself staring long and hard at the regal flags, the double sets of oar holes lining either side. "But these aren't the ships of privateers. Look at the carvings. If you ask me, I'd say they were royal."

Royal? Sinbad snapped his fingers. "I *knew* I'd seen those banners before! Three years ago, on my way to the kingdom of the Franks. Look! Those are the royal crests of Denmark. King Harald's ships!"

"King Harald," Felicia repeated breathlessly. "Then the stories were true—his envoys have come at last."

"What stories? What envoys?"

The pirate second mate of the *Scheherazade* smiled bemusedly. "For more than a year now we've been hearing rumors of an alliance between Denmark and Byzantium, a trade alliance to be solidified by the marriage of King Harald's eldest daughter, Princess Thruna, to the new young king of Crete. Such an event could usher in a whole new era of trade between the Christians of Northern Europe and the Eastern Christians of Byzantium. Can you imagine the weath to be plied upon the sea?" She shook her head sadly, thinking of the lost opportunities for a privateer.

From their close distance Sinbad could see a flurry of activity throughout the city. Church bells were ringing, citizens were thronging the plazas. It looked as though Felicia had been right. Crete was preparing for a grand wedding, and Sinbad hoped he might have a first-hand look at the festivities.

"Take her in easy, Abu," he called with a grin. "Let's make a show of it. We'll select one of Melissa's stolen treasures for a wedding gift to present to the king himself."

Abu saluted and beamed. A royal feast was surely waiting, and he hadn't been to a really good party in years.

The marriage was the talk of the Aegean; from far and wide, dignitaries of many lands had traveled to be here at the celebration. The city of Chandrax was in an absolute tizzy of preparation to entertain the hundreds of foreign nobles who had come from as far away as Constantinople and gathered at the great palace of Crete to await the momentous event.

And what an event it was going to be! The finest wedding of all time, it was already being called, a glorious pageant in which the entire island would bask for decades to come. Harald's eldest daughter had arrived in true Danish splendor with a retinue to make even the wealthiest of kings flush with envy. Her handmaidens alone numbered seventy-two, tall blond Nordic girls, blue-eyed and proud, as firm and noble as their feared ancestors had been. There were blood relatives from all over the North, also come in fine array, bearing gifts and promises of the united kingdoms to be. There were three hundred guests from the North alone, fully half of these representatives of the Danish royal court at Roskilde.

The king of Crete for his part greeted them royally and more than matched them in luxury. He had sent for bishops and priests from Constantinople to be in attendance as well as members of his own family from across the Aegean. There came to Crete the feared king of Rhodes, the noble Prince of Corinth, the fine lords and ladies of Thrace and Peloponnesus, Macedonia, Hellas, and the city of Athens itself. Wines and exotic foods and spices were shipped from every court in the East and even the most remote desert kingdoms. The finest chefs of Rome, Alexandria, yes, even Tyre and Jaffa, had been paid extravagant sums to come and plan the banquet, in which upwards of a thousand invited guests would partake.

So it was that Chandrax was a frantic place indeed that day when the *Scheherazade* reached her rocky shores. And when it was learned that Captain Sinbad of Baghdad had come, local dignitaries lost no time in securing Islam's most noted mariner his own special invitation to the nuptial banquet, scheduled for the following evening. As the Byzantines were currently at peace with the nations of Araby, Sinbad gratefully accepted, on behalf of Islam and of the Sultan of Baghdad, whose flag he still flew.

All day the happy people of Crete celebrated, consuming wine and food bestowed upon them by their monarch. The bells of the churches, of which there were many, rang out continuously, reverberating across the city and far into the countryside, along the dales and meadows where humble shepherds tended their flocks and prayed for the happiness of the royal couple. Kindhearted peasants held banquets of their own, feasting joyously in the villages on this holiday of holidays. No man or woman worked; no cobbler, no fisherman, no tinker or baker. This was a time to rejoice; never would there come another quite like it.

On the morning of the marriage, blacked-robed priests formed a solemn procession and marched from the plazas of Chandrax to the palace cathedral, blessing the common folk as they passed, singing hymns and asking God to invoke his blessings upon the island and upon the betrothed couple.

While Sinbad, his officers, Methelese, and Clair made ready for the feast at night, the crew lost little time in joining the celebration. Eating, drinking, toasting the local citizenry, they amused themselves fully, for the first time forgetting the ordeals of Phalus and their rigorous voyage. The girls of Crete were lovely, olive-skinned, eyes shaped like almonds, and eager to befriend the strangers from so far away. It did not take very long for new bonds to be formed and, holding hands, the couples enjoyed the carnival together, laughing at the jugglers and clowns, listening to the poets with respectful severity, joining with the ballad singers in merry tunes befitting of the occasion.

Sinbad, meanwhile, carefully chose his gift for the bride. It was a dazzling fleur-de-lis brooch, about the size of a man's palm, in white gold inlaid with precious stones— dark rubies and translucent emeralds. A perfect piece of exotic jewelry worth a ransom in any land.

"What do you think?" Sinbad asked, displaying it with both hands to the breathless Don Giovanni.

The frog examined it goggle-eyed; he pulled himself away and peered up at his smiling captain. "A gift worthy of any queen," he said. "Princess Thruna will be most appreciative."

Sinbad carefully wrapped the brooch in a silk scarf and tucked it away in his trunk for safekeeping. "I hope so," he sighed, pushing back the thin curtain from his window and gazing from the heights of his room toward the rooftops of the city. Chandrax spread before him in an arc, glistening in the sun. From here he could see the harbor, and the sea calm beneath blue skies.

"This wedding," he went on thoughtfully, "could be more important than any of us realize. Our world is changing, Giovanni. Expanding, growing with new discoveries, new nations sprouting like wildflowers. Tonight we must all be Araby's finest emissaries—and show these men of Byzantium and Denmark that we are like them, sharing the same goals, the same desires for trade and peace."

Don Giovanni listened to his friend and smiled. "Don't worry, Sinbad. All shall go well. Your presence here is going to have more benefits than you think. Why, the king of Crete was honored to learn of your arrival. Methelese predicts he'll treat you as royally as he does King Harald himself."

Sinbad grinned. "I doubt that, but I'll give as good a performance as I can." He knitted his fingers as if in prayer. "I only hope nothing goes amiss."

Don Giovanni, used to Sinbad's worrying, scoffed. "Of course it will. But tell me, who have you decided will be your companion at the king's table?"

At this Sinbad frowned. He folded his arms and faced the frog again. "I can't take Clair without making Felicia angry," he confided honestly, "nor can I escort Felicia without upsetting Clair." He sat down at the end of the bed beside his companion. "They're both expecting to be at my side, although I never promised either one."

Giovanni nodded with understanding. Both were unusually beautiful, both charming and intelligent. Except for Felicia's fiery temper, they were an even match.

"What would you do if you were me?" Sinbad asked.

The frog thought for a while, tapping a webbed foot against a fold in the blanket, and then he said, "Do as any good diplomat, Sinbad. Bring them both."

With a broad smile the captain agreed. "Ah, I wish I were as wise as you, my friend. This way I can enjoy the company of both while offending neither."

"Exactly. But be careful, Sinbad. Twice the pleasure can also lead to twice the trouble." And on that grim note Don Giovanni hopped away, leaving a suddenly soured Sinbad to his thoughts while he bathed and dressed.

Trumpets heralded the arrival of the guests at the great hall of the castle. Milling crowds of Cretan nobles stood on hand to greet everyone personally. The patriarchs of the island, decked out in their finest robes, formed a long line

253

across the red carpet, bowing graciously before lords, kissing the bejeweled hands of ladies, thanking them one and all for coming and congenially gesturing for them to find their places at the many round tables in the hall.

Musicians played softly upon their lutes and harps, servants by the hundreds bustled back and forth. Slowly the huge room filled. Bathed in the light of crystal chandeliers holding ten thousand candles, and a dozen crackling fireplaces, Greeks and honored aristocrats from Constantinople mingled for the first time with the stout, rough-looking fellows of the North, with their flowing yellow beards. Coarse, lacking the refinements of the ancient Aegean peoples, they entered the hall with swagger and bravado, hailing their hosts while keeping watchful eyes on the abundance of riches.

Upon a large platform at the front of the hall stood a long table apart from the others below. Here the king of Crete and his royal family held personal court for their most special guests. When King Harald himself had entered, amid a barrage of trumpet blasts, his blushing daughter left her husband's side and led him by the hand to the place of honor. The two kings stood eye to eye, shook hands and kissed, then, while the crowds waited in silence, smiled and sat. The din rose, all guests took their places, the banquet was ready to begin.

Sinbad had arrived only moments before. All eyes turned at the announcement of his name, and with Felicia and Clair flanking him, he boldly strode to the platform, bowing graciously before both kings. Milo and Methelese found their own places at a table near the kitchen, and looked on uneasily as King Harald himself stood from his place and greeted the mariner.

"So you're Sinbad of Baghdad," he thundered, hands on hips, horned helmet imposing upon his large head.

"I am, Your Majesty," replied Sinbad, his hand sweeping before him. He wore a tan Damascan robe, stitched with gold thread at the sleeves and hem; on his head was a fine turban, covering all his dark hair except for a shock that slanted across his forehead.

"By the gods of old," roared Harald, "I've heard so many stories of you that I expected a far older man!"

Sinbad smiled warmly. "And I, Majesty, have also heard tales of you and your Norsemen. All the cities of the East hold your name in great respect."

Harald's ice-blue eyes crinkled, and his chest swelled with pride. "Indeed, good Captain?"

"Indeed, yes. Sire, I venture to say that the name of Harald shall live when all others are long forgotten."

The king of Denmark, a barbarian until his early manhood when his conversion to Christianity had taken place, laughed heartily. "By Odin!" he bellowed, forgetting himself as he frequently did, "I like this fellow!" He pounded a heavy fist upon the tablecloth, almost spilling an urn of wine. "Give him and his companions chairs closer to me! I think I'm going to enjoy his company."

The king of Crete jumped to his feet in respect for his father-in-law's wishes and had the servants move three members of his family to farther places.

"We are honored," said Clair with a polite curtsy, her low-cut gown hinting at the firm breasts beneath.

"Most honored," added Felicia, with a spicy and alluring smile.

Harald laughed again, helping them to their seats. Glad that his wife, Inga, had not made the voyage with him, and relieved to have the equally distressing Thruna already married, he now looked toward the evening with renewed interest. The stuffy Greeks had been most boring; he had wondered how he might stay awake for the rest of the evening. But now, this young stranger from Baghdad had brought new life into the party. And with such beautiful women at his side, Harald was convinced he would yet have a good time.

All manner of foods were swiftly placed before the hosts. From stuck pig to the finest lamb and skewered beef.

Casseroles of every description; pots laden with stew, covered with onions, smothered with a peppery tomato sauce; mountain-high husks of corn on platters swollen with garnished potatoes; baked chicken, dashed with ground cinnamon and cloved garlic, sprinkled with a rich cheese sauce. Skewered roast, fried eggplant, hams basted and covered with breadcrumbs and nutmeg. There were thick muttons and mutton chops, oxtail, gut and veal, doused in sour cream atop sliced cucumber. Fish and fowl, vegetables galore. Many of them strange foods to the eyes of Sinbad, but all readily devoured with relish by the Norsemen for whom most were specially prepared.

Wine flowed freely, but to Sinbad's surprise he saw that most of the guests from Denmark spurned it, preferring instead to drink the bitter barreled ale they had brought themselves. It did not take long for bellies to be filled and thirsts quenched. Tongues spoke more freely as more and more of the ale and wines were consumed. And Sinbad noted that, like her father, Princess Thruna, now queen of Crete, had a most healthy appetite for the heady, home-brewed ale. Holding her flagon high with one hand, a soft layer of foam nestled like a moustache above her lip, she laughed and drank, toasting everybody at the table in true Nordic fashion. The braided princess seemed more than a match for her dour and austere husband, Sinbad noted with a chuckle, thinking that the king had probably let himself in for more than he realized.

King Harald joined in the merriment, insisting that Felicia and Clair share with him their lives and pasts, rollicking at the tales Felicia had to tell, pinching both women in embarassing places and, much to the consternation of his Greek hosts, turning the atmosphere of the banquet into one decidedly Viking in nature.

Harald roared good-naturedly as several of his men started to brawl. The combatants cleared off a table top and, while other guests fled their seats in horror, the king stood and offered a fine prize to the winner. When the flushed king of Crete bade them to stop and behave like gentlemen, good Harald shut him up with a deadly glance.

"Such patsies these Greeks are," he mumbled to Sinbad with a wink. "Tell me, is there sport among the peoples of the Mediterranean?"

Sinbad laughed, himself growing heady on the strong brew. "Indeed there is, my lord," he replied boastfully, returning the wink. "Why, among my crew is a man, a man . . . Not a man, my lord. A *giant*. The strongest giant in all of Islam—the world's greatest wrestler."

Harald's blond brows narrowed with interest.

Thruna leaned across her husband and looked to Sinbad. "Is this man here now?"

"Unfortunately no, my lady. He enjoys the banquet in the plaza, along with the rest of my crew and the good people of Crete."

"Then bring him," demanded Thruna, ignoring her husband completely. "Let him fight one of our own to determine which land bears the true champion . . ."

Harald pounded his fists on the tables. "An excellent idea! Bring on this giant!" He looked distastefully at the two warriors having it out with swords atop the table and commanded them to cease. As the crowd of onlookers voiced their displeasure with hoots, Harald raised his arms and calmed them. "Enough of these amateurs," he growled. "We're going to have some real fighting. Between Captain Sinbad's best warrior and our own!" At this a mighty cheer went up from the hundreds of Norsemen.

"Balox, come forward!"

All eyes turned as the powerful viking stood from his chair at a distant table, wiped his mouth with the back of his hand, strode forward with awesome strides, and bowed before his liege.

"Are you ready for a contest, good Balox?"

The hirsute warrior's sharp teeth glinted; he grinned. "At your command, sire." He looked about the room distastefully. "But which of these effeminate Greeks am I to fight?"

The Hellenic guests murmured at the insult. The king of Crete rose to his feet and tried to intercede before things got out of control. "I . . . I don't think this is a very good idea," he stammered.

"Oh, shut up!" barked Thruna. "Don't you ever have *any* fun?"

At this the Norsemen chuckled. The king sat back humbled, his face as long as his sigh.

Sinbad bowed to him. "Sire, do not be upset. This will only be a friendly match. I promise you. No weapons. A bout of wrestling to entertain your noble guests."

But the king was still hesitant; he didn't very much like the thought of his carefully planned party being taken over by all these foreigners.

"Please, my dear," cooed Thruna, now snuggling up to him. "For me? Just this once?"

The king growled but assented. He stood again. "Have the wrestler from Sinbad's crew brought here," he commanded his guards.

Harald laughed. "What? And deny his shipmates the honor of seeing him?" He, too, looked to the perplexed guards. "Bring all of Captain Sinbad's crew! Let's see what kind of men these Easterners really are!"

And the crowd of Vikings applauded while the Greeks shrank. Balox quickly stripped himself of his furs and jacket and stood proudly flexing his muscles before the oohing and ahhing audience.

Harald laughed again, clapping Sinbad on the shoulder. "I must warn you, my friend: Balox is my finest soldier. Why, once in the German black forests I saw him kill a bear with his hands!"

Sinbad smiled. "Thank you for your concern, King Harald. But I, too, must give warning. If Mongo breaks your man's back, don't blame me."

The king bellowed. He held out his empty flagon and

called for more ale. Twenty serving girls scurried to do his bidding.

It was not long before the arched doors of the hall flew open and in came the crew of the *Scheherazade,* all slightly drunk, all staggering up toward Sinbad at the platform. In the middle of the group, a full head above everyone else, came Mongo. The jolly giant was already set for the match, naked save for a small covering about his loins. His body, in preparation, had been gently smeared with fat so that his flesh glistened in the candlelight. He glanced briefly at the waiting Balox, then politely bowed before Harald and the king of Crete.

Harald turned to Sinbad. He rubbed at his flowing beard with obvious admiration. "Hmmm. It seems you told me no lies, my young friend. . . ."

"I never lie, sire," replied the beaming captain, realizing that even the mighty Balox seemed to be dwarfed by his giant.

Harald clapped his hands. The center of the floor was cleared, tables dragged out of the way. Many of the Greek ladies in attendance turned away their eyes. "Let the fight begin!" roared Harald. "A hundred pieces of silver to the winner! Paid by our host, the king of Crete!"

The crowd cheered madly while the king of Crete put his head to his hands and groaned.

And so the fight began. Balox and Mongo circled each other for some long moments, then both charged, each seeking a quick pin. Though the Libyan showed an advantage in height and reach, the wily Balox proved a tough competitor. Used to such combat in his raiding days along the Northern European coasts, he gave Mongo more than a fair fight. Indeed, for a long time he not only kept the giant at bay but actually almost pinned him several times through the use of a number of tricks unknown to the East.

Harald munched upon a great leg of lamb, enjoying every second. Thruna leaned forward, her blue eyes wide, and shouted vulgar epithets at Balox every time Mongo slipped away unharmed.

The wrestlers tumbled across the floor, smacked into tables, crushed urns, and sent silverware flying. Balox grunted when Mongo's fist met his mouth; spitting teeth and blood the Viking delivered a blow of his own to the giant's solar plexus. Then they grappled again, twisting, cavorting, slamming themselves against the draperies and pulling valuable tapestries from the walls.

The Norsemen loved it. So did Sinbad's crew. And so did many of the younger Greeks who also considered themselves athletes. But Thruna's husband could only simmer with anger. He was beginning to dislike his barbaric father-in-law and his rugged new bride. Was the palace of Crete to be turned into an arena for brawling? He shuddered and grew determined to keep family visits to a minimum.

"Hit him, Balox!" screamed a nervous Thruna, swinging a fist through the air. "Or must I get in there and do it for you?"

Felicia was jumping up and down, her own fists flailing. "Come on, Mongo! Pin him! Pin the oaf!"

Both fighters were growing weary; they squared off panting, sweat dripping from their bodies like rain.

Harald looked to Sinbad and frowned. "Seems to be a draw," he mumbled with disappointment.

"I think so, sire. Your man Balox is much sturdier than I thought."

"My man? What about your own? Why, I'd give anything to bring him back to Denmark with me. A man like that . . ." He sucked in air and sighed wistfully. Then he said, "What about it, Captain? Come back to Roskilde with me. Join my fleet, you and all your men. Why, together I bet we could teach those German and Irish dogs a trick or two, eh?"

Sinbad was certainly flattered. He would have loved to share some adventure with the king of the Danes. But how could he go when so many matters were yet unsettled? When Sherry still languished in the caliph's court as a wife and prisoner?

"I thank you for the offer, my lord," he said. "And were it possible I would gladly accept your hospitality. But"—he lowered his gaze—"alas, it just isn't possible. Not now. One day, perhaps. . . ."

Suddenly the crowd roared; Mongo had all but finished off the clever Viking, but as he drew close to a pin, Balox somehow managed to wiggle out of his grasp. The Norsemen became excited and many of them were clearly itching to get involved in a little bout of their own.

Then it happened. One of Sinbad's crewmen accidently jostled the Viking behind him. The Norseman used the bump as a pretex to start a brawl. He hauled back his fist without warning, connected, and sent the startled crewman sprawling. At this, several other members of the *Scheherazade* leaped upon the attacker—and the fight was on. Seconds later, all of the crew, joined by a handful of sturdy Greek youths in training for the Olympics, charged the willing Vikings.

Casseroles smashed to the floor, women screamed and ran, priests dumbfoundedly ducked for cover. The brawl rippled outward until it encompassed the entire hall.

The king of Crete was on his feet in an instant. Veins popping, he shrieked at the sight of valuable treasures being smashed all over the place.

"Stop it!" he screamed, crimson with rage. "I demand you stop at once!"

But the noise was so great that no one had heard. Harald turned to his son-in-law and looked at him as though he were mad. "What's the matter with you, eh?" he asked. "Don't you like your people to enjoy themselves? In my court we do this all the time. There's no harm—"

"Be quiet, you old fool!" yelled the king of Crete. "Just look at the hall! It's a shambles! Those vases your men broke are priceless! Those tapestries—"

261

Burly Harald would have killed the little Greek without batting an eye had it not been for the marriage and the trade agreements whose ink was still wet. "Sit down, you weakling," he seethed. He glanced to his grinning daughter. "And count yourself lucky. . . ." His intent was not lost on the king of Crete who, knees quivering, sat down in silence. Every time another valuable artifact was heaved against the wall, he flinched.

Sinbad, hoping to rekindle the strained friendship, quickly took out the silk-wrapped present and drew both Harald and the king away from the fight. "My lords," he announced, "I would like at this moment to present Thruna with the present I have brought. Had I more time to select, I might have found something even more worthy, but as I've been at sea . . ." He crouched as a large gaily painted urn sailed above his head and shattered behind him. Then he unwrapped the brooch and held it out for all to see.

Felicia took one look and gasped; her eyes grew wild. Sinbad saw the look and smiled. "It is dazzling, isn't it?"

She tugged at his sleeve, breathless. "Sinbad" she stammered. "Sinbad, listen to me. Don't—"

But before she could finish her thought, Thruna squealed with pleasure. "Let me see it!" she pleaded, and Sinbad was all too eager to hand it over. "For your wedding, good lady. May you and your husband know many happy—"

Felicia was pulling at him more frantically. He turned around, annoyed. "What is it, girl? Why are you—?"

"We must get that brooch back!" she panted. "Now! Quickly, before the king of Crete sees it!"

"What in Allah's name are you talking about? It's their gift. Our goodwill effort on the part of Baghdad."

"Oh, it's *stunning*!" cried Thruna, clutching it to her breast while her pleased father looked on.

"Yes, my lady. Rare as a star. The finest handiwork you shall ever see. The famed craftsmen of both Baghdad and Damascus toiled for fully a year to design and forge it—"

A dark pall came over the king of Crete's face. "May *I* see this present?" he demanded, his hand brazenly stuck out to accept it.

Thruna was still beside herself with excitement. "Isn't it marvelous, my husband? What fine work! These men of the East should be well rewarded for their art."

The king scowled. "Give it to me." Thruna handed it over with growing puzzlement. Her husband was obviously upset, and she didn't understand why.

The king took it with both hands and examined it carefully, all the while growing more livid.

"What's the matter with him?" Sinbad muttered.

Felicia gulped. "That brooch, Sinbad. Melissa took it from—"

"Where did you get this?" barked the king of Crete, rising from his chair and glaring at the puzzled mariner.

"My lord? Why, that gift was forged just for this occasion. It—"

"You're a *liar!*"

Sinbad stared back at him. The king's lips were trembling, saliva was dripping off his lolling tongue. "A liar, sire?" He began to rise, but before he could, King Harald, suspecting that something was amiss, kept him in his place.

"What seems to be the matter?" he asked.

"The matter? The matter?" The king's eyes were popping from their sockets. "You dare even *ask* such a question? An outrage! In my own home, no less!" And he pounded his fists on the table.

Harald looked at Sinbad and shrugged. "Poor fellow's had too much to drink, I suppose. I can't think of any other reason—"

"I'll give you plenty of reasons!" he boomed. And he stuck the brooch directly beneath Harald's nose. "Do you see this? Do you *see* it?"

Harald nodded. "Yes. And I think it's lovely. Too feminine, perhaps, but lovely. You should thank Captain Sinbad for bringing it here."

"Oh, I'll thank him, all right. I'll *thank* him! Guards! Guards!"

Felicia, Sinbad, and Clair all jumped up.

"See here!" growled Harald.

"You're a fool, Harald!" sneered the king of Crete. "This gift belongs to me! It was my grandmother's! An heirloom in our family for nearly three hundred years! Two years ago it was stolen—my family's treasures were being shipped for safekeeping to Rhodes when pirates attacked and stole everything aboard. This brooch that our good Captain bears is not a gift of Baghdad but my own precious jewel! No doubt this rogue"—he pointed at Sinbad contemptuously—"was the very pirate who stole it! And now he dares return it as a gift. What an insult! Guards! Call the guards!"

"Is this true?" asked Harald.

Sinbad lifted his right hand solemnly. "I swear to you, my lord, I didn't know. If what the king says be true, I honestly didn't know it. . . ."

"Liar! Liar!" hollered the king, searching frantically for his guards, who were standing far across the room and didn't hear his calls over the commotion of the brawl.

Felicia faced the shaking king. "Sinbad tells the truth," she said. "He didn't steal the brooch—it was captured by the Scarlet Pirate."

The raving king gasped. Tales of the Scarlet Pirate were rife throughout the Aegean; the very mention of her name sent shudders down every spine.

Harald glanced over at Felicia. "How do you know all of this?"

"Because," there was an air of defiance in her tone, "I was there. I was one of the pirates."

More gasps from the sputtering king. "See? I told you! I told you!"

But Harald seemed more amused than anything else. Hands to his paunchy belly, he laughed. "All's fair upon the open sea," he reminded his son-in-law. "Anyway, now that you have the brooch back safely, why be angry? Sinbad did you a favor—"

"A *favor?*" Spittle sprayed in every direction, some landing on Harald's face. The Dane frowned.

"Guards!" bellowed the king again, so loud that this time they couldn't help but hear. "Arrest this man!" he shouted, waving a bony finger in Sinbad's direction. "And all of his crew! Put the lot of them in the dungeons!"

Sinbad pulled his knife and shielded Clair with his body. Felicia drew her own weapon. "We've got to get away!" she cried.

Sinbad nodded. From down the hall came a squad of spear-carrying Greeks. Their clatter broke up the friendly fight, leaving all the parties struggling to their feet and gazing on in wonder and puzzlement.

"How are we going to get out of here?" rasped Sinbad, looking about frantically.

Harald shook his head. "There is no way. Put down your weapons. Perhaps I can see to it that no harm comes to you. Perhaps—"

Sinbad wavered, knowing instinctively he could trust the bulky viking. But the king was so enraged . . .

"I'll see you all drawn and quartered!" hissed the monarch, a maniacal grin splitting his hawkish features. "Not one of you will leave Crete alive!"

The guards were bounding closer. "That settles it!" called Felicia. She swiftly pressed her knife against Thruna's breast. The princess felt her heart skip a beat.

"On your feet!" demanded Felicia.

Thruna got up slowly, her eyes darting to her father. Harald rose as well. "I warn you, woman. Leave my daughter or—"

"We need a hostage," shot back Felicia. "Your daughter is our only chance to get off this insufferable island."

The guards made ready to throw their spears, but the king stayed them. "You'll never get away with this," he roared.

There was laughter in fiery Felicia's eyes. "Oh no? Well, then, Thruna dies with us. The first one to make a move is responsible for her death. Budge an inch from your places and I'll slit her throat."

"She means it," said Sinbad.

Harald flushed a shade of purple. "If one hair on my daughter's head is split . . ."

Sinbad snapped his fingers at his men, barked for them to relieve the Greek guards of their weapons and clear a path for them all down to the quay.

As the guests were huddled into the corners, the bold fighting men of Denmark seemed ready to strike, knowing a swift charge could easily overtake the badly outnumbered followers of Islam. In ordinary circumstances Harald would have gladly given the command, even if it had cost him his own life. Better death than humiliation, he always said. But now it was Felicia's knife at the throat of his darling Thruna, and he was wise enough to realize that the pirate girl would not hesitate. So he signaled for his men to let them pass and watched with consternation as his daughter was hustled from the banquet hall.

"I'll not rest until she's back!" he growled, shaking a fist.

Sinbad turned and looked at him. "No harm will come to her, King Harald. All we want is the chance to escape. . . ."

"And Thruna?"

"We'll release her after we're safe."

"He lies!" wailed the king of Crete. He gritted his teeth, stepped amid the rubble of his once resplendent hall, and glared angrily. "I'll follow you till the ends of the world for this," he vowed. "If your ships ever come within a hundred leagues of Crete again I'll—"

Harald stepped in front of his son-in-law. "All I want is my daughter, Captain. Give her to me now and we can part in peace."

Sinbad shook his head. He glanced over his shoulder through the open doors and saw that half his men had already reached the docks. "I can't do that, sire. Believe that I wish I could. But Thruna's all we have to make sure we sail safely."

The Viking grumbled beneath his breath. He had come to like this brazen Easterner. Truly he had. But if forced to choose between Thruna's life and this friendship, he knew he would cleave Sinbad's head in half and not bat an eye.

"My ships shall be following you, too," he promised. "We shall not rest until this matter is resolved."

Sinbad nodded. "I understand. I'll have to take my chances." Then he bowed his head to the king of Crete. "I enjoyed your party, sire. My only regret is that it had to end as it has." And before the infuriated leige could reply, Sinbad had turned and fled out into the evening shadows.

PART SIX:

OF THE CHASE AND THRUNA
AND METHELESE'S BAG OF
TRICKS WHICH WERE REALLY
MORE THAN THE GOOD CAP-
TAIN BARGAINED FOR.

The deck of the *Scheherazade* bustled with life, the sails gaily swelled, and the ship heeled slightly to port as she set upon her course. She sailed west, against her own shadow cast by the rising sun, toward the Ionian sea and the coasts of Sicily.

Sinbad had been up all night, directing the new course and keeping out a wary eye for their pursuers. With his shirt open to his waist, he crossed the bridge to the weather side and studied the morning stars intently. The isle of Malta lay perhaps ten days ahead he knew, but that was providing the wind, which had seemed so promising all night, did not continue to fall off.

"A warm drink, sir?"

Sinbad turned to see a smiling Abu holding a mug of spiced tea. He took the drink gratefully and sipped at the steaming brew; then he glanced upwards to his man perched high in the crow's nest. "Can you see them yet?" he called.

The sailor shaded his eyes from the rising sun and peered along the horizon in the direction of Crete. "Aye, capt'n," he replied at last. "A whole fleet of them—coming fast at five points off the stern."

Sinbad looked back at Abu and grimaced. "They'll spare no effort in trying to catch us," he said uneasily.

The first mate spat into the wind. Felicia leaned against the rail and scowled. "We can outrace those Greeks," she huffed.

Sinbad nodded as a low cloud crossed the sun and a pall

271

covered the ship. "Maybe. But I'm less certain about these long ships of King Harald. They're fast, the fastest I've ever seen. A leaky tub like ours won't win any races against them."

"We've been chased before, Capt'n," said Abu, a daring note in his voice. "It's not the first time—and I daresay it shan't be the last."

Small comfort, thought Sinbad. He turned to Felicia. "How's Princess Thruna? Giving anyone a hard time?"

The second mate grinned. "Not a peep out of her, Sinbad. Still drunk, snoring like a sailor. When she comes round I'm not sure she'll remember what happened."

"Perhaps we should wake her and bring her on deck. It won't be long before Harald's ships start to bear down."

Abu looked at the captain uncertainly. "What's up your sleeve?" he asked.

"Not much. We can't fight a whole fleet, and Thruna's our only bargaining chip. Harald won't dare attack us and put his daughter's life in jeopardy . . ."

"I doubt the king of Crete will feel the same," rejoined Felicia dryly. "He's got his pride at stake; he won't give a brass plate's worth of a damn for his bride."

Felicia was right, Sinbad knew. Thruna meant nothing to the king now. Until honor was satisfied he would never rest. Their only hope was to somehow remove King Harald from the chase and hope to elude the Cretans. On an open sea in fair weather it would be hard, but once they reached the rugged coasts of Sicily . . .

"Three leagues and coming fast!" cried the lookout.

Three leagues! The *Scheherazade's* lead wasn't holding up very well. By nightfall the Norsemen could easily whittle that distance in half.

Sinbad called for the officer of the watch, who proved to be Milo, and instructed him to keep a steady course into the wind. Then he turned back to Felicia. "Bring the princess to my cabin; I think we'd better have a little talk with her."

The ship had begun to pitch in rougher weather by the time the tall Viking girl was brought. Escorted by Felicia, Thruna stood passive and proud, her blond braids glinting sunlight at the edges, her sea-blue eyes coldly taking in the captain seated at the corner of his desk. Shoulders back, breasts thrust out, she appeared a perfect picture of Nordic womanhood.

Sinbad met her stare and sighed. She must hate him for what he'd done—and with good reason. After all, he'd spoiled her wedding banquet, made a laughingstock of her husband, kidnapped her at the threat of her life.

He gestured for her to sit. Thruna refused with a shake of her head. As Don Giovanni hopped onto his shoulder, Sinbad said, "I don't expect you to believe this, Princess, but I'm truly sorry for what happened."

Thruna didn't move a muscle and said nothing.

Sinbad fidgeted uncomfortably. "No harm is going to come to you; you have my word. But you must understand the predicament we're in. As you must know, both your husband's fleet and your father's ships are following behind. . . ."

A small smile broke across her thin lips.

Sinbad continued. "Anyway, our only chance seems to be to outsail them all if we can. But we have to hold onto you, Princess, although I'm loath to cause you any more suffering. We can't risk King Harald trying to attack or burn our ship. He won't—as long as you're with us and safe." He looked at her sternly. "Now do you understand our plight?" No answer was forthcoming, so Sinbad went on. "This ship is bound for the west, and once we're well out of danger I plan to put you ashore. We might touch many ports—Corsica, Sardinia perhaps, or even the Balearic Islands. Whichever is best for you is where we'll head. Sooner or later you'll be found, I'm sure, and brought safely back to your husband. I'm sorry, Princess Thruna, but right now it's the best I can do."

Her smile suddenly vanished. She said, "Thank you for

273

your concern, but I don't want to go back to Crete."

Felicia exchanged a shocked look with Sinbad who turned back to Thruna scratching his head. "You don't . . . *want* to go back?"

The Nordic princess laughed, leaving her companions dumbfounded. She proceeded to sit down on the chair, cross her legs so that her thighs showed milky white through the slit in her gown, and grin.

"But he's your *husband!*" protested Sinbad.

"*Piff!*" She waved an imperious hand, sloughing off the thought. "He's a bore. An absolute *bore*. A dullard and a dimwit. A piece of pastry. In Denmark we laugh at men like this. . . ."

"Then why did you marry him?" asked an incredulous Felicia.

She looked at the pirate girl with no hatred at all. "Ah, you're so young, dear child. I've dreaded this silly marriage since I can remember. But King Harald,"—she sighed and turned down her lip distastefully—"my father, cannot be disobeyed. Once something is planted in his mind, not even the wrath of the gods can persuade him. Thor knows I've tried! He's dreamed of such a foolish alliance ever since I was a child, hoping to bring new prosperity to our land. High and low he searched for a worthy husband"—her stare hardened—"and when one wasn't forthcoming he settled on *that* clown. A marriage of state, nothing more. Time and time again I pleaded with him to forget this nonsense, but as I said . . ." And she finished her remarks with a shrug.

Stunned, Sinbad could find no words; Thruna had more than taken the wind out of his sails; she had left him breathless.

"So you see," Thruna continued easily, "you've freed me from a life bound to be as boring as it is useless. If anything, good captain, it is *I* who should be grateful to you." She leaned forward, her hands forming a pyramid, fingertips tapping together. "Where is it that we sail for?"

Felicia's eyes widened. "You don't want to be rescued? Not even by your father?"

"Not unless he has my marriage annuled and takes me back to Denmark. Otherwise, I think I'll just go with you." She was as calm as a lake on a mild summer's day.

"Come with *us?*" cried Sinbad. "Are you crazy? As it is, the whole Cretan fleet is chasing me! Do you think I want to add the fleet of Denmark as well?"

Thruna wasn't disturbed. "You'll manage. You can outsail the Cretans."

"I'm not as sure of that as you are," Sinbad said. "But even if we do, what about King Harald's ships?"

Thruna smiled, her eyes bright. "My father's captains are no match for the world's finest sailor. Surely you can keep them at a safe distance and find some way to slip away. Anyway, for your own sakes you have to try. What other options do you have?" And she complacently sat back, knowing that Sinbad's dilemma forced him to accept her whether he liked it or not.

Felicia looked at the captain and groaned. Fate had played a curious joke, and now it was they who had been outsmarted.

"What are we going to do?" she asked after Thruna had been returned to her quarters.

Sinbad shrugged. "For now, nothing. Just hope that the princess is right, and those long ships aren't as fast as we think they are."

By evening, with a good wind still prevailing, the *Scheherazade* had almost managed to maintain its three-league lead. But as the sun dipped, the sails and banners of Denmark were still too close for comfort. And not far behind, lagging but doggedly staying in the race, came the Cretan fleet.

"There's grim humor in this voyage of ours," Sinbad told Don Giovanni as he restlessly paced in his cabin that night. "We set sail from Jaffa as a peaceful merchant. Since then we've been chased by pirates and by poor

Dormo's ship from Baghdad, incurred the wrath of the whole Cretan navy, and found ourselves the enemy of King Harald. All this while our intentions were peaceful. What might have happened to us were they otherwise?"

Sinbad came to the deck the next morning in glum spirits. He found his trusted officers gathered together on the bridge, all looking terribly worried as they peered across the stern. He didn't have to ask what was wrong.

The billowing golden sails of the long ships were twice as large as they had been the night before. Sinbad's zig-zag course in darkness had done nothing to lose them. In fact, King Harald had even managed to cut the distance. Two leagues at best, perhaps only one in a day or two, and then . . .

Milo turned and faced the chagrined captain. "We did our best, Capt'n. Followed your orders to the letter; changed tacks three times, cut our sailing time—"

A small wave of Sinbad's hand stopped him abruptly. There was no point in hearing the story—it wasn't the fault of his crew at all. Just that they were battling a determined adversary—determined and angry.

"We made a mistake in taking Thruna has hostage," he said at length.

"That's to say now," countered Felicia. "But if it wasn't for her, we'd all still be on Crete—chained in a Greek dungeon for the rest of our lives."

Sinbad stood by the poop-deck rail, peering through the spyglass, shadowed from the morning sun's glare by the mast. Those Vikings were a rugged bunch, he saw, working at a sweat to inch their ships nearer to his own. Carefully altering course with the subtlest shifts in wind, exploiting the swells below them and taking full advantage of their speed. Inwardly Sinbad had to admire them—Harald as well. A pity they couldn't be on the same side. If only Felicia had choosen a different hostage! Anyone. Even the king of Crete himself. But no, he thought. This whole, mess was his own fault; there was no one else to blame. If he had chosen the wedding gift more carefully, made sure of its origin . . .

"What are we going to do, Sinbad?" asked Milo.

"Let's give the princess back," grumbled Abu. "At least that might get Harald off our backs. Then we can concentrate on the Greeks."

Sinbad lifted his gaze toward the heavens. "By Allah, if only we could! But she won't go! She refuses—not while Harald insists on taking her back to Crete."

"Maybe he can be persuaded to change his mind?" offered Methelese.

"Small chance of that. This alliance is his lifelong goal. He'll mend the fences with the Greeks any way he can—at Thruna's expense as well as our own. . . ."

Felicia turned, her hair blowing freely in the gusts, and said, "Then if we can't change Harald's mind, we've got to change Thruna's."

"Are you serious? You heard the way she spoke. She's adamant. She's—"

Felicia smiled coyly. "She need not agree, Sinbad, only be unable to struggle when we transfer her to her father's ship. . . ."

"What do you mean?"

The pirate laughed, her large eyes filled with mischief. "There are ways, Captain. Women—er—seem to succumb to your charms. . . ."

Sinbad gulped. "You want me to seduce a princess of Denmark? The wife of a Greek king?"

"Not seduce, Captain. *Soothe* her. . . ." She put a strong emphasis on the word, leaving its meaning both clear and foggy.

"You're crazy."

"Am I?" Then, as Sinbad and the others stood perplexed, Felicia drew them all closer and explained.

Sinbad's face was impassive when she had done. "It's risky," he said nervously. "We'll be letting Harald's ships come awfully close; and we'd lose any chance of outrunning him should the plan fail."

Felicia's eyes twinkled. "It won't, Sinbad. You won't."

He looked to the others. One by one, they all avoided his gaze, leaving him to carry the burden. At length he sighed, put his hands on his hips, and nodded. "All right; we might as well try it. Abu, you know what to do. Keep our course and speed exactly the same until twilight. Then proceed with half sails. By dawn I want Harald's ships to be within shouting distance. Leave the rest to me."

Thruna was lounging in her cramped quarters when Sinbad knocked at sunset. The tall girl was more than surprised when he pleasantly invited her to his cabin for supper. Gone was all his anger and frustration with her, and seemingly even his concern about her father's closing range.

Thruna had spent the day happily. Glad to be rid of the yoke of her husband and her imposing father, she contemplated this new and exciting life she had embarked upon. Oh, one day she would show up in Denmark again, she was sure. But not for a long time. Not until she had sailed with Sinbad and the *Scheherazade*, seen the world, and experienced the freedom of the sea. Not until this nonsense of marriage was a dim memory and her unconsummated wedlock annulled forever.

The meal began merrily enough, with Clair preparing, and Mongo delivering, a tasty flounder gently sprinkled with lemon and dry wine. Exhilarated by the sea air, the Nordic princess displayed a monstrous appetite, cleaning her plate with crusty bread and finishing long before Sinbad.

"So, what is this city called Roskilde like?" asked Sinbad, pouring the large-boned girl a mug full of fine wine.

Thruna took a healthy draught and said, "Fogs and winds, winds and fogs. Ice-locked in winter. *Brrr*. I wonder how I ever put up with that! I like these climes much better. What's Baghdad like?"

278

Sinbad leaned back in his chair with folded arms. "Oh, heat and flies, Sand . . ."

The princess giggled. "Are you playing games with me, Captain?"

There's more intelligence behind those sea-blue eyes that she lets on, thought Sinbad. *I'll have to be careful.* "Not at all, my Princess. I'm merely reminding you of the ancient maxim that grass seems always greener in another's yard."

Thruna laughed and held out her mug, which Sinbad, readily refilled. Then she pulled a face. "Aren't you going to drink?" she asked.

"Certainly." And he refilled his own, careful not to put in quite as much as he had given her. He held his goblet high, and the two mugs clinked. "A toast, my lady, to Denmark—"

"And to Baghdad." Her smile was sly. Then they both drank to the dregs. Sinbad flushed with the feel of wine spilling through his veins. Thruna, though, used to many a drinking bout, merely smacked her lips.

"More, Princess?"

She nodded eagerly. "Yes, please."

And again he poured for her and then for himself. Thruna sipped more slowly this time and glanced at ease around the cabin. She found it spartan, but neat. Comfortable, although far too small.

"I've been thinking," she said, running her finger around the rim of the mug. "This ship of yours, the *Sch*—?"

"The *Scheherazade*, my lady, named after another lady of quality like yourself. But those of us who sail her call her the *Sherry*."

"Yes, the *Sherry*, then. It seems to be a good ship. . . ."

"It is. Well fitted for long voyages."

Thruna frowned slightly. She shifted her weight and this time poured from the pitcher herself. "It's not that I'm complaining, you understand," she continued, "but I find my cabin, indeed all the quarters aboard, a trifle stuffy."

"My lady?"

"Come come, Captain. You know what I mean. There's so little room. Why, even your cabin is not much larger than an oversized closet. We're too cramped. We should have something bigger. . . ."

Sinbad swallowed. "Ah, I realize that you've been accustomed to far more spacious quarters, Princess, but if you intend to stay with us I'm afraid you'll have to make do."

Her smile was full, and crafty. "Hmm. Perhaps—for a while. But I was wondering if we might not sell her somewhere and get ourselves a bigger ship," Sinbad was flabbergasted. *We, ourselves?* "You know," Thruna went on, "Something to give us more freedom. Something—er—shall we say, more worthy?"

"More worthy of what?"

"Of our voyages, Captain."

Hiding his consternation, Sinbad smiled and said, "Have another drink."

Thruna's milky flesh showed through the sheer gown she still wore. "You're trying to get me drunk, aren't you?"

He refilled his mug also. "We'll both get drunk," he replied, trying to keep the festive mood alive.

Thruna narrowed her eyes and looked him over carefully. *She suspects,* Sinbad thought. The Nordic princess, however, didn't seem cautious. With a grin and a wink she downed the entire mug in a few quick swallows—and politely waited for Sinbad to finish his as well.

"Haven't you any ale?" she asked when he was done.

"No, my lady. Sorry. Only wine."

"Never mind." She sighed and again let him refill the cup. "I don't know what you're planning," she said as he emptied the last contents of the pitcher and called for another, "but it's not going to work." She put her elbows on the table, folded her hands, and rested her chin on them, all the while looking at Sinbad and smiling.

Sinbad returned the smile but secretly groaned. This

280

was going to be harder than he thought; Thruna was determined to match him drink for drink, to make a contest of it, to see him pass out long before she did. And knowing the ways of Harald's court at Roskilde, he knew she just might succeed.

There was a knock on the door and Mongo entered, carrying a small barrel filled with strong Egyptian wine. He placed it on the table and withdrew silently, though not before noticing Sinbad's reddened face and the slur in his speech when he thanked him.

Thruna opened the spout and filled the mugs, pushing his in front of his eyes. "Drink it," she said in a tone that was as much command as request.

He lifted the cup, uttered a toast, and put it to his lips. Thruna did the same and they drained the mugs immediately. Sinbad was tipsy by the time he put the cup down; his eyes were fogging, his cheeks shading scarlet.

Thruna giggled. "You underestimated me," she said, yawning and pouring them both more wine. She untied her braids and swung her head so that her hair flowed freely. "In Denmark we're used to drinking matches. But of course we prefer a stronger brew . . ." And he frowned at the wine.

Sinbad sighed, cursing Felicia for letting her talk him into this. The brazen Viking woman downed her wine as though it were water! And the contest was taking an insidious turn; now it was she who was testing him, analyzing his stamina and weighing it against that of the lords of Roskilde whose bellies were never satisfied.

"More?" she asked, her brows raised.

Sinbad forced a pleasant smile. "Certainly."

How much of the brew they consumed between them it was impossible to say. All Sinbad knew was that no matter how much he took, her own intake was at least the same. Clearly her purpose was to prove that she could beat him at his own game, prove that she was his better, and thus settle once and for all the question of leadership. For the first time Sinbad felt pity for the weak king of Crete, who had agreed to take such a determined woman to wife.

"Hot, isn't it?" said Thruna. She rose and opened the porthole. Sinbad drew a deep breath of sea air and drew upon every inner resource he could muster. By Allah, no Nordic princess was going to get the better of him!

This time he poured the wine, filling the mugs evenly.

"I have great plans for us, Sinbad," Thurna said, raising her arm in yet another toast. "With your nautical skills and my leadership—"

He hardly heard. It took all his committment and energy just to keep up at her pace; while she rattled on about adventure and daring, he focused on keeping his mind clear. One way or another.

Thruna was laughing grandly now. Banging an open palm on the table like a drum, she went into a series of Norse songs—songs of the ancient gods, songs of battle, of seafaring, of the life her people had led for a thousand years. Her loud voice carried far past the door of his cabin, along the corridors, up to the deck, where many a head turned in wonder.

"What's going on down there?" said Abu, scratching his head.

Felicia, on watch, shuddered. She didn't know—but she had a good idea.

It was well past midnight, and the trimmed sails had slowed the ship's speed dramatically. Already the crew could see Harald's long ships gaining, even under the stars, as the *Scheherazade* purposely slowed.

Thruna burped. "Excuse me."

Sinbad nodded feebly. He felt nauseated; his eyes followed the gentle swinging of the hanging lamp above and he gripped the sides of the table fiercely to keep from falling over.

Thruna saw this and chortled; she filled her own cup but left his empty. The clash of wills was all but finished, she knew. It would not be long before Sinbad threw in the towel and collapsed into a stupor.

She twiddled her thumbs and smiled brightly. "Had enough?"

Her voice seemed distant and it was all he could do to turn his head and look at her. "E . . . nuff?"

Thruna slammed down her fist and roared. "Give in, Captain. You made a valiant effort and I respect you for it. But—*hic*—you know you're defeated. Why not admit it? Look." She glanced to the porthole, where the faintest glimmer of morning gray had begun to tease the far horizon. "It's almost dawn. Why don't you sleep? Later when you feel better we'll talk again, discuss our next destination. By then I hope to have some good ideas. . . ."

She had won. Already she was speaking as though she were the commander of the ship. Sinbad put his head to his hands and groaned. What was he to do? Harald's ships would be close—too close to escape now. He was lost for sure. But at least Thruna didn't know her father was so near. At least one good thing would come of this, for even though he might spend the rest of his days in a Cretan dungeon, she would be returned to her husband after all. That would be his feeble revenge.

Thruna leaned back wearily, her own eyes red and blurry, and inhaled deeply. "Ah, fresh air. . . ."

Fresh air! Yes, there was still a chance. . . .

He picked himself up, mug in hand, and wobbled over to the porthole. "T-the . . . contest is—isn't over yet, Princess. I—I need air. . . ."

Thruna chuckled. "You never give up, do you? All right, Sinbad. Have your air. I'll be waiting." Then she tauntingly opened the spout and filled her cup once more.

Sinbad staggered to the wall. Thruna was not facing him; he lifted the thick clay mug and stepped slowly toward her. "Sorry, Princess," he slurred. "I really hate to cheat . . ." And he brought the mug down on her head, shattering it into a hundred fragments and spilling the wine over her golden hair.

Thruna spun round. She gaped, started to rise with balled fists and eyes fit to kill. Then with a gurgle and a moan she slumped forward, toppled from the chair and fell unconscious on the floor.

Sinbad fought his way to the door and flung it open wide. Felicia came running from the end of the corridor. The pirate girl took one look inside and gasped. "You killed her!"

He shook his head and spoke with effort. "Not . . . blood. Wine . . . Pick her up. You . . . know . . . what . . . to do. . . ."

Felicia nodded. With Mongo's help she scraped the dazed princess off the floor and carried her to the deck. Sinbad stood alone, watching from the porthole as the two Viking ships pulled aside. Hundreds of burly Norsemen, horned helmets glinting in the predawn light, made ready to attack.

"Give me my daughter!" raved a frenzied Harald, bedecked in full battle armor and shaking a menacing fist as he stood boldly at the prow of his vessel. "I *warn* you, Sinbad!"

On deck a barrel had been prepared. Mongo held Thruna upright in full display. "The princess is well," shouted Felicia to the king. "See for yourself. And we're returning her to you—with but one small condition . . ."

The enraged king of Denmark scowled. "What condition?"

"That you give up the chase. Take Thurna but turn back. Give no aid to the Cretans."

Harald stared at the brazen girl responsible for this whole episode. He looked mad enough to have everyone aboard the *Scheherazade* beheaded. He squinted hard into the light and peered at his wobbly daughter. "The princess is all right?"

Felicia nodded. "Drunk—but all right."

The king, knowing his child very well, smirked. "And your captain? Where is he?"

Felicia flushed. "Indisposed, my lord. . . . Too drunk to greet you . . ."

Harold roared with laughter. The crews of both his ships laughed in similar fashion.

"Then we have a bargain?"

The king chuckled. "We do. Bring the girl to me."

Felicia nodded and Mongo gingerly packed the princess into the waiting barrel. She began to snore as he covered her with a blanket to keep her warm.

Ropes were swiftly connected and the barrel was lowered over the side, where the swells soon carried Thruna closer to her father's ship. From his side ropes were also lowered, this time to receive the package.

"You'll keep your promise?" called a worried Felicia. "No aid to the Greeks?"

At the very mention of the word Harald's face changed color. "Assist those *dogs?*" he barked, sputtering. "After the way that jellyfish of a king insulted me? *Bah!* I must have been demented to seek such a ridiculous alliance! The king of Crete can count himself lucky that I don't declare war on *him!* No, now that my child is safe, it's back to Denmark. I've had enough of warm seas and hot air. Cultured races indeed!"

Felicia beamed. "Good-bye, my lord. May Allah protect you."

"And may He keep you as well. But remember—if your captain ever decides he's had enough of these fools and their islands, you all have a place at Roskilde. I'll keep a thousand barrels of ale waiting. Farewell, my pirate! Farewell, Captain Sinbad!"

And with that, Harald strode from the prow and signaled his captains to set a new course, back to icebound Denmark.

Sinbad smiled from his vantage point at the porthole. Although the blustery king might have claimed his head, he was sorry to see him leave. And he made a special point of promising himself that he would one day come to Roskilde.

The he vomited out the window and fell upon his bunk to sleep.

With full sails and good winds the *Scheherazade* continued to head west. Within a week they were in sight of the cliffs of Sicily, but the crazed king of Crete and his fleet had not given up. Although still far behind, and slipping farther back every day. The king pressed forward in the hope of finding and catching Sinbad at some nearby port. And dock the ship must, for the weather was changing and the *Scheherazade's* supplies were running precariously low.

"Stopping at Malta or Sicily is too risky," said Sinbad gravely to the small group gathered in his cabin. "Give those Cretans a few days' time and they'll be swarming all over us."

"Aye," agreed a dour Milo. "But what are we to do? Our fresh water is dangerously low, Sinbad. Not to mention the stores . . ."

Nods of agreement from every face met him as he glanced around: Felicia, Abu, Methelese, Clair, even Don Giovanni, who sat meekly at the side of the desk.

"We just can't risk it," Sinbad went on firmly. He took his map and spread it out across the desk; everyone peered over his shoulder.

"Perhaps we can make it to Corsica," said Abu hopefully, adding, "That is, if we don't run into any rough weather. The gale season is upon us, you know."

Sinbad nodded. "That's what I'm counting on."

"What?" Methelese was incredulous. So were the others. This was the worst time of year. The changing seasons made these Mediterranean waters as dangerous as any in the world.

"Hear me out," said Sinbad hastily over the protests. "Our only hope is to force the Cretans back. While the waters are calm the king will follow us forever, but"—he

286

let a small grin break over his otherwise stoic features—
"should we lead him to danger—"

"He'll have no choice but to turn around," said Felicia,
completing the thought.

"Precisely. He'll run like a hound for a safe harbor to
wait the season out. In the meantime we'll have lost him,
with no chance of his finding our route again."

"All well and good," said Milo uneasily. "But what
about ourselves? Your're purposely taking us into these
storms—risking *our* lives every bit as much. And frankly,"—
he frowned and looked at his companions—"I'd rather face
the Greeks than these gales. By Allah, we'd have a better
go of it!"

Sinbad rubbed at his chin. "Maybe, maybe not. Look."
He pointed to the map again. "My plan is to swing north
by west here,"—his finger landed in the Tyrrhenian Sea
and tracked a pattern upward—"pass close to Sardinia,
letting the Cretans think we're going to port. Then, we
shoot through the narrow strait between Sardinia and
Corsica, heading again toward the Pillars of Hercules.
Sooner or later these spring gales are going to hit;
somewhere along the way the Cretans will have to seek
shelter. And we'll be on our way."

"Good plan," said Felicia, "but aren't you overlooking
one thing? We'll never reach the Pillars of Hercules without
supplies—and a Greek sword is certainly a preferable
death to starvation."

"Hear, hear," chimed Don Giovanni.

"Ah, but we *are* going to stop. Here. At Mallorca, in
the Balearic Islands. Or even Tarragona in Córdoba, if we
have to."

The faces were still long.

"Well, what do you think?"

Abu frowned, keeping in mind the near-empty barrels
of fresh water. "I think," he answered, speaking for them
all, "that we had better pray for rain."

* * *

The ship went on half rations immediately. Under a hot sun, growing hotter day by day, it passed the peaceful coasts of Sicily and headed north, on the route that Sinbad had outlined. With the warmer months at hand, the temperature steadily increased, and there was also a noticeable shift in the sky's turbulence. But one full week after the plan had been discussed there was still no sign of rain.

Less than a hundred leagues from Sardinia, quarter rations were imposed. A cupful of water a day for everyone. That and a subsistence ration of fish and salted beef. Each day the lookout would scour the horizon from edge to edge and dutifully report that the Cretan fleet was yet within sight, doggedly trailing behind and never once failing to reappear even after a cloudy and foggy night.

Sinbad spent long hours alone, especially in the time before dawn, staring forlornly up at the stars, praying for rain, and hoping that his decision had been the right one. At moments of despair it was Don Giovanni who offered solace. The little frog alone understood Sinbad's loneliness and frustration, the heavy burdens always imposed upon those in authority. But something would have to break soon—if not, the ship might not be able to survive long enough to even reach the next port.

It was during the critical passage between Corsica and Sardinia that matters began to change. While Sinbad stood forlornly at his post, thinking of the advancing Cretans and his perilous survival, Methelese came to the bridge, Clair meekly at his side.

"How goes it?" the wise Greek asked somberly.

Sinbad grimaced, staring out at the cloudless night sky. "Fair weather for as far as a man can see," he replied glumly. "I fear we'll never reach our destination."

Methelese studied the face of the worried mariner. Their predicament was certainly becoming drastic, he knew, and such a happenstance called for drastic solutions.

"Perhaps you should sleep for a while," said Clair to the captain.

Sinbad smiled and shook his head. "I've tried, dear lady. It's no use; I can't rest. Not while our lives are in such peril."

Methelese clasped his shoulder in a fatherly fashion. "You must rest, my friend. No man can carry all the burdens by himself. Perhaps I can find some potion in my bags to make your nights more comfortable—"

Again Sinbad shook his head. "Better you should find a potion to make it rain," he answered, his eyes gazing once more to the heavens. "A strong rain, and a stronger wind. Something to carry us far away from the Cretan navy."

"Aye," chimed Milo, listening from afar and joining the grim conversation. "A storm is what we need."

"A storm, *hmmm?*" responded the philosopher, scratching his shock of silver hair.

"It's our only hope," added Sinbad. He folded his arms and drew a deep lungful of salty air. "I just don't understand it. By this time of year these climes should be swollen with tempests. And yet . . ."

"Nature hasn't been very cooperative," agreed Felicia. She put her hands to her hips and stared over the rail.

Methelese took all this in and then, with his fingers toying at the side of his nose, pursed his lips and nodded. "I wonder," he mumbled almost inaudibly. "I wonder . . ." And then he looked to his daughter. "Can you fetch me my black bag, child?" he asked.

Clair winced. "Now, Father?" She seemed most reluctant to do his bidding.

"Yes, now," Methelese replied impatiently. "You know our predicament. Good captain Sinbad here just finished saying—"

"I know, I know," said Clair. "But your *black bag?* You know what happened the last time. . . ."

"Bah!"

289

Sinbad and Felicia felt totally bewildered. "What black bag is this?" asked the captain.

"Why, my potions, of course," answered the philosopher with a tone that implied the question was superfluous.

"His tricks," added Clair quickly. "He's carried them around for half his life, as often as not getting us both into hot water. And I mean *hot*. Once, he promised the prince of Venice to recede the waters of his city,"—Methelese looked at her angrily as she spoke—"but instead, the potion backfired . . ."

"It did *not!*" huffed the wise man.

"It did too!" rejoined the girl. "Recede the waters? *Ha!* Do you want to know what happened? He created a flood, that's what! We had to leave Venice like thieves in the middle of night—and with a troop of soldiers on our heels all the way to Rome!"

"I wish you wouldn't talk like that," said her embarrassed father. He looked to Sinbad shyly. "My potions were good, but you see I estimated my amounts a bit too liberally. Instead of less water, we found we had more. Much more. . . ." Methelese shrugged.

There was a bemused grin upon Sinbad's face as he pictured the poor, well-meaning philosopher becoming so fouled up. Felicia, though, seemed to receive the story quite a bit more seriously. "Wait a moment," she said, turning around and facing Methelese fully so that her sharp eyes were keenly fixed upon his own. "What exactly are you telling us? That you can perform magic?"

The philosopher was genuinely offended. "Magic? Am I a wizard? A magician to entertain kings and children? No, my dear Felicia. Please do not place me in such an unenviable category."

Felicia was unperturbed by his outburst. "Forgive me if I seem rash," she said, "but what then is it that's in this black bag of yours."

"Wisdom," came the somber reply.

"Would you mind explaining that?" said Sinbad.

290

Methelese shrugged, then sighed. "As you all know," he began, "I've spent my life studying the ancient civilizations of the world—"

"Yes, yes," said Milo impatiently. "But to the point, man! What's in the bag?"

Methelese ignored his impatience. "Many things," he replied flatly. "Many strange potions whose workings it would take a lifetime to explain. Suffice to say that in my hands is the full knowledge of lands and peoples long since vanished. From the secrets of ancient Egypt to the wonders of Atlantis, from the miracles of the Cretan Caves to the blasphemies of Sodom and Gomorrah, all this can I recount. And all of their arts as well—"

Felicia pulled him by his sleeve. "And magic?" she panted. "Do you know their magic?"

Methelese reddened. "I told you not to use that word!"

"I'm sorry. Knowledge, then. Call it what you like. But do you possess it?"

"But naturally! Why was I being kept prisoner so long on Phalus if not for this very knowledge?"

There was a long pause as Sinbad looked first to the pirate girl, then to Milo, then to Clair. "Is this so?" he asked the girl.

Clair nodded slowly. "I'm afraid it is," she conceded. "But my father has never learned to use his potions properly. One way or another, he always seems to make a mess of things."

Methelese eyed his daughter with shock. "How can you say such a thing, child? Have I ever misused these powers?"

She shook her head. "No . . . . Not intentionally, anyway."

"Well then?" Methelese felt better now that he had proved his point.

Sinbad held up his hands. "Never mind all this," he said. "What I think Felicia wants to know—what we all want to know—is whether there is something in this bag of tricks of yours than can be of help to us?"

A smile broke across the philosopher's marred features. "You mean can I make your storm for you?" he asked. "Is that it?"

"Exactly!" cried Felicia. "Can you do it?"

"No."

"What?" She was astounded. "After all you just finished telling us about the Egyptians, about Atlantis . . ."

"No man can *make* a storm," Methelese told her. "It is quite impossible. Nature alone governs such matters."

"By Allah, then, what *can* you do?" the pirate cried with despair.

Methelese smiled slyly. "I can lend nature a hand."

"Lend . . . nature . . . a *hand?*" wondered Milo.

"Certainly. It's really quite simple." He rested his hands on the rail and peered out toward the starry western sky. "As Sinbad noted before, the tempest season is already upon us, although we have yet to see a storm . . ."

"So?"

Here the Greek turned back to them in triumph. "I possess the very powders needed to stir the clouds, block the sun, raise the wind—"

"And make rain?" said Sinbad, breathless.

Methelese grinned like a schoolboy. "And make rain."

Clair hastened to stand between her father and the others. "Don't listen to him!" she pleaded. "It won't work. It will go wrong. It always goes wrong!"

Sinbad studied the philosopher's expressionless face. "Is Clair right?" he demanded. "Are your tricks safe?"

"Safe enough for the ancient pharaohs to use," he replied dourly. "Time after time these very powders—with the right incantations of course—saved the land of Egypt from drought. And this trick was taught to them by no less than the Persians a thousand years earlier. Naturally, it was during the Golden Age of Atlantis that these potions were originally devised. . . ."

Milo looked at the captain darkly. "I don't like the

292

sound of this," he warned. "By Allah, we should not have to resort to such sorcery."

"I disagree," said Felicia, shaking her head vehemently. "I put great trust in the ancients. After all, it was their civilizations that flourished long enough to give us our own. Everything we know we learned from them in one way or another. Let's give Methelese a chance."

"She's right," said the Greek. "Wisdom such as this has never been matched. Would you hide it because of superstitions?"

"You say Atlantis used these powers," said Milo, unconvinced. "Well? What happened then? Is it not so that that mighty nation sank beneath the very sea? The entire land with all its peoples? What powers caused such catastrophe? I warn you, Sinbad, use these potions and we will bring down the wrath of nature upon our own heads!"

Felicia scoffed. "What is there to fear? A tempest?" She laughed caustically. "Come now, gentlemen. We have the entire Cretan navy at our backs, poised to ram and burn us. Bad weather is our only chance—are we to willingly slip into the king's grubby hands? I say no." She faced Methelese sternly. "Bring this bag of yours, Greek. Quickly. If you have the powers you claim, then use them. Remember, your own throat and Clair's will cut as easily as mine at the wrong end of a Cretan blade."

With that sobering judgment Sinbad was forced to agree. "Now is no time to fear superstition," he told the old sailor. "Besides, what choice do we really have?"

Milo remained silent and nodded submissively. The captain had been honest enough; right now the *Scheherazade* was a desperate ship.

"Bring the black bag," said Sinbad to Clair. "Let's not waste any more time." Then to Methelese, when the girl scampered below, "What can we do to help?"

With a piece of white chalk from his pocket, Methelese drew a rough circle about two meters in circumference on

293

the deck of the bridge. "While I spread the potion to the wind," he said soberly, "Clair shall do her rain dance. Meanwhile I'll need you all to concentrate as hard as you can—thinking only of the rain. The rain and nothing else. Understood?"

Milo grimaced; Felicia nodded; Sinbad shrugged. "All right. What else?"

"That's all. Just keep the picture of rain in your minds for as long as you can."

"All night?" asked Milo.

The Greek's face was stony and glum. "And all day if necessary. We'll wait for the dark clouds to appear; at the first rumble of thunder we'll know we've succeeded."

Milo snickered but said nothing as an out-of-breath Clair clambered back onto the bridge, a small leather satchel in her right hand. She gave it to her father with obvious misgivings, and the look in her eye clearly pleaded for him to use the potion sparingly and carefully.

The philosopher put the bag down slowly; taking a tiny key from the gold chain around his neck, he unlocked it. Sinbad peered over his shoulder at the incredible clutter inside. The bag was crammed with a vast variety of devices, some as crude as rough rocks, others seemingly so sophisticated that Sinbad could only speculate as to what they might be.

"Now let me see," muttered Methelese, rummaging through these items. He tossed aside a worn volume of curious writings and proceeded to mull among a dozen or more stoppered vials with liquid contents. He held out a green one and frowned. "No, this is for rendering genies helpless," he reminded himself. "I think I need the pink one . . . yes. But where is it? Dear me, what could have happened to it?"

Clair lent a ready hand. She shuffled aside a parchment of Persian script, pulled out a few geological specimens and placed them gently at her side. It did not take long

294

before half the bridge had become cluttered with Methelese's varied prizes.

"Aha!" cried the Greek at last. He stuck his hand deep, deep inside and came up with a vial so tiny that he could easily hold the whole thing within his palm. "Here we are," he said triumphantly. "I knew we'd find it sooner or later."

"What is that stuff?" asked Felicia with a shudder, the foul smell from the vial creeping into her nostrils.

"A potion concocted by the wise men of Imhotep the Eighth's court," Methelese replied. "He was pharaoh of all Egypt two thousand years before the first pyramids."

Sinbad whistled. "And the liquid still holds its powers?"

"We shall see," answered the Greek. Then he stood up and looked darkly at Clair. "You may begin, child," he told her, gesturing for her to take her place inside the drawn circle.

Clair grimaced. "Are you sure, Father? Are you—"

"Positive," he replied sternly. "You know what to do?"

She nodded. "I remember the dance, Father. Don't worry."

"Good." Methelese smiled and turned back to his companions. "Now remember what I said. Concentrate as hard as you can. . . ."

"And what will you do with that stuff?" Milo wanted to know.

With his teeth, Methelese uncorked the vial; a thin vapor immediately began to rise, slowly curling in the breeze and working its way upward to the sky. The pink changed color almost immediately upon contact with the air; Sinbad watched amazed as a flaming orange cloud spread lightly above their heads.

"I am ready," said Clair.

"Then begin."

She threw off the hood from her cloak, unclasped the pin, and let the garment fall to the floor. Then she started to sway her hips, her arms lifting above her head, hands forming weird and mysterious patterns in the air.

Milo watched her with interest; Clair's dance was unlike any he had seen before. Her long hair waving in the breeze, she spun round and round and sang a curious song in a tongue no one save her father could name, much less understand. Methelese, meanwhile, lifted the vial higher and soundlessly mouthed an incantation. This continued for a very long while, with no results to be seen. Undaunted, he repeated the prayer again; Clair, although tired and dubious, went on with her vital part of the ceremony.

Milo grew weary of concentrating. He glanced at Sinbad and frowned. "Bag of tricks indeed," he scoffed. "I feel like a fool. How much longer are we going to play this silly little game?"

"Quiet!" barked Methelese, "Do you want to ruin everything?"

Scowling, the old sailor went back to his thoughts of rain, and Sinbad and Felicia did likewise. It was nearly dawn; Mongo and Abu had come from below to take over the watch. When they reached the bridge, they stood frozen and speechless at the scene before them. There were the captain and his mates, standing mute and still like dolls, Methelese mumbling queerly to himself, and the lovely Clair cavorting around inside a chalk circle like a Ceylonese snake-charmer.

"By Allah!" cried Abu. "What goes on here?"

"Shhh!"

They peered down and saw Don Giovanni sitting quietly beside the black bag watching the proceedings. The frog hopped to Abu's side and cautioned the first mate to stay silent. Perplexed, thinking Sinbad and the others mad, both he and Mongo complied.

The contents of the vial had all but evaporated and Methelese pulled a long face. His chant over, he started it again, this time stamping his feet in time with the lyrics, singing louder, and gesturing for Abu and Mongo to clap their hands in time. The two sailors looked at each other, shrugged, and did as asked. Clair's own song grew stronger as the light of day began to glow in the east. And on and on the group continued with the ceremony, until all, save Methelese himself, were stamping their feet, clapping their hands, and concentrating on rain.

Rain, thought Sinbad, over and over. *Rain. Rain!* Eyes shut, body swaying, he summoned all his mental strength to this desperate effort.

Suddenly Methelese stopped. His eyes shot to the eastern sky. "Did you hear?" he cried.

Felicia opened her eyes also. "Hear what?"

"The rumble! The rumble! Thunder!"

Milo peered out as well. Shaking his head, he said, "I didn't hear a thing."

"Nor I," admitted Sinbad. "Let's keep going . . ."

"No, wait." Methelese was clearly excited. Clair stopped in her dance as her father ran to the rail and beamed. A dull haze had begun to cover the morning stars in the east; he could almost make out the outlines of thick black clouds growing across the far horizon. "Do you see?" he called. "Do you see?"

Sinbad rushed to his side. "See what? What?" And then he felt it. A single drop of water splashed on his nose. He touched it with his finger and tasted. There was no salt; the water was fresh. "Rain," he whispered. "It *is* rain."

Methelese clapped his hands delightedly. "Yes, rain! It worked, by Heaven, it worked!" And he gleefully threw his arms around Felicia and swept her off the ground.

Milo stared in disbelief. This time the rumble of thunder could not be missed. It was real all right, as real as the ominous clouds scudding in from the east. And while the sun still shone in the straight between Corsica and Sardinia, they saw ahead the first fearful strokes of lightning.

Abu took to the helm, gazing at the nearby shores of Corsica. "That looks like a bad one," he marveled. "Allah's mercy, feel the wind!"

Indeed, the wind had gained incredible speed and force; already the *Scheherazade* had begun to roll with the early swells.

"I've never seen a storm look so fierce," Felicia said. "It could last for days. . . ."

Methelese laughed buoyantly. "Days, yes! Maybe more! Ah, Clair! Isn't it *wonderful?* I've done it; *we've* done it. This time we've really succeeded!"

Milo shook his head. "We need a storm, my friend. Not a deluge. Just look at that! Do you realize what we could be in for?"

Sinbad glanced behind and saw the sails of the Cretans, barely in sight of the straight but pressing on still, unaware of what was ahead. He had wanted a chance to get away from the Cretan navy, and now he had one. "Steady the course," he told Abu. "Keep her three points off the eye. Everybody not on duty get below. I have a feeling we're going to get more than we bargained for."

They rounded the finger-peninsula of Corsica in trepidation, as the sky overhead grew still darker as if in final warning to those sailors upon the sea, and then with a violent clap let loose a terrible barrage of pelting rain. Using the weather as cover, they attempted to slip across the strait, but the king was not to be deterred—at least not yet, and even under the bleak stormy night Sinbad could see his fleet also enter the straight and round the peninsula.

Out in the open again, the winds seemed to moderate but they veered sharply south. Sinbad's crew had to struggle to avoid being swept too far off their course for Mallorca near the Moorish coast.

By morning, Sinbad found that the trip from the deck to the bridge ladder had become in itself a torturous ordeal. Spray and foam were lashing over the bulwark and a ferocious wind screamed from the starboard side. *Wild horses,* Sinbad thought, recalling the unbroken Arabian stallions whose natures could never be tamed. Those stallions and the storm had much in common, and only the steadiest hand might hope to master them.

Gray-black thunderheads tumbled and churned above, and a thick pea-soup mist was fast bearing down on the battling ship. At times the tips of the masts were already being obscured, only to reappear as the ship tumbled into a trough before climbing the next mountainous wave. And the driving rain increased in intensity. Forward progress had been more than stalled; by evening, they were still in sight of Corsica.

"Can't we turn round and go back to land?" Sinbad heard a frightened Clair ask of the second mate.

Felicia scowled. "That's the worst thing we can do! The ship won't be running away from the tempest if she heads for Corsica. Look at those winds—she'll be running with them! And we'd be smashed before we even reached the strait!"

The crew at the halyards as well as those on the bridge lashed themselves to the lines to keep from being swept overboard by the huge waves breaking in steady rhythm across the deck. The ship steered badly, when at all, and heaved and yawed again and again under what had become a virtual battering-ram of water.

The wind continued to pick up; foaming waves exploded against the hull, cascading like waterfalls over the deck. The crew slipped and slid at their posts while they worked the rigging waist-deep, tugging at the lines with hands raw and bloodied.

"Sinbad, look!" cried Felicia. The captain spun, shading his eyes from the downpour as he stared back toward the coast. The Cretan fleet was still there, but caught amid a barrage that pinned it to its place like glue. Swirling winds battered it from every side. Waves, tearing like demons across the reefs, crashed upon it time after time. One wave, higher than any other, formed a solid wall of water, bearing down on the fleet like a gruesome ogre frothing with malevolent rage.

The lead ship, the king's ship, fell off to port side in a trough and took the battering broadside. Sinbad watched with a mixture of dread and fascination. The lofty masts spun, the mainmast cracked. Timber went flying in a thousand different directions, and in his imagination he could hear a dozen sailors screaming as they were hurled into the air and dragged down deep beneath the black waters. The Greek ship reeled, almost capsized, then straightened. Behind it, the captains of the other ships were turning for land. The flagship listlessly spun, floundered as tremors rippled her from stem to stern.

Sinbad fought his way to the rail, Felicia and Milo on his heels. There was no doubt about it—if the king's ship survived at all, it could not go on anymore. The Cretan fleet would have to hobble to safety and give up the hunt. Besides, what sane captain would dare continue on in such a storm? If nothing else, the Greeks would be certain of one thing: that Captain Sinbad and his ship would go down long before the tempest subsided. Wisely would they let nature do what they were unable to accomplish.

"They're running!" chortled Felicia, her uncovered hair moplike in the torrential downpour. She looked at Sinbad and grinned. "We've won! You were right! They've given up!"

Sinbad sighed. Yes, he'd been right; the Greeks were no longer the enemy. But now there was another: the tempest itself. And there was no going back now. Nothing but open sea and the storm lay between them and Córdoba.

For the hundredth time the wind shifted, and through blinding scud Sinbad kept them going. The exhausted sailors worked in shifts, four hours on, four off. Creaking and groaning, sails tattered and furled, the *Sherry* did not give up. Sinbad worked with them all, pulling his way hand over hand along the anchoring ropes, lending encouragement, extolling his men, calling for courage and

300

pride. And in no respect was he disappointed. His men were the best, from giant Mongo, who did the work of three, to old Milo, whose hands were always ready.

Day came again, a cold dismal day in which the awful chill cut to the bone. Then night. Bleak as it was black. No stars, no sky, only the rumbles of thunder and the opened bellies of grim turbulent clouds.

The ship bobbed like a cork, shaking herself to shed water from the single unfurled sail that ballooned from the mainmast. For a full forty-eight hours Sinbad stayed on deck, until, dropping from exhaustion, he was forcibly taken to his cabin for a few hours sleep.

"Wake me before dawn," he had barked to Abu, and the first mate had nodded somberly. But when Sinbad finally did wake, he learned that he had been purposely allowed to rest for ten hours. In a fury he clambered to the bridge, the late afternoon of the third day of the storm. And there a bone-weary Felicia greeted him with a smile. She and Abu had taken control themselves while Sinbad slept, and grudgingly he had to admit they had done a fine job of it. With somewhat slackened winds, they had made more headway these past hours than the ship had made in the previous two days.

"If the wind stays with us," said Milo, sharing the helm with the captain, "We could reach sight of the coast in another twenty-four hours."

"Tarragona," replied Sinbad, feeling well rested. His hands grasped firmly at the steering oar and he kept the course as steady as he could. "We'll head for Tarragona if we can. It's a small port, but at least we'll be able to make some repairs."

The spars buckled and groaned with the lashing wind. The bow dipped and rose, the ship pitched and tossed. And still there was no end in sight. Without question it was one of the worst storms Sinbad had ever seen. Had he known then what he knew now, he wondered if he would have enlisted Methelese's aid.

The sharp cry of the lookout snapped him from his thoughts.

"A ship, Sinbad!" came the furtive call. "A ship off the starboard side!"

Calling for Mongo to take the helm, Sinbad wiped his eyes and grasped at the splintering rail at the edge of the bridge. There *was* another ship. Far back, to the east, fighting the gales just as the *Scheherazade* was doing.

A wave crashed over the side, causing him to lose his balance. By the time he picked himself up from the foam a series of lightning bolts lit up the sky. He stared ahead again. Before he could get a good fix, though, the day had returned to night and the other ship once more became a dark silhouette.

Felicia fought her way to his side as the ship reeled lopsidedly. "Who can they be?" she asked, panting to fill her lungs with spray-filled air.

Sinbad shook his head. "It can't be the Greeks; they turned back, we saw them . . ."

Felicia frowned. "Maybe they had second thoughts. Maybe the king—"

Thunder crashed and shook the very planks beneath their feet. The *Scheherazade* dived into another trough and, while new mountains of waves stertched above them, the second ship disappeared from view.

Sinbad held tightly onto the girl and they picked themselves up together, careful to keep firm hold of the lashline. "Could it *be?*" asked Sinbad rhetorically. Then he shook his head again, water wildly spilling from his hair. "No. Impossible. . . ."

She took his arm. "Who?"

His face was grim in the shadows, his eyes flickering with the mystery of unsolved questions.

Felicia gasped. "*Melissa!* You think it's Melissa, don't you?"

He shrugged. "I don't know what to think. But it's pos—

sible. She *could* have been following us since Phalus. . . ."

A renewed gust punched violently into the heaving vessel. Felicia fell back helplessly, her hand letting go of the rope, sliding across the bridge. Sinbad dived for her, only to be knocked back sharply. Felicia tumbled and rolled, almost to the far side of the rail where she would have been thrown overboard, had it not been for the quick hands of Mongo. Letting go of the steering oar, he grabbed for her a split second before the deck tilted again and the *Scherherazade* twisted helplessly.

Sinbad rushed to the scene, sighing thankfully as the giant hand-signaled through the terrible din of rain and thunder that she was all right. Shaken, Felicia sat and spewed saltwater from her lungs.

The ship lurched; Sinbad spun, arm covering his face, and listened to the awful sound of groaning timber. The boom was swinging loosely and dangerously. Then another wave toppled over the side and from the corner of his eye he could see the lashed water barrels snap free from their bindings and go sailing into the air. A deluge of water shattered them into hundreds of fragments.

The whitecaps were growing larger again, hurling the tiny vessel, looming like a majestic mountain range as they carried the ship forward at breathtaking speed.

"We're losing control!" groaned Abu, trying to draw air into his waterlogged lungs.

Flat on his stomach, clinging to the lashline, Sinbad struggled to regain his feet. All around was total pandemonium, a vortex of raging whirlpools and furious sea. Allah alone knew where they were being dragged by the violent westerly winds and the roaring waves.

"Run with her, Abu!" he shouted above the noise. "Stay with her as long as you can!"

"We'll never make Tarragona!" rejoined the mate.

Sinbad wiped the pools of water from his face and glared at his anguished first officer. "We *can!* We've come this far—we can make the rest!" And he worked his way to the steering oar, grappling at it with Abu and trying to keep it on some semblance of a course.

The air pressure began to drop, then rise, only to drop again. And the crazed quilt-patch of winds shifted, battering from the south, then from the southeast. The ship made a frantic effort to ride the waves, succeeding against all odds but throwing them farther and farther away from their destination.

During flashes of lightning Sinbad again saw the other ship, also fighting a desperate war against the sea, also struggling for its very survival. Who they were no longer mattered—both vessels were now in a life-and-death match against the full force of nature gone rampant and wild.

Long hours passed—it seemed an eternity—and still the fury raged around them. But the pelting rain at times had begun to momentarily ease, and that, with the erratic shifting patterns of wind and air pressure, indicated that the storm was beginning to break.

The sky remained as dismal as ever. Was it dawn or dusk, Sinbad wondered, as a dim distant scrape of light appeared against the black horizon. No matter. Not now. Not until the worst was over. Not until—

He jumped to his feet, screaming for his men to get out of the way of the swinging boom. A yard cracked, split, sent one of his younger men sprawling over the side, dragged down into the frenzied whitecaps. Another wave crashed from the prow, spilling like a tide from one end of the ship to the other. For an instant Sinbad's head was under water. And then he found himself swimming, swimming in an ocean of freezing water that raged over the ship. His head bobbed up from the pouring tide. The brave ship managed a full half turn before she hit the bottom of the slant, dark waters rushing up, up, up on all sides. Then the bow finished the arc of its turn, to await the next onslaught.

Sinbad went under again, a mouthful of air to sustain

him. When he next came up he saw the great mainsail looming before him, its mangled lines pulling loose, whipping and lashing any who got in its way. The yards strained to maintain their angles. Sinbad grabbed for a stay at the port-side rail, then sank below the water as the ship plunged to one side.

He wallowed helplessly in the sloshing waters, desperately trying to take hold of anything. Twisting, seeking air for his bursting lungs, he came up again, feeling himself being pulled without restraint toward the bulwark.

Dizzying crests swept over and the *Scheherazade* once more plunged to the troughs. Wind-driven spits hit him harshly; his water-clogged eyes opened and caught sight of the burly silhouette of Mongo screaming and pointing to him as he stood against a backdrop of slashing lightning. But there was nothing the giant could do, nothing anyone could do. Not while the reeling and pitching convulsed the ship in a horrid dance for life.

A white-ridged swell proved the final blow. The well-secured skiff snapped from its ropes and began a grisly dance of its own, planks flying as it heaved into the sea. And Sinbad was with it every step of the way. Over the side, tumbling down, crashing into wet blackness colder than he had ever imagined. The ship's natural roll brought her one way, a malignant lash of wind hurled Sinbad and the little skiff the other. He whirled forcefully into the maelstrom and with every ounce of effort began to swim upward to reach air.

Barely conscious, he made it to the top, lost in the dark shadows of his ship. He saw the frail and battered skiff floundering nearby and fought against the waves to swim to her. It seemed like forever, but make it he did; he managed to grab hold of a splintered plank and haul himself up and over, falling into the skiff head-first. The *Scheherazade* loomed before him like a monster in the throes of death; he was like a spinning bottle crushed in

305

her wake. And bit by bit the ship was pulling away, dragged out of its trough and sent tearing prow first into the gigantic whitecaps.

The skiff climbed its next slope, then fell back and nearly capsized. Sinbad clung to the tiller; he cried out in futility to his shipmates, knowing full well no one could possibly hear him above the roar. But someone—he couldn't tell who—had seen him and was shouting to the others. For a brief time the *Scheherazade* righted itself and through the slant of the rain Sinbad could make out his men cluttering at the foredeck as they anxiously watched him drift farther and farther into the maelstrom.

He was on his own, no chance of being rescued. And it would take a miracle for him to save himself against *this*. All around the waves lashed, driven water wreaking havoc upon the already waterlogged boat. The shoreward currents played a treacherous game, sweeping him to dizzying heights on the back of frothing whitecaps, then plunging him to the darkest depths while all the time he kept his grip on the tiller. He wrenched his gaze from the sad sight of the faraway ship struggling for her own life, and grimly kept as much control as he could.

This will be the end, he thought. And with eyes more melancholy than frightened, he stared at the raging sea around him. *I've fought many fights with you before, dear lover—and won every one. Now it's your turn to even the score. I'm ready. Claim me when you will* . . .

But it seemed incomprehensible to him that these could really be the final moments of a life once so promising and fulfilled, yet with so much left undone.

As the sea smashed over the skiff, Sinbad's thoughts turned to Sherry, for the last time, he was sure. There would be no triumphant return to Baghdad. No new love to share with her, no way of freeing her from her bondage. The quest for the Red Dahlia, barely begun, was now ended. A failure. Sherry could never be saved. Nor could Don Giovanni. Sinbad sighed at the thought of the little frog, probably shivering and petrified at this very moment, hidden beneath his bed. *Poor Don Giovanni. I've failed you, too. Failed my ship. Failed my crew. Nothing is left.*

With a mighty roar the skiff was upended and sent spinning, thrown a dozen feet above the water, above the peaks of the waves, and came crashing down again. Lightning flashed, bolts racing three at a time across the sky. Through the murk and the gloom, holding on for dear life, Sinbad winced. He wiped his eyes as the skiff crashed clumsily onto water and rode another whitecap.

A hint of color; dark forms, ragged and solid . . . Land!

He shut his eyes and prayed. *Merciful Allah, let it be so! Don't deceive me, not now!*

He daringly reopened his eyes, heart thumping, almost too afraid to look. More lightning flashed, culminating amidst a terrible barrage of thunder. And there it stood, still distant to be sure, but as real as could be. Not a figment of imagination or dreams, but a true shoreline.

The Córdoba coasts! he cried jubilantly. It had to be! It could be nothing less!

No time for all your self-pity now, Sinbad, he said to himself, pulling up into a sitting position and clutching the brace as the boat rode the wave. *If only I can keep afloat long enough to reach the shore. . . .*

A swirling wind sent the broken skiff into a somersault; water flooded over his head and obliterated everything. Then the skiff heeled leeward in a madcap race across tumultuous sea, finally shooting back up beyond the surface and riding once again upon the back of a wave. It thundered along with the powerful swell and dipped sharply back down into a trough, wildly spinning. Sinbad could feel the boards beneath his feet split asunder as the skiff smashed like kindling. A large board drifted by and Sinbad clung to it. Swimming now, submerging and surfacing out of control, he stiffened his resolve, wrapped his arm around the splintered wood, and rode the wave toward the shore.

From behind came a growing roar. He glanced back over his shoulder only to gasp at the sight. The sea was gathering itself and rising behind him in a new wave twenty or more feet high. And still the land was so far away!

He was rising again toward the crest of the mighty mountain as it climbed upon itself, gaining strength and speed, and rolled in a fury toward the beach. Soon it peaked, curved in a terrific arch, and came tearing down upon him, the roar filling his ears like a hideous laughter.

Sinbad filled his lungs with air, the last air he would breathe. And as he did so, he saw that the wave's arc began to look more and more like a grin, a sardonic death mask waiting to capture him and claim him for the sea. Sinbad swam as fast as he could, the board now the only thing keeping him above the waterline.

Before he could even shut his eyes, the wave thundered over, the impact knocking the board out of his hand and sending him flying head over heels beneath the murk. Its incredible weight pressed; his struggling was useless. Deeper and deeper into the depths, the ocean whirled him like a hapless matchstick until he scoured the very sands of the seabed.

He gagged, felt his lungs bursting for air. With his last few seconds of consciousness he fought a valiant fight to regain the surface, to reach the cap of the churning foam. But he'd never make it, not now, not with so far to go.

It was then he waited for the end, the sea rushing in on him and burying him in her tomb. It was over. He'd been so close, though. So very close. If only he might have lasted a few precious seconds longer.

Then he lost himself in the abyss of wet darkness from which there could be no return. A true sailor lives by the sea and dies by her as well; Sinbad's jealous lover had finally claimed him.

PART SEVEN:

**ONE TALE IS DONE, ANOTHER
UNFOLDS: HOW SINBAD LOSES
ALL HE HAS GAINED, AND GAINS
WHAT IS LOST**

"So there you have it. That's all I know. When I finally awoke, I found myself here, right in this very room."

María Elisa remained still for a time; then she inched her head from his chest and nestled it more comfortably against the crook of his arm. Through the window she could see a small gray patch begin to nudge upward against the sky; from the barn a rooster crowed, heralding the new day.

Sinbad stirred; he kissed María Elisa lightly on the top of her head and forced himself to sit up straighter. His mouth was very dry, he realized; he'd been talking through the night. Neither he nor the girl had slept for a single moment.

Sinbad's fabulous and incredible saga had left Elisa spellbound and awed; she had nothing she could compare it to. Oh, the old fishermen of Pansa often told stories of their own, tales of the sea and the faraway places they'd seen during their lives—but nothing like this. Nothing even remotely similiar. She felt overwhelmed by it, and a little bit saddened as well, for she knew she would now have to add to his pain.

Sinbad sat and stroked her hair for a time, watching peacefully while the gray of dawn spread, turning first to indigo, then to blue, and a trickle of majestic sunlight shimmered along the sea. He gazed wistfully at the tiny fishing boats of Pansa, bobbing in the little harbor. Then, feeling the swell of his memories rush up at him, he shut his eyes.

Elisa opened her own and peered into his face. A single tear appeared between his thick lashes and rolled slowly down upon his cheek. Her lover, so strong and capable, so much the master of his fate as he sailed the limits of the world, had begun to cry. And right now he seemed far more the lost little boy than the daring mariner every land admired.

She kissed his lips softly, tasting the salt of his tear. "You're safe now, Sinbad," she assured him. "All these things are past, soon to be forgotten. Now you'll start life again—a new and better life . . ."

He shook his head, the sadness etched into his features only deepening. "I don't think so, Elisa," he whispered. "You see, I've failed—failed for the last time, and failed miserably. What kind of a future can there be for me? Everything I've set out to do is lost. Better that I should have died in the storm—"

She shuddered as he spoke, and squeezed his hand. "No, Sinbad . . ."

Looking down at her wide eyes, he smiled. "All those whom I love," he said, "all those who love me, had put their faith and trust in me. Counted on me. Now, I've let them all down. My crew, my ship, Sherry . . ." He reflected for a moment, adding, "Even poor little Don Giovanni, whom I vowed to help find a cure for his affliction." Sinbad sighed; he slumped his shoulders and pinched the bridge of his nose with his thumb and forefinger, feeling tired, incurably tired. "It was all for nothing, Elisa. All of it. None of my hopes can be realized, none of my goals achieved. It's as impossible a dream as the search for the Red Dahlia. I was a fool to believe in any of it. It doesn't exist."

Elisa lifted herself up and wiped away a second tear that had streaked down his face. He opened his eyes to find her holding back tears of her own. "It does exist, Sinbad," she whispered.

"No, Elisa. Because of a broken heart I've spent all

these months chasing rainbows. I see that now. I only wish I hadn't made those around me believe in them, too."

Elisa looked at him evenly, biting her lip. "Listen to me, Sinbad. I don't know what I can do to help you find your ship or return to Baghdad, but as for the flower, the dahlia . . ."

His eyes narrowed. "What are you trying to tell me?"

And here it would come, she thought. Perhaps the cruelest blow of all, and she dreaded having to be the one to tell him. "The Red Dahlia you've sought. It's real. I can show you—"

His expression turned to stone. "*You?* You know of it? You can tell me where it can be found?" Trembling, he held her by the shoulders and stared at her with pleading in his eyes.

Elisa sniffed. "Oh, Sinbad! How can I be the one to tell you this? Yes, your strange flower exists. It's as real as you or I. But I fear you've searched so long and hard only to be disappointed. You needn't pass the Pillars of Hercules to find it. These hills, right here in Barcelona, abound with wildflowers. Many of them dahlias, many of them red . . ." She cast her gaze away.

"Where?" he panted. "I must see for myself!"

Pity for him overtook her and she started to cry. "A dahlia isn't rare, Sinbad. Not even a red one. It holds no magic, no cures. Both you and Don Giovanni have put your hopes in a fantasy." She clasped him tenderly, sorrowfully. "It's . . . it's only a flower. A common flower. . . ."

What she was saying hit him with the weight of a sledgehammer. Disbelief filled his features and he shook his head. "No, Elisa. It can't be . . . It can't be. . . ." But even as he spoke he knew she was telling the truth. From the beginning he had known, although he had never allowed himself to admit it. Love and misery had caused him to cling to a myth; truth was hard to swallow. He had embarked upon a futile journey for a useless weed.

"Then . . . there is no hope?" he asked, his voice cracking.

"None. I know what I'm telling you only hurts you further. But it's better to face it now than to go on believing. Perhaps in Baghdad a red dahlia is so rare that to find one is said to bring magic. But here"—she gestured about her—"there are fields filled with them; they hold no attraction for us. I know, I've picked them many times. They're beautiful flowers, Sinbad. Perhaps the most beautiful that God ever created. But there is no magic. None."

Sinbad lifted his gaze toward the rising sun, a bitter laugh upon his lips. How cruel the fates had been! How mean, how spiteful to have been given hope only to have it shattered now like everything else.

Still, dreams die hard, and Sinbad, although convinced of Elisa's sincerity, could not let himself accept. Not just yet. . . .

It wasn't hard for her to read his thoughts; she could well understand his doubts. "Would you like to see for yourself?" she asked. "I can take you into the fields and show you—"

He nodded with a mixture of enthusiasm and fear. "Yes, Elisa. Please. It still means a lot to me, more than I can explain. I have to see for myself . . ."

She put a finger to his lips. "I understand. We'll go. This very morning."

Sinbad closed his arms around her, and as her dark lashes meshed, she could feel the wetness in her eyes. At that moment she wished and prayed that he would prove to be right about the flower. She wanted to be wrong, she wanted him to find the magic he sought if only to see him happy once again, knowing he could return home and claim everything that had so unjustly been taken away.

From the house she heard the stirrings of her sisters. Elisa slipped from the bed and hastily dressed. Her father was already up; she could see him from the window as he sleepily strode from the house and made his way, buckets in hand, toward the barn.

"You'd better hurry," Sinbad told her as she combed her hair and slipped into her sandals.

Elisa nodded. "I have a few chores to do. Wait for me. I'll be back as soon as I can."

He watched as she threw him a kiss and stole quietly from the room. She hid near the hedges and, after making sure no one was about, sneaked back to the house.

Sinbad smiled, thinking fondly of the girl, then shivering in the chilly morning air, he pulled on his shirt, and waited tensely for her to come back.

The minutes ticked by like hours. His own breakfast was brought by María Vanessa and left untouched as he anxiously paced back and forth. And then she came, breathless and smiling, her duties finished.

"Don't let anybody see us," she said as she took him by the hand.

Sinbad nodded. He opened the door slowly, peered outside, then dashed with her beyond the garden toward the line of trees atop the hill.

"Where's the field?" he asked, peering from the heights across the village and the harbor.

Elisa pointed down to a meadow where a herd of sheep grazed peacefully in the damp thick grass. A shepherd boy sat perched on a boulder, playing a flute as he kept an eye on the herd.

"Not far," replied Elisa, taking his hand again. "There's a ridge over the next hill. We'll cross the meadow and come to a stream. The field is beside it."

They ran through the grass like a pair of young lovers, unmindful of the smiling shepherd boy who watched or the *baa*ing sheep who crossed their path.

Warm sunlight filtered through the branches of the trees onto the cold waters of the rippling stream. Sinbad and Elisa splashed across and, barely pausing to catch their breath, raced up a rise. The girl reached the top first

315

and beckoned. He followed slowly, almost too frightened now to look at what he had come so far to find.

"There, Sinbad," said Elisa, pointing down a sharp slope covered with knee-deep grass and a multitude of wildflowers.

Sinbad shaded his eyes from the sun and peered into the field. Below him lay a full spectrum of color: roses, violets, daisies as bright as the sun, bloodroots as crimson as a sky at dusk. Slowly he picked a path downward, Elisa following in his footsteps.

Pausing in a patch of white lilies, he stooped over and plucked a single orange blossom that had fallen among them. His mind flashed back to Baghdad and to Sherry with such a flower in her hair. Orange blossoms were her favorite, and it hurt him deeply now to be reminded of his loss.

Elisa took his hand again, they made their way to the foot of the hill. Sinbad dropped the blossom and stared ahead. As Elisa had promised, growing in the field were a multitude of lovely dahlias. He walked among the array and gazed at the red petals. Each flower was a work of art, a masterpiece in itself.

The girl kept back while he knelt down and choose one from among the many. The delightful fragrance of the flower filled his nostrils; he took it by the stem and gently yanked it from the soil. Then he held it between his fingers and looked at it with wonder. The Red Dahlia of his dreams was at last in his possession. It, and a hundred like it, all his to claim, as few and as many as he desired.

What was it that Don Giovanni had told him so long ago? Yes; *to grasp it within your palm, to shut your eyes, to make your wish as you squeezed it . . .*

Sinbad swallowed, his mouth dry, his hand shaking, his heart beating like a drum. Afraid to find out once and for all the secrets of the flower, he wished that the little frog could be here with him now, sharing this crucial moment. As his fingers began to tighten around the soft petals he prayed with all his heart that Elisa was wrong, that the dahlia was every bit as strange and powerful as the legends of Baghdad said. And a thousand different wishes swam through his thoughts; he found himself struggling to blot them all out and think of only one. Yes, that was it. Just one thought. One wish. Maybe the flower might yet provide it. . . .

The petals started to crush as he squeezed. He shut his eyes fiercely and concentrated all his will and energy on this single moment.

Take me far, far from this place, he entreated. *Take me back across the sea, across the desert sands to my home. Take me now to Baghdad, to the caliph's palace, and even should I die for it, allow me to take Sherry one last time into my arms. . . .*

He stood perfectly still, waiting, intensifying his concentration. The sun was strong, and he could feel the beads of perspiration on his face and hands. A calm breeze cooled his flesh, and in his agonized mind he thought he could feel the magic of the dahlia flowing mysteriously through him. On his knees now, he rocked his pained body back and forth, wishing, praying, begging. Elisa looked on with sadness while over and over Sinbad repeated his desire.

Then, head bent low as if in prayer at a mosque, Sinbad dared to open his eyes. At first the salty tears blurred his vision, allowing him to make out only the vaguest forms of land and sky. But soon reality washed away hope and belief; he plainly saw the gentle field, the slope of the rise, the patch of lilies and the silent girl standing tearfully among them. Slowly he got to his feet, and with sagging shoulders opened his hand. The pretty flower had been crushed almost beyond recognition. One by one its petals floated away in the wind and the bent stem dropped forlornly to the grass, to be lost among the tall blades.

Elisa hesitantly took a step forward. She held out her hand to him. "Sinbad . . . I—I'm . . . sorry. . . ."

The mariner stared at her for a time, and then he smiled. "Don't be silly. Of course you were right. I had no reason to believe . . ."

"Yes, you did. Everyone has at least that much reason. What good is living without it?"

She bit her lip, sorry she had said that. Sinbad sighed; he kneeled and plucked another dahlia. Then he twirled it around and watched its petals spin. "You'd be lovely in the gardens of Baghdad," he said wistfully to the flower. "A pity I can't bring you home to bloom. . . ."

María Elisa came beside him. "What will you do now?" she asked. "Now that your search seems to be over . . ."

Sinbad shrugged. He turned to her and rose. "I suppose what I planned to do all along. Sneak a boat from the village tonight and make my way south across the Córdoba border. There's a good chance still that my ship is looking for me. With luck maybe I can catch up with her at Tarragona as planned."

Elisa nodded. "You will, Sinbad. I know you will. And I'll help you steal that boat. I promise I will."

She locked her eyes with his, smiling as he said, "You mean that? You'll help me get away from here?"

"I swear. Just tell me what must be done."

A faraway voice grew louder, a woman's voice shouting from the top of the rise.

Elisa let go of Sinbad and turned sharply. "It's my sister!" she gasped. "She's seen us! And now she'll tell Papá!"

María Victoria had indeed seen the couple holding hands in the field, but if jealousy was in her heart it did not show itself now. Instead, Victoria was frantically waving her arms, madly beckoning both Sinbad and her sister to come up quickly, urging then with near-screams.

Neither Sinbad nor Elisa could make out what she was saying, but the mariner knew that anguished look well enough. Victoria was frightened—frightened out of her wits.

318

Pulling Elisa by the hand, Sinbad raced up toward the crest of the rise. Just then the church bell began to ring; Sinbad turned toward the village, where he could see Father Augusto in the bell tower calling the citizens of Pansa to hurry to the plaza.

"*Qué es?*" cried Elisa, panting. "What is it?"

Victoria looked through her sister and focused her attention upon Sinbad. "It's them!" she raved. "They've come! They've come!"

"Who?" shouted Sinbad, grabbing her by the shoulders and shaking her out of her panic. "Who's come?"

Victoria's face was the color of cotton clouds. She shuddered as she spoke. "Suliman. Suliman and his band of cutthroats."

Elisa's hand leaped to her mouth.

"Are you sure?" asked Sinbad. "How do you know? How can you be certain?"

"The shepherds, Sinbad. Last . . . Last night. They saw the campfires," she pointed in a southerly direction. "Dozens of fires. Everywhere, farms burned, destroyed. Prisoners . . . *slaves*. . . ." She blurted the last word and shook uncontrollably as Elisa shielded her in her arms.

Sinbad looked at the older sister. "She must be right," Elisa said firmly, looking to the village. "Father Augusto would never ring the signal at this hour unless . . ."

Sinbad nodded, saying quickly, "Can you take care of her while I get to the plaza?"

"She's all right. I can manage. Go, Sinbad. Do what you can. Please. For my sake . . ."

He squeezed her hand. "For Pansa's sake." Then he turned and ran ahead, listening to the shrill gong of the church bell and the dim wailing of the old women. Absentmindedly he stuffed the fresh dahlia in his pocket, forgetting all about the flower and thinking only of what he could do to help.

The plaza was filled by the time he reached it. The old men of the village had gathered near the steps of the church, hollering above the din of crying children, trying to restore order amid the pandemonium.

Sinbad tried to reach the priest and found himself blocked by a dozen anguished mothers sheltering babies in their arms. Pablo the cobbler was trying to calm a number of fisherwives whose husbands were still out upon the sea, and Francisco the smithy had his hands full holding back a crowd of farmers and shepherds from the nearby hills.

Sinbad looked around frantically for someone he could talk to, someone who might be able to explain exactly what was happening. Hearing his name called from behind, he turned, stumbling over a running dog, to see Manuel de León huffing and puffing his way through the crowd. Sinbad grappled past others and finally forced his way to the innkeeper's side.

"What's going on, Don Manuel?" he called, nearly drowned out despite his closeness to the other man.

Manuel narrowed his dark eyes. "Haven't you heard? It's Suliman! The bandit has crossed the border! His men can be here in a day!"

A shepherd's wife fainted away after hearing what Manuel said. And without meaning to, the peaceful innkeeper had added to the panic. Manuel bent down to revive her, feeling the frightened eyes of a dozen others upon him. They expected him, as village leader, to do something. To take some action, to band them all together and tell them what to do. But poor Manuel was as frightened as any—and with good reason, for Suliman commanded an army of hundreds, and with the young men of Pansa gone off to fight with el Cid, the village was left totally helpless against the onslaught.

At the top of the church steps Father Augusto was bravely trying to restore some order. Sinbad bolted from the innkeeper and struggled to make his way to the priest. Then through both their pleadings the citizens finally were quieted.

"We must not panic, my children," Father Augusto told

them severely. "We must pray and seek courage. . . ."

"But Suliman comes!" wailed a fisherwife. "Who shall protect us?"

"We'll be murdered!" screamed Pepe the goatherd. And he looked upon the faces of his companions. "You all remember the last time Suliman came into Barcelona?"

Virtually everyone in the crowd crossed himself. The incident was still vividly remembered, though it had been some time before. Dozens of their daughters had been butchered or raped or taken to be sold as slaves or prostitutes. Their sons had been killed like animals, beheaded, and castrated. No vile or foul thing had been left undone. These memories made the townspeople cringe with horror.

"We must flee Pansa!" shouted Francisco. "Gather our families and run while we can!"

"But to where?" shouted someone from well back in the crowd. "Where is it that we can flee? What refuge can we seek?"

"The City!" rejoined Pepe the goatherd. "Barcelona. It's our only chance!"

"But the city is so far," cautioned Manuel, now on his feet and regaining his composure. All eyes turned to him. "Suliman's men will catch us on the road long before Barcelona is in sight. We'll be cut down like dogs!"

"Then what shall we do?" yelled Tomasina de Cordobal, wife of Sancho the candlemaker.

Manuel shook his head.

"Run to the hills!" shouted Pablo.

"Are you mad?" rebuffed Francisco. "Suliman is *in* the hills! His spies must be near Pansa already!"

Gasps abounded and the crowd fell into a despondent silence. Indeed, things looked bleak.

Sinbad held out his arms, catching their attention. "Just a minute," he said. "We must get organized. We must know exactly what we're up against before making any decisions. The wrong choice could kill us all."

The crowd stared, awed by his words and his command of them. But some had doubts.

"And who are you to speak for Pansa?" called Pablo. "You are not of this village!"

"Yes!" shouted a fisherwife. "I was on the beach the day you were found. You are not of us. You are a foreigner!"

"A Moor! He's a Moor!" somebody called angrily, and the crowd turned hostile.

"Kill him! Kill him! He's a spy!"

"Yes! He's a spy for Suliman!"

A handful of citizens began to mount the steps in rage, sticks in their hands to be used as clubs. Sinbad stepped back toward the church door, his hand slipping to his knife.

Stop this!" cried Father Augusto, before the mob had taken over. "Dare you defile this church?"

"But, Father," protested Francisco. "He is a Moor—"

"He's not!" The voice was loud and strong; the crowd looked away to where María Elisa de León and her two sisters came striding across the road. They bristled past the startled onlookers and climbed the church steps. Elisa pushed Pablo out of the way and the cobbler's mouth hung open in amazement.

Elisa scanned the gathering and looked at them with scorn. "This man, this *foreigner*, is the only chance we have," she snapped. "Yes, he's from across the sea. But were not the Three Wise Men? And the disciples? Would you condemn them as well?"

The crowd stood in shocked silence. Elisa's lips trembled as she addressed them again. "This man is *not* a Moor. But he knows their ways, and he can help us fight against them—"

"Fight?" mimicked an amazed Francisco. "How can we fight against Suliman and his army? This is madness!"

"Then run!" shouted Victoria, taking her sister's place at the forefront. "Go on! Cowards! Let Suliman sack Pansa. Let him burn our homes and our farms, steal our livestock

322

and take with him everything we've ever held dear." She gestured to the bell tower above. "Even our church will be destroyed. Desecrated. Left in ruins at the hands of the infidels. Is this what you want?"

"No! No!" came the response of everyone. "Never! Never!"

María Vanessa smiled thinly. "Good. Then it's agreed. We hold our ground. We keep our homes. That is,"—she turned meekly to Sinbad, who was standing in the shadowed doorway of the church too dumbfounded by these most recent events to speak—"that is, if our Captain still wants to aid us. . . ."

Sinbad slowly stepped into the open, a smiling Father Augusto at his side. "The girls are right," the priest said to the crowd. "If we leave Pansa now, we shall never return. And even I, a man of the cloth, say that it is better to meet the infidel than flee before him." He held out his hand for Sinbad to shake. "Well, Captain? Can our humble village entrust itself to you?"

Sinbad bit tensely at his lip. They all sounded very noble in this dark hour, very courageous. But what would happen when the moment itself came and Suliman's hordes swept down upon them all? How could this ragtag group of well-meaning old men and girls possibly defend an entire village?

"I'll do what I can," he said at last. "But no promises." Then he took the priest's hand and shook it.

Manuel de León came forward. "What shall we do, Captain Sinbad? What do you want us to do?"

Sinbad thought fast. "First of all, I want us all to learn as much about the enemy as we can. Which among you saw the campfires last night?"

A small hand stuck out from among the crowd and Sinbad peered to see. A young boy, not more than thirteen, stepped from the group and came to the foot of the steps. "I saw them, sir," the youth said hesitantly. "In the early hours, before my father came to tend the flocks."

323

Sinbad beckoned him closer. "What is your name, son?"

"Rudolpho, sir."

The mariner smiled. "You needn't be frightened, Rudolpho. Just tell me, tell us all, what you say."

The dark-haired, scruffy youth gulped. "At first," he began, "I heard only the hooves of horses, many horses. And then I peered beyond the meadows and saw them riding. A hundred horsemen, señor. Perhaps more; I cannot tell. They made their camp near the flat. I heard much laughter, much singing as they set up their tents and built their fires. In the darkness I crept closer, as close as I dared." Here he shuddered, making the sign of the cross. "I saw him. Suliman the Filthy." He spat. "A pig of a man. I watched as he commanded his lieutenants to fortify their positions. Then, while these horsemen ate and drank, other bandits came. On foot. Dark, dirty men, carrying spears and swords, dragging behind them dozens of prisoners with ankles and hands bound by rope. These prisoners cowered under the lash; I heard one beg, heard his guards laughing cruelly as they beat him again and yet again. It was terrible, señor . . ."

"Go on," urged Sinbad.

Young Rudolpho shivered as though a cold wind had swept over him. "Then I saw the poor man fall to the ground, whimpering. A friend of his came to his side and spoke a few words in a tongue I could not understand. Suliman's soldiers knocked him down as well, and then, while the first man screamed, they cut his tongue from his mouth."

The crowd looked away, sickened at the awful tale. Rudolpho looked up and said, "Must . . . must I go on, señor?"

Sinbad nodded firmly. "Yes, Rudolpho. As painful as it may be for you, it's vital that everyone hears it. Please, young friend, do continue."

The lad sighed deeply and began again. "There were women as well among the prisoners. Girls from nearby

324

villages, one of whom I recognized. Carmen, daughter of Paulo the swineherd. . . ."

Faces of stone cracked in horror as many among the gathering acknowledged that they knew her also. "What happened?" asked Father Augusto.

Rudolpho swallowed hard. "I saw Suliman's men take her and bind her to a tree. Then, filled with the fire of wine, they . . . they used her. . . ."

The priest was aghast. "*Dios mío!*" he mumbled beneath his breath, making the sign of the cross.

"Never mind that," said Sinbad softly. "What else can you tell us about Suliman's army?"

"Very little, señor," admitted the boy. "The sentries became suspicious and began to scour the wood where I lay hidden. Frightened of being found out and captured, I ran back to my home as quickly as I could to tell my father. He, of course, came here to Pansa this morning and told Father Augusto of the things I had seen. The rest you already know."

Sinbad frowned. The lad's story had been vivid and truthful, yet it provided little in the way of real information about Suliman's forces—information that he must have if Pansa were to try and hold her own against him.

He mussed the boy's hair and smiled. "Thank you, Rudolpho. You've done a very fine job; we're all proud of you. But,"—and he sighed, shaking his head slowly— "we're going to have to find out a lot more."

"What more is there to know?" questioned Manuel, now over the shock of the tale. "Suliman is coming. Is that not enough?"

"I'm afraid not, my friend. If we are to defend the village, we have to learn something more than this about our enemy's strength. For example, how many men does Suliman really command? One hundred? Two? Three? Are they seasoned fighters or rabble? Are they planning to attack us at night while they think Pansa is asleep? Or do they plan a frontal assault at dawn, with the sun before their eyes? How skilled are these bandits, will they run if challenged? Or will they fight to the death? All this we need to find out, in order to plan our own defense and strategy."

Father Augusto understood what the mariner meant and he looked at Sinbad darkly. "How do you propose we obtain this knowledge?" he asked.

Sinbad met his stare and didn't flinch. "There can only be one way, Father: sneak right into Suliman's camp and take a prisoner."

María Elisa gasped; she flew to Sinbad's side and clung to his shirtsleeve. Breathlessly, she said, "And who shall be the one to capture the prisoner?"

Sinbad smiled glumly. "There's only one person here who has even a chance of pulling it off. Me."

Victoria paled and tottered; it seemed she was going to faint. Father Augusto and her sister steadied her until the shock had worn off.

"Don't worry," said Sinbad, looking at the distraught girl but really addressing everyone. "I've been in scrapes like this before. I'll manage."

"You'll be killed!" cried Manuel de León. "Caught long before you even reach their camp."

"No he won't!" called young Rudolpho boldly. All eyes looked upon the boy as he said to Sinbad, "I'll take you, señor. I'll show you the way through the hidden trail. . . ."

Sinbad clasped him by the shoulders. "You'd risk your life again?" he asked.

Rudolpho nodded somberly. "For my village and my friends, yes."

"Then it's settled. At dusk the boy and I shall leave for Suliman's tents."

"And what about us?" shouted Francisco. "We thought you were going to stay and help us!"

"And so I am!" He turned to Father Augusto. "Father, while I'm gone you and Manuel are in charge. . . ."

326

The priest nodded. "I understand, Captain Sinbad. What do you want us to do?"

Sinbad lost no time; he pointed to the narrow street at the end of the plaza. "I want a barricade set up beyond the well," he said. "Use any materials you have—wood, brick, anything . . ."

A short, balding man stepped forward. "I can build your wall," he said. "I am Javier, the mason." And he bowed politely.

Sinbad smiled. "Good, Javier. Round up as many able-bodied men as you can. I want it up before tomorrow."

"And what can *we* do?" asked Miguel the fisherman.

"Gather all of Pansa's supplies. Take the children and keep them out of the streets. Gather them in the church."

Miguel nodded. He called his fellow fishermen and they set to the task even before Sinbad had finished.

"And what about us?" said Elisa. "We want to help also."

"That's right," chimed Victoria. "We all want to do our part."

"Everyone will have to," replied the mariner dourly. He peered up at the morning sun. "My guess is that we have forty-eight hours at the most before Suliman and his band are ready to march again. Forty-eight hours until all of Pansa is under siege. Find every available weapon you can. Knives, bows, rolling pins and kitchen boards if necessary. Come the day after tomorrow, we're going to be fighting for our very lives."

Crossing a copse, Rudolpho dashed among the thick trees and indicated for Sinbad to hurry up and follow. Impulsively, the boy ran forward, plunging himself among the long, lengthening shadows. In a half a dozen full steps he had cleared the trees and made his way onto a small rise that looked down upon a lush field of tall grasses.

Sinbad hunched down and crawled beside him. Rudolpho

327

was busy scooping handfuls of earth and smearing it across his face. "It will help keep us unseen," he assured the mariner. Sinbad nodded and spread a thin layer of dirt over his own face. Now their faces almost blended with the approaching night.

"How far to the camp?" Sinbad asked.

Rudolpho lifted his hand and pointed far across the field. It was then that the first flame of a campfire suddenly appeared, a thin crimson finger dancing gently in the mildest of breezes. Luck was with them, Sinbad knew. Since yesterday, when the boy first came upon the camp, Suliman had not moved his forces. It was obvious that he was resting his men, feeding them, letting them enjoy the spoils of the last campaign before moving on to the next. And this brief respite was exactly what Sinbad had been hoping for. Now if only everything else would go as well . . .

"We must be doubly careful from here on out," said Rudolpho. "Suliman's sentries patrol the perimeter as far as here. They must not have any opportunity to grow suspicious."

"Don't worry," said Sinbad. "I know exactly what to do. I'm going down first. You follow, but linger behind. Don't stay too close." Then he looked at the youth darkly. "If I should get caught, you run back to Pansa as quick as you can, understand? I don't want any heroics."

Rudolpho nodded. "I understand completely. Good luck, Sinbad."

The mariner mussed the boy's hair, then in a slow belly-crawl he inched his way into the field and hid among the grass. It was a tedious process to make his way toward the glowing fires. As he crawled, he could hear the laughter of Suliman's swarthy villains growing louder, hear their cruel jokes and exultations about what they would do to the villages that lay between here and the walled city of Barcelona itself.

There was a narrow path in the grass, marked by a tall cherry tree. Sinbad crouched beside the trunk and peered out at the lone sentry, curved sword dangling from his side, who patroled the perimeter. As the leaves rustled with the breeze, Sinbad slid back down, this time on his back, and slipped out his dagger. Then he patiently waited. He could feel the sentry coming closer by the heavy step of his boots. Sinbad tightened his grip on the blade and held his breath. Like lightning he was up; he caught the man from behind, choked him with his free hand, and plunged the blade up into the small of his back with the other. The sentry's eyes widened, he gurgled and then crumpled into Sinbad's arms. Sinbad dragged him behind the tree and tucked him out of sight among a patch of high weed and scrub. With a thin smile of satisfaction the mariner continued his journey toward the camp.

By now he could smell the aroma of stuck pig on the skillets and of the heady wine being passed around in goatskin pouches. He could almost see the lustful fires burning in the eyes of the bandits as they contemplated the spoils to come, vengeful eyes, filled with hate and malice. Oh, Sinbad knew he'd seen their kind before; scavengers, always there in any land, waiting for the opportunity to rape and plunder and gather the spoils that war spilled carelessly all around.

A scream brought him back to reality. Across the camp, near a cluster of trees, he saw for the first time the groups of prisoners. Set apart from Suliman's soldiers, they had been herded into bunches, just as Rudolpho had said, hands and feet bound, waiting meekly while the guards taunted them. A girl had been dragged from her companions screaming and kicking and pulled roughly into the darkness behind the trees. Sinbad winced at the sound of her agonized shrieks, not even daring to conjecture what those spineless animals might be doing to her. As for the other prisoners, several had tried to protest, but angry kicks in the face and groin by Suliman's laughing troops were the only reward for their concern.

Knife blade firmly clenched between his teeth, Sinbad pushed himself forward on his elbows and slowly began to circle the camp, heading in the direction of the prisoners. From everything he had observed, those guarding the hapless groups were both drunk and careless. With any sort of luck, he knew he might be able to slip inside the camp itself unnoticed—and free at least some of the hostages before anyone even realized he was there.

Foul-mouthed and crude, the soldiers went on with their sport. Sinbad looked back over his shoulder and, hooting like an owl, gave waiting Rudolpho the signal that everything was well. Then he crept on again, this time purposely away from the dim light of the fires and back into high grass. The ground was rough and damp; he strained every meter of the way, every few moments freezing in his place when another sentry passed on his rounds nearby.

Soon the silent silhouettes of the prisoners were in full sight. Tied in small units of five or six, women mingled with men at random, they sat crosslegged and weary, tattered clothes giving testimony to the cruelty they had endured since their capture.

Sinbad studied them all before making another move. Right now he had to be prudent and select from their number one or two of the fittest, healthy men who could run fast enough to elude the guards who would surely give chase.

Raucous laughter arose from nearby. A handful of grinning soldiers, their needs satisfied, came stumbling out of the bushes. Behind lay the wimpering form of a girl—the girl they had dragged away only minutes before. While the guards snickered among themselves, complimenting each other on their virility, Sinbad tucked his knife into his shirt and stole to the very edge of the camp. A pair of startled eyes caught his fleeting shadow and stared. Sinbad stared back, catching a glimpse of the man's features as a crackling ember sent a quick needle of light his way. Sinbad rubbed his eyes, disbelieving what he had seen.

But no, there was no doubt. The craggy face, sunken eyes, strong hands . . . It could be no other.

Milo!

At that moment, bolts of anguish shot through him like blue-charged lightning. *It couldn't be! Not Milo!* How, how was all this possible? And he felt his heart sink like a leaden weight. If Milo had been caught, then so must have the others. Were all from aboard the *Scheherazade* now slaves in the hands of Suliman? He remembered what Ruldopho had said to him at the meeting, about the foreign voices he had heard among the captives, and Sinbad knew then that his worst fears must be true. For days he had hoped his shipmates would be looking for him, and now, irony of ironies, he had found them instead.

Sleepy after their fill of food and drink, the close-by guards paid little attention to their bound charges. As several returned to the whimpering girl for another moment of pleasure, Sinbad deftly inched into the camp, shielding his face and throwing himself among the startled prisoners.

"Allah be blessed!" cried a mournful Milo, staring at his captain. "Is it really you? We feared you dead!"

Sinbad pressed a finger to his lips. "A long story, Milo, but to be told another time. Right now we have other needs . . ." And with a cunning smile he withdrew his knife and split Milo's wrist bonds with a single thrust.

The old sailor rubbed his reddened wrists thankfully.

"Has all the crew been taken?" Sinbad asked as he cut the leg ropes.

Milo shook his head. "No, only three. Me, Mongo, and Methelese." His eyes shifted to the edge of the group, and there, uncharacteristically silent, sat the giant. Double knots held his powerful hands together and leather straps his feet; his mouth was gagged with a dirty cloth.

Sinbad slipped over and freed the giant.

Mongo groaned with relief and grinned at his captain.

331

"Am I glad to see you," he moaned. "I thought we were done for."

"How did this happen?" Sinbad whispered. "How did you fall into Suliman's hands?"

Mongo spat upon the ground. "A sorry tale. After the storm, we were certain you were dead, but we had to be sure. We found a safe cove north of Tarragona and Felicia dispatched a longboat with a search party to look for you. The odds against your being alive were long, but every one of us wanted to try anyway. Milo, Methelese, and myself set out to the north while the others went inland. During that very night, when we came close to the borders of Barcelona, we were attacked. We fought these brigands off as best we could, but as we were outnumbered by ten to one"—he sighed—"we couldn't hold them off. Our captors made us prisoners and brought us to the main camp of Suliman's army. Then we were thrown together with all these other poor souls, doomed to be led into slavery when the war is done."

Sinbad gloomily peered around at the sad faces of the captured prisoners, dozens of them, all trapped here at the mercy of this ragtag horde descending upon Barcelona. He wanted to free them all, to stay right here and make a fight of it against Suliman. Yet his mission demanded that he return to Pansa as quickly as possible. Releasing everyone now would only rouse the rebels into an earlier attack upon the village. With a heavy heart, Sinbad resigned himself to leaving the others behind.

As the laughter of the drunken guards became louder again, he slipped away from Mongo toward another group of captives where he had spotted Methelese. The stunned Greek sat speechless while his bonds were cut. "Follow me," whispered Sinbad, crouching down and starting to crawl toward the trees.

Methelese bent forward, eager to follow. It was then that a dark, tiny head appeared in the shadows amid the folds of his tunic. Sinbad stared with utter disbelief, his stony expression at length turning into a full and delighted smile.

"Hail Captain Sinbad!" croaked the frog.

"Don Giovanni!" gasped the captain.

Methelese grinned. "I brought him with me, Captain Sinbad. I knew he wanted to help in the search. . . ."

The bullfrog hopped from his host and landed squarely on Sinbad's shoulder. He looked at Giovanni and laughed. So glad was he to see his old friend again, he almost forgot the dangers that faced them all.

Quickly Sinbad surveyed the way to the grass. A thick-necked sentry crossed from the bushes and planted his feet almost directly in front of the sailor. Silently, Sinbad raised his knife and, with a quick flick of the wrist, threw it. The blade whistled in the stale night air; the sentry groaned as it sliced between his shoulder blades. He tottered, sputtered as if trying to call for help. Out of nowhere the great silhouette of Mongo leaped over him and pummeled him to the earth.

Mongo grinned as he tossed the knife back to Sinbad. And with the way to the trees clear at least for the moment, the small group scurried like ants from the camp.

A beaming Rudolpho greeted them all at the edge of the clearing. "We must hurry, señor," he said to Sinbad after they had gathered. And he pointed to the array of tents lining the folds of the knoll. Men were stirring, buckling on their curved and straight swords, preparing to begin a new watch until dawn.

"Lead the way, Rudolpho," said Sinbad. "We've learned all we need to know. When Suliman strikes, we're going to be ready."

"It will never work!" cried Francisco. "Suliman has cavalry—you saw it yourself. Our wall will never hold him back."

Father Augusto looked at Sinbad and sighed deeply. His face darkened by the slanting shadows cast inside the church, the priest peered down once more at the map Sinbad had sketched. The configurations of the village were plain. The sea on one side, the hills on the other. The winding road to Barcelona a long, curling slash in between. "Our wall cannot hold back Suliman's horsemen," he said at last. "Even had we enough able-bodied men to man it."

Sinbad gritted his teeth. He glanced quickly out the window, where he could see the hasty mud, brick, and wood barrier nearing completion at the far side of the plaza.

"It's not meant to *stop* Suliman," he said strongly. "Only to slow him down and make his riders come down from their mounts . . ."

Don Manuel de León threw up his hands. "'Tis useless! We'll never hold him off. Never! Perhaps it would have been better after all had we fled the village and run for Barcelona."

The small group of elders gathered inside the church gravely nodded in assent. Upon Sinbad's return they had been told all they needed to know—the true size and force of Suliman's hill army had left them terrified. Milo and Mongo readily attested to what they had seen, a fully coordinated army ready to move at a moment's notice, the scum of the earth gathered beneath the banners of the vile Suliman ready to march upon tiny Pansa. They were the worst dregs in all of Iberia—renegades, thieves, rapists, murderers, a cruel and cunning band who had lived all their lives on wits and brawn, fearing no man or God.

Javier, the mason, swung wide the doors of the church and anxiously strode inside. He made the sign of the cross, looked first to the priest and then to Sinbad. "The wall is almost complete, Captain," he said, as he wiped caked mud and straw from his hands onto his apron.

Sinbad nodded. The first part of his plan was almost complete; he was ready for the second. If only he could keep the villagers calm. . . .

"Good, Javier. Now go back and block the road from the other side. Turn over every cart and wagon you can find. Fishing boats, too. I want the town secure before nightfall."

The elders mumbled among themselves; pleading, desperate eyes confronted the mariner. "We are fooling ourselves, Captain Sinbad," sighed Don Manuel. "Even if Suliman is held at bay, with what weapons shall we fight? These?" He glanced at the butcher knife strapped to his belt, then to the various other weapons his companions wore. Knives and bats against cavalry and barbarian swords?"

Sinbad faced them all. "Now listen to me, all of you. We *must* stand our ground; it's the best defence we can make. Running may seem easier now—but it isn't. On the open road we'll be cut down like sheep."

"And how shall we fare here?" asked Pablo the cobbler. He waited for the nods of agreement from his friends. "A thousand men and more you say Suliman commands, is this not so?" His eyes darted to the new strangers standing silently beside the altar. Mongo and Milo nodded and looked away. "And what are we?" he continued after the point was made.

Sinbad tensely glanced about at his pitiful grouping of old men and young girls, his brave army of defenders.

"You forget one thing, cobbler," snapped María Elisa. Her mouth turned down angrily as she spoke. "Captain Sinbad has found his ship."

Francisco threw up his hands, defying the brazen girl. "Is this to be our salvation? Why, we don't even know where it is!"

"Ah, but we do," Sinbad told him. "And that's the second part of my plan." He beckoned to Paulo the fisherman. "Do you know the cove near Tarragona?"

The old man weakly nodded. "I think so, señor; but it is far . . ."

"How far?"

He shrugged.

335

"It can be reached by dawn," announced Milo. "Give me a boat and a few good oarsmen and I'll find it, all right."

"Good," said Sinbad. "That's exactly what I want." He looked at Milo and Mongo. "As much as I need both of you here, it's more important that you reach the *Sherry* and sail her to Pansa as quickly as possible. With the ship, our strength will be tripled, and if worse comes to worse, we can evacuate as many as we can from Pansa . . ."

"How do we know the ship is still at anchor in this cove of yours?" demanded Francisco. "How do we know it did not sail away days ago?"

Milo grew crimson with anger; veins bulged in his sinewy neck. "A shipmate will never strand another," he hissed. "The *Scheherazade* will wait, this much I promise you."

"Bah." It was Pablo who grumbled. "Is this what we are asked to rest our lives upon?" he asked of the group. "The word of these . . . these *foreigners?*" He glowered at Milo. "And even should you reach the cove and find the ship in waiting? What then? What makes you think you can reach our harbor in time, eh? In less than twenty-four hours Suliman will attack—you told us this yourselves—and by the hour you arrive we may all be dead!"

María Elisa put her hands to her hips and faced down the troublesome cobbler. "Then run," she flared. "Flee to the hills, you billygoat. But I for one shall stay." She spun and faced Sinbad. "I am not afraid, nor are my sisters. Give us weapons and a place to fight. If I am to die it is going to be right here in Pansa."

And her sisters shouted in agreement.

Sinbad looked at them proudly, knowing they meant every word of it, even if poor Manuel was beside himself at the thought.

"We've talked enough," said Father Augusto. "Our commitment was made before you went to spy upon Suliman's camp. For good or ill, our village is in your hands. What is to be done next?"

336

Sinbad clasped the priest on the shoulder, then addressed Milo. "Find the best boat you can, take her out with Paulo and his stoutest fellows. It's imperative that you reach the cove by first light."

"And bring the *Sherry* to Pansa by nightfall," said Milo, completing the thought. "Don't worry, you can leave it to me."

Leaving a fretful Methelese to stay behind with Sinbad, the two sailors and the fisherman scurried from the church. Before the oaken doors had time to properly shut, a worried Father Augusto whispered to Sinbad on the sly, "What chance do they have of succeeding?"

Sinbad pulled a long face. A hairsbreadth of time, he knew, could make the difference in saving all their lives. The priest nodded solemnly, needing no words for his answer. He turned to the gathered villagers, and said, "As for the rest of us, we had better get back outside and give poor Javier a hand in blocking the road."

Sinbad was quick to agree, but added, "We'll need all the help we can get; don't you think that first we should pray?"

It was a peaceful and serene twilight that bathed the roofs and hills of tiny Pansa. Amber and gold leaves shimmered in the evening moonlight as the lone fishing vessel slipped quietly from its berth and, her single sail unfurled, made her way across the bay and out toward the southern frontiers of Córdoba.

Sinbad looked on silently for a long while, wondering if he would ever see his friends again. Don Giovanni, equally pensive, sat upon his shoulder and uttered not a sound, content to keep his gaze firm across the tranquil sweep of meadows and hills sloping away from either side of the dusty road that bisected the village.

By nightfall, amid the soft chirping of the crickets and the hoots of unseen owls, all final preparations for the coming attack were completed. While Sinbad gathered the farmers together and inspected their weapons, a hodge-podge of knives and pitchforks, hatchets and anything else they could get their hands on, Methelese, flanked by María Elisa and a small band of village girls, ventured past the outermost barricade and onto the road.

Tense eyes watched from the doubly fortified plaza as Methelese and his group dug small random holes in the soft dirt. The clever Greek took a razor-sharp sliver of glass, bent down, and placed it carefully in the dirt, sharpest edge up. The girls repeated the deed until hundreds of unseen pieces dotted the way back to the plaza. This roadway of glass would surely cause havoc among the lead ranks of Suliman's fearless cavalry.

Sinbad positioned Francisco and a number of others along the low mud roofs. Torches yet to be lighted, they hid among the shadows, keenly observing the front perimeters of the village, where bushels of dried hay had been carefully placed.

Sinbad patrolled from one side of the plaza to the other. Ever intent on making certain that everything was just right, he refused to leave his posts unchecked for a single moment.

"Which way will they come first?" asked Don Manuel, nervously fondling the hilt of his sheathed kitchen knife.

Sinbad rubbed at his sunken jowls. "Both sides at once, I fear," he answered with a frown.

Methelese agreed. "Of course. If you were Suliman, wouldn't you do the same?"

Manuel de León heaved a long sigh; he gazed around at the darkened plaza. From inside the church, where the mothers and children were huddled without protection, he could dimly hear the noise of crying infants.

"Get some rest," Sinbad told him. "I doubt they'll attack before first light."

But the battle-weary veteran of many wars shook his head. And, returning to the south wall, he leaned beside the overturned wagons and silently waited.

"It's going to be a long vigil, Sinbad," Giovanni said to the mariner.

Sinbad hardly had the strength to nod. He hoped he had not raised the hopes of all the village for nothing. The *Sherry* would have to make it back before dusk tomorrow. No two ways about it. In daylight, with luck, his small force, barricaded as they were, could just conceivably hold off Suliman. But at night? No, it wasn't possible. Brave as the villagers were, a well-coordinated night attack was more than they could stand. The village would be razed; the day after tomorrow would find not even a goat or dog left in Pansa to feed among the rubble.

Low clouds swept in from the sea about midnight. Here and there among the defenders he heard singing, old folk melodies, softly hummed upon the lips of the dozens of young girls, untrained, who bravely stood in defense of the town. Sinbad looked at them all, his pitiful army of women bolstered by old men, and smiled with emotion. He was proud of them, proud of them all. And he could not recall a time in his life when he had been prouder.

As the minutes ticked away, the battle was drawing closer to hand. María Elisa, exhausted after the long day's preparation, stood at her post along the highest point of the north wall. Eyes weary and bloodshot, at first she almost missed the faint hints of firelight appearing from beyond the ridge west of the road. It did not take her long to realize what was happening.

"Sinbad!" she called, spinning around and waving her arms.

The mariner and the Greek dashed from their places and crept over the top of the barricade to where the girl stood. Squinting, Sinbad scanned the horizon. Torches were burning dully in the distance, a pale orange glow against the moonless velvet night. And from somewhere distant he could hear the whinnying of horses and the trample of marching men.

"They're here," mumbled Methelese, wiping a hand across his dry mouth.

"A pity you don't have your bag of tricks now," said the captain.

The Greek glumly sighed.

"What do we do?" asked Elisa.

"Alert everyone; take up positions. It's all we can do—that, and wait."

While the walls were reinforced with every man and woman in Pansa, Sinbad kept his place and waited. Suliman would never expect to find such resistance from a tiny village like Pansa; the element of surprise was Sinbad's only advantage. Caught badly off guard, the bandit might be forced to retreat and ponder a new strategy for his assault, all the while buying Sinbad more time. Once the *Scheherazade* arrived, Suliman might even give up entirely; after all, any losses in taking Pansa would surely not be worth the few spoils to be found there. At least this is what Sinbad was counting on. Anything else, as everyone knew, would spell disaster for them all.

Slowly, slowly, a thin line of gray spread across the western horizon, the first glimmer of coming dawn. A low whistle sounded from a rooftop beyond the plaza. Sinbad peered up to see someone's arm waving a bright kerchief. It was Paulo, he knew, giving the signal that the enemy was on the march toward the road.

All around him the dozens of girls and fishermen and shepherds and farmers were concealed across the perimeters, hidden in dark doorways, behind brush and wagons, poised over flat mud roofs, inside cesspool ditches. There was no more to be done.

The coming swarm were stirring up dust along the paths. Odors of horses and sweaty men filled Sinbad's nostrils, igniting a pang for the open sea, where he feared he would never sail again. His sense of the past became heightened in these few minutes before the battle. He thought once more of Baghdad, his home, once again of all those he loved. As through a murky veil, he could see Sherry's face before his eyes. He sighed, thinking that death would not be half so bad if only she were beside him.

A moist warm wind blew in from the sea. The brightening sky revealed a bank of clouds that hinted at rain. In the distance, Sinbad could see a smoky outline upon the hills: horses and riders, moving in a single line, slowly making their way to the grass fields at the side of the roads. There were no whoops or war cries, no drunken oaths or vilifications. Only a host of grim, dark riders, weapons in hand, ready to mercilessly destroy everything in their path.

Sinbad slid his hand to his waist and unsheathed his dagger. Then he reached into his boot and withdrew the small concealed knife he had bought in the marketplace so long ago, with Don Giovanni perched upon his shoulder as he was now, before their shared adventures began.

"Are you frightened, my little friend?" he asked the frog.

Giovanni nodded his head solemnly.

"You know you don't have to be a part of this. You can hop away now, while there's time, get out of the village, and hide in the thickets. Suliman won't be looking for you. . . ."

The frog looked at his friend with bulging eyes. "Leave you now, Sinbad? After we've come through so much together?"

"It could save your life . . ."

Don Giovanni shook his head vehemently. "Our bargain was to stay together," he reminded the sailor, recalling the agreement made that long-past day at the pond. "No, Sinbad. We set out on our search together, and we'll stay that way. At least until we find our flower."

The Red Dahlia!

Sinbad realized that, in the urgency of frantic preparations for protecting Pansa, he had completely forgotten about the mysterious flower—and the sad news he now had to relate to his friend.

341

He sighed heavily and rested the frog on his lap. "There's something I forgot to tell you, Giovanni," he began in a low tone. "About the dahlia . . . You see—"

A multitude of shouts filled the air. Sinbad leaped to his feet, eyes wide, and stared at the full force of Suliman's cavalry charging down the road.

"Here they come!" María Victoria shouted from her advance position.

While Father Augusto led the mothers and children in prayer inside the church, young Rudolpho climbed to his post in the tower and rang the bell. The tolling reverberated throughout the plaza amid the frenzy of last-second activity. Machetes gleamed in early morning sunlight; knives glistened, bows were loaded with homemade arrows. Huge clouds of dust rose behind the advancing horses, Suliman's men now whooping and shouting at the top of their lungs.

"Hold your fire until I give the word!" called Sinbad, bounding to the top of the wall, a handful of anxious defenders at his side.

Like bats out of hell the horsemen rode, swinging their animals out and fanning across the road in ranks of twenty. The sun was in their eyes; they could as yet make out little of what lay ahead. On the flat roofs the torches were lit, ready to be thrown; the defenders watched numbly as the cavalry hurtled closer and closer.

"Now!" cried Sinbad.

Streams of black smoke followed the thrown torches as they fell into the carefully placed bales of hay. The hay ignited instantly, sending great orange tongues of flame licking toward the sky. The front line of horses broke amid the tumult; balls of fire sent stallions rearing and panicking, riders yanking at the reins, trying to calm their frightened steeds.

Arrows whistled from the roofs. Ruldolpho slowly aimed his homade bow and let loose. The whistling shaft slammed fiercely into the throat of the foremost rider. The burly fellow's head shot back and he plummeted from his saddle, screaming as he tumbled into a bale of flaming hay.

From both sides of the road the villagers hurled their missiles, bricks and bats and clubs and sticks, slowing down any attempt on the part of the riders to regroup and form another assault. The northern path to the village became completely blocked with raging fires and stumbling horses, the air filled with the awful screams of Suliman's stunned legions.

From the south came another cavalry charge. Sinbad jumped from his barricade and ran across the plaza to direct the defense. Fifty meters away he could see the first galloping steed break stride and fall, its hoof pads cut to pieces by the slivers of glass Methelese and the girls had laid during the night. A second horse stumbled, then a third. A fourth whinnyed high on its rear legs and came crashing down upon the road; a half dozen horses charging on behind could not slow in time and tumbled over it. Riders were thrown sprawling onto the caked earth. As they scrambled to their feet, ten farmers jumped from their hiding places in the cesspools and hurled pitchforks as though they were spears. Sharpened prongs struck horses that crumpled to the earth, leaving their riders helpless amid the barrage of arrows loosed from the barricades.

More farmers jumped out into the open, waving clubs and machetes above their heads. Wails of anguish permeated the air as the villagers set upon the stricken attackers and hacked and slashed their way through men and horseflesh alike. Right through the struggling line of stallions they dashed, some quickly cut down by advancing cavalry riding low and swinging words, others boldly standing up to the onslaught, machetes turned to wheels of death at every spin. Left and right, horsemen were falling, yanked from their saddles and thrown to the ground. María Vanessa led a group of girls from the barricades and charged into the fray. Knives and sticks in their hands, they blocked the retreat of the furthermost riders and forced them to flee from the road to what seemed to be the safety of the village.

Methelese and his own band were waiting. Vats of boiling water were spilled from the roofs onto the surging mob of dazed attackers. Their wails and shrieks sent shivers through everyone who heard them; men fell grappling at their burning faces, raw flesh afire, the pain only growing worse as the skin blistered.

The struggle proved long and difficult. Although the bulk of the cavalry had been stopped before penetrating Pansa's defenses, it was the charging foot soldiers, well behind the horsemen, who now threatened the town from every side.

From the bell tower Rudolpho signaled the warning. Sinbad jumped from the barricade onto a nearby roof and surveyed the scene. Ahead, along the northern road, fires were still burning; dozens of Suliman's men were sprawled helter-skelter across the ravine and ditches, their wounded animals bolting and kicking mindlessly amid the fury. But behind these, forming shoulder-to-shoulder ranks three and four deep, was the infantry; hundreds of ragged men, coming in a charge as fast as their legs could carry them.

Sinbad put two fingers to his mouth and whistled loudly. At his signal, María Elisa and her father came pulling a mule-drawn wagon loaded with hay. An opening was quickly made between the barricades and Sinbad, lighted torch in hand, leaped onto the buckboard. Then without a word he drove the wagon onto the road and fought his way beyond the fires. The front ranks of infantry were almost upon him; he could see the looks of hate and lust in their eyes, the malice etched into their faces. He spurred the frightened mules forward, tossed the torch behind and jumped off as the hay lit into a huge bonfire. The wagon rolled out of control, heading straight for the enemy. It overturned beside the gulley, spewing hay, igniting the fields of dry grass, and turning the whole scape into a massive inferno in a matter of seconds.

The attacking ranks turned in panic; their flight was swift and soundless, back up to the meadow, far away from the approaches to the village. Billows of thick smoke formed black clouds over Pansa. Dust swirled behind the kicking hooves of fleeing horses. Charred bodies lay still upon the road, nestled in tiny pools of blood. Weapons yet in hand, the corpses gave grim testimony to what had happened here this morning—testimony that could not be refuted. Pansa had taken the enemy by surprise and had sent him reeling back. Suliman's outlaw army had been defeated by a handful of old men and girls. But as the bandit chief shook his fist and cursed at the sight of his retreating forces, he made a vow: For what Pansa had done, they would be repaid.

The battle had lasted well into the morning, and by the time the last of the smoke cleared it was already past noon. A hot sun blazed high in the perfect blue sky as Sinbad and his defenders got their first clear look at the battlefield spread before them. It was a gruesome sight, but encouraging. At the cost of only a handful of lives they had cut down the cream of Suliman's cavalry, forcing the bandit to think twice before sending his men on another such assault.

"We've won!" cried a jubilant María Elisa, throwing her arms around Sinbad. "We've beaten them off!"

Don Manuel stood at her side, a small chuckle on his lips. "Did you see them run, Sinbad? Suliman the Conqueror—*Ha!*" He spat upon the ground. "We taught him a lesson or two, didn't we? He won't be so quick to come again."

And from everywhere across the plaza came added cries of glee. Panting, Francisco came running from his own advance position, blood still wet on his machete. "They've gone behind the hills," he told Sinbad proudly. "Back to their campsite, I'm sure; perhaps back to Córdoba—if they have any sense."

Everybody laughed. Everybody except Sinbad. He looked into their smiling faces and saw the relief that had replaced anguish, the sudden belief in the impossible miracle that had happened here this morning.

"It isn't over yet," he reminded them. "Suliman, as much as we may want to believe it, is not going to run. He'll regroup and come at us again—only this time knowing what to expect. No more surprises. He knows our weaknesses and he'll exploit them."

"In the meantime," added Methelese, his eyes to the hills, "we had better do some regrouping of our own. As surely as night follows day, this bandit Suliman means to take Pansa—and set an example for all Barcelona."

It proved to be a hot, clammy afternoon, with no breezes to freshen the stale air that hovered above the village. Feeling the pressure of the long wait before the next attack, Sinbad inspected the fortifications and bantered with his troops, trying to keep morale as high as possible. Always, though, he kept a watchful eye toward the harbor in hopes of seeing his ship come sailing in.

Afternoon shadows lengthened; it would not be long before the first evening star appeared. And still there was no sign of the *Scheherazade*. When Rudolpho called from the bell tower, Sinbad's heart pounded. Expecting to see the youth pointing toward the sea, he was severely disappointed to find Rudolpho's excitement raised from another direction.

"The ridges, Captain!" shouted Paulo, who was first on the wall to catch a glimpse of what Rudolpho had already noticed: a grim procession of bedraggled troops, hundreds of them marching slowly, lining the gently sloping hills and surrounding the village on all sides save for the harbor.

"Prepare for the attack!" shouted Sinbad, and the bell in the church rang loudly again. Prayerfully all resumed their posts, knowing that this time they would fight without the benefit of surprise. Suliman's men, once fully dominating the heights, made no move to march down to the road. Instead, they kneeled in groups, drew bows, and waited.

Don Manuel scratched forlornly at his smudged cheek. "What are they up to?"

Sinbad shook his head. He wasn't sure what Suliman had in mind, but one thing was certain: The bandit had been badly burned the first time; he wasn't going to chance another frontal attack until he was absolutely positive his men would meet only the scantest resistance.

As Sinbad watched in growing trepidation, wagons rumbled from behind the ridges, bringing forth barrels and buckets of oil. When the barrels were placed at random points throughout the line of archers, Suliman's men lit the oil. Thin wisps of black smoke trailed thickly heavenward and a hundred arrows were lit.

Methelese gasped. "Hit the dirt!" he shouted, throwing himself against an overturned wagon.

Muffled screams rose from every side as the hundred burning arrows whistled overhead. Leaving black smoke behind, the volley scattered and crashed throughout the plaza, slamming into dirt, brushing against the stone of the church, sticking into wooden barricades and doorways where tiny fires immediately sprang to life.

Sinbad lifted his head and stared. "Keep down," he cried to the defenders. And just then the next volley let loose, only this time there were more arrows, hundreds more, pouring down like rain from one end of Pansa to the other.

From somewhere near the south barricade a frightened farmer broke from his position. He dashed madly for the safety of the church, ignoring the pleas of his comrades. Arrows smacked to the ground all around him; he ran faster, leaping to reach the arched doors. Three snubbed darts caught him from behind, singeing his flesh with burning oil. Like a human torch he fell, screaming and writhing, digging his fingernails into the dirt and pleading for help.

"Stay where you are!" Sinbad called out to those closest to him.

But the good-hearted defenders didn't listen. They scrambled to his aid, three more of them immediately falling victim to the shower of flaming arrows.

Within moments, fires were burning in every direction. Houses and barns, stables, the pier itself.

"Pansa will be burned to the ground!" cried Francisco. And his shout fed the panic growing among them all.

Sinbad spun, fell to his knees, and crawled from one end of the barricade to the other. The defenders were slowly moving back from their postions, smoke and fire forcing them to abandon all of the outermost strongholds along either side of the road. Weapons discarded, they ran madly back to the plaza, seeking the shelter of Javier's wall.

Time after time the arrows spewed across the sky. One by one the villagers were being cut down, hurled from their postions upon the roofs, forced to retreat from the ditches where, suddenly out in the open, the deadly rain riddled them until they fell in heaps, wailing as their bodies became torches and they were consumed.

The smoke was terrible. Coughing, wheezing, Sinbad led those near the north wall back to the second line of defense. Smoldering wood sent great billows upward. All eyes were stinging from the fumes.

"We'll never hold against this," said Methelese, protecting himself as best he could.

Sinbad stared warily at the sun; the light had started to wane, night would not be far off. And still no sign of his ship.

From the wings of the rows of archers, at the blare of a trumpet, infantry marched, wheeling inward toward the road even as the deadly rain of arrows continued unabated. In a bold move, the bandit had committed his forces to strike from both the front and rear in an effort to gain the village in one swift blow.

Once again the church bell was ringing, but this time the brave defenders were unable to regain the outermost positions. With María Elisa on one side, Methelese on the other, Sinbad regrouped his forces along the lower level of Javier's wall. Bows were raised and aimed, machetes lifted. *Tramp, tramp,* came the sound of marching feet, over the gulleys, across the ditches, between the lifeless corpses of slain comrades still smoldering upon the road. The grim cohort, covered with shields and helmets of mail, marched straight into Sinbad's line of fire, prepared to scale the low barricade and set upon the plaza.

"Steady," called Sinbad to his own archers, holding them back until the last possible moment.

In an unwavering line of lifted weapons, spears, broadswords, scimitars, axes, and the like, the enemy started to run at double time, reaching the outskirts of the village in seconds and then tearing along the road. Once on level ground there seemed no stopping them; between them and the wall stood nothing.

"Fire!" shouted Sinbad.

A dozen Spanish arrows tore from their bowstrings. Three deep-chested, thick-necked attackers fell back, shields flying from their hands. A loud cry ensued as their compatriots charged with renewed fury.

A second time the villagers let loose. Two attackers tangled and dizzly plumeted, necks crimson with spouting blood, arrows stuck through their throats. But for every one of the enemy who had been hit, there were ten who had not. Whooping now, brandishing their swords and axes above their heads, they came on undaunted, right to the foot of the wall.

Heavy smoke swirled, fueled by a sudden wind from the bay. The fighting became hand-to-hand as Sinbad, Methelese, and a handful of farmers stood atop the wall and fended off the grappling enemy clambering up the ragged face of mud bricks.

Twang!

Sinbad ducked; a charging bandit, clad in heavy mail and swinging a chain, stopped in his tracks at the broad height of the wall's crest, a short arrow piercing his left eye. He spun around in a horrible dance, hands to his face, and careened back below, falling on top of a group of frenzied attackers. Sinbad peered up to the church tower and grinned; he waved at young Rudolpho, acknowledging that the boy had probably saved his life.

From the sides came a hundred more marauders, scrambling onto roofs of burning thatch previously held by Pansa's defenders. From their new positions, they kept up a steady barrage that prevented the defenders in the plaza from mending the breeches in the north wall.

Sinbad jumped down from the wall. He drew back his fist and smashed the jaw of a matted-haired bandit racing for Don Manuel. As the bandit staggered, pirouetting before he hit the ground, Sinbad grabbed the innkeeper by the collar and yanked him away. All around, more of the villagers were falling. Still wielding machetes, they put up good fights before being overwhelmed one by one by the never-ending onslaught.

Rudolpho aimed again; straight through the heart went his arrow, piercing a vest of thin mail, causing the bearded, sinewy leader of the charge to slam back against the inside of the wall and slump over. His astounded companions crouched, hid, looked to the bell tower and cursed. Rudolpho had been seen—and marked.

"Retreat!" yelled Sinbad. Behind him ran María Elisa and a group of her girls. María Victoria came rushing from the southern wall with her own surviving defenders. The battle on the other side of the plaza had been every bit as furious as had the one here. No matter how brave an effort they had made, the sheer numbers of Suliman's forces had them completely overwhelmed.

Fire arrows continued to rain, fires were burning everywhere. Methelese, face blackened, body wracked with small wounds, came running to Sinbad, his bloody knife in hand.

"We can't hold anymore," he hissed through his pain. "There are too many breeches. Too many—"

Sinbad brought his knife up just in time. A powerfully built bandit, with gold earrings and a jewel in his nostril, flung himself at the captain from the roof of the burning stable. The two men fell to the ground and grappled. In that instant of horror and surging panic, Sinbad felt the muscular hands of his adversary around his throat, strangling his own effort to scream. But Sinbad's knife was still in his hand. Afterwards he could not remember drawing it back and stabbing blindly at the grisly flesh encumbering him. Nor could he remember feeling the blade of the knife meet soft flesh and sink deeply in. An almost fiendish wail brought him back to awareness and, amid the rising clamor and tumult, he pushed the attacker off, leaving him to lie face down, a pulsing, gaping wound in the back of his neck sending forth a torrent of crimson.

He stood up to find Methelese locked in combat of his own. Using the skill of the ancients, the wily Greek kicked to the groin, delivered an elbow to the face as the bandit howled, and, his blade firmly clenched in his bloodied fist, brought it up deeply into the solar plexus. The attacker convulsed as Methelese twisted the knife and withdrew. Then, panting, the Greek exchanged a brief look of triumph with the captain.

Villagers were running helter-skelter, abandoning their places and seeking some new refuge, some new place to stand and fight. From the corner of his eye, Sinbad could see Francisco and a few others boldly trying to maintain their line at the near edge of the southern barricade. But Suliman's forces had sensed the collapse of the defenses and were now pressing from every side, even working their way completely around the village and coming from the quay. Fishing boats raged with fire, the few villagers left in the pier's defence lay scattered and still upon the dock, triumphant attackers trampling over them in their race to the plaza.

Overhead, the sky had changed color. The indigo of evening had replaced the blue of day. Stars were twinkling the moon bright and full. Sinbad stared and gritted his teeth, harshly swearing. Where was the ship? Where was Milo?

"To the church!" he cried, gathering those around him And together they bounded from the wall and rushed toward the oval doors of the sanctuary.

Methelese covered while the girls ran up the steps Sinbad blocked the thrust of a wildly wielded scimitar threw its owner to the ground, and dashed to the landing With a fallen bandit's shield in his hand, he warded off the rush of flying arrows and urged everyone to come through the doors as quickly as possible. All the survivors of the attack, including the three de León daughters as well as Don Manuel, managed to dodge arrows and spears and axes, and fling themselves inside. Barely in time, for no sooner had they gained entry than a host of new cavalry broke over the barricades and overran the plaza.

Methelese, with Don Giovanni hopping behind him and Sinbad, shield held high over his head, were the last to make it in. The very second the doors shut, a hundred arrows slammed into wood, shafts shaking with the force.

Huddled mothers and children were crying; Sinbad stared about the grim pews and shuddered. All that remained of Pansa was here in this one place, gathered together and prime for taking. He could not have chosen a worse defensive position had he tried.

"Man those windows!" he barked to the farmers. Then to the ashen priest, "Gather the children in the front—it's the safest place we have."

Father Augusto nodded, and while this was being done Sinbad called together a small handful of his best fighters

352

Both María Elisa and María Victoria stood beside grimy-faced Methelese and weary Francisco.

"Gather up as many arrows as you can find," he told them all. "Bring them to the tower." He turned to Javier. "Suliman is going to storm the walls—what do we have that can stop him?"

The mason darkly shook his head. That there was pitifully little to be found needed no telling.

"There is some pitch in the cellar," said the priest, leaving the grouped women and children and coming to Sinbad's side. "And a barrel of oil, I think. . . ."

A small smile of satisfaction broke over Sinbad's face. Pitch and oil! What better could he ask for? He snapped his fingers, shouted for Manuel. "Follow the father to the cellar," he barked. "And bring everything of use to the tower right away."

The priest led the way below; Sinbad, only Don Giovanni accompanying him, rushed up the narrow stone stairway beside the rectory and made his way to the tower. There he found young Rudolpho, bow in hand, fingers taut on the string, taking dead aim at a bellicose attacker running from the fallen barricades toward the church steps. The youth held his breath, let loose. Whistling, the snubbed arrow sailed in a direct line and smacked cleanly through the attacker's gut. The man whirled, grasped at the shaft, and doubled over before he fell dead.

"Got him!" laughed Rudolpho, tiny fires glinting in his eyes.

"Fine shooting, my boy," said Sinbad with admiration.

Surprised to find the Eastern mariner behind him, Rudolpho grinned. He made the sign of the cross. "So far I've been lucky."

Sinbad laughed. "Skillful as well. But tell me, what have you seen?"

Rudolpho uncrossed his legs and half-slid to the farthest edge of the platform, a spot that afforded an excellent view of almost the entire plaza. "See for yourself," he told Sinbad.

Sinbad crouched and poked his head just over the top. His eyes scanned the full scene below. Suliman's men had overrun everything, it was certain; all of Pansa's carefully planned defenses were now smashed or burned, with a scattering of fires still sending up billows of dark smoke in every direction. The ground was littered with corpses, many of them defenders, but many more Suliman's own men. The battle for the village had been more costly than the bandit chief could ever have dreamed. So much so that now, while his forces were busily overrunning the buildings, looting what meager spoils they could find and putting swords to anything yet alive, Suliman had called off his frontal attack on the church. Clearly, he was consolidating again before the final assault. It was a wise move for the bandit, Sinbad knew, yet it also provided just a little more time for his own plan.

Amid muffled shouts in the now chilly night air, the firelight provided Sinbad a good view of what was happening below. Captains were regrouping their archers, spreading them out thinly in an arc, positioning them in the very ditches that Sinbad's own men had dug. Beyond the road, there was a rumble of wagons, fresh supplies and weaponry being hauled to the plaza to ensure a successful siege. The whitewashed church was caught in a vise, surrounded on three sides by the bandit army, ever gathering strength as stronghold after stronghold was fortified, and the defenders trapped with their backs to the sea, where the tiny harbor blazed out of control, every fishing boat put to the torch to assure that no one might escape. Suliman's revenge would be complete and total.

Sinbad gritted his teeth and hissed. His gaze turned to the sea for the hundredth time since afternoon—and still there was no sight of the *Scheherazade* on the horizon.

"Watch this, Sinbad," growled Rudolpho, drawing another arrow. The mariner squinted and saw a burly wagon master directing three wagons to a new position where the south barricade had been. The dirty fellow stood brazenly in the open, barking commands to his drivers, a whip in his hand, his eyes intent upon the church. Rudolpho expertly took aim; he swung the bow horizontally and fired. The wagon master screamed, head thrown back with sudden and petrifying force, eyes popping as the arrow slammed through his throat, ripping it apart, the tip of the arrowhead protruding from the back of his neck.

There was a flurry of cries and activity below as his companions dragged him away and hid behind the walls, loudly swearing and vowing revenge on the unseen tower archer.

Rudolpho gloated but Sinbad frowned; there were hundreds more like roaches, to take the dead man's place, and all were ready to swarm over the townspeople the moment the signal was given.

Just then Sinbad heard footsteps on the stairs. He peered down at Elisa and Victoria, their arms bundled with arrows. Behind them lumbered Methelese, Manuel, Francisco, and the priest, slowly and carefully carrying up buckets of already heated pitch and oil.

It was just in time—for no sooner had they reached the landing than Suliman's archers began to pound the church with fearful vollies again, their flaming missiles sailing through the recessed windows downstairs and causing panic among the huddled citizens. The farmers posted at the windows stood by helpless, themselves cowering, unable to return the fire.

"We'll not hold long like this," said Methelese, putting down his buckets of flaming pitch. He peered over the wall but quickly ducked as archers across the plaza saw his silhouette and let loose a barrage. The arrows sailed over his head, slamming into the cast-iron bell and causing a gentle tingle.

A flank of footmen lifted themselves from hidden darkness and began to march openly. Elisa and her sister drew their bows, aimed. Rudolpho did the same. But they were only three—and the front rank of the phalanx numbered at least forty.

Father Augusto crossed himself and shut his eyes. With a shudder, he said, "All is lost."

"Not yet!" snapped Sinbad. He stood up, a bucket of oil sloshing from side to side in his hands. And he leaned closer to the edge of the precipitous wall. "Wait until they get within ten paces," he told the others. "Then toss the buckets."

Methelese nodded glumly; Francisco and Manuel silently said a prayer and lifted their own pitch. Meanwhile, in the plaza, the army had begun to break into a run, rank after rank fanning out and spreading over the charred battlefield. Their peculiar formations closed in swiftly; already they were gaining a strong foothold around the church while their archers kept the defenders at the windows ineffective.

A horn blasted. Running amok, the bandits launched their offensive. A confused medley of sound rose all around, men's cries and screams, mingled with the whistling of arrows, the whinnying of frightened horses, the roaring of fueled fires spreading everywhere.

Sinbad heaved his bucket of pitch. The black liquid, scorched and scalding, spread like a wet blanket as it poured over the front row of frenzied attackers. Men reeled back and howled, stumbled, fell, trampled over each other, and drew back. Methelese's bucket was quick to follow. The boiling oil thickly scattered, lumping and landing squarely upon a group of scimitar-wielding bandits who, with broad gaits, had almost reached the church steps. Scalded and singed, they too staggered back, dropping their weapons and wailing as they ran off aflame into the night, lighting the way to the road like human beacons.

Horsemen came tearing through the plaza, chains

spinning dizzily above their heads, balls of iron let loose and sent crashing into the fragile walls.

Whump!

Again and again they struck, causing huge cracks in the stone to deepen, the edges to crumble. And then came more bandits, dozens more, heaving an enormous battering ram. Straight for the church doors they trotted, grim and silent, paying heed neither to the hurled pitch nor the agonized screams of comrades fallen and writhing upon the ground.

Manuel's bucket went sailing onto their heads. Then Francisco's. Then Sinbad's second. The pitch splatted every which way. Havoc reigned among the battering-ram carriers; as the front bearers fell, those behind could no longer carry the weight. The great lumbering log, cut from a giant tree more than a thousand years old, thudded to the ground, many of its bearers pinned underneath. They screeched and yowled, cursed and pleaded, but to no avail. Those nearby left them lying helplessly, as the charge to gain entry only increased in ferocity.

"They're at the doors!" cried Elisa, staring down from the tower, watching the ugly host of men who had eluded the pitch and were at this very moment banging hatchets and axes into the aged wood.

Rudolpho's bow sang; the arrow hit true, one attacker spun, stared up through glassy eyes, and gurgled as he toppled over. Elisa's arrow slowed down another; the bandit hobbled, his left leg buckling under; but it was Victoria's shot that stopped him completely. Her aim had been wild but lucky. Calloused hands shot to his face; the bandit opened his mouth and screamed soundlessly. Stuck through his right eye was her dart; he tried vainly to pluck it out. His face turned to a pulp of oozing red and he twisted aimlessly until finally he slipped into a pool of burning pitch and was consumed.

More iron balls slammed into the walls, many into the

tower itself, whose fragile foundations had begun to crumble. Then more horses and more charging footmen came roaring into the plaza. Thundering over debris, they led a vicious new attack from the shattered north wall and poured like ants over every inch of the field of battle.

Sinbad hurled the last bucket of pitch, gaining little satisfaction when a stallion reared and threw its rider high into the air with such force and fury that every bone in the man's body broke when he at last crashed to earth.

The fires downstairs in the church, up until now contained, were suddenly raging out of control. Archers hidden along the rooftops still relentlessly rained their deadly arrows, and the screams of anguished villagers were the most horrible sound Sinbad had ever heard.

It was over at last, he knew. Pansa had given her best fight—and a bloody good one it had been—but now she was doomed. There were no more resources for him to call upon. No more tricks, no more last-ditch efforts at trying to regroup. He had promised the townsfolk a chance at survival, and now, while the peaceful village was sacked, burned and plundered before his eyes, he knew that he had failed. Failed miserably.

With his knife in his hand, he observed the carnage. His place in the shattered tower still allowed a clear view of the foot of the church steps, where now he saw the doors crack under the blows of axes. The bandit army blurred across the plaza, leaping and jumping, howling war cries and shouts of victory. Suliman was about to have his revenge. Pansa was destroyed—and from here to the gates of Barcelona there was nothing to stop him.

While Rudolpho and Elisa fired arrow after arrow, the captain from Baghdad watched in sorrow. Even Don Giovanni, still upon his shoulder, had no words of comfort. Sinbad clenched his knife between his teeth and waited for the bandits to start to scale the walls to reach the tower. Already ladders were being brought forward, ropes and iron hooks hurled from every side. Disconsolately,

Sinbad's hand fell to his side and felt at his pocket. There was something inside, and without thinking he pulled it out. It was a flower, a crushed red dahlia—the one he had saved from the field. A sour smile crossed his lips as he held it in the palm of his hand and stared. The splendorous flower that was going to be the answer to all his problems. He laughed bitterly and balled his hand into a fist. If only he hadn't been such a fool; if only he had never believed in its magic; how very different life would be for him today. . . .

Then, with rising smoke filling his lungs and the clatter of boots scaling the wall, he shut his eyes.

> *By Allah, he prayed, if this flower has any powers at all, give them to me now. Save Pansa, save these good people of Barcelona who have given me their trust and their faith. Spare the lives of the innocent, let them not die with me because of my folly. Grant me this one wish, and this one wish alone. . . .*

"Sinbad, look out!"

He opened his eyes to find a hairy beast of a bandit coming over the top of the wall. He wheeled and ducked as a thick blade *swooshed* centimeters from his scalp. Then, dropping the flower, he took his knife from between his teeth and lunged. The bandit caught his wrist; the tip of the blade licked at Sinbad's throat. Sinbad yanked hard and they fell to the ledge together, each grappling at the other's throat, rolling over and over until they were at the very edge of the steps. Sinbad fought the beast of a man with every bit of strength he could muster. He drove his knee straight up into the bandit's groin; the attacker loosened his hold only for a split second, but it was enough. Sinbad's knife slashed then and ripped the man's throat at the jugular; with a heave he sent the corpse hurtling down the steps to crash head-first at the bottom of the landing. Then onto his feet he sprang, leopardlike, no longer feeling sorry for himself. A bandit rushed for Elisa; before he could grab the girl, Sinbad slammed the full weight of his body against him, and the bandit reeled back with the blow. The pitiful wall, battered and broken, crumbled and then gave way suddenly so that the attacker fell backwards, his sinewy arms flailing, and tumbled to the plaza, knocking over a siege ladder and taking with him the three or four climbing bandits. As they splattered, Sinbad grabbed Elisa and pulled her from harm's way. Across the other side of the tower more ropes had been thrown; a half-dozen fiery-eyed bandits were swarming up. Rudolpho drew back, let go one last shot. The arrow smacked through the lead attacker's belly and, as he stumbled, Father Augusto swept up his fallen sword, swung it over his head and whirled it. Three bandits staggered, oozing wounds slashed across their faces. Manuel hurled an empty bucket, flung his knife. Another bandit cried, the blade firmly stuck through his heart.

All around was screaming. Sinbad, through the smoke and fire and thunder of battle, vainly tried to force a path to get both Elisa and Victoria off the tower and back down to the rectory. From every side they were now blocked, with swarthy men clambering like an army of dreaded tarantulas. With Methelese beside him, Sinbad held as many at bay as he could. Francisco fell, a hatchet buried in his skull. Young Rudolpho took a severe wound in the side and dropped to his knees, his last arrow spent. Manuel fended off another and desperately tried to reach his daughters, but the body-strewn tower made the venture impossible.

Below, horns were sounding the charge; Suliman's forces boldly rushed the doors and windows. Through the din and dark there was little to be seen; sound alone told the story. It was only moments before the church would be totally overrun, the last survivor put to the sword.

Sinbad kicked a bandit sharply in the groin, slitting his throat as he tumbled, and forced his way to the wounded

Rudolpho. The boy, eyes shut with pain, brow burning feverishly, tried to smile as Sinbad took his hand. Don Giovanni, perched beside the fallen lad, looked at Sinbad and shook his head sadly. There was nothing anyone could do.

"I—I'm sorry I let you down, *mi capitán*," choked Rudolpho, opening blurry eyes and straining to see.

Sinbad mopped the sweat from his brow. "You didn't let me down, young friend. You fought well, as well as any man I've ever known. . . ."

Rudolpho smiled through his pain and sighed. Father Augusto, sword still in hand, stood over him and prayed softly. The child was dying, but perhaps it was well, for at least he would not have to witness the end, when Pansa would burn to rubble and its people to ashes.

Rudolpho pulled at Sinbad's collar; his lips trembled and he fought to get the words out. "I can hear them, Captain Sinbad," he mumbled. "The horns of your ship, come to save the village. . . ."

Sinbad stared at him briefly, then turned to Methelese. The wise Greek shook his head. "He's delirious, Sinbad. . . ."

The grip tightened, and Rudolpho sputtered, "Listen, Sinbad. *Listen!*" Then the grip released; Rudolpho took a long breath and slumped his head on the captain's shoulder.

Sinbad got up slowly, tears in his eyes, hands trembling. "They'll pay for this," he vowed, and he spun around, knife in hand, to greet the next line of bandits scurrying over the wall. To his shock, there were none. The ropes and ladders were still there—but no one was climbing.

Elisa stared at him bewildered. Methelese began to say something but stopped at the low wail of a horn coming from the direction of the harbor.

Sinbad scampered across the tower and leaned himself far over the parapet. Amid the haze of battle he could see only a jumble of activity throughout the village. His eyes burned like the devil from the rising smoke and he held his breath as he stared through the mist.

361

"What's going on?" cried Elisa.

The dumbfounded mariner held out his hands and shrugged. And then it came again, the same blast, only louder and closer.

Father Augusto and Methelese ran to his side. The priest wiped grime and splattered blood from his eyes and peered into the distance. "Sails," he whispered. "I see sails. . . ."

Sinbad clutched at the wall, not daring to believe. Then he saw them, too, the wide, billowing sails of a great ship. But it was not the *Sherry*, no certainly not the *Sherry*; he would recognize his own vessel at once.

He stared and gasped. The swan-necked prow came into view. It was a long ship, a Nordic ship. And another right beside it.

"King Harald!"

Onto the fiery dock, brandishing battleaxes and heavy broadswords, charged a hundred and more of Denmark's finest Vikings. Sinbad looked on dumbly, disbelieving his eyes. It wasn't possible. It couldn't be. . . . Yet there they were, rampaging into Pansa like swarming locusts, routing Suliman's forces in the plaza, sending the bandit army reeling back in the direction of the hills.

"A miracle!" cried the priest, crossing himself.

"More than that, Father," responded Methelese.

Don Manuel and his daughters began to cheer, clapping their hands and urging the new attackers on.

"Stay put," Sinbad barked to his companions. Then he looked to the frog and grinned. "Well, Giovanni? Are you coming—or do you want to miss all the fun?"

With a croak, the frog hopped to Sinbad's shoulders. Then the mariner grasped a siege rope and before the startled eyes of everyone swung himself down into the fray.

Cries of "Odin!" and "Thor!" and "For Denmark!" resounded through the air. Bandits were fleeing this way and that, running like crazed men at the very sight of the furred Vikings setting upon them. Sinbad held his ground only briefly; he stuck out his foot, tripped a bandit, and watched as the fellow cringed when a mighty Viking ax came sailing down to split his skull. The victor of the skirmish stood over the lifeless body, hands on hips, and bellowed a laugh before raising his weapon and cleaning the blood off the blade. In the darkness and the heavy smoke, Sinbad recognized that laugh. It was the fearsome king of Denmark himself.

"My liege!"

Harald turned abruptly, squinted his steely eyes, and searched the dark to see who had called him. Sinbad stepped from the shadows, his features flickering in the glow of the fires.

Harald stared at him and roared, "Ah, so it's you! Captain Sinbad! By Odin, I'm glad to find you alive!"

Sinbad glanced at the menacing ax, almost as big as he was, and gulped. He quickly remembered that the last time the king had laid eyes on him he had vowed to kill him.

Harald chuckled and scratched at his flowing beard. All around him more Vikings were rushing helter-skelter, flinging weapons, heaving screaming bandits into ditches and cesspools and fires.

"How . . . How did you get here? . . . I don't understand. . . ."

Harald slapped the mariner so hard on the back that Sinbad almost toppled over. "The storm," bellowed the king. "The storm that Methelese conjured up so you could escape the Cretans. The weather was *so* bad, for *so* long, that even my ships could not weather it. We put into harbor, off course, and found ourselves in your damned Moorish Córdoba."

Sinbad was astounded; events were happening so fast that he could not keep up with them. "But how did you know where we were? Who told you of Pansa?"

Here the king's eyes gleamed; he turned Sinbad around,

pointing him in the direction of the flaming harbor. And there she stood, quietly in the bay, not a hundred meters from the village. The *Scheherazade*, sails furled, as shipshape as ever. Milo had not let him down.

"We anchored off Tarragona," went on the blustery Harald, "and stayed on a few days to make repairs. Moors attacked us several days ago, and took a few of my men prisoner . . ."

"Suliman!" gasped Sinbad.

"Aye. The very same. We would have made short shrift of his filthy little army had they not all fled for the hills." Here he shrugged. "And we were ready to set sail for home when your own ship slipped from her hiding place at the cove." He laughed jovially. "What a storm, Sinbad! I've never seen one like it!"

Sinbad groaned at the memory. "But continue," he said, "what happened next?"

"Well," said Harald with a sigh, "the sight of the *Scheherazade* was certainly one we did not expect, as I'm sure I don't have to tell you. As a matter of fact, my first inclination was to burn and sink you, hang your crew, and drag you home to Roskilde in chains. . . ."

Sinbad swallowed hard; Harald's broad smile remained. "However, I must admit that I was talked into not taking such rash action."

Scratching his head, Sinbad said, "By whom?"

Harald squeezed the mariner's shoulder. "By my daughter, Thruna, that's who! Come, come, my dear Arabic friend, surely you know that Thruna fell in love with you the minute she first saw you!"

"My lord! Never! Why, I . . ." He turned crimson.

Harald bellowed again. "Don't seem so shocked; believe it or not, Thruna saved your life. Had she not begged—begged at my feet, I tell you—I would have taken your puny ship and . . ." He closed his fist slowly, saying nothing, but the implication was all too clear.

"Anyway," Harald went on, "We stopped your vessel

and Felicia implored me to let bygones by bygones. She offered all your treasures stolen from Phalus if I would only make haste and follow the *Sherry* to this place, Pansa."

Sinbad's eyes narrowed. "All the treasures?"

Harald nodded somberly. "Everything."

"And you took it?"

Here the wily king smiled. "All of it—including Felicia herself, whom I intend to make my next wife."

The captain from Baghdad was astounded; he took a deep breath of smoke-filled air and whistled.

"Never mind," said Harald in fatherly fashion. "All's fair in love and war, as they say. But you need not feel angered or jealous, Captain. I'll tell you what: Why don't you come back to Roskilde with me? Perhaps we can have a double wedding."

Sinbad held up his hands, palms forward, and shook his head with a slightly bemused grin. "Forgive me, my liege, but—er—your daughter, lovely though she is, is not the woman I intend to marry. I already have someone waiting for me, someone far, far away, back home in Baghdad."

The king of Denmark frowned. "A pity; I think I would have enjoyed having you for a son-in-law. Are you certain you won't change your mind?"

The two men faced each other evenly and Sinbad shook his head. "I'm sorry, Harald, but I can't. . . ."

At first the king's features darkened at the rebuke, but slowly a smile worked its way over his chiseled face and soon he was grinning. "I think I understand," he said with a sigh. "Thruna is going to be very disappointed. Still, she'll find another." He rubbed thoughtfully at his chin. "Perhaps one of those Britons. . . ."

Trumpets were blasting from the direction of the road; a vanguard of Suliman's horsemen were forming to block the Viking thrust from the plaza. The Norsemen were pressing on undaunted but taking a terrible toll as at last the bandit army had mustered its strength and, smarting from the licking they had taken from the foreigners, were now attempting to regain the upper hand.

Stoically the Vikings formed a shielded wedge and, with heaving axes and shouts to the gods of old, forced their penetration through the strongest mounted ranks.

Seeing the battle wax hot before him, Harald tightened the grip on his ax and darted for the fray. "Stand beside me, Sinbad," he shouted back to the mariner, "Let's show these bandits a thing or two about war!" And into the tumult he dove.

The frog on Sinbad's shoulder looked at him curiously, and Sinbad shrugged. Sweeping up a fallen sword, he quickly followed the burly Norseman's footsteps.

With fires raging all around, Harald sprang up like a cat and smashed his blows against Suliman's best men. Lancers were sent sprawling from their steeds, footmen reeling back and toppling over one another. A mounted bandit lowered in the saddle, arched forward and brandished his curved blade, heading straight ahead to cut down the king. Harald deftly spun, eyes afire, and with a whoop and a *swish* of his ax flailed upward and clove the attacker from collarbone to groin. As the rider tumbled into the dirt, those charging on his heels took one look at the fearsome Lion of Roskilde and threw down their blades. Harald's ax sailed as they turned to run; its recipient never felt the blow—his neatly severed head went flying in one direction, his torso cavorting in another before tumbling in a crimson heap.

Shouts everywhere, calls to arms, attack and retreat trumpet blasts swelled in a terrible crescendo; Sinbad fought boldly alongside the laughing king, pushing back the Moorish bandits and clambering over their fallen corpses. He whirled at the sound of racing footsteps behind and held his sword with both hands, ready to swing out at the attackers. Silhouettes were racing through the smoke, and as he prepared to meet them head on, it was Don Giovanni who called, "Still your blade; it's our crew!"

And there they came, Mongo leading the charge of the *Sherry's* crew; beside him on one side Abu, brandishing a sword and clenching a pirate knife firmly between his teeth; flanking him, faithful Milo, come back to Pansa as promised, heaving a farmer's scythe above his head and urging on the sailors behind. Sinbad stared at the incredible sight, tears in his eyes.

Elisa hurried from the tower and ran down the steps of the church. It took her only a moment to find Sinbad and she threw her arms about him gleefully, letting him lift her off her feet, smothering him with wet kisses as she squealed with delight. "We're saved, Sinbad! We're really saved!"

Sinbad kissed her fully on the lips, oblivious of the hotly contested battle still raging all around him.

"A pretty sight this is," came a voice.

He put Elisa down and turned to find Felicia, the future queen of the Danes, with her shoulders back, her hands to her hips, and her hair tossing freely in the morning breeze. The fiery pirate glared up and down at the clinging Elisa, tapping her boot impatiently in the dirt. "I thought you needed to be rescued," she commented icily to Sinbad, "But it looks like your time has been well spent."

King Harald bellowed with laughter at the sight of the two women smoldering with mutual jealousy.

"Thank *Allah* you made it here in time," said Sinbad to Felicia.

Without answering, Felicia turned, her skirt swirling, and threw her arms around Harald. The king of Denmark winked back at the mariner from Baghdad. "I'll wager there'll be hell to pay when this fight is finished," he said with a laugh.

Sinbad bit his lip and didn't answer. Nearby, Thruna stood impassively watching, and the sight of the longlegged, hard-drinking Viking girl only made matters worse.

By this time the church doors were opened wide and the villagers were streaming into the plaza, ready to give a hand in pushing back the last of Suliman's forces. They scooped up clubs and bows, knives and axes, and followed Harald's men into battle. Sinbad looked on in wonder. It was truly something extraordinary to behold, these Norsemen and Spaniards and Arabic sailors joining together to swamp the bandit army.

Over splintered limbs and broken bodies the defenders pressed, thoroughly routing the last vestiges of Suliman's army. By the first cracks of dawn the battle was all but over. Fully nine-tenths of the bandit army lay scattered across the plaza and roads, in the ditches, or hung limply and luridly over the crumbling walls. Those who managed to escape had been forced to flee on foot, hobbling in the direction of the southern hills and the frontier of Córdoba. As for the Suliman himself, he was never found. It was rumored in years to come that, disgraced and made a laughingstock at Pansa, he was forced to give up all aspirations to military glories and spend the remaining years of his life as a beggar in the back alleys of Tarragona, broken and embittered, spat upon by children and barked at by dogs.

And so morning came to Pansa. The last of the smoke was blown away by a strong wind off the sea. Face smeared with grease and sweat, a weary Sinbad observed the carnage. Here and there an occasional arrow sailed, and a scream would pierce the air as a hiding bandit was found and swiftly put to death. The sad-hearted women of the village roamed through the plaza and examined the dead, weeping as the stilled form of a loved one was found. Then Father Augusto would come, Bible in hand, and whisper a prayer in Latin before the body was wrapped in a blanket and brought to the church for burial.

"I can't believe it's done," Sinbad sighed, squeezing Elisa's hand and walking slowly toward the church.

Elisa nodded and gazed down sadly at the blood-splattered steps. "Nor I. It's going to take the village a very long time to rebuild."

Sinbad looked around at the flattened roofs, the cinders where the fishing docks had been. Save for the church, the village was totally destroyed. Yet the people of Pansa had doggedly fought adversity all their lives. Surely now was a new beginning for them.

"And you, Sinbad," Elisa asked. "Now that your ship is here, what will you do?"

He stopped on the steps, glanced up at the perfect blue sky, and sighed deeply. "I don't suppose there's any point in going on with our voyage past the Pillars of Hercules," he said wistfully. "Now that we've found the Red Dahlia. . . ."

Eliasa sniffed; she gently put her hand to his chin and lifted his head so that he was forced to look at her. Then she kissed him softly. "I only wish I could have been more help to you. I'm sorry, Sinbad, sorry you didn't find the magic you need. . . ."

The bell rang again in the tower, causing all eyes to look up. A hand was frantically waving, and Sinbad saw that María Victoria was leaning over the crumbled wall, trying to get his attention. "The harbor, Sinbad!" she cried. "There's a ship coming into the harbor!"

Sinbad ran from the church, past the burned-out homes that lined the sandy path to the dock, and stared out at the calm waters. Felicia was already there; so was King Harald. The Viking squinted his eyes and focused on the strangely shaped vessel flying flags he had never seen before.

But to Felicia the ship was no stranger—nor was it to Sinbad. "It . . . it can't be!" muttered the mariner, exchanging a stunned look with the pirate.

"But it is," whispered the girl in reply.

The gold and speckled black of the banners left no doubt: The vessel flew the seals of Baghdad. And Sinbad knew he had seen this very ship before. Its carved bowsprit and silken sails left no doubt about that. This was the very vessel that had followed the *Scheherazade* all the way from Jaffa, the same one that Sinbad saw attacked by pirates so long before, attacked and nearly sunk. . . .

Sinbad swallowed hard as the sails slacked and the bow dipped into the half-moon bay. As she drew closer he could make out the forms of a captain and officers upon the bridge shouting commands to the crew; and among the officers one stood out from the rest. A stout fellow, tall and proud, dressed in the flowing robes of a minister—a caliph's minister.

Sinbad held his breath as the anchor was thrown, and soundlessly mouthed the name, "Dormo."

Felicia paled and looked at the captain. "What . . . what are we to do?"

Sinbad shook his head; King Harald put his thick hand on his future bride's shoulder and asked, "What is this ship, Sinbad? Why are you so concerned?"

"It is a very long tale, my liege, but this very ship has been after us since the day we set sail. Indeed, it's been following me since I was forced to flee Baghdad. And can you see the hawk-nosed fellow in the crimson robe? He's the First Minister of Schahriar's court—come to arrest me and drag me back in chains."

Harald furrowed thick brows and peered at the Arabian ship. "Never fear, my friend. They won't harm a single hair on your head. Not while I'm alive." A roaring shout brought forward dozens of his fiercest Vikings. Shields in hand, they formed two lines along the edge of the burnt pier, first rank kneeling, second rank standing behind it, axes in hand.

"We mustn't fight them, my liege," said Sinbad. "Look, my lord. They have hundreds of soldiers aboard, fresh troops unscarred from any battle. We are too few—"

"*Bah*," growled Harald, spitting contemptuously into the water. "I'll handle it; I'll take your First Minister and break his spine with my own hands. I'll let my axe shave the hair from his head and then I'll—"

"Please, Harald! You mustn't!"

The king was more than puzzled. "But why not, man?
370

Surely you don't want to return to Baghdad in chains? And if killing the minister is the only way, then . . ." He shrugged.

Sinbad sighed and shook his head; he was in a quandary as never before. "You don't understand," he said at last. "That man, the minister, is the father of the girl I love, the woman I yearn for every moment of my existence."

Harald looked to Felicia in disbelief.

"It's true, my lord," said the pirate. "Sinbad told me of it long ago. Dormo was to be his father-in-law. You can't just kill him."

"It's a very complicated situation," broke in Sinbad. "But believe me, Dormo loves me—and I love him. No harm must come to him."

"Then you *are* in a pickle," observed the Viking king.

"That, sire, I am." And his shoulders slumped dejectedly.

All along the Arabian ship soldiers were massing to counter the array of Danes deployed along the shore. Bows drawn, quivers jammed with arrows, they took up strong positions from stem to stern, patiently waiting for commands.

"Better make up your mind, Captain," said Harald. "It won't be long before they lower their skiffs. Look— already a landing party is being formed."

Sinbad looked away, not knowing what to do. Should he fight Dormo, this man who had been more than a friend for so many years? Or should he put an end to all the bloodshed here and now, give himself up with no questions asked and be taken back to Baghdad to wait at the caliph's pleasure? He shook with the thought. But one thing he *did* know: No matter what the consequences, he could never stand by and see Sherry's father slain. Not by his hand or any other; it was better to die.

Even as he pondered this grave decision the lonely church bell rang again. The startled mariner and his companions turned to see a terrible commotion in the village. The survivors of Pansa had begun to cheer and shout, laugh

371

and sing, hug one another and run madly from the plaza up toward the road.

"By Allah, what's going on?" cried Sinbad, momentarily forgetting his dilemma.

María Victoria was shouting to him again, her voice carrying on the breeze all the way from the tower to the harbor. "Come see!" she yelled, "Come and see for yourselves!"

Perplexed, the band quickly moved from the dock to the plaza, and there they watched as thousands upon thousands of armed knights and footmen came marching over the distant hills in their direction.

"What is it?" cried Sinbad to Father Augusto.

The priest made the sign of the cross and smiled. "It can only be one thing, my friend—el Cid, victorious from the plains of Navarre, come now to meet the Moorish threat along Barcelona's frontier."

And indeed they came, mounted knights resplendent in their fine armor, vests of mail, plumed helmets, and cloaks flowing behind. Drums beat slowly, trumpets blared; the tramping of feet in steady rhythm filled their ears as the powerful army swiftly crossed the hills and approached the regions of the dusty road.

"*El Cid*," whispered Sinbad in awe.

Felicia nodded darkly. She gazed from one end of the horizon to the other, her eyes tearing from the flashes of sunlight reflected off shields and armor.

"By Odin, I've never seen such an army as this," swore Harald. "Just look at them! There must be at least ten thousand!"

"I'd like to meet this Cid," said Sinbad, recalling the tales he had heard of the prophetlike leader of Castile's forces.

María Elisa shook her head violently and looked at him with pleading in her eyes. "Sinbad," she begged, "You must get away from here at once!"

"Don't be silly, girl," laughed Harald, every bit as

impressed as the others. "Look how happy your villagers are to see them. Look at them running over the road, cheering and throwing flowers—"

"But they're not Moors!" cried Elisa. She tugged at Sinbad's sleeve. "Please, listen to me," she entreated. "To the Cid you are one of the enemy, no different from Suliman—"

Sinbad was aghast. "What are you saying? Me and my crew saved Pansa! We're not his enemy!"

"No matter," said Elisa, her cheeks streaming with tears. "El Cid is sworn to rid all nonbelievers from Castile. And you are one."

"*I'm* not a heathen," barked King Harald angrily.

Elisa lowered her gaze from his royal stare. "Perhaps you are not, my lord. But think—what of your bride-to-be? Felicia is as much of a heathen as Sinbad is, at least in the eyes of the Cid. Would you want to stand by and see her harmed?"

Harald's face flushed crimson. "By the gods of old," he roared. "If one of those Spaniards touches a single hair on her head, I'll—"

"Then you must flee as well," pleaded Elisa. She grabbed Sinbad tightly and forced him to look at her. "As much as I love you," she said, "I'd rather see you gone, far away and never to return, than stand by and watch you suffer. Go, Sinbad! Get to your ship before it's too late!"

Harald scowled. He called again for his men to take battle positions, this time along the broken barricades of the wall. The Vikings grimly took places over the corpses of Suliman's slain followers, their eyes darkly set upon the locustlike swarm of men moving down from the heights.

"Are you crazy, Harald?" sputtered Sinbad. "They have an army of ten thousand! Ten thousand!"

The king was unmoved. "Norsemen fear no odds, young captain. We'll stand and fight—and mark my words, this . . . this *Cid*, whatever that is, won't be so quick to take us on."

"And what of Dormo's ship?" added Sinbad. "Have you forgotten the hundreds of Baghdad soldiers ready to come ashore? *By Allah!* Has all the world gone insane? We haven't got a chance!"

"He's right, you know," said an impassive Felicia to her future husband. "Perhaps it *is* better if we gracefully withdraw. . . ."

"It may already be too late," said Father Augusto, pointing behind. A great longboat had already been lowered from the Baghdad warship, carrying a dozen soldiers with hands at the hilts of their swords. Dormo, standing in the middle of the crowd, was stern-faced and somber as the shirtless oarsmen brought them closer to berth.

"Prepare to fight!" shouted Harald.

To the dock scrambled half his force along with Mongo and Milo and the crew of the *Scheherazade*.

"This is madness," mumbled Sinbad, his anguish growing by the second. He and his band were trapped in a vise, with no escape possible. On one side marched el Cid in all his pomp and splendor, prepared to wipe him and his crew off the face of Iberia forever; from the other side came an equally determined Dormo in the name of the caliph, also determined to see the name of Sinbad erased from the world.

Felicia scurried from the king's arms to take command of the forces on the dock. She gave the order for bows and swords to be drawn, for the longboat bearing Dormo to be stopped from reaching shore.

"Wait!" shouted Sinbad, dashing as fast as he could to reach the pirate. "Listen," he said, panting, "hold off for a second; let me talk to Dormo, maybe we can reach an accommodation . . ."

"Don't be a fool, Captain," said Milo with knitted brows. "Dormo's been waiting for this moment for how long? Only Allah knows how he found us, but now that he's here, he'll get what he came for."

The longboat came surging through the rippling water,

with Dormo pushing his way to the bow. He cupped his hands around his mouth and called, "Sinbad! Sinbad, is that you?"

The mariner looked to the angry pirate girl. "Felicia, please. Give me a minute to talk to him, just a minute. . . ."

She bit tensely at her lip and sighed. "All right, then. Speak with him if you think it will do any good. But remember—I'll not hold off for long. Warn Dormo not to touch shore, otherwise . . ." Her thought did not have to be finished; Sinbad took one glance at the readied Vikings and shivered. The crew and soldiers aboard the Arabian ship also watched tensely, their weapons in hand, prepared to fight should a single arrow fly from shore.

Sinbad ran over the smoldering planks of the dock and stood at the very edge. The bows of sunken fishing boats protruded from the water like tiny black icebergs.

"By Allah, I've been searching for you since the day you left home!" shouted Dormo to Sinbad. "At last I've found you!"

Sinbad held up a hand. "Don't come any closer, Dormo. Lift your oars at once! You mustn't set foot on land."

The minister grimaced. "Sinbad, what's this all about? Why are you—?"

"Please, Dormo. Don't make it worse. Turn your longboat around and get to your ship. Sail from here at once—and never look back."

"But," sputtered Dormo, "but I've been trying to reach you for so long! We have to speak; I almost caught up with you near Crete, but—"

"I know about the pirates that attacked you, Dormo; and believe me, I thank Allah that you're alive. . . ."

"It was close, Sinbad. They almost had us. Our sails were ablaze, their grappling hooks were already thrown. But we fought them off; by the time repairs were made you had already gone. I thought I'd lost you forever."

"Better if you had, Dormo! I don't know how you found

us now, but it would have been better for us all if you hadn't."

The hawk-nosed minister signaled for his oarsmen to draw in their oars. Twenty meters from land the long boat came to a halt and bobbed gently in the shallow water. "Now listen to me, Sinbad," Dormo called, his voice becoming harsh. "This ship of mine has faced more perils than you can imagine to find you. In fact, we almost gave up, until we reached the channel of Corsica and met up with the fleet of the Cretan king."

Were the Greeks still after him, too? Sinbad shuddered with the thought.

Dormo continued, "It was because of him that we knew we were still on the right trail. I'd have caught up with you before you reached Mallorca if it hadn't been for that ferocious storm. . . ."

Sinbad groaned. "Then you should have turned around, just like the Greeks. Coming here is useless. Go back, my friend. Go back now. I don't want to have to see you killed."

Dormo's eyes grew wide. "Killed? You would have me murdered?"

"For Sherry's sake, no. And for the sake of the friendship we once shared. But turn about, Dormo. Tax me no more; these companions of mine are growing impatient."

The minister snapped his fingers and the oarsmen took up their strokes again, coming closer to shore.

"Draw your weapons!" cried Felicia, and the front rank took dead aim for Dormo's heart.

"Go back!" pleaded Sinbad. "I warned you—you must not come any closer!"

Dormo set his jaw; he stood brazenly at the fore, almost daring the Norsemen to fire. "Now listen to me, Sinbad," he called as the longboat nearly reached the shattered quay. "I didn't chase you all this way for nothing. I want you to come back with me to Baghdad today. There is no time to lose."

"Never!" flared the mariner. He clenched his fist around his knife and held it menacingly. "I'll not let you take me, Dormo. Not alive. I'll not wear your chains; I'll not languish in the caliph's dungeons. I'm not a criminal—no matter what Schahriar claims!"

Dormo's mouth hung wide. "But of course you're not, my boy! No one ever said—"

"Then why are you here? Why have you chased me all the way from Baghdad?"

The minister heaved a long sigh and shook his head sadly. "Oh, my poor Sinbad. If only you had not fled home so rashly. If only you had stayed in Baghdad but a single day more. . . ."

"Why? So the caliph could imprison me—and laugh even as Sherry was made his bride?"

Dormo threw up his hands in exasperation. "But this is what I'm trying to tell you, son! For love of Prophet! Won't you listen to me now? Sherry never wed the caliph!"

Sinbad stared at his old friend. "I . . . I don't believe you. . . ."

"It's true! Allah be my judge, won't you hear me out?"

The skiff had all but reached shore; Sinbad turned to Felicia, who had been listening to the entire conversation. For a second she hesitated, then, seeing the pleading in Sinbad's eyes, she ordered her force to hold off.

Dormo leaped to shore and stood face to face with the man who once was to be his son-in-law. "There was no wedding, Sinbad," he said. "There shall never be. Sherry is free—and waiting for you now."

Sinbad gasped. "Sherry . . . is . . . free . . . ?"

"That's right. You see, after the order for your arrest was given, all Baghdad was incensed. There was not a man in the whole city who did not know that you were innocent of the charges. There was a terrible demonstration, an uproar as never before. Riots broke out against Schahriar's injustices. Even his own court and ministers turned against him. . . ."

377

"Including you?"

Dormo nodded gravely. "Including me. A petition was brought before the caliph demanding his abdication at once upon peril of death. He had little choice but to sign it. Schahriar is no longer ruler of Baghdad. He has been expelled from the city, sent to his summer home on the Tigris where he may live out his waning years in peace. Baghdad has a new caliph."

"Who?"

The First Minister smiled thinly. "Me."

"You?" Sinbad's lips sputtered, unable to form words or thoughts.

Dormo put his hand upon Sinbad's shoulder. "Yes, my son; it is so. My first order was to have all charges against you dropped, all your properties returned, and your good name restored. My second command was that you marry my daughter, Scheherazade. . . ."

Sinbad numbly dropped to his knees; he took Dormo's bejeweled hand and kissed his ring. "My lord," he stammered, "if . . if only I had known. . . ."

"But there was no way for you to know, was there?" went on the new caliph. "As rumors said you had left for Damascus and then Jaffa, I knew that you must be tracked at once and told of your fortunes. Another man in my stead would never have been believed; I knew that only I myself might convince you of the truth. Arise, Sinbad, my son. And come with me now, back home where a special place awaits you. Court Poet and Philosopher shall be your newest title. That, and, husband to my daughter."

Sinbad rose slowly, tears forming in the corners of his eyes. "Yes," he cried, "yes, I'll come with you. Forgive me, my lord, for not having believed you before. . . ."

With an imperial wave of the hand Dormo dismissed the matter. "How soon can you be ready?"

Before Sinbad could reply, the sound of trumpets shattered the air. King Harald and his men were at their battle positions, calmly waiting as the army of el Cid reached the Pansa road and headed straight for the village.

"By Allah, I almost forgot!" rasped Sinbad, staring at the advancing knights of Barcelona and Navarre. "Excuse me, sire," he begged, and before Dormo could as much as nod, he bounded off back to the plaza and the battle-hardened King of Denmark.

"To the ships, Harald!" he shouted. "No time to lose; let's get away before this Cid reaches the village!"

"But how?" said the Viking. "What about that Arabian ship at our backs?"

"They're friends," cried Sinbad gleefully. And he threw his arms around the Lion of Roskilde. "I'm going home!" he shouted. "Home to Baghdad; home to Sherry!" He implanted a fat kiss on Harald's hoary cheek, leaving the king astounded.

"Have you lost all sanity, man?"

Sinbad shook his head. "No, sire. For the first time I think I found it. Now hurry! Gather your men and get to your ships. In minutes el Cid will be here."

At the sight of Felicia waving him on, the burly liege grinned, grabbed Thruna by the hand, and scurried as quickly as he could toward the quay.

"Come on, come," called Sinbad, urging everybody to hurry.

María Elisa slipped to his side and took both of his hands. "Good-bye, my captain," she whispered.

Sinbad paused to wipe a tear from her round eyes. "Good-bye, Elisa. I'll never forget you. In my heart a candle shall always burn for you. . . ."

She smiled and kissed him softly. "And in my own as well, Sinbad. *Vaya con Dios*. Go with God."

Sinbad embraced her tightly and then turned away, pained to be leaving tiny Pansa and all his new friends, but hoping that one day he would come back to a rebuilt village where everybody dwelled in peace.

"All set," said Methelese, who had been supervising the skiffs to the waiting ships. "Let's be on our way."

Sinbad nodded happily, but suddenly he stopped. His face darkened and he looked around with worry.

"What's the matter?" asked the Greek.

"Don Giovanni! Where is he? I haven't seen him since . . ." He recalled the little frog's being on his shoulder as he fought side by side with King Harald. But now the frog was gone, and in the excitement Sinbad had completely forgotten about him.

"I can't go," he said. "Not without my closest friend."

"We cannot linger," said Milo, his eyes upon the advancing forces of the knights of Castile.

But Sinbad was adamant. "No; go on ahead if you like. I'll stay until Giovanni's found."

The Greek and the old sailor exchanged furtive glances; they knew their captain was serious. Rather than leave a friend behind, he would risk his very life, even at a time when all his wishes had been fulfilled.

Milo sighed. "Then we'll look together."

With María Elisa helping, the three men scoured the plaza, calling the frog by name, digging by hand through the rubble, kicking over grim corpses of Suliman's bandits. Time pressed; the drums grew louder, the first knights and pages were reaching the perimeter of the destroyed village.

Sinbad looked about in trepidation and prayed. *By Allah, let me find him. Let him not be lost to me now. . . .*

"Sinbad, come quick!"

He spun around to find Elisa calling to him frantically from the crumbled wall that Javier the mason had built only yesterday. Running, his face broken out in beads of sweat and his heart wildly beating, he kneeled down beside the girl and gasped. There was Don Giovanni, motionless amid the rubble. On the side of his head was a small gash.

Sinbad picked him up carefully and held him in the palms of his hands. "Giovanni! Giovanni, speak to me!"

But the frog didn't move. Methelese ran over and put a

380

finger to the bullfrog's heart. There was a faint beat. "He's still alive," he said sourly, "but that was a bad knock in the head that he took. Any other frog would be dead."

Sinbad began to cry loudly. "Oh, please, my tiny friend. Don't desert me now, not after all we've been through. Not when we can go home at last. . . ."

And just then, Don Giovanni stirred; he opened one bulging eye, stared up at the mariner, and croaked.

Sinbad jumped for joy. "You're alive! Praise be to *Allah!* You're alive!"

Don Giovanni croaked again.

Wiping away his tears, Sinbad grinned. "Come on, Giovanni. Speak to me. It's only your friends here now. You can talk."

Another croak.

"It's all right," implored Sinbad. "Speak! Don't pretend!"

But the frog only croaked. Sinbad looked to Methelese and the wise Greek sadly shook his head. "I don't think he can talk to us any more," he said gently, putting a hand on Sinbad's shoulder. "That knock on the head he received must have really jarred him. Now he's just a frog again. No different than any other."

"Impossible!" cried Sinbad. He held the frog tightly. "Come on, Giovanni. Show him that he's wrong. Speak to me! Speak to me, please!"

No words came. The bullfrog gazed up at the human faces around him and watched them with apparent puzzlement.

"Let him go, Sinbad," advised Milo. "Let him return to a pond where he can be happy."

"Milo's right," added Methelese. "It's no use trying to make him back into what he was. . . ."

Sinbad nodded slowly; somehow he knew that his little friend would never return to him, at least not in the way he had known him before. It was strange, though; Don Giovanni, through an accidental blow, had gone back to what he had been—which was all he really wanted anyway.

"All right," said Sinbad at last. "We'll take him to a pond. But not here. I'll bring him home to Baghdad, to the pond where we first met. I think he'll like that. There he can be happy again, seeing his friends and his family."

"But we'd better hurry," said Milo, an eye to the road. Sinbad looked to see the procession of knights almost upon them. Father Augusto ran from the church and hurriedly escorted them to the last skiff waiting at the quay. Sinbad and the others jumped in barely in time, for no sooner had the oars been lifted and dropped into water than el Cid himself, upon a magnificent white charger, came sweeping into Pansa.

"Good-bye, Sinbad," called María Victoria from the bell tower. And Sinbad stood up and waved, fondly recalling the youngest of the de León sisters, who had found him that day on the beach.

"Good-bye, Victoria," he called. Beside her came Vanessa, also waving. Then Elisa, crying and laughing, waving a silk scarf. "Good-bye to you all; I shall always think of you." With Father Augusto standing alone on the quay, a tear in his own eyes, Sinbad's boat reached the waiting rope ladder of the *Scheherazade*.

Into the sunset sailed the four ships. Once out of the harbor, King Harald's long ships turned south and headed for the Pillars of Hercules and the Atlantic Ocean. With Felicia in his arms, the Lion of Roskilde bid a fond farewell to the bold mariner from Baghdad, hoping that soon Sinbad would take him up on his invitation to visit with him and Felicia in Denmark.

Sinbad stood at the bridge, his hands holding the rail, his black hair tossing in the wind. The *Sherry* set an easterly course that would take them to Jaffa. Dormo's escort ship was right beside him, and he gazed fondly at the new caliph, knowing that Baghdad had at last found a truly wise and noble leader. He could hardly wait to gain his new position at court, and was understandably even more eager to see Sherry. His mind swam with the memory of her, and right now her embrace was all he could dream of.

It was peculiar, though, that these adventures had all been in search of the mythical flower. He laughed and shook his head at his own foolishness, his intense hope of finding the magic to make all things right again.

Yet somehow, all things *were* right again. Pansa was saved; he was on his way home to his beloved; even Don Giovanni had what he wanted. The voyage could not have been more successful.

Feeling the cool breeze against his skin, Sinbad sighed. Twenty-four hours ago, as he stood upon the tower of the church while the battle raged below, all indeed seemed lost. Since then everything had changed—a total reversal. But how? When did it all happen?

A sudden chill crawled down his spine as he remembered. There had been a flower in his pocket, a red dahlia. . . .

He had taken it, crushed it and closed his eyes, making his tearful wishes. Pansa . . . Sherry . . . Giovanni. . . . They had all come true!

"The flower!" he gasped. "The flower has magic after all!" *But it couldn't! It can't! It's only a flower!*

He stared out at the sandy shores of Barcelona, his mind whirling at the mystery. Was it really possible? Might the dahlia have . . . ? He shrugged and sighed, putting the matter aside and thinking of home again.

Sinbad of Baghdad was a sailor and an adventurer, a poet and a philosopher, a wise man and a fool. He knew that sometimes a mystery is better left unsolved.

Great Adventures in Reading

THE GREEN RIPPER   14345 $2.50
by John D. MacDonald
  Gretel, the one girl the hard-boiled Travis McGee had actually fallen for—dead of a "mysterous illness." McGee calls it murder. This time he's out for blood.

SCANDAL OF FALCONHURST   14334 $2.50
by Ashley Carter
  Ellen, the lovely mustee, through a trick of fate marries into the wealthiest family in New Orleans. But she must somehow free the man she really loves, the son of a white plantation owner, sold to die as a slave. In the exciting tradition of MANDINGO.

WINGED PRIESTESS   14329 $2.50
by Joyce Verrette
  The slave: Ilbaya, of noble birth, in love with his master's concubine. He risks death with each encounter. The Queen: beautiful Nefrytatanen. To keep the love of her husband she must undergo the dangerous ritual that will make her the "winged" priestess—or destroy her! An epic of ancient Egypt.

FAWCETT GOLD MEDAL BOOKS